IN EVERY LAUGH A TEAR

A Novel by
Lesléa Newman

Novels
Good Enough To Eat
Fat Chance

Short Stories
Secrets
A Letter To Harvey Milk
Every Woman's Dream

Poetry
Sweet Dark Places
Love Me Like You Mean It
Just Looking For My Shoes
Still Life With Buddy

Non-fiction
SomeBODY To Love: A Guide To Loving The Body You Have
Writing From The Heart: Inspiration and Exercises for Women Who Want to Write

Humor
Out of the Closet and Nothing to Wear
The Little Butch Book

Children's Books
Heather Has Two Mommies
Gloria Goes To Gay Pride
Belinda's Bouquet
Saturday is Pattyday
Too Far Away To Touch
Remember That
Matzo Ball Moon

Anthologies
Bubbe Meisehs By Shayneh Maidelehs:Poetry by Jewish Granddaughters About Our Grandmothers
Eating Our Hearts Out: Personal Accounts of Women's Relationship to Food
A Loving Testimony: Remembering Loved Ones Lost to AIDS
The Femme Mystique
My Lover Is A Women: Contemporary Lesbian Love Poems
Pillow Talk: Lesbian Stories Between the Covers

IN EVERY LAUGH A TEAR

A Novel by
Lesléa Newman

New Victoria Publishers, Inc.

Published by New Victoria Publishers Inc., PO Box 27 Norwich, Vt. 05055
A Feminist Literary and Cultural Organization founded in 1976

New Edition 1998
Printed and Bound in Canada

Cover design Claudia McKay
Back cover photo by Mary Vazquez

Excerpts from 'Morning' © 1989 Gail Kadison Golden and 'Immigrant' © 1989 Linda Watskin, reprinted from *Bubbe Meisehs by Shayneh Maidelehs: An Anthology of Poetry By Jewish Granddaughters About Our Grandmothers,* edited by Lesléa Newman, published by HerBooks, Santa Cruz, CA 1989. Used with permission of publisher and authors.

Note: The characters and events portrayed in *In Every Laugh A Tear* are fictitious inventions of the author's imagination.

Library of Congress Cataloging-in-Publication Data

Newman, Lesléa.
In every laugh a tear : a novel / by Lesléa Newman. -- New ed.
       p.   cm.
   ISBN 0-934678-92-8
    1. Jewish families -- United States -- Fiction. 2. Nursing home patients -- Fiction. 3. Jews -- United States -- Fiction.
4. Grandmothers-- Fiction. 5. Jewish aged -- Fiction.
6. Aged women -- Fiction. I. Title.
PS3564. E9162815   1998
813' .54-- dc21

                                                       98-22696
                                                          CIP

For Ruth Levin

may her memory be a blessing

"mother of my mother
by your thin blue-veined hands
I have been anointed
strong…"
—Gail Kadison Golden
Morning

"I taught her to write
her name in American.
She taught me to rest
my head between her breasts
and listen."
—Linda Watskin
Immigrant

Acknowledgements

I'd like to thank the following people who were there when I needed them: Nickie Albert, Mollie Babize, Janet Feld, Sharon Gensler, Joanne Gold, Tzivia Gover, Jon Hirsch, Tryna Hope, Michele Karlsberg, Sue Krause, Barry Levin, Sara Northrop, Judy O'Brien, Arachne Rachel, Irene Reti, Deliah Rosel, Jodie Shapiro, Shlomit Shalfy, Marilyn Silberglied-Stewart, Prudy Smith, Sue Tyler, Susan Waldman, Jess Wells, and Irene Zahava.

I appreciate the immense support and encouragement of my agent, Charlotte Raymond, and I would also like to thank the women of New Victoria Publishers, Claudia Lamperti, Beth Dingman, ReBecca Beguin and Mattie Richardson for the care they took in shaping my manuscript into a finished book.

A special heartfelt thank you to Mary Vazquez, my saving Grace, and to my parents, Florence and Edward Newman, for their patience, kindness, good humor and generosity.

And to my beloved grandmother, Ruth Levin:

Grandma, you always knew I'd be a rich and famous writer someday. I don't know about the rich, but I'm working on the famous (maybe someday they'll make my book into a picture, yet). Thank you for your stories, your wisdom, your courage, your never-ending love. Zie gezunt, Bubbe. Ich hob der libe.

Forward

My beloved grandmother, Ruth Levin, passed from this world to the next on November 13, 1989, just a few months shy of her one-hundredth birthday. At that time a quote, attributed to the playwright Andrea Hairston hung over my desk: If you don't tell your story, you die twice. And since losing my grandmother once was almost more than I could bear, I decided I would indeed tell her story, so I would not lose her again.

By her own definition, my grandmother was not an extraordinary woman. "What's there to tell?" she'd shrug, her palms turned up towards the ceiling. "I was born in Europe—all right, sometimes they called it Poland, sometimes they call in Russia, what's the difference?—I came here with my mother, I went to school for a year, then worked in the lace factory, then married your grandfather, then I had three children, then I had grandchildren and that's all." Oh, but there was so much more, for no woman's life, ordinary or extraordinary, could possibly be summed up in one sentence, even a run-on sentence at that.

What makes my grandmother extraordinary, in my eyes, is not the events of her life, but rather her response to those events. She accepted whatever came her way—a new country, a new language, marriage, motherhood, widowhood, old age—with courage, dignity and humor. And she never lost her appetite for life; everyone's business was her business. She was the matriarch of my family and the ambassador of her neighborhood (it's not for nothing her nickname was the Mayor of Brighton Beach).

My grandmother had a remarkable gift for bestowing unconditional love on her family and friends. She accepted me, her lesbian granddaughter, long before anyone else in my family got used to the idea. In fact, accepted is hardly the right word. My grandmother did more than accept me. She loved me, rejoiced in me, kvelled over me. When I sent her copies of the books I had written, she proudly displayed them on her coffee table. When I won a Creative Writing Fellowship from the state of Massachusetts, she gathered all the residents of her nursing home floor around the phone, so they could chorus "Mazel tov!" into my delighted ear. She was my cheerleader, my confidante, my very best friend.

Like all her grandchildren, I like to think I was her favorite and even she admitted I had a bit of an edge: I am my grandmother's only daughter's only daughter. "A tochter's tochter is special," she reminded me more than once. Which is perhaps why, when my grandmother was moved into a nursing home, it was understood by everyone in my family (though not a word was spoken) that I would be the one to take care of her during the last, difficult chapter of her life.

So why did I choose the form of a novel rather than a memoir, to tell my grandmother's story? The obvious and easy answer is, because I'm a novelist. But beyond that, my grandmother, like her fictitious alter-ego Tzydl Zimmerman, is larger than life. She has huge emotions, attitudes, ideas, and heart. The thought of writing a memoir and sticking to the 'facts' felt enormously constraining to me; on the other hand, by writing a novel, I had free reign to expound, exaggerate, and fuss with the facts in order to bring out larger truths of my grandmother's life, and of my own. As all fiction writers do, I lie in order to tell the truth. And the truth is, my grandmother and I carried on a special kind of love affair, from the day I was born until the day she died.

I miss her more than words can say.

Lesléa Newman
May 1998

Chapter One

"I'll get it, I'll get it," Shayna yelled to Tzimmy, though Porky Pig could turn kosher long before her fourteen year old cat would ever answer the phone. "Tzimmy, c'mon." Shayna ran through her apartment, the red bandanna she was using as a shmate waving from her hand like a flag. *I hope it's Luz, I hope it's Luz, I hope it's Luz,* Shayna breathed, as she pretended to dust off Tzimmy (short for Tzimmes) who had beat her to the phone, and was now plotzed on top of the answering machine.

"Shmutz patrol, Tzimmy." Shayna continued dusting off the cat's back as she counted the telephone rings. "I know what you're thinking, Tzimmy," she said. "But Bubbe always says never to pick up before the fifth ring. 'A girl shouldn't be so eager, mamela. Boys like a girl to be a little more reserved.'" Shayna shook her finger at the cat in a perfect imitation of her bubbe. "But what about butches, huh, Tzimmy? What do they like?" Shayna had always wanted to ask her grandmother, but so far she had never gotten up the nerve. *Though let me assure you, in all other areas, Shayna P. Steinblatt is A-Okay in the chutzpah department.*

Shayna waited one more ring before she snatched up the receiver, winked at Tzimmy, and said in her coolest, toughest, oh-is-the-phone-ringing?-as-if-I-really-care voice, "Hello?"

"Hello. Is this Linda Steinblatt?"

No, it's Martha Washington. Who do you think it is? "Yes," Shayna snapped, keeping the annoyance evident in her voice. *Wouldn't you know it,* she thought, rolling her eyes at Tzimmes. *Here I am, futzing around in my apartment, happy as a pig in shit (you should pardon the expression) dusting off my tchotchkes for once in my life, when who should call? Not Luz Maria Borges, the girl of my dreams, God forbid, but some putz who doesn't even know I changed my name from Linda to Shayna when I came out ten years ago.* "Who is this, please?"

"I'm calling from the telephone company and—"

"My phone's fine."

"Listen ma'am, this is the New York telephone company, calling from your grandmother's apartment, and if you don't wanna talk to her, it's no skin off my nose."

Calling from Bubbe's? What was going on? Shayna spoke in a softer tone. "Why are you calling from my grandmother's house?"

Note: A Yiddish and Hebrew glossary appears at the end of the book.

"Listen ma'am," the man said again. "You gotta tell her there's nothing wrong with her phone. She keeps calling the phone company and saying she can't get through to nobody. Next time we send someone up here, we're gonna hafta charge her fifty bucks. I'm the third guy that's looked at her phone this week."

"Well, she just got back from Florida and no one's used the phone in six months. Do they get rusty or something?" A long shot, but you never knew.

"I'm telling you, there's nothing wrong with this phone. She got me to dial your number, and it works just fine. You wanna talk to her?"

"Of course I want to talk to her." Shayna sank down on the couch and tossed the shmate on the floor. It landed right next to a huge dustball, supporting Shayna's Theory of Cleanliness: shmutz begets shmutz, so why bother cleaning, when the more you clean, the more there is to clean? She leaned her head back on the couch as she heard the man say, "It's your granddaughter," and her grandmother say, "Who?" before she spoke into the phone in a shaky voice. "Linda, is that you, darling?"

"Yes Bubbe, it's me." Shayna didn't mind that her grandmother still called her Linda. It was one of the few remnants of her 'former life' she allowed. Besides, more often than not, her grandmother called her darling, or bubbeleh, or mamela anyway.

"How's by you, darling?"

"I'm okay, Bubbe. How's by you?" Shayna automatically raised her voice about fifty decibels so her grandmother could hear her, since she absolutely refused to wear the hearing aid Shayna's mother had bought her two years ago.

"Oh by me it's terrible. Terrible."

"What's the matter?"

"Wait, let me switch ears. I can't hear you."

"Bubbe, do you have your hearing aid on?"

"What? The ear aid? Oy mamela it's no good, it only makes it worse."

Shayna decided to let that one go for now. "Bubbe, what's wrong with your phone?"

"My phone? Oy, that lousy superintendent there wired the phone, and every time they hear my voice, they cut me right off. I been calling you and calling you, but they hear my voice and off it goes. So I went next door by Tillie. She came over and dialed—her, they put through—but the minute they heard my voice, off it went."

"Maybe you dialed wrong, Bubbe. Did you remember to dial a 'one' before my number?"

"I'm telling you, it's no good. The super wired everything; there's wires all over the apartment and I hear them all night long, talking, talking, talking, and the phone they don't let me use for love or money, oy, I'm telling you. Wait a minute, darling, he's packing up his tools there, he's leaving." Shayna heard her grandmother bang down the phone on the kitchen table and say, "Thank you. Thank you very much." She waited as her grandmother let the man out, locked the three locks behind him, and shuffled back to the phone.

"Bubbe, are you all right?" Shayna asked "Maybe you should call Sylvia to

4

come over."

"Don't send your mother. Her they'll kill for sure. I heard them talking about it over the wires." Her voice rose, bordering on hysteria, and Shayna had to hold the phone a little away from her ear. "Don't send your mother! Linda, listen to me. Her they'll kill for sure, and I want she should live. Send your father. Him they'll let through. Just your father."

"Bubbe, what are you talking about? Who would kill Sylvia?" Shayna sat up and leaned forward on the couch, as if that would help her hear better, help her make sense of what her grandmother was saying. This was very strange. Shayna had just talked to her grandmother last week when she was still in Florida and they'd had a perfectly normal conversation: first her grandmother had kvetched about the weather, it was too hot; then she reminded Shayna to send her cousin Abbie a card for the new baby, kinehora; and then she'd oy-veyed about the sad state of Shayna's marital status. It was the same conversation Shayna had been having with her grandmother for the past twelve years, ever since she'd left home, and it either annoyed her, or comforted her, depending on her mood.

"Listen, Bubbe, I'm going to hang up the phone now and call Sol, okay? Just Sol. He won't bring Sylvia, I promise. Maybe you should go next door by Tillie and wait."

"Okay, darling." There was a pause and then Shayna winced in disbelief as her grandmother started to scream. "Bastards! Get off the phone, you lousy momsers! Get away from here!"

"Bubbe, it's me. It's Linda."

"You dirty bastard. Get the hell away from here. Shut up. Shut up, you filthy momser!"

"Bubbe!" Shayna jumped as her grandmother slammed down the phone. She hung up too, and remained motionless on the couch, her head in her hands, staring at the pile of shmutz on the floor.

Tzimmy stood right in front of her, gazing into her eyes. "You always know, don't you?" Shayna murmured. "C'mon." She leaned back and patted her lap. The cat leapt up immediately, sat down and began to purr. "Tzimmy, did you hear that? Do you think Bubbe's having a nervous breakdown? I never even heard her curse before. Oy gevalt." Shayna ran her hand along Tzimmy's back as she tried to figure out what to do. I could drive down to Brooklyn, she thought. I mean, what the hell, it's not like I've got a wild Saturday night date or anything. I can make it in three hours if I don't get caught in traffic or stopped for speeding. Shayna picked up the phone again and dialed her grandmother's number, but all she got was a busy signal.

"Now what?" Shayna asked Tzimmy. She knew the obvious thing to do was call her parents, but the prospect didn't exactly thrill her. Shayna didn't get along with her mother and father very well, or to rephrase the understatement of the year, Sol and Sylvia Steinblatt were absolutely mortified by the fact that their only daughter was a lesbian. A drop-out, a junkie, an unwed mother, even a werewolf they could cope with, but a lesbian? Nothing they had ever been through, even in their wildest dreams had prepared them for their daughter's 'selfish, self-cen-

5

tered, self-absorbed, self-indulgent' behavior, as they succinctly put it. They did everything but sit shiva when Shayna told them eight years ago, and things hadn't changed much since.

Not that Shayna's adolescence had been a hunky-dory time for the Steinblatt family either. Shayna had gone through a long rebellious stage, starting at age thirteen, when she began calling her parents by their first names. ("After all, we're all adults now," she'd said. "I would have been Bat Mitzvahed already, if I'd ever gone to Hebrew School.") She'd gone through a pot-smoking stage, an I-won't-wear-anything-but-torn-jeans stage, and the famous I'm-not-going-to-college-I-want-to-live-on-a-commune stage. Shayna had calmed down considerably when she turned twenty and discovered the delights of loving women. She'd stopped taking drugs altogether, started wearing dresses again, and lo and behold, gone off to college to major in journalism. Despite all that, her parents were still convinced, even after all these years, that Shayna was a lesbian for one reason and one reason only: to torture her mother and father and drag the family name down into the mud.

"Well, here goes nothing." Shayna picked up the phone and dialed her parents' number. No answer, thank God. She dialed her father's work number, and was informed by his secretary that Mr. Steinblatt was not in the office. That's weird, Shayna thought. Mr. Steinblatt is always in the office. He's a workaholic; it's his job to always be in the office. Even on a Saturday.

Shayna called her grandmother's number again and let the busy signal rattle against her ear for a minute before hanging up the phone.

"Okay world, let me know what to do." Shayna lay her head back against the couch, letting her long brown hair cascade over the arm in a jumble of curls. She put her feet up and scrunched over, as Tzimmy adjusted herself alongside Shayna's body. Woman and cat stared out the open bay window, enjoying the fresh May air. It was May twentieth, and hallelujah! school was over. Shayna had made her students turn in all their papers a week early, despite their grumbling, so she could grade them and be through with them by the end of finals week. That way, she had a whole month off before summer school began. Well not off, exactly. She was planning on using this month to write some of the articles she hadn't had a chance to get to, but hell, today was her first day of freedom; she deserved a little break, didn't she?

Instead of relaxing though, Shayna, who never was one to sit still, had decided to do a little spring cleaning. Scattered about the floor all around her were various piles of clothes: soft wool sweaters and corduroy pants to be put in boxes she would slide under the bed; skimpy tank tops and shorts to be put in dresser drawers; and cool cotton skirts to be hung up in the closet, and some day, God willing, ironed. It wasn't that different from her apartment's usual state of affairs, though she was trying to do a little better. "I can't tell if you're coming or going," her grandmother used to say, when she'd visit Shayna's family on Long Island. She slept in Shayna's room on the extra bed that Shayna usually kept covered with books, papers, cassettes, clothes, stuffed animals, bobby pins and rollers. When her grandmother came, she'd just dump everything onto the floor with

6

one grand sweep of her arm.

But this year, Shayna had turned thirty, and vowed to become what her grandmother called a neatnik, not to be confused with a beatnik, which Shayna used to love dressing up as every Halloween of her childhood. Sorting out her clothes by season was her first step. "I suppose we should get back to the task at hand, huh, Tzimmy?" Shayna turned her head to survey her cluttered living room. "But maybe we should take a little cat nap first, don't you think?" Tzimmy purred in agreement, nudging Shayna's hand with her nose.

"Oh, so you want me to pet you, huh? What'll you give me? A trip to San Francisco? A year's supply of carob-coated rice cakes? A phone call from Luz Maria Borges, the handsomest butch this side of the Mississippi? Probably the other side, too." Shayna sighed and let a pair of dark bedroom eyes set in smooth golden-brown skin under a shock of jet black hair form on the blank TV screen of her mind. After nine months of celibacy, Shayna P. Steinblatt was hot to trot. She'd promised herself she'd be celibate for a year, wanting to move out of her lesbian adolescence, as she called it, into a more mature, committed relationship. She had spent the fall and the winter alone, and she'd learned a lot about herself. But it seemed cruel and unusual punishment to force herself to go without sex all spring. And besides, nine months was long enough; long enough to have a baby, for God's sake. And besides that, it wasn't her fault that Luz had a pair of strong arms, a tight ass, and a smile that could melt matzo balls.

Shayna had also vowed, after one too many women had said to her, "You're Jewish? Really? With those green eyes? You don't look Jewish," that she wouldn't get seriously involved with a gentile again. But the problem was Jewish butches were awfully hard to find. And besides, Luz was Puerto Rican, so even though she wasn't Jewish, she did come from a strong culture, and she had to know something about feeling like an alien in New England, the WASP capital of the world. And besides that, who knew what was really going to happen, Shayna thought. She hasn't even called to ask me out on our first date yet.

Rumor had it, via the lesbian grapevine, that Luz had a crush on Shayna. They'd known each other for years, or known of each other, rather, both of them being high profile dykes. Luz owned a local flower shop and had surprised more than one girl in town by delivering flowers from her sweetie at unexpected moments. And Shayna, in addition to teaching English 101 at the local community college, had had numerous articles published in *Gay Community News*, *Sojourner* and the *Boston Phoenix*, as well as the local papers. They'd both lived in the area for a long time now: Luz, having grown up here was an official townie; and Shayna, having gone to school and just stayed put, was doomed to be forever branded a transplanted New Yorker. Shayna had come out in this town and had no intention of going back to Long Island and being a suburbanite, which to her was the equivalent of being a sub-humanite, though she was trying to be less judgmental.

In fact, Shayna and Luz had found themselves at the same party a few weeks ago and they'd had some promising eye contact. Normally that would have been enough to inspire Shayna to walk over, introduce herself and start flirting her little tuchus off. But there was something about Luz that stopped Shayna from pouring on the charm. Maybe it was the quiet way she stood in the corner taking everything in, or the gentle way she reached up to help the hostess's six week old kitten down from on top of the refrigerator. Or maybe it was those deep dark mysterious serious eyes. Whatever it was, Shayna knew this was not someone to tease or someone to play with. So even though she did go over and say hello, she didn't bat those great big green eyes of hers, and she didn't touch Luz on the shoulder or arm with every other word. Their conversation only lasted a few minutes anyway before some new butch in town rudely interrupted them by asking Shayna to dance.

"Go ahead," Luz had said gallantly. "I'll catch a dance with you some other time." Shayna went off reluctantly and came back as soon as she could, only to find that Luz had gone. Now however, whenever they saw each other on the street, their 'hi-how-ya-doing?' always ended with 'see-ya-on-the-dance-floor.'

Shayna supposed that was progress. She had recently heard from her best friend Pearl, who'd heard from the catcher on her softball team Kim, who'd heard from her roommate Gwen, who'd heard from her massage therapist Rosie, who'd heard from her piano tuner Jean, who'd heard from her ex-lover Diana who happened to be Luz's hairdresser, that Luz was planning on asking Shayna out to the next chem-free dance at the grange, which was only two weeks away. I wish she'd call already, Shayna thought, idly twisting her fingers through a lock of her hair. If she doesn't call soon, I'll have to call her myself and ask her to ask me out.

Shayna half sat up, reaching for the phone, then lay back down again. "Patience, girl, patience," she said aloud to herself. "Oy Tzimmy, when the Goddess was handing out patience, I was standing on the wrong line, you know what I mean?" Shayna scratched the cat between the ears. "It's just like the line at the food co-op, you know, Tzimmy? It always looks like an okay line, and then the register tape breaks, or the person in front of me has to run to get an extra can of tuna fish." Shayna rubbed the cat under the chin and Tzimmy arched her neck in delight. "Ummm, you like that, huh Tzimmeleh? Want me to go to the store and get you some tuna? What do you think Luz likes to eat? I sure hope she knows how to cook." Shayna was a very fussy eater, a health food nudnik, as her father called her. Once, in high school, in her most obnoxious stage when it wasn't enough that she had stopped eating red meat, the whole world had to stop as well, she had cooked her family a supper of brown rice and stir-fried tofu and veggies. Her mother and father both had diarrhea for a week, and her grandmother insisted they all have a little coffee and prune danish after the meal, it would help with the digestion.

Speaking of her grandmother, Shayna had to do something about the present situation. She sat up and dialed her bubbe's number once more. This time, thank the Goddess, it rang.

"Hello?"

"Sol, it's your daughter. What's going on? Is Bubbe all right?"

"Who is it? Who is it?" Shayna could hear her grandmother screaming in the background, her high-pitched voice cracking like a Bar Mitzvah boy's. "Is that the lousy super? Don't talk to him, Sol. Hang up the phone, don't talk to nobody, don't let them know you're here. Sol!"

"Linda, we'll call you later, okay? We're taking her home with us."

"Okay, but listen. Some guy from the telephone company called. She keeps thinking her phone's broken and she says there's these voices coming over the wires. She—"

"I know, I know. Listen, I gotta go, I'm double-parked. We'll call you." And again, Shayna was left with a click and the buzz of the dial tone.

Shit. She placed the receiver back in its cradle, and as soon as she let go, the phone rang again. Shayna grabbed it immediately, forgetting for a moment her bubbe's always-play-hard-to-get advice.

"Hello?"

"Hello Mrs. Bubbelinski?"

"Hello Mrs. Mamelinski?"

"So nu, how's by you?"

"By me, it's terrible, Pearl. Just terrible. Oy, by me I got enough tsouris here for the whole Israeli army."

"What's the matter, Shayna?"

"It's my bubbe, Pearl. She's hearing voices. I think she's flipping out. My father was at her apartment, and you know it was bad if he took a day off from work."

"Oy, Mrs. Bubbelinski, that's terrible." Pearl listened as Shayna told her the whole story, putting in a few oys, gevalts, and even a vey iss mir or two. Pearl was Shayna's best friend. They had met several years ago, at their favorite clothing store, *Wear It In Good Health*, a boutique obviously owned by another transplanted New Yorker. They had both been tugging at a red and black tiger-striped bikini on the sales rack, when their eyes met.

"You take it," Shayna had said.

"No, you," Pearl answered. "I insist."

"No, really, it was made just for you." Finally Shayna had suggested they see what size the bathing suit was, and they both bent their heads in search of a tag. "Size three?" Pearl had read. "Feh! Who wears a size three? What kind of cocka-mammy size is that?" She held the bottom of the suit up to her body. "Look at this. My whole tuchus would stick out."

That's when Shayna noticed the button pinned to Pearl's coat: THE BEST THINGS IN LIFE ARE HALF OFF, and cracked up. A girl after my own heart, she thought. "Look at this," she said to Pearl, pointing to the button pinned to her own lapel: I CAME, I SAW, I DID A LITTLE SHOPPING. "A match made in heaven," Pearl said. "Pleased to meet you. I'm Pearl Gold."

"Shayna P. Steinblatt." Shayna took Pearl's outstretched hand. "Just plain Gold?" she asked. "Not Goldman, or Goldstein, or Goldberg? Just Gold?"

"Yeah," Pearl said. "We shortened it."

"From what?"

"Kennedy." Pearl winked and Shayna cracked up again. "C'mon," Pearl said.

9

"I just saved myself fifteen-ninety-five, I'll buy you some coffee and cake." Over tea, Shayna had found out Pearl was from Great Neck, which she referred to as Great Drek, just a stone's throw from Woodmere, Shayna's old stomping grounds, which Shayna of course called Vey Iss Mir. They'd talked and laughed for hours, and it had been Mrs. Bubbelinski and Mrs. Mamelinksi ever since.

"You want I should come over with some chicken soup and an Allen Sherman record?" Pearl now offered. "I'll even go to Bread and Tsouris and get the chicken special for you, organic."

"Thanks, Pearlie," Shayna said, her eyes wandering around the living room, "but I'm right in the middle of spring cleaning and I've got other work to do after that and—"

"Listen Shayna," Pearl interrupted. "You want my advice?"

"Do I have a choice?"

"No. Now listen, Shayna. I know you. You're gonna clean up your apartment and write five articles you've been putting off and then you're going to bake sourdough bread from scratch and before you know it, your shoulders will be stuck up around your ears and you'll have a migraine from all that futile activity you're doing to try to avoid feeling your feelings." Pearl paused and then gentled her voice. "Take a break, Shayna. You must be scared or sad, or something. Your bubbe's really important to you."

There was a long silence. "I hate you, Mrs. Mamelinski."

"I know you do, Mrs. Bubbelinski. That's what friends are for. But how do you feel?"

"I don't know. Pretty numb, I guess. I can't believe it happened. I'm not even sure what happened. Or what I should do. Now she's at my parents' house and if I want to talk to her I have to go through them."

"Well, give it a day or two. At least she's not by herself."

"Yeah, okay. Maybe I'll light a candle and send her some energy or something groovy like that." Shayna put her hand across her forehead and began rubbing the space between her eyebrows which had begun to furrow.

"Well, call me later if you want. I'm probably just going to play sofa spud in front of the VCR tonight. Your dream girl call you yet?"

"No, but she's kinda shy. I'm giving her a little time."

"Oh my God, you're giving her a little time? She must be pretty special."

"She is, Pearlie. I don't know, I just have this feeling about her. She's so quiet, and gentle and soft-spoken. She's just not your average girl."

"I'll say. She must be something else to weasel five minutes out of Ms. I-Gotta-Have-It-Yesterday."

Shayna laughed. "It's so nice to be known, you know. Makes me feel truly appreciated. Hey, how come you're being a couch latke tonight? Aren't the girls still knocking down your door?"

"Hardly. To tell you the truth, at this point I'd like to knock both their heads together." Pearl, in her quest for Princess Charming, was dating two women at once. It took half the time, she pointed out to Shayna, but caused twice the aggravation. You can't with one tuchus dance at two weddings, Shayna reminded Pearl, who promptly reminded her that she, unlike Shayna, was not the marrying kind.

"Listen, Mrs. Bubbelinski, I'll talk to you later."

"Okay, Mrs. Mamelinski. See ya." Shayna hung up the phone, picked up the shmate from the floor and wandered into the kitchen. She stuffed the rag into a bucket under the sink and then walked over to the last cabinet on the left, where she kept her 'Jewish supplies': a jar of gefilte fish, a bottle of borsht, a box of matzo meal, the North Shore Hadassah cookbook, and some candles.

"Not a yarzheit candle, Tzimmy," Shayna said as she moved things around. Tzimmy had followed Shayna into the kitchen and was crunching on a piece of dry cat food, pretending she still had teeth. "She may have just turned ninety-nine, but she's still alive and kicking. Don't I have any Shabbas candles left?" Shayna fished around in a blue and white box, pulled out two candle stubs and pointed one at Tzimmy. "Yes, I know it's hard to believe she's ninety-nine," Shayna said, as though addressing every shocked person she had ever told her bubbe's age to, "but she is. Lots of people live past their hundredth birthday: Rose Kennedy, Grandma Moses…" Shayna had written an article the year before about people who live to be a hundred. She'd uncovered lots of fascinating information about centenarians. The man who had posed for the Indian nickel had actually lived to be one-hundred-fourteen, and there was also a man from North Carolina, who at age one-hundred, had run for Congress (he didn't win.) There was even an organization called the American Centenarian Committee, with a good, strong membership. Shayna had been inspired to write the article partly because she thought it would make a good story, but mostly to reassure herself that her grandmother wasn't quite at death's door yet. When her bubbe had first turned ninety, Shayna had gone into an absolute panic that the end was near. But as the years passed and her grandmother stayed healthy and active, it seemed as if her bubbe could, and would live forever. But today's turn of events cut through Shayna's denial like a knife piercing her heart.

Shayna put the candles into two pewter candlesticks and set them on the kitchen table. Then she went into her study, untacked a photo from her bulletin board and brought it back into the kitchen. The picture was taken two years ago: Shayna and her grandmother were laughing, their heads bent together, standing on the boardwalk at Brighton Beach. Shayna propped up the photo and lit the candles, her hands automatically making three small circles to gather the light of the flames toward her, as though it were Shabbas. "Brucha Aht Shekhina, Elohanu, Malka, Ha-Olam. Blessed Art Thou, Oh Lordess, Our Goddess, Queen of the Universe, Whoever You Are. Please, oh please take care of my Bubbe." Shayna's chin quivered, her voice broke, her shoulders relaxed, and the tears finally came.

Chapter Two

Shayna sat in her study, a notebook on her lap and several other notebooks spread out on a small table in front of her, along with pens, pencils, two teacups, half a bag of whole wheat pretzels, the last two issues of the Sunday *New York Times*, the current issue of *off our backs*, a pile of photos, a small blue eraser shaped like a tiny typewriter, nail scissors, a pair of earrings made of sea shells, and a slinky. She was curled up in a big green overstuffed easy chair that was getting funky around the edges, due to the persistence of Tzimmy's claws. Pearl (as well as many other people) couldn't understand how Shayna could work in such a mess. "Cluttered house, clear mind," Shayna would say, in answer to Pearl's kvetching.

"I just don't know how you stand it," Pearl often said. "If we lived together, it would be just like Felix and Oscar in *The Odd Couple*. I'd be picking up after you all the time."

"Your house is so neat, it scares me," Shayna would comment whenever she visited Pearl. "Nothing moves, nothing breathes. Every tchotchke has its place. I'm scared to touch anything."

"Touch, touch. I can't help it if I'm compulsive. C'mere, I'll show you something." Early in their friendship, Pearl had taken Shayna by the hand through her living room and into her kitchen pantry. "Open the bottom drawer," she said. Shayna did, and to her delight found a regular, normal junk drawer. Loose nails and screws nestled in bits of wrapping paper, along with a hammer, a screwdriver, several light bulbs, two rulers, a length of rope, scissors, a flashlight, crumpled maps, candles, batteries of all sizes, a couple of draydls, and one or two stray M&M's. Shayna was visibly relieved. "Thank Goddess, you're only human like the rest of us."

There's always one thing, Shayna thought, tapping her pen against her right cheek. One thing, one little idiosyncrasy that makes them human. That makes them imperfect. It has to be unexpected, but predictable at the same time. Unexpected enough to be interesting and out of character, but predictable enough to be believable.

Shayna was trying to put together a profile of Doris White for her bi-monthly column, *Women To Watch*, which she wrote for the local newspaper. The paper was quite conservative, and in the year and a half she'd done the column, Shayna had only interviewed two lesbians, neither of whom felt safe enough to come out in print. Shayna had often thought of making some suggestions to her editor: she could do a piece on Janet and Cynthia, who had just had turkey baster triplets; or Donna and Lizette, who had just celebrated their twentieth anniversary (now that was lesbian news); or Sue Jackson who had been a first place triathlon winner at the Gay Games. But Shayna knew her editor would never go for those kind of ideas, so here she was, stuck with Doris White, whose only claim to fame seemed to be the fact that she had stayed married to the same staunch Republican for fifty years, raised their five kids, knit sweaters for their thirteen grandchildren, and baked award-winning peach pies for the Ladies Auxiliary Club.

Not that I'm any better than she is, Shayna thought, for after all Shayna P. Steinblatt was a bona fide feminist who firmly believed every woman had the right to choose. But who, given the choice, would actually pick a life like that? Well, you love to knit, a voice inside Shayna's head reminded her, and you baked carob macaroons for the Women's Softball League's fundraiser last year.

"But I'm not married," Shayna said aloud, beginning to doodle on the blank page of her notebook. But you'd like to be, the voice inside her head shot back. Shayna drew a three tiered wedding cake with a bride and bride on the top layer, and stared at it. Maybe I'm just jealous of Mr. and Mrs. Doris White, she thought, picking up their photo from the table. The article was a profile of Doris, but when the photographer had gone to her house, she'd insisted on a family portrait, with Ralph right by her side on the sofa.

Shayna studied the picture, looking for inspiration. It's true, she thought, when people live together for that long, they do begin to resemble each other. Both Mr. and Mrs. W. (Shayna was sure Doris White would rather die than be called Ms.) had short gray hair, round faces and thick, wire-rimmed glasses. "I want that," Shayna said out loud, tears from nowhere springing to her eyes. "I'm an old-fashioned girl. I believe in happily ever after, or maybe not so happily ever after, but ever after anyway. There's gotta be someone out there who wants only me." Shayna wiped her eyes with the back of her hand and put the photo down. I'm such a sap, she thought. The next thing you know, I'll be listening to a Ferron tape and bawling my head off. What's with me today? One minute I'm trying to get an angle on Doris White and the next minute I'm a mess. Maybe I'm pre-menstrual.

But Shayna knew that wasn't it. She had just finished bleeding on Thursday, and it was only Sunday. Sundays were hard for Shayna. Sunday was the day lovers spent reading the New York Times, eating bagels and lox, making love and doing the laundry. Sunday was the day families spent together, taking the kids to the park, going for long drives and eating out. Sunday was the day Shayna felt most alone, so Sunday was the day she reserved for writing articles. "I'm not a worka-holic like my father," Shayna flatly told Pearl, when thusly accused. "I just like working on Sundays when it's nice and quiet."

"Bullshit," Pearl answered. "Nobody likes working on Sundays, Mrs. Bubbelinski, not even Brenda Starr. C'mon, let's go have brunch somewhere," she'd say to Shayna, "the quiche is on me." Or she'd call Shayna to take in a matinee if it was rainy, a walk if it was sunny, or a trip to the mall if they were having a sale.

Today though, Pearl was visiting her family in Boston. Who else can I call, Shayna asked herself. Everyone seemed so busy lately. Trudy had a new lover and was off to New York every weekend; Monica had just joined AA and went to meetings every Sunday; Alice was totally depressed because her therapist and her ex had both just gone straight. Shayna had heard there was a pot luck dinner for menopausal women happening as well as a brunch for women just coming out, but unfortunately (or maybe fortunately) she wasn't qualified, at this point in her life, to attend either.

Wasn't there anyone else around with the Sunday blues? Even Tzimmy was outside, stretched across the lawn, soaking up the sun. Shayna looked out the window at the cat and then stared down at her wedding cake drawing again. "Bubbe's right, I really should get married. It's no good to be alone," she said, letting her eyes take in the emptiness of her apartment. "Sometimes I talk to the walls at night, just so I can have someone to talk to," she said, mimicking her grandmother, who did in fact talk to the walls and had told Shayna so many times. "It's no big deal, Bubbe," Shayna had said. "You don't have a thing to worry about, until the walls start talking back."

Should I call my parents' house, Shayna wondered, biting the tip of her pen in an effort not to chomp on her nails. I'm worried about Bubbe. Is she getting Alzheimer's? Or just going senile? What will they do with her? They, being of course Shayna's mother and father. They'd been talking about putting Shayna's grandmother in a nursing home for years. They'd even found a place in Florida that wasn't far from the hotel she stayed at every winter between Chanukah and Pesach.

But Shayna's grandmother didn't want to move. "Florida, who lives in Florida? Old people, that's who," she'd say to Shayna with disdain, for after all, she didn't belong in that category. "What would I do all year in Florida? Here I got the apartment; I got friends; I go down on the avenue, I do a little shopping; I go down to the boardwalk, I sit a little by the water. What's in Florida? One room. Four walls and a bed, that's all. Don't let them take from me the apartment, mamela. This is my home."

"Don't worry, Bubbe. No one's going to take the apartment from you. It's your house, they can't take it away." Shayna would reassure her grandmother with words she wanted to, but couldn't quite believe, especially after the phone conversations she had with her mother.

"Linda, we've talked about this a hundred times already," her mother would say, and Shayna would scowl, wishing for the millionth time her mother would call her Shayna, the name she had chosen for herself, instead of the name her parents had given her. "Your grandmother can't stay there much longer, the place is falling down all around her. Look up next time you're there: the ceiling is full of cracks. And the elevator's been broken for a week—is that what you want for her—a woman your grandmother's age shlepping groceries up five flights of stairs? At a home she wouldn't have to shop, she wouldn't have to cook, everything would be done for her." Mrs. Steinblatt had obviously looked into the joys of nursing home life. "She wouldn't have to wash out her panties by hand every night, she wouldn't have to dust all that furniture. There's activities there—card games and singing circles—it would be the best thing for her. She's by herself too much, your grandmother. If you really love her, if you really want to do her a favor, you'll help me convince her to get out of that crummy apartment."

"But Sylvia, that's the point: she doesn't want everything done for her. She likes to shop and cook and clean. What's she going to do in a nursing home all day, sit and twiddle her thumbs? You can't just take a person's home away from her."

"Linda, you're impossible. You're just as stubborn as she is. What if she wakes up dead one morning, God forbid? Who's going to find her? What if she falls and breaks her hip and she can't crawl to the phone? Use your head, Linda. Your grandmother is ninety-nine years old."

"And she's done fine up till now, hasn't she?" Shayna's voice rose, as what little patience she had ebbed away. "She hasn't fallen down and broken her hip. She hasn't dropped dead in the living room. Would you like to live in a nursing home, Sylvia? Would you like to live the last years of your life among strangers?"

Mrs. Steinblatt was not one to be outshouted. "What if she forgets to take her pills and gets dizzy and falls down in the street? What if she gets hit by a car? Is that what you want?"

The apple, as they say, does not fall far from the tree. "Yes, Sylvia, that's exactly what I want," Shayna screamed. "I want Bubbe should get run over on Coney Island Avenue and left out there to rot under the boardwalk."

"Linda." Mrs. Steinblatt shocked. "That's a terrible thing to say."

Shayna let out a long breath. "Sylvia why do we have to fight like this?"

"Fighting? Who's fighting?" Shayna heard the click of a lighter as her mother lit a cigarette to calm her nerves. "I'm not fighting with you, Linda," she said in an even voice. "I'm trying to have a civil conversation with you, but you just don't seem to understand that your grandmother is no longer capable of taking care of herself."

"And you just don't seem to understand," Shayna matched her mother's tone of voice perfectly, "what it means to force someone to give up their home."

"Don't be fresh, young lady. This is your mother you're talking to."

As if I could forget, Shayna thought, her eyebrows meeting in the center of her forehead for a conference, the outcome of which was to try a different tactic. "Sylvia, put yourself in Bubbe's place. If you were that old, what would you want me to do with you?"

"Take me out in the back yard and shoot me."

"Fine. I'll remember that. Look, I gotta go." Shayna had hung up the phone upset, but not too concerned. Her mother had been worrying about her grandmother for years now, just like her grandmother had been worrying about Shayna. There's nothing wrong with women living alone, Shayna thought. We can make it. We can take care of ourselves just fine. Except on Sundays.

On Sundays, Shayna's grandmother usually called her, even though Shayna would say, Bubbe, let me call you, I can afford it. Most of the time, Shayna wound up calling her back anyway, since more often than not, she was out with Pearl, and her grandmother got her answering machine, which she was finally getting the hang of. At first she didn't understand the concept at all, and thought someone else was in Shayna's apartment, answering her phone.

"You shouldn't let strangers come in the house to use the phone when you ain't home," she said to Shayna.

"No, Bubbe, it's a machine," Shayna tried to explain. "I turn it on when I'm not home and then I know who to call back. It's me, it's my voice on the machine."

"So if you're there talking on the machine, why don't you pick up the phone when I call?"

Shayna finally got her grandmother to say a few words after the beep, but she still didn't seem to believe that Shayna wasn't there. "It's Bubbe. Bubbe Tzeydl," she would say, just in case Shayna might mix her up with all the other bubbes that regularly called her on Sunday mornings. "Call me. Call me right back. I'm sitting right here by the telephone, waiting for your call. I ain't gonna move until I hear from you."

But this Sunday, Tzeydl hadn't called and it was already after three o'clock. Talking to her grandmother every week helped Shayna feel a little less alone on the planet. Shayna would tell her what she did over the weekend, and what she was planning to have for supper, and Tzeydl would fill Shayna in on the family gossip and kvetch a little about her aches and pains, and they would both hang up fortified to face the beginning of another week. What if something happens to Bubbe, Shayna thought, her eyes wandering over to the phone. Then I'll be all alone in the world. I know she's ninety-nine, but she's gotta make it to her hundredth birthday at least. That's only eight months away. I know she's old, but she's been old ever since I can remember, ever since I was born. I know she can't live forever, but I want her to. Tears rose in Shayna's eyes again, and her chin began to tremble.

"C'mon, get a grip, Shayna." She clutched the arms of the chair as she scolded herself. "You've been crying on and off all day and there's nothing to worry about. No news is good news, remember? You'll call tomorrow when Sol's in the office. That'll be one less parent to deal with. Now let's get back to our regularly scheduled program: Doris White."

Shayna dried her eyes and tried to concentrate on the notes she'd taken last week, sitting in Doris White's living room. They might as well have been the original Ten Commandments for all the sense she could make of them.

"Maybe I need a cup of tea and a little nosh." Shayna pushed herself out of her chair and picked up the two teacups on the table. "Tea for two?" she asked her friend the wall. "Don't you dare answer me," she called over her shoulder. "Then I'll know I'm really meshugeh."

She took the teacups into the kitchen and put up some water to boil. Maybe Luz will call today, Shayna thought, checking the kitchen clock. It was shaped like a cat and its eyeballs and tail wandered back and forth with every tick of the second hand. Three-thirty-five. Was Luz out on a date? Hanging out with a friend? Having wild sex with some lucky girl? All alone, day-dreaming about Shayna?

Fantasizing about her with her hand in her crotch? You pig, Shayna scolded herself. She's not that kind of girl. At least she doesn't seem like it. Too bad.

Shayna sauntered over to the refrigerator while the water was boiling and opened the door. "Pitiful," she murmured, surveying the dismal scene before her. "Bubbe would plotz if she knew her favorite granddaughter lived like this." Shayna opened a Brown Cow yogurt container and peered in at some leftover millet that had definitely seen better days. "Kind of an interesting effect," she said, prodding the white fuzz with the container's lid. "Like snow on a mountain top. Lucky for the world I'm not a poet." She reclosed the lid and tossed the container into the trash. "Yes! Two points." Shayna spun on her heels to see what else she could chuck across the room. She moved aside a jar of granola, a bottle of unfiltered apple juice, a loaf of seven grain bread, and a package of soy pups. "Nothing to write home about," she muttered, opening the vegetable bin. She picked up a soggy plastic baggy and her thumb went through what used to be a cucumber. "Yuk."

Shayna took the mess over to the trash and dumped it as the tea kettle whistled on the stove. "Oh well, I wasn't that hungry anyway," she said, making herself a cup of peppermint tea in her favorite Betty Boop mug. She went back into her study and plopped herself down in her chair. Notebook on lap and pen in hand, she tried again. But it was no use. Doris White could have been Bette Midler, Barbra Streisand or any one of Shayna's many strong Jewish women idols, and still her attention span would have been as short as a wick on a Chanukah candle. Finally Shayna decided to try an old trick she used with her writing students at least once a semester as a last resort, usually on a gorgeous sunny day, when her students would rather be doing anything but writing. When all else fails, write about not writing, she'd tell them. What the hell, Shayna thought. She turned to a fresh doodle-free page and wrote at the top of it:

How To Write An Article......Not!

1. Sit down.
2. Pick up notebook.
3. Pick up pen.

Well, that was a start, anyway. Shayna looked around her study. Her eyes wandered through the doorway into the adjoining living room and landed on the pile of shmutz she hadn't picked up yesterday.

4. Notice shmutz on living room floor.
5. Take a sip of tea.

Shayna picked up her mug and quickly put it down. The tea was still way too hot.

6. Almost burn hands.
7. Study hands.
8. Notice freckle on pointer of left hand and snake ring with ruby eye on fourth finger.
9. Wish snake ring was wedding band.
10. Marvel at your incredible political incorrectness.
11. Look at hands again.

12. Decide hands don't look like hands of a journalist.

13. Study hands closely. Decide fingers are too short for playing piano and nails are too uneven to model for hand lotion commercials with Madge.

14. Decide, by process of elimination, that you might as well be a journalist.

15. Notice ink smudge on palm and callus on top of third finger: sure signs of a roving reporter.

16. Feel relieved.

17. Wonder why, if you really are a writer, you've been sitting here all afternoon, unable to pull together one lousy little article about Doris White.

18. Decide that even though you really are a writer, you're really not a very good writer.

19. Feel bad.

20. Feel very bad.

21. Feel bad for feeling bad. Remember how much money you spent in five years of therapy learning to love and accept yourself, and what a waste that's been.

22. Think about how disappointed your therapist, or rather your ex-therapist would be in you.

23. Think of all the great things you could have done with that money.

24. Feel guilty for even thinking that.

25. Feel shitty in general.

26. Think about what your ex-therapist would suggest.

27. "Do something nice for yourself."

28. Decide to take her advice. Decide to walk downtown and buy yourself a piece of ruggelech.

29. Okay, but what about the article?

30. Skip it. Your deadline's not until Wednesday and you work better under pressure anyway.

31. Okay, but am I a lazy, good-for-nothing shlemiel who'll never get anything published in the *New York Times* and is doomed to teach Intro to Composition forever?

32. Yes, but I love you anyway.

Shayna put down her pen with satisfaction. So that's why I paid my therapist forty bucks an hour every week for all those years: so I could goof off and not feel bad about it. Okay. She took a sip of tea, which was finally lukewarm, just the way she liked it, and then stood up to shut off the overhead light.

"The office is closed," she announced to the world in general. "Ms. Steinblatt is not in. Ms. Steinblatt is not a workaholic. Ms. Steinblatt is out, and no, we don't know when we expect her back. Hold my calls." Shayna switched on her answering machine on the way to the kitchen. She lifted her pocketbook from the back of one of her pink vinyl chairs and slung it onto her shoulder. "I deserve a little treat," she said, stopping off in the bathroom to check her reflection in the full length mirror. "Can I really let myself be seen in public in sweats?" she asked her twin in the mirror, who was busy brushing her waist length hair, trying to tame her unruly curls. "Oh, what the hell, there's probably no one at Nosh A Bissl at this hour anyway."

Nosh A Bissl, a bakery owned by yet another transplanted New Yorker smack in the middle of downtown, was Shayna's home away from home. You see, the unexpected, yet predictable thing about Shayna, the thing that made her human like the rest of us, was that even though she'd get herself a buzz cut long before she'd let a Twinkle or an Oreo cookie pass between her lips, when it came to Jewish food, she relaxed her no-white-flour-no-white-sugar regiment and let the flavors of her childhood soothe her soul, even if they did unsettle her stomach.

Shayna left the house, slamming the door behind her, and ran down the steps, stopping of course to bid a fond farewell to Tzimmy. "No, don't bother getting up Tzimmy. It's okay. Don't knock yourself out." Shayna bent over to run her hand along the length of the comatose cat's back. "Maybe I'll get inspired," she said, hiking her shoulder bag back up her arm. "Maybe Doris White will be downtown doing something exotic. Or erotic. You never know." Shayna shook her head at herself. "Shayna, Shayna, Shayna, you have a one track mind. Who's going to put up with you? Uh-oh, that's not a very self-loving thing to say." She turned the corner and stopped, waiting for the light to change. "Mwah!" She suddenly planted a kiss smack dab in the middle of her own left palm. "Shayna P. Steinblatt, you are a wonderful prize that some lucky girl is going to treasure someday, even if you do have this strange habit of talking to yourself in public. Now shut your mouth, before you put your flat foot in it." The light turned green and Shayna crossed the street with a smile on her punim. Maybe, just maybe, she really was lovable after all.

Chapter Three

Shayna sauntered up Main Street soaking up the late afternoon sun. It was warmer out on the street than it was inside her uninsulated apartment and she began to feel a little better as she neared the center of town. The street was crowded for a Sunday: a bunch of high school kids in black leather jackets with green and orange mohawk haircuts were leaning against the plate glass window of a music store; a few artsy-fartsy types sat at an outdoor cafe, drinking cappuccino and smoking clove cigarettes, and some dykes stood outside the women's bookstore, the butches fingering the loose change in their pockets and the femmes with their arms folded, shifting their weight from side to side. They weren't women Shayna knew very well, so she just nodded hi and sauntered on.

There was a crowd gathered outside Nosh A Bissl. Probably a street musician, Shayna thought, slowing her pace in spite of the fact that she hated street musicians. "They're all lousy imitations of Ani Difranco," she'd say to Pearl, who always made her stop and listen, and worse yet, throw a few coins into their beat-up, open guitar cases. As soon as it got warm, Main Street turned into a three ring circus, and Shayna wondered what it was this time—a juggler tossing fire into the air, a ventriloquist with a dummy that looked like a chimpanzee on his lap, a musician playing Beethoven's Fifth by rubbing the rims of wine glasses filled with various amounts of water—Main Street and Shayna had seen them all. Some of the acts were so bad she sometimes wondered if the whole thing was a set-up: while one person was distracting everyone with their lack of talent and their chutzpah in displaying it, their crony was probably busily picking pockets and stealing purses.

You can take the girl out of New York, but you can't take the New York out of the girl, Shayna thought, clutching her shoulder bag to her side, with the part that opens pressed tightly to her body as she joined the crowd, for after all, she was a part-time reporter and it was her job to keep her shnozzola out for anything that might make an interesting story. Shayna craned her neck, but being five foot one and three quarters, she couldn't see much, especially since a teenage boy whose hormones had gone wild had planted himself right in front of her. I wonder what this kid eats. He must be over seven feet tall, Shayna thought, staring into the skull and cross-bones painted on the back of his jacket and decorated with safety pins at exactly her eye level. She moved to the side, just as the boy gave a low whistle and said to his companion, a shorter version of himself, "Man, that's some pig."

From her new vantage point, Shayna could just make out a middle-aged woman in the center of the crowd, who seemed to be the focus of this attention. Shayna could see she had something on the end of a leash, but she couldn't see what. Probably a ferret—they were pretty popular these days—or some kind of exotic dog. But Shayna didn't really care what it was at the moment, for after all, what was a rare spectacle of Mother Nature, compared to an all too common every day occurrence of Women's Oppression?

"Excuse me," Shayna said, tapping the boy on his shoulder, which was all she could reach. "You have no right to call that woman a pig." Shayna spoke in her most authoritative Ms.-Steinblatt-is-the-teacher-and-if-you-don't-watch-your-step-she'll-make-you-stay-after-school-even-if-this-is-a-community-college voice.

"A woman is a human being. She is not a pig. She is not a chick. She was not put on this planet so you could rate her sexual attributes. Contrary to what the patriarchy would have you believe, not every woman is tall, thin, blonde, eighteen and panting for your approval. Do you understand me?"

"Hey, chill out." The boy flipped some metallic blue hair our of his eyes. "I wasn't talking about the lady, man. I was talking about the pig." He pointed a bony finger.

"What pig?"

"That pig," someone behind Shayna said. She followed the boy's finger with her eyes, and there, sure enough, at the end of the woman's leash was a fat little black pig.

"Cute little porker, ain't he?"

Shayna turned around to see who had spoken to her and almost died, for who of all people was standing there listening to her ranting and raving like Miss or rather Ms. Obnoxious Feminist of 1997? Not Pearl, who was used to her and loved her anyway; not Alix Dobkin, who would at least be proud of her for opening her big Jewish mouth; not even some guy from the New York Telephone Company who Shayna didn't give two knadlech about, but Luz Maria Borges, Shayna's crush, and we sure ain't talking about orange soda here. "Hi." Shayna's left hand automatically flew up to her hopelessly farshimmeled hair, and her right hand swung her shoulderbag across her body in a desperate attempt at hiding her less-than-glamorous sweat shirt.

"Hi," Luz chuckled. "Look at that little pig. Cute as a button. I wonder what she feeds it."

"Walk this way," Shayna said, bending over, clasping her hands behind her back and pointing her feet out like a duck. Luz laughed and followed Shayna, who wove her way through the crowd, nonchalantly tucking in her sweatshirt. When they got close to the pig, Shayna straightened up and put her finger to her lips. Luz nodded, and watched Shayna pull a notebook and pen out of her pocketbook and step right up to the woman holding the leash. She cleared her throat. "Excuse me, I'm Shayna P. Steinblatt, reporter extraordinaire," she said, this time in her friendly, interested, yes-I-did-say-reporter-but-I'm-not-like-all-the-rest-you-can-trust-me-with-your-most-intimate-secrets voice.

Only you, Shayna thought to herself. One minute Gloria Steinem, the next minute Lois Lane. "I see you have a most unusual pet there. A pig, isn't it?"

"Oh yes, she's a pig. An African pygmy pig." The woman half turned around and momentarily disappointed Shayna by not being Doris White.

"A pygmie pig," Shayna repeated, writing it down. "What's her name? What does she eat? Where does she sleep?"

"Watch her ears. Don't pull them." The woman turned toward the pig and the three children who were petting her. One of the children squealed and stepped back as the pig started nibbling on her shoelace. "Her name is Wilma, after Wilbur in Charlotte's Web. That was my favorite book when I was a little girl. Ever since I read it, I've always wanted a pig. So this year I decided it was now or never. They can live twenty-five, thirty years, and I'm not getting any younger." The woman laughed. "They're much smarter than dogs, you know. You can train them to do anything. Watch this." She reached into her pocket and pulled out a dog biscuit, which, in this reincarnation was destined to become a pig biscuit. "Sit down, Wilma. That's a good girl. Now sit pretty." The pig raised her two front hoofs off the ground. The woman fed her a biscuit and then told her to sit again. "Now shake hands." The pig extended her right hoof which Shayna shook vigorously. "That's a good piggy-wiggy. Here." Once more Wilma was rewarded. "She eats special pig food I get at the vet's. And she has her own bed. I made it out of a laundry basket."

"Fascinating," Shayna said, still taking notes. "Might I have your phone number? Maybe I'll do a story. If you're interested, of course."

"Oh, sure. I love showing Wilma off. I think more people should have pigs for pets. They're very affectionate and they bring a smile to everyone's face. Why, we've emptied out three entire restaurants just this afternoon." As the woman spoke, she wrote her phone number down in Shayna's notebook.

"There," Shayna said, stepping back to stand next to Luz. "Got any more questions?"

"Just one. Do women always give you their phone numbers so easily?"

Shayna laughed. "Yeah, everyone loves to talk about themselves. That's one of the first things you learn in this business. Hey, look at that." Shayna pointed at a mother with her two year old daughter on a kiddie leash, approaching Wilma. The child strained on her leash trying to touch the pig, and the pig strained at her leash trying to touch the child. "Oh Goddess, where's my camera? Is that a prize-winning picture or what? I bet the A.P. would give me a thousand bucks for that picture. Shit." Shayna watched, as a month's rent, food, utilities and printer cartridges flashed before her eyes. Oh well, a reporter's motto, just like the Boy Scouts was Be Prepared, and obviously Shayna wasn't.

"What's the A.P.?" Luz asked.

"The Associated Press. Now what I'd really like to do," Shayna said, besides kiss your pupik that is, "is interview the pig. I mean, how do you think Wilma felt walking past the butcher shop on Adams Street? Does she go wild when that woman eats bacon and eggs for breakfast? Does she like living high on the hog, if you know what I mean?"

Luz laughed. "Why don't you ask her?"

Shayna stood with her hands on her hips, watching Wilma who was sitting pretty again, waiting for a treat. "I don't know. You think she speaks English? Maybe she understands pig-latin. Goddess, a pig in the house, how unkosher can you get? My grandmother would plotz."

"Well, you'd never see a pet pig in Puerto Rico, that's for sure. The only pigs there are served on a plate."

"That pig's never gonna wind up on a plate," Shayna said, wondering if her sweatshirt looked better untucked after all, and if she should casually pull it out again. "Wilma probably eats off a plate. And sleeps on a pink satin pillow and gets breakfast in bed every morning."

"On a silver tray with one long-stemmed red rose." Luz grinned down at Shayna, who lowered her eyes demurely as a soft blush spread across her cheeks. Stop it, she ordered her face. She took a deep breath and looked up at Luz, who was now staring at the tips of her sneakers.

Shayna studied her closely. She seemed to be alone. She didn't look like she had just been fucking her brains out. Every short black hair was perfectly in place; the collar of her white shirt was freshly ironed, if not starched, and stood up stiffly around her tan hickey-free neck. Her jeans were creased down the front and her keys were clipped to a belt loop on the side. A good old-fashioned butch, Shayna thought with admiration. But will she break my heart? What if she's into non-monogamy? What if she hates cats? What if she wants to move to a big city? What if she's allergic to matzo meal? Whoa, slow down, girl. Shayna held onto the strap of her shoulder bag for dear life, as if it were an anchor, keeping her moored to the moment as the tide of the future threatened to carry her away.

"So, um, what are you doing out in town on such a beautiful day?" Shayna asked, not daring to add, besides being beautiful yourself.

"I'm working. I just closed the shop for a minute to see what all the fuss was about. It's slow today anyway." Luz half-turned toward the corner of Oak and Main. "Walk me back?"

"Sure."

They both turned and headed up Main Street, Luz with her hands thrust deep in her pockets, and Shayna playing with the clasp of her shoulderbag. Shayna shlepped along, trying to stretch the time it would take to walk the block and a half to Petal Pushers, the florist where Luz worked. Now how can I slip dancing into the conversation so she'll ask me out, Shayna wondered. Well, first we have to start talking to each other so there'll be a conversation to slip it into. She looked at Luz, who said nothing, but started whistling a tune to walk by. Oh great, Shayna thought, she's no help. Oy, I'm such a social shlemiel. Just say anything: dancing, prancing, glancing, advancing, romancing. No, that's all too obvious. Let her bring it up. Remember what you've learned in the last nine months of solitude? You're fine without a girlfriend. You're not going to control things this time. You're going to let someone else chase you for a change.

Okay, fine. I'll talk about the weather. "Gorgeous day," Shayna said. "Kind of makes me feel like dancing." She looked up, but Luz wasn't standing to her right as she had been a moment ago. Now what? Shayna turned around and saw her a few yards back, flipping through her keys and fitting them into a door.

"Hey, back it up, Jack," Luz called, motioning with her hand.

"Sorry." Shayna backtracked with an embarrassed smile on her face as Luz peeled a Gone-Fishing-Be-Back-In-Five-Minutes sign off the door.

"After you," Luz said, stepping back to let Shayna in.

"Oh, it smells so good in here." Shayna stepped into the shop, shut her eyes and inhaled deeply. "Oh, I wish I could wear this smell. This is a great place to work." She opened her eyes and looked around. "All these beautiful flowers. Look, what a gorgeous African violet." Shayna took a step towards the flowering plant and reached out to touch its furry leaves.

"Don't touch it." Luz's hand shot out and stopped Shayna's arm. "Their leaves are very sensitive." Speaking of sensitive, Shayna could feel the warmth of Luz's skin through her sweatshirt, giving her a little thrill. "That's my special plant. It's not for sale. I rescued it from a dumpster and the poor thing was so brown and dry, I didn't know if it would make it. I took care of it for six months and then it bloomed on my birthday."

"Wow, that's magic," Shayna said, duly impressed.

"C'mere, look at these." Luz touched Shayna's shoulder and steered her toward the back of the store, to a cooler with sliding glass doors. "See the roses? They're my favorite. Aren't they pretty?" Luz pointed proudly. "I'm in charge of roses."

"They're beautiful. Do you own the store?"

"As a matter of fact, I do."

"Do you always work on Sundays?"

"Hell, no. You gotta be nuts to work on Sundays. I'm just filling in for someone who's sick."

"Oh." Great. It's unanimous, then. Both my best friend and my potential girlfriend think I'm a jerk for working on Sundays. Oh well. Shayna studied the flowers. "Are those irises? I love irises. Too bad those aren't open yet."

"Watch this." Luz slid open the glass door and extracted an iris from the bunch in the vase, shaking it briskly to get the water off its stem. Then she flicked her middle finger against the bud four or five times, until the flower burst open.

"Wow, you really do know magic."

"Nah, anyone can do it. Wanna try?"

"Okay."

Luz reached into the cooler again and offered a soon-to-bloom iris to Shayna. She tapped the flower gently but nothing happened.

"You have to do it a little harder," Luz said, taking the flower. "See?" And once more she made the flower open. "Try again."

Shayna tapped her finger against another iris. "Look, it's working, it's working," she said as the iris spread its petals. "Just one more should do it." Shayna tapped the flower again and the iris fell off its stem. "Oh, I ruined it." Shayna felt like a little kid who licked her ice cream cone just a tad too hard and wound up with an empty cone and a chocolate chip puddle at her feet.

"It takes practice," Luz said, as Shayna bent to pick up the flower. "You have to do it a little rough, but not too rough."

"Kind of like a rough fluff?"

"A what?"

"You know, someone who's tough on the outside but a mush underneath. Kind of like butch on the streets, femme in the sheets." Shayna stared down at the blossom in her hand as she started to blush again. How did we ever get on this topic, she wondered, marveling at the way the mind of a dyke who's been celibate for nine months worked. Well, I might as well go all out. "Speaking of dancing," she said, even though they weren't. "do you happen to know when the next dance at the grange is?"

Luz took the iris out of Shayna's hand and wove it into her hair. "That looks pretty," she said, turning Shayna around so she could see her reflection in the glass.

Wow, we would make a handsome couple, if I do say so myself, Shayna thought, as her eyes met Luz's in their reflection. Shayna turned back around and started futzing with her purse. "Let me pay you for it. I mean, I broke it and everything."

"Don't worry about it. Take these, too." Luz held out the other two irises.

"No I couldn't. I mean those you can still sell."

"No we can't. Once they're open they only last a day or so." Luz held them out further. "Please."

"Well, okay. You won't lose your shirt?"

Luz laughed. "Are you kidding? I 'm not going to lose my profit over three little irises. Besides, you're the kind of girl that's just made for giving flowers to. I should give you the whole place." She made a sweeping gesture with her hand and then ripped a big sheet of white paper off a roll on the counter. She placed the irises in lavender tissue paper, rolled the whole thing up and stapled it. "Here."

"Thank you," Shayna said. "Don't I get a card?"

"Sure." Luz twirled the rack on the counter and took down a little white card. She looked at Shayna, then looked down and started writing. Shayna pretended to be fascinated with a tiny bonsai plant set in a miniature rock garden, which actually was quite intriguing, though not half as much as the woman across the room. She's worked here thirteen years, Shayna thought. That's about twelve years more than I've stuck with anything. She sure doesn't seem like the love-'em-and-leave-'em type. Hmmm.

Luz put the card in a small envelope, which she licked and sealed. "Here you are, Miss," she said, extending the note to Shayna.

"That's Ms.," she said automatically.

"Oh, are you married?" Luz asked.

"No," Shayna said, "but I think it's important for women to not be labeled according to their marital status, which is just a convenient way for men to keep track of us anyway, and…" Shayna's voice trailed off as she let herself drown in

Luz's dark eyes. "I don't know what I'm saying," she mumbled, waving her hand in front of her face as if to clear away smoke. "Never mind." She shook her head a little. "No, I'm not married. Are you?"

"No, not yet anyway. Maybe someday."

"Really?" Shayna's eyes widened.

"Sure, why not? Why should we give up everything just because we're lesbians? Marriage is a wonderful thing. The longer you're with someone, the more you love her."

Shayna nodded, bug-eyed, and then realized she was staring. "Well, I better let you close up shop," she said. "Thanks for the flowers."

"Sure. Cut them under water, warm water, and put half that packet of powder in when you get home and the other half tomorrow when you change the water. They'll last longer."

"Yeah, okay," Shayna muttered, not hearing a word Luz was saying. Talk about tall, dark and handsome. Gevalt. And not only that, Shayna thought. she believes in marriage. I'm going to plotz. "Well, see you on the dance floor sometime."

"Yeah." Luz leaned forward, resting both elbows on the counter. "Listen, I'm here Monday through Friday, nine to five, except when I'm out on deliveries. Or pig-watching. Come by sometime."

"Okay." Shayna looked into Luz's eyes once more and felt her belly drop, as if she was in an elevator that had just rushed up to the ninety-ninth floor in three seconds flat. "Bye." She left Petal Pushers holding her flowers high like a trophy, and walked right past Nosh A Bissl, where the cinnamon-glazed ruggelech glistened in the window like bits of golden amber. Shayna didn't notice though. She was off in another world: a world where pigs shake hands, flowers open up like magic, and girls fall in love and maybe, just maybe, live together happily ever after, after all.

Chapter Four

"What's it say? What's it say?" Pearl dropped the grocery bag she was shlepping on her hip like a baby onto Shayna's kitchen table with an oy. "What'd we buy, rocks?" She reached into the bag and pulled out a bunch of celery and a bag of organic carrots.

"C'mon, Shayna. You've tortured me long enough."

"We've got to learn to have a little patience, Mrs. Mamelinski."

"What's this collective we business? *I've* never had a problem with patience."

Shayna nudged Pearl away from the grocery bag with her elbow, reached in with both hands and pulled out a chicken. "Ooh, such a nice chicken you picked out, Pearl, not a skinny chicken, a nice, big, fat one. Get out the soup pot, wouldja?"

Pearl threw up her hands. "All right, all right. What's the big deal? Just because you got a love letter from the girl of your dreams yesterday, is no reason why you should let your best friend in the whole world see it."

"It's not a love letter," Shayna called, as Pearl disappeared into the pantry. A moment later she emerged with a huge pot she heaved onto the stove.

"Give me the chicken."

"Here, catch." Shayna hoisted the chicken onto her shoulder like a football, but before she could back up for the winning pass, Pearl ran behind her and grabbed it out of her hands. She slapped it onto the counter and reached her hand inside.

"Feh." Pearl made a face as she pulled out a plastic bag of parts. "You want these for Tzimmy?"

"Sure, why not? My little purr box deserves a treat, don't you, Ms. Tzimmy?" Shayna looked at the cat who was sitting on a kitchen chair, her green eyes going back and forth between Shayna and Pearl, like she was watching a tennis match, for it was hard to tell who was really in charge of the chicken here.

Pearl rinsed off her hands and then took the lid off the soup pot. "Oh my God, no wonder it was so heavy." She paused, with the lid in mid-air. "What are you trying to do, bring back *Get Smart?*"

Shayna turned from making goo-goo eyes at Tzimmes and peered into the pot. "Oh, my phone, my phone! That's great, I've been looking for that phone for months!" She removed the red cordless phone from the pot and held it up to her ear. "Yes, yes, this is Shayna P. Steinblatt, ace international reporter. What's that?

27

You'd like me to fly to London and do a joint interview with Queen Mother and Fergie? Oh, I'm terribly sorry, but I'm about to fly off to Rome to do an exclusive interview with the Pope." She put the phone down on the counter and shrugged at Pearl. "Oh well, easy come, easy go. You better rinse that pot good, Mrs. Mamelinksi. I haven't made soup in a long time."

"I'll say." Pearl washed out the pot while Shayna got a knife and cutting board out of the dish drain, brought them over to the table and started slicing vegetables.

Pearl shut the faucet and came over to supervise. She picked up a piece of carrot and held it up between her thumb and forefinger. "Not like that, Shayna. These are too thick. They look like Lincoln logs."

"Oh Pearl, don't be such a kvetch. They're perfect, just the way Bubbe makes them."

"But this is how Oma used to make them." Pearl took the knife from Shayna and sliced one of her carrot chunks into four thin rounds. "See?"

"I see we have a problem here. That's how you cut them for salad, not for soup." Shayna lined up Pearl's thin slices next to her thick ones. "What do you think?"

Pearl studied the cutting board with her hand on her hip. "I'll tell you what. We'll process for a few hours until we come to a completely fair, mutually acceptable decision in which each party gets her needs totally met. We'll even call in a mediator to act as a referee. What d'ya say?"

"Nah, I'm too hungry for that." Shayna picked up a thick carrot slice and started chomping on it.

Pearl noshed on a piece of celery. "Got it," she said with her mouth full. "We'll just eat the vegetables raw. We'll arrange them all fancy-shmancy on a platter, charge thirty-seven dollars and call it crudité." She moved the carrot and celery pieces into a little circle on the cutting board.

Shayna shook her head. "We gotta have vegetables in the soup or else it won't taste right. And besides, that's the only time most Jews eat vegetables anyway."

"True." Pearl nodded her head. "All right, then, we'll do what we always do." She walked over to Shayna's dish drain and got herself a knife. "We'll chop half your way and half my way."

"I did it my way," Shayna sang, in her best imitation of Frank Sinatra. Or was it Sammy Davis Jr.? She wasn't sure. "Oy Pearl, such a smart kop you got there." She rose on tip-toe to kiss the top of Pearl's dirty-blonde head. "A genius she is, my best friend. A regular Einstein."

"And you're a regular Gertrude Stein."

"Thank you. Here, finish chopping." Shayna slid three carrots over to Pearl. "Now, where'd you put the chicken?"

"Over by the stove." She pointed with her elbow. Shayna put the chicken in the pot and brought it over to the table, where Pearl dumped in the veggies, then took the soup-to-be over to the sink and added enough water to cover the chicken. "Anything else?" Shayna asked, lifting the whole thing onto the stove.

"We forgot the parsley," Pearl said. "Got some?"

Shayna shrugged. "I don't know, look. But you enter my fridge at your own risk. I'll start the matzo balls." She got a box of matzo meal out of the pantry and started reading the back of it.

"Let's see, matzo balls. Two tablespoons fat, two eggs. Hey, get me some eggs and some margarine, wouldja, Pearl?"

Pearl closed Shayna's vegetable bin with her foot and turned around with a foul looking object in her hand. "What do you call this?" she asked, extending a lemon that looked like it pre-dated the invention of the wheel.

"That's called the world's oldest fruit. I was saving it for the Guiness Book of Records."

"I thought I was the world's oldest fruit." Pearl crossed the kitchen holding the lemon as far away from her as was humanly possible, which wasn't far at all, given the fact that her hand was attached to the end of her arm. She threw out the lemon and then dug around in the refrigerator for the matzo ball makings. "Here's some eggs. What's this, soy margarine? Don't you have any butter?"

"No, no, this is much better for your…" Shayna lowered her voice to a whisper, "…cholesterol." She measured out two tablespoons of the margarine and cracked the two eggs into a bowl.

"Let's see, half a cup of matzo meal, two tablespoons soup broth, and a bissl salt which we can do without."

"No salt? Shayna please, it's gotta have a little taste."

"Salt is terrible for you, Pearl. Here, I'll put in a little tamari."

"Oy." Pearl winced as Shayna added a little soy sauce to the batter.

"Okay, now, a little broth…" Shayna moved toward the soup pot but Pearl stopped her. "No, wait. Don't use broth, use seltzer."

"Seltzer? Are you kidding?"

"No, really. Oma used to put seltzer in her matzo balls all the time. It makes them float."

"You never told me that."

"I just remembered. They'll be really good. Trust me."

"Well, I don't know. Selzer in knaydlech? I wonder what Bubbe would say." Shayna opened the refrigerator. "Uh-oh. All I have is mandarin-orange."

"Mandarin-orange? What kind of goyishe seltzer is that?"

Shayna shrugged. "Take it or leave it."

"I'll take it. It'll go good with the tamari." Pearl took the bottle and loosened the top to let out the fizz. "How is your Bubbe? Have you talked to her yet?"

"No, I was waiting until after five."

Pearl looked up at the kitty-clock. "Shayna, it's already half-past-six."

"Oh, is it? Time sure flies when you're having fun." She stared down into the meshugeneh matzo ball concoction Pearl was now stirring with a wooden spoon. "Hey, mix it good."

"I'm mixing, I'm mixing. I thought you were going to call this morning when your father was still at work."

"I'll call, I'll call, alright? What are you, my mother?" Shayna's voice rose as she spun on her heels and started pacing around the kitchen, her arms folded tightly across her chest. Pearl dropped her spoon, turned around, and took two steps forward, blocking Shayna's path.

"Hey," she said softly.

"Oh Pearl, I'm sorry." Shayna lay her head on Pearl's shoulder and let Pearl hug her. "I know I have to call, but I'm scared."

"I know, Shayna. But you have to face it. Avoiding things doesn't help."

"Yes it does," Shayna mumbled into Pearl's chest. "It got me through my whole childhood." She shut her eyes for a minute and watched her bubbe's face, round as a matzo ball, float across the surface of her mind. "All right, I'll call. But let me show you Luz's note first."

"Luz? Who's Luz?" Pearl stepped back and looked at Shayna, puzzled.

"Pearl!"

"Well, I thought you'd never ask."

"Let me just put the batter in the fridge." Shayna covered the bowl with a plate and handed it to Pearl, who put it on the second shelf, next to a seaweed and miso concoction she didn't even bother asking Shayna about.

Shayna led Pearl into the living room. "Have a seat."

Pearl looked around. "Where?"

Shayna surveyed the room. "Oh, c'mon Pearl, this isn't so bad." She moved two sweaters, the *Times Book Review,* a plate with a stale carob brownie on it, a ball of yarn and an emery board off the couch with one sweep of her arm. "Here."

Pearl pretended to dust off the couch before delicately lowering her tuchus onto it. "Honestly, Shayna, how do you stand it?"

"Stand what?"

"That." Pearl pointed to the cluttered floor.

"C'mon, Pearl. This is a vast improvement. I told you, by the end of my Saturn Return, this house will be spotless. Anyway at least you can see the floor."

"That's true. So nu?" Pearl extended her hand, palm up. Shayna stared at Pearl's fingers, refusing to meet her eye, as a little smile flickered across her lips. "What, all of a sudden you're bashful? C'mon, Shayna." Pearl crooked her index finger and motioned it.

"Well, all right." Shayna dug into the back pocket of her jeans, pulled out a small white envelope and handed it over.

"That's more like it," Pearl said, taking the card out of the envelope.

"Careful," Shayna shrieked. "Don't rip it. Give it to me, I'll read it to you." She lunged for the card, but Pearl held it overhead, out of reach.

"Ah-ha! Now I've got you where I want you. What'll you give me for it?"

"All my politically incorrect feather earrings. A year's subscription to *Lilith Magazine.* Breakfast in bed for a thousand years. Please, Pearl." Shayna clasped her hands to her chest and kneeled on the couch.

"I love it when you beg like that. All right, it's a deal."

Shayna relaxed. "You're a sick woman, Mrs. Mamelinski. You know that?"

"Yeah, well, that's what happens when you grow up with three older broth-ers. You're an only child, what do you know?" Pearl took the card out of the envelope and read it out loud, though she knew Shayna had probably read it at least a million times by now, and committed it to heart. "'Roses are red, irises are violet; here's my phone number, I hope that you dial it. Shayna, you are a lovely woman, and speaking of dancing, I would be proud to take you to the dance next Saturday night. Call me. Love, Luz. 555-0202.' Wow, she used the L-word and everything, Shayna."

"I know, I know." Shayna took the card from Pearl and read it again. "Pretty hot, huh?"

"Yeah. So what'd she say?"

"Who?"

"Luz."

"When?"

"When you called her."

"I haven't called her yet."

"Shayna, what are you, allergic to the phone all of a sudden? Get on the horn, girl."

"Pearl, wait a minute. I don't want to seem too eager."

"Too eager?" Pearl shook her head. "Shayna, did you read this card? 'Lovely woman.' 'Love, Luz.' This woman is smitten with you. Not calling her is down-right cruel. She's probably plotzing in her pants by the telephone."

Shayna shrugged. "So, let her plotz a little. Listen, I'm doing it different this time, Pearl. I'm playing hard to get. Bubbe always said I should. Every femme fatale knows that makes those butches appreciate us a little more."

"Oh yeah?" Pearl lazily crossed her legs. "You know what's best, Mrs. Bubbelinski. I just hope Luz hasn't given up by now and asked someone else."

"Give me that phone!" Shayna jumped off the couch and snatched up the telephone from the coffee table. "What's the number? Quick, Pearl. What if I'm too late?"

"Relax, relax." Pearl picked up the card that Shayna had dropped in her haste. "Here. You want me to go in the other room?"

"Of course not. What do you think, we're gonna have phone sex?" Shayna dialed Luz's number and let it ring a few times. "Not home," she whispered to Pearl, her hand covering the mouthpiece. "I'll bet she's out on a date with some-one else. Shit."

"Maybe she threw herself out the window because she thinks you don't want to go out with her."

"Oh, great. One more thing to feel guilty about." Shayna heard a click. "Oh no, it's her answering machine. What should I say?"

"Give me that." Pearl grabbed the phone just in time to hear the beep, and before Shayna could stop her, said, "Hello, Luz. This is Pearl Gold, Shayna P. Steinblatt's social secretary. I have checked Ms. Steinblatt's calendar and by some strange, uncanny twist of fate, she happens to be free next Saturday night, though I must warn you, this is the first free Saturday night she's had since 1969, so next time, please give her a little more advanced notice."

"Pearl!" Shayna was plotzing on the couch.

31

Pearl put her hand over the mouthpiece. "Well, you wanted to play hard to get." She spoke back into the phone. "Now, Ms. Steinblatt would like to know if this is strictly a dancing engagement, or also a dinner engagement, and if this really is an engagement, Ms. Steinblatt would like a nice, big, fat diamond ring, sort of along the lines of the Hope Diamond, but on second thought, maybe just a tad smaller, we wouldn't want some jerk on the subway to knock her off for it when she goes to visit her bubbe…"

"Pearl, give me that phone!" Shayna jumped off the couch and wrestled the phone away from Pearl. "Hi, Luz. This is Shayna. Pearl didn't mean that about the ring."

"I did, too," Pearl shouted.

"I mean, I know you said lesbians shouldn't give up marriage, but do you really think we should get rings? Oh Goddess, I don't mean me and you should get rings, I mean we hardly know each other, I mean lesbians in general, you know, I mean the ones that are getting married." Shayna paused for a second, no longer sure who or what she was talking about. Then she spoke in a rush, in case Luz's machine was voice-activated. "Listen, Luz, I'd love to go out dancing with you, so why don't you call me later on next week, and we'll make plans, okay? I'm going to go kill Pearl now. Bye."

Shayna hung up the phone and glared at Pearl. "I can't believe you said that. And then I just made it worse. Oy." Shayna flung up her hands and began to moan. "What if she thinks I'm too meshugeneh to go out with?"

"Won't she think it's funny?"

"Pearl, this may shock you, but not every lesbian on the planet has the same sick sense of humor you do."

Pearl shrugged. "Well, fuck her if she can't take a joke."

"I'd love to."

"I'll call her and tell her." Pearl reached for the phone.

"No!" Shayna screamed. "You've done enough damage for one evening. Now sit down."

"Yes, ma'am." Pearl retreated to the couch and Shayna followed, holding the phone tightly. She sat down next to Pearl and threw her another dirty look. "I should never have told you that she believes in marriage."

"Oh, c'mon, Shayna. If she doesn't have a sense of humor, she's no good for you anyway and you might as well find that out now."

"I suppose. Well, I might as well call my parents. Want to check the soup?"

"Okie-doke." Pearl went into the kitchen while Shayna dialed. She let the phone ring half a dozen times, tapping Luz's card on the arm of the couch while she waited.

"Hello?"

"Hi, Sol, it's your daughter." Shayna was surprised to hear her father's voice. He usually worked until at least eight o'clock. "How's Bubbe? Is she all right?"

Shayna heard her father sigh. "It's very bad here, Linda. Very bad. Your grandmother's in the hospital."

"In the hospital? What happened?"

"It's very bad, Linda, very bad," Mr. Steinblatt repeated. "We took her home on Saturday, and she seemed to calm down. She went to bed early, about eight o'clock. But on Sunday morning she woke up and started screaming the minute she opened her eyes and she didn't let up for a second. I'm telling you, she yelled from seven o'clock in the morning until way past midnight."

Wow. Shayna's eyes widened. "What was she screaming about?"

"Never mind. It's not important."

"Sol, tell me."

"Linda, what do you want to know for? It'll only upset you." God forbid anyone should get upset, Shayna thought. She waited silently.

Mr. Steinblatt sighed again. "She just kept on insisting that the super had wired her apartment and that they were after her, and when we tried to tell her it wasn't true, she yelled even louder that we must be in on it, since we refused to believe her. I'm telling you, Linda, your grandmother did not shut her mouth from seven o'clock in the morning until twelve o'clock at night. We tried to take her to the hospital, she wouldn't go; we tried to get her into an ambulance, she wouldn't go; finally we had to call the police and they took her to the hospital."

"You called the cops on Bubbe?" Shayna's voice rose three octaves. "I don't believe it."

"Now, Linda, don't start with me. We did it for her own good. I told you, it was after midnight already and we had no choice. She was keeping up the entire neighborhood and besides, we were afraid she was going to have a heart attack, the way she was carrying on."

"The cops took Bubbe away," Shayna repeated, shaking her head in disbelief. Pearl, who had just come back into the living room, stopped in her tracks and raised her eyebrows. Shayna motioned for her to come and sit on the couch, so Pearl did so, taking Shayna's hand. "So, what now?" Shayna asked her father.

"I don't know what."

"Should I come home?"

"I don't think so. The doctor said we should wait for a few days before we see her."

"Can I at least call her?"

"I don't think so, Linda."

"Sol, let me get this straight. Bubbe's all alone in the hospital, and no one's allowed to see her or call her? Don't you think that's a little extreme? I'm sure she'd want to talk to me." Shayna's voice cracked.

"Now, don't get upset, Linda. I'm sure the doctor knows what he's doing. This is exactly why I didn't want to call you. I knew you'd get upset."

"Of course I'm upset. Bubbe's in the hospital!"

"Well, we spoke to the doctor today, and they're running a whole bunch of tests. We'll call you as soon as we know anything. Okay?"

"Yeah, swell." Shayna squeezed Pearl's hand. "Can I talk to Sylvia?"

"Your mother's not feeling well. She's lying down and I don't think she wants to talk to anyone."

"I'm not anyone. I'm her daughter."

33

"I'm very well aware of that, young lady, and I can tell from your tone of voice that it would not be a good idea to let you talk to your mother right now." Mr. Steinblatt's voice had a tone of finality to it that Shayna wasn't in the mood to argue with.

"Well, tell her to call me tomorrow, okay? Bye." Shayna hung up and then sat quietly, staring at her and Pearl's clasped hands. "They called the cops to take Bubbe to the hospital," Shayna said to Pearl's pinky. "I can't fucking believe it. They said she screamed for seventeen hours. Can you imagine?" Shayna looked up at Pearl and giggled. "Think of it, Pearl. A quiet night in Vey Iss Mir. All of a sudden a paddy wagon with its sirens roaring and its lights flashing comes tearing down the street. It screeches to a halt in front of the Steinblatt establishment, and two cops race inside. And what dangerous criminal do they drag out, restoring law and order to the neighborhood? Not Jack the Ripper, not the Boston Strangler, not Bonnie and Clyde, but Tzeydl Zimmerman, all one-hundred-and-seven pounds of her."

Pearl smiled. "Your mother must have been slightly embarrassed."

"Slightly embarrassed? Pearl, she must have been totally mortified." Shayna started to laugh. "I mean, can you see this? Mrs. Rosenbloom out on her lawn in her flannel nightgown; the Eisenbergs peering out through their ventilation blinds next door; and the Greenbergs standing in their driveway with their two toy poodles yapping, and out of the house, the cops come with my little bubbe?" Shayna was laughing in earnest now, bent over from the waist, slapping her knee.

Pearl rubbed her back. "Take it easy, now Shayna. It's okay."

"But Pearl," Shayna gasped, "don't you think it's funny?" She looked up at Pearl until she stopped laughing and her eyes filled with tears. "Oh, Pearl," she said softly. "My bubbe's in the hospital. What should I do?"

Pearl wiped Shayna's cheek with her finger. "I don't know if there's anything you can do at this point, Shayna," she said, taking her hand again. "At least you know she's in a safe place, if anything happens to her. Maybe she had a stroke or something. It doesn't sound like she's dying or anything. Your father would tell you that, wouldn't he? He knows how much you love her."

"I don't know, Pearl. I wouldn't put it past him." Shayna frowned. "He wasn't even going to tell me about this. Mr. Emotional is too afraid his crazy daughter will get upset."

"Well, at least you know where you learned the fine art of avoidance." Pearl offered Shayna the sleeve of her work shirt to dry her tears. "Think, Shayna. What would your bubbe want you to do?"

Shayna smiled through her tears. "Oh, that's easy. She'd say I should eat a bissl soup, no matter what happens, you gotta eat a good supper, mamela, how can you think on an empty stomach?"

"Thatta girl." Pearl stood up and pulled Shayna to her feet. "C'mon, we'll go make knaydlech your bubbe would be proud of." Pearl put her arm around Shayna's shoulder and steered her into the kitchen, where Tzimmy was still holding down the fort, her eyes glued to the soup pot, just in case the chicken had plans to escape.

Shayna took the matzo ball batter out of the refrigerator and Pearl put up a pot of water to boil.

"You know, Pearl, the first time I made matzo balls, I put them right into the soup, instead of boiling them in a separate pot." As Shayna spoke, she rolled a bit of dough between the palms of her hands. "I let it boil for forty minutes and when I came back and lifted the lid, all the soup was gone and I had eight knaydlech the size of cantaloupes. Boy, did Bubbe laugh over that." Shayna dropped the matzo ball into the bubbling water and started shaping another one. "Do you think it's my fault, Pearl? Maybe I should have driven down there on Saturday. Maybe then none of this would have happened."

"How could it be your fault, Shayna?" Pearl lifted the lid off the soup pot and dipped a wooden spoon in for a taste. "Well, then again, maybe it is. The soup's a bissl bland. A little authentic Jewish guilt is exactly what it needs."

"Oh, you." Shayna pretended to throw the next matzo ball at Pearl, but dropped it into the boiling water instead. When the matzo balls were done, she added them to the soup and measured out two generous helpings, and a smaller one, minus knaydlech for Tzimmy.

"Thanks." Pearl took the two bowls over to the table, sat down and tasted her soup. "Yum. It's great."

Shayna sat down too, and lifted a spoonful of soup to her lips. The first bite brought a fresh batch of tears to her eyes and she dropped her spoon. "I'm sorry, Pearl. I just can't help it. She's my bubbe."

"I know, Shayna, I know. Don't worry, Mrs. Bubbelinski, we forgot to put salt in the soup anyway." Pearl scraped back her chair, stood up and cradled Shayna's head against her soft belly, as Shayna cried and cried.

Chapter Five

Shayna called her parents every day for a week and a half, and by Thursday evening, she could barely force her fingers to dial the number once more. *I've talked to them more in the past two weeks than I have in the past ten years,* Shayna thought, as she waited yet again for one of her parents to pick up the phone.

"Hello?"

"Hi, Sol. It's your daughter. Any news?"

"Nothing, Linda. Everything's the same."

"When's Bubbe coming home?"

"We don't know yet."

"When can I see her?"

"We don't know that, either."

"Can I call her at least?"

"The doctor doesn't think it's a good idea."

Shayna sighed and slouched down on the couch, until her head rested on the couch's seat and her tuchus was on the floor. Talking to her father always had this strange lulling effect on her, as if someone had drained all the blood out of her veins and replaced it with wet cement, while at the same time removing the wooden floor of her living room and replacing it with quicksand. In other words, our girl Shayna was sinking fast. "Well," she said, "how's Sylvia?"

"She's all right."

"Can I talk to her?"

"Not now, Linda. She's lying down on the couch, resting."

"Okay, I'll call you tomorrow." As Shayna hung up the phone, she heard her kitchen door open and close. "Hi, Shayna, it's me," she heard Pearl call. Shayna remained motionless, half on the couch and half on the floor, listening to Pearl's footsteps approaching the room.

"Let me guess. You just won the lottery." Pearl looked at Shayna from the doorway.

Shayna smiled, in spite of herself. "How'd you know?"

"Well, I've just never seen anyone look so ecstatic in my entire life." Pearl crossed the room, rummaging in her backpack. "I can hardly see in here. You're positively glowing with joy." She took her cool, mirror sunglasses out of her pack, put them on, and sat down next to Shayna. "There, that's better. But must we sit on the floor?"

"I guess not." Shayna hoisted herself onto the couch and Pearl did the same. "Did you see Tzimmy out there?"

"Yeah, she's sleeping under the dogwood tree. So, what's new, pussycat?"

"Nothing. I just talked to my father." Shayna scooted over to rest her head on Pearl's shoulder. "Want something to eat, Pearl?"

"No thanks. I just ate half a pizza. I'm telling you, this construction work is making me eat like a horse. Do I have garlic breath?" Pearl took off her sunglasses and breathed out through her mouth in Shayna's direction.

"No, but let me feel those arms." Shayna sat up and gave Pearl's upper right arm a squeeze. "Ooh, Mrs. Mamelinski. By the time you finish building that house, you'll be Ms. Biceps of 1997."

"Well, the competition on my crew's tough, but not bad, not bad." Pearl tightened her muscle and poked it with her finger. "All I ever wanted out of life was the woman of my dreams and muscle definition. One out of two's not so bad." She flexed her other arm and admired it, then turned to Shayna. "So, nu? What'd your father say?"

"Nothing. Absolutely nothing." Shayna placed her hand over her eyes and shook her head. "I don't know what the hell to do."

Pearl stroked Shayna's hair. "Listen, Mrs. Bubbelinski, this has gone on long enough. You've been totally stressed out, not to mention a bissl depressed. Look, I can practically play tic-tac-toe on your forehead." She traced the lines in Shayna's brow with her fingers. "If you don't relax, your forehead will stay like that forever."

Shayna shrugged. "Big deal."

"Oy, Shayna, you gotta snap out of this." Pearl started massaging Shayna's temples. "I know you're worried about your bubbe, but isn't there anything to smile about? Like the fact that your best friend is here to entertain you? Or how about your date with Luz Saturday night?"

"Luz who?"

"Oy, vey iss mir, this is worse than I thought." Pearl sat Shayna up and put her ear to her chest. "Ka-thunk, ka-thunk, ka-thunk. I think you're still alive, Mrs. Bubbelinski, but let me check your pulse." She reached for Shayna's wrist and held two fingers against it. "Just as I suspected."

"Is it very bad, Dr. Mamelinski?" Shayna looked from her wrist up into Pearl's worried eyes.

"Well, I'm sorry to be the one to break the news to you, but frankly my dear, you are suffering from a very serious disease known as nuclear family-itis. In many cases, this disease has proven fatal, especially among lesbians, for some mysterious reason. However, in your case, there may still be hope."

"Hope? Is there a cure?"

"The cure, the cure, let's see." Pearl picked up her sunglasses and bit at the ends of one of the ear pieces thoughtfully. "Many studies have been done, and it seems the most effective treatment is cold turkey."

"But I don't eat turkey."

"How about hot pastrami?"

Shayna shook her head. "Would a soy dog on a whole wheat bun do?"

"I'm afraid not." Pearl picked up one of Shayna's notebooks from the couch and started taking imaginary notes on it. "Hmmm," she said, "since cold turkey is out, my advice, young lady, is to have only minimal contact with your parents, and only under strict supervision by your private physician, yours truly. Now, I usually charge fifty bucks an hour for my services, but I'll give you an hour and a half for seventy-five. What do you say?"

Shayna shrugged. "What can I say? A bargain is a bargain."

"Good." Pearl got up and started pacing around the room, her left hand stroking her chin. "Now, let's review the situation here. Your mother's not talking, your father, ditto, and you haven't been able to contact your bubbe all week. Hmm." She continued to pace as Shayna watched from the couch, a little life coming back into her eyes. Pearl spun around, picked up a New York Yankees baseball cap from Shayna's rocking chair, and pulled it on her head, backwards. "All right, my dear Watson. What we need are clues."

"Miss Scarlet in the dining room with the lead pipe."

"Good guess, but your Bubbe doesn't have a dining room. Try again, Watson."

"That's Watsonblatt," Shayna said, sitting up a littler straighter on the couch.

"Watsonblatt, of course." Pearl stopped pacing in front of Shayna. "Well, Watsonblatt, why would the doctors and your parents want to keep you and your bubbe apart? I mean, what's in it for them?"

"I'm sure they're after bubbe's vast fortune that she smuggled over on the boat from Russia."

"That's it!" Pearl raised a finger in the air. "Why didn't you tell me, Watsonblatt? What are we talking here; diamonds, rubies, pearls—which I admit I'm a bit partial to—emeralds, gold, silver..."

"Not quite, Sherlockski. We're talking one pair of Shabbas candlesticks. Maybe you better try again."

"One pair of candlesticks? That's all she took?"

"That's all she took," Shayna said, nodding. "They took what they could carry, and she was only a little girl. Listen, I don't mean to insult you, Sherlockski, but maybe we should consult Nancy Drewberg on this case."

"That's it!" Pearl raised her finger again. "I'll call Nancy Jacobs, you know, she's the femme on my crew with the rhinestone labyris on her hard hat?"

"Yeah, so? What's she got to do with anything?"

"Don't you see, Watsonblatt? She used to be a nurse." Pearl sat down on the arm of the couch. "We'll ask her if, in her ten year nursing career, she ever heard of a doctor isolating a patient from their family like that. It just sounds a little too fishy to me, Shayna. How can that be good for your bubbe?"

"I don't know, but I'd love it if a doctor ordered me to isolate myself from my family."

"Dr. Mamelinski just did, remember? Hmm, short term memory loss. Your condition is worse than I thought. You better lie down." Pearl picked up Shayna's feet and swung her legs up onto the couch.

"There, that's better," she said, as Shayna leaned back. "Let me call Nancy, Shayna. It's time for action here. I don't know why they're not letting you talk to your grandmother, but it can't be good for her. It's certainly not good for you. You're a mess."

Shayna fluffed up her hair. "Thanks a lot."

"You know what I mean. You haven't written all week, you haven't called your editor about doing a profile on Wilma the pig, and you certainly don't look like a dyke who's about to go out with the girl of her dreams Saturday night." Pearl slid off the arm of the couch onto a cushion next to Shayna. "As an outstanding lesbian of our illustrious community, it is my civic duty to help you get a grip. The romance of the century is in jeopardy, for God's sake. Now," Pearl began rummaging in her pack. "The question is, do I have Nancy's number on me?"

"You're a jewel, you know that, Pearl?" Shayna leaned up on her elbow to watch Pearl go through her pack. "Amazing. It's like a file cabinet in there."

"Checkbook, bankbook, here it is." Pearl pulled out a small lavender address book and thumbed through it. "Nancy Jacobs."

"Under J, I suppose."

"Of course. Phone, please."

"Right there." Shayna pointed to the end table and lay back as Pearl dialed. She shut her eyes, listening to Pearl explain the situation. Then there was a long silence, broken only by Pearl's periodic "uh-huh's" and "I see's."

"Just as I suspected again," Pearl said, as she hung up the phone. Shayna opened her eyes. "What?"

"Nancy Drew Jacobs was horrified. She said in her whole decade of nursing, she never heard of such a thing. She said contact with the family is always the best thing for a patient."

"Obviously she doesn't know my family," Shayna said. "So nu? Now what?"

"Now we still need some clues." Pearl started pacing again, stopping to pick up a pair of pinking shears that were lying next to the telephone. She peered through the scissors' thumbhole as if it were a magnifying glass as she inspected Shayna's punim.

"Pearl," Shayna said in a small voice. "Do you think my bubbe's dead, and they're not telling me?"

"Oh, Shayna." Pearl put down the scissors and kneeled down in front of Shayna. "Even your parents wouldn't do that, would they?" She looked into Shayna's eyes.

"I don't know."

"I don't think she's dead, Shayna. C'mon now, let's not think the worst here."

"Hey, I'm Jewish, I can't help it."

"Believe me, I know." Pearl picked up the pinking shears again and conducted a thorough investigation of the living room. "There's gotta be a clue here. Dust, lots of dust." Pearl peered through the scissors at the tchotchkes on the

39

mantle over the fake fireplace. "Candles, sea shells, driftwood, card from Luz, menorah, hmm…" Pearl paused for a minute."…That's it, that's it. Card from Luz."

Shayna narrowed her eyes at Pearl. "What does Luz's card have to do with finding out what's wrong with Bubbe?"

"Don't you see?" Pearl brought the card over to Shayna.

"No."

"We'll call your parents and ask them the address of the hospital your bubbe's in, so you can send her a card. Then we'll know where she is and you can call her." Pearl sat down and waved Luz's card in Shayna's face. "They can't say there's anything wrong with sending her a get well card. If they do, we'll know for sure something really unkosher is going on here."

"That's brilliant, Pearl. Why didn't I think of that? I'm such a shmegeggie, I never even asked them what hospital she's in."

"Shayna, do me a favor and berate yourself on your own time, okay? You're too upset to think. It's a classic symptom of your condition here. Now, are you strong enough to sit up and use the phone?"

"I guess." Shayna sat up, dialed and made a face at the sound of her father's voice.

"Hello?"

"Hi Sol, it's your daughter."

"Nothing's changed, Linda."

"I know, Sol. I spoke to you an hour ago, remember?"

Pearl poked Shayna with her elbow. "Be nice," she whispered. "You're on a mission here."

"Listen, I called to find out what hospital Bubbe's in, so I can send her a card." Shayna pantomimed writing in the air and Pearl got up to get her a pen.

"Why don't you just send it here and we'll forward it?" Mr. Steinblatt asked.

"Why?"

"Well, we were going to send her a card, too, and it would be nice for her to get them together, don't you think?"

"No." Shayna's belly started to shake. Something fishy really was going on. "Sol, level with me for a minute here, okay? What exactly is going on? Why won't you tell me where Bubbe is?"

"Nothing is going on, Linda. We're just following the doctor's orders, that's all. We've got nothing to hide from you."

"All right, I'll call you tomorrow." Shayna hung up the phone and repeated the conversation to Pearl. "And you know, whenever anyone says they've got nothing to hide, you can bet your kishkes they're hiding something. Now I'm really worried."

"Okay, we gave them a chance," Pearl said. "Now we go directly to the cops."

"And have them arrested?" Shayna asked hopefully.

"Not quite. Allow me, toots." Pearl picked up the phone and dialed. "Yes, I'd like Woodmere, New York information please. Hello? I need to speak to the police. Thank you." Pearl cupped her hand over the phone. "God, even 911 has muzak. Hello?" She spoke into the receiver again. "Yes, this is Mrs. Mamelinski, and I'm visiting my daughter in Woodmere here, and I'm wondering where the closest hospital is, in case there's an emergency." Pearl paused. "No no, everything's fine at the moment, but one can't be too careful these days, Officer, you know how it is. I always call the police whenever I'm away from home for this information, and they've always been very polite and helpful to me, at least so far." She paused again. "Yes, yes. Do you happen to know their telephone numbers?" Pearl wrote the information down and hung up.

Shayna looked at her. "Nu?"

"We're getting somewhere, don't worry. Maybe I'll give up construction and become a private eye. Now, what's your bubbe's full name?"

"Tzeydl Zimmerman."

Pearl wrote it down. "Sit tight. I got two hospitals to call. We'll find your bubbe." She dialed the first hospital, as Shayna watched, fascinated. Is this a movie or my life, she wondered, as Pearl spoke into the phone.

"Let me check. Just a minute." Pearl cupped her hand over the mouthpiece again. "What day did they bring her in?"

"Umm…let me think. I talked to her Saturday, my parents took her home Saturday night, she yelled all day Sunday… Sunday night it was, no very early Monday morning. So that was, let me see, May twenty-second."

Pearl spoke into the phone again, waited, and then hung up. "No luck there," she said. "I'll try the other one. Stop that." She interrupted her dialing to take Shayna's finger out of her mouth. "You can't go out on a date with chewed up cuticles."

"Sorry." Shayna clasped her hands in her lap and listened.

"Yes. I'm looking for information about Tzeydl Zimmerman. I believe she checked in May twenty-second at about one a.m.?" Pearl looked at Shayna, who nodded. "Yes, I am a relative, her sister. Oh. Do you have that address? And when was that again?" Pearl scribbled something down. "Thank you. Do you happen to have that number? I don't have a New York book here. Thanks." Pearl put down the phone and re-read the piece of paper on her lap.

Shayna watched her, bracing herself for the worst. Finally Pearl spoke. "You got a little shnapps, maybe, Mrs. Bubbelinski?"

"Pearl, you don't drink."

"I know, but your family's driving me to it."

"Is she dead?" Shayna searched Pearl's eyes.

"No, honey, but…oy." Pearl sighed and patted Shayna's hand.

"What? What?"

"Well, it seems that Tzeydl Zimmerman was discharged from the hospital last Friday, May twenty-sixth, that's about a week ago, under the care of a Mr. Sol Steinblatt, and her forwarding address is the Rosenbaum Estate Nursing Home on Forest Avenue in Brooklyn."

"What?" Shayna gasped. "Give me that." She grabbed the piece of paper Pearl was still holding, as if the written words offered something beyond the spoken ones. "How can that be? She has her own apartment on Brighton Tenth Street."

"I don't know, Shayna. You want to call?"

"Yeah, I better." She dialed the unfamiliar number with trembling fingers.

"Good evening," a male voice said. "Rosenbaum Estate Nursing Home."

Shayna leaned back, resting her weight against Pearl. "I'd like to speak to Tzeydl Zimmerman, please."

"Who?"

"Tzeydl Zimmerman. She just got there about a week ago."

"Oh, you mean the new one. She's on the third floor, hold on." Shayna waited.

"Hello, third floor." This time a female voice spoke.

"Yes, I'd like to speak to Tzeydl Zimmerman."

"Tzeydl? I'm sorry, Miss, she isn't speaking to anyone at the moment."

"What do you mean?"

"I mean, she is one angry lady. She won't come down to meals, she won't sleep in her bed, she just hollers if anyone comes near her."

Yep, that's my bubbe all right, Shayna thought, feeling slightly relieved. "Well, listen. Tell her her granddaughter Linda is on the phone. She'll talk to me."

"I'm telling you, Miss, she won't talk to a soul."

"Please, just humor me. Do me a favor, tell her it's Linda."

"All right." Shayna could practically hear the woman shrug. "Hold on." Shayna waited and after a minute she could hear her grandmother's voice in the background. "I ain't talking to nobody until they take me home. I don't care if it's the goddamn president. Who? Linda? Really? Oh, if it's Linda, well, that's a different story. Of course I'll talk to my Linda."

The woman picked up the phone. "I don't know who you are, but she's coming."

Shayna sat up. "Thank you."

"Hello?"

"Bubbe, it's me. It's Linda."

"Linda who?" Her voice was suspicious.

"Linda Steinblatt, your granddaughter."

"What's your mother's name?"

"Sylvia."

"What's your father's name?"

"Sol."

"What's your cousin's name?"

"I have a cousin Sam in Israel and a cousin Abbie in California who just had a baby Melinda..."

"Oh, it's you, it's really you." Tzeydl burst into tears.

"Yes, it's me, Bubbe. It's me." Shayna was crying too, not to mention Pearl, who was also sniffling on the other end of couch. "I love you, Bubbe."

"I love you too, darling. How's by you? Everything all right? Did you eat your supper?"

"Yes, Bubbe, I had some chicken. How are you?"

"Oy, by me it's terrible. Terrible. They put me in this lousy dump, and I'm going crazy in here, I don't know what's what anymore. They don't let me make a phone call, no one comes to tell me what's going on… it's like I'm in jail or something. I don't know why they won't let me go home."

"I don't know why either, Bubbe."

"I don't got no pocketbook, no lipstick, nothing. They took from me my watch, you know that I always wear, and my medal from the club. One change of clothes is all I got here. I'm telling you, I don't even feel like a person no more." She started to cry again.

"Bubbe, they took away all your things?" Shayna couldn't believe it.

"Yes, I'm telling you, I ain't got nothing in here. Nothing. That's why I didn't call you—you know I call every Sunday—I don't got my book with my numbers in it. Your mother took from me everything. Everything. Oy, I didn't think I'd ever talk to you again."

Shayna felt a tearing in her chest, as if her heart was ripping in two. "Listen, Bubbe, try to hold on there. I'm coming down tomorrow, okay? After lunch I'll be there. I'll bring you your pocketbook and some clothes and your watch. Okay?"

"Oy, a laybn on dine kop. Such an angel you are. Only you could do it, Linda. You're the only one that still cares for her old bubbe."

Shayna wiped her eyes with her sleeve. "Try and get some sleep, okay, Bubbe? What's the matter with the bed there, you don't wanna sleep on it?"

"The bed? I couldn't lay down on it, so aggravated I was. But I'll sleep all right tonight, because I know tomorrow you'll come."

"After lunch, okay? Don't forget."

"Okay, darling. As long as I know you're coming. Be careful how you drive and eat a good breakfast before you leave, it's a long trip."

"Okay, Bubbe. I love you."

"I love you, too, mamela. Bye-bye."

"Bye." Shayna let out a long sigh and looked at Pearl. "They put her in a fucking nursing home without telling me. Can you believe it?" She shook her head. "Oy, my poor bubbe."

"So, you're going down there tomorrow?"

"I have to. She was practically hysterical. She drilled me on our family history to make sure it was really me. Goddess, who can blame her for not trusting anyone? They probably didn't tell her either and they put her in a goddamn nursing home. A nursing home," Shayna said again to herself, still unable to believe it. "They took her pocketbook, her watch, this medal she always wears…"

"She has a medal?"

"Well, she calls it a medal. It's this pendant she got years ago for raising money for charity. She's so proud of it, she wears it all the time. And her watch; that was the first mother's day present she ever got from my mother and my uncle. I mean my grandfather really bought it for her of course, but still, those are her things…" Shayna shook her head again and sighed. "Oh, I just can't believe this. I don't know what to do first, kill my parents or go rescue Bubbe."

"Well, if you want my advice," Pearl said, "I'd say we skip the homicide for

43

now and concentrate on your bubbe."

"You're probably right." Shayna looked around the room. "Do you see my datebook anywhere?" She felt behind her tuchus underneath the couch cushions. "Never mind, I got it. I'll have to cancel my acupuncture appointment tomorrow. And my lunch date with Angel. Thank the Goddess this didn't happen three weeks ago when I was grading term papers. Looks like I don't have a deadline coming up for another week and a half."

"How long are you planning on staying?"

"I don't know. I'll have to see what's what down there."

"But Shayna, what about your date?"

"Oh no!" Shayna slapped her forehead lightly. "My date! What'll I do? Oh, why me? Why now?"

"Now, let's not panic here." Pearl picked up a pile of paper from the floor and started straightening it out.

"What are you doing?"

"Oh, don't mind me, I'm compulsing. It helps me think." Pearl put the papers down and arranged three pens in a neat line on top of the stack. "Want me to call Luz and explain?"

"Hell, no. You did enough damage last week. She hasn't even called me yet to make definite plans." Crisis number one, Luz's failure to call again, had been shuffled to the back of Shayna's mind temporarily by crisis number two, her bubbe's situation, but now the tables, or rather the crises had turned. "Do you think she's changed her mind? Maybe she was never really interested in me at all."

"Shayna, today is Thursday, right? You told her to call later on next week, as I recall. And you said she was shy. She's still got the rest of tonight, all day tomorrow, tomorrow night and all day Saturday."

"But I won't be here."

Pearl picked up a green sweater off the back of the couch and folded it. "You'll have to call her."

"Oh, Goddess," Shayna moaned. "How can I cancel our first date? The first date I've had in almost a year?"

"That's tough, alright." Pearl unfolded Shayna's sweater and folded it again. "But you know, explain that your family's in crisis and it has nothing to do with her. Tell her you wouldn't even be able to go if it was a date with Madonna. What else can I clean?" She looked around. "Hey, you are getting better."

"I told you." Shayna followed Pearl's gaze. "I know. I'll stop in at the flower store tomorrow on my way to the turnpike and tell her in person. You think she'll believe me?"

"Sure, why not? You're not lying. She'll probably think you're a mensch for rushing down there. She'll respect you for it."

"I hope so." Shayna got up. "I better throw a few things together."

Pearl handed her the sweater. "Where will you stay?"

"I don't know yet." Shayna walked into her bedroom and Pearl followed.

"Well, as your medical doctor, social secretary, best friend and private eye, I forbid you to stay with your parents."

"I guess I'll stay at Bubbe's apartment. I have keys. I'll go there first and bring her some stuff." Shayna flopped down on her bed.

"You are a mensch, Shayna." Pearl sat down beside her.

"Thanks. You were great, Pearl. You can keep the hat."

"I forgot I still had it on." She took off the baseball cap and ran her fingers through her short blonde hair. "Now, no packing tonight. Get some sleep and you can pull it together in the morning."

"Will you take care of Tzimmy?"

"You don't even have to ask. Half a can in the morning and half a can at night."

"And some Brewer's yeast for a treat sprinkled on top."

"Got it. Call me from Brooklyn, okay?"

"I will. Thanks for everything."

"Hey, what are friends for? Sweet dreams." Pearl kissed Shayna's forehead and let herself out as Shayna prepared herself for a night of restless sleep.

Chapter Six

Shayna sped down the highway with Chava Alberstein's Yiddish *Greatest Hits* blaring on the tape deck and tears streaming from her eyes. There's nothing like a good cry in the car at sixty-six miles an hour, she thought as she fumbled through her purse with her right hand. Her fingers sorted through packs of sugarless cough drops, two combs, her Swiss army knife, a notebook, her checkbook, address book, wallet, Luz's card, photos of Tzimmy, several rose quartz good luck stones, a tiny sewing kit just in case, a roll of stamps, a pocket mirror, used and unused tissues, three pairs of earrings, forty-two pennies and seventeen pens, until they found her sunglasses, biding their time at the bottom of her bag like a kid playing hide and seek. Shayna breathed on her glasses, wiped them with a light blue tissue and put them on, all the while keeping her eyes on the road, squinting in the glare of the morning sun.

She had left the house at eight-thirty, for she'd woken up much earlier than she'd expected, though woken aren't exactly the right words, since she hadn't slept much during the night. Instead she'd tossed and turned, drifting in and out of half-dreams/half-memories of herself and Tzeydl: standing in Tzeydl's kitchen frying latkes and draining them on brown paper bags; or walking along the boardwalk tossing crusts of rye bread to the seagulls; or sitting by the counter at Mrs. Stahl's, eating kasha knishes on Coney Island Avenue. In one dream, Shayna was a very little girl, and Tzeydl was lifting her high in the air and then tilting her backwards on her lap, until the whole world looked upside-down. Shayna was laughing and laughing as Tzeydl took her two small hands in her own and crooned, "Patty cake, patty cake, baker's man," bringing all four of their hands together. Shayna could see Tzeydl's hands vividly in her mind: they were full of raised blue veins and brown age spots, with perfectly filed nails painted bright red; her diamond wedding ring circling the fourth finger of her left hand. Shayna had startled herself awake with the sound of her own two hands clapping together, and sat up in the early morning light, her cheeks wet with tears.

"That's it, Tzimmy, I'm outta here," she'd said, flinging aside the covers. Shayna showered and dressed as quickly as she could, which wasn't very, since morning is not our girl's favorite time of day. She emptied out her dresser and closet, throwing half her clothes on the floor and the other half in her suitcase, vowing to resume her neatnik regime upon her return from New York. Finally Shayna had a couple of skirts and blouses she knew Tzeydl would approve of in her suitcase, as well as some pants, sweaters, shoes, socks, underwear, pajamas, and jewelry. "I know I'm forgetting something, Tzimmy, but I can't think of what," Shayna said, putting her toothbrush in a plastic bag. She checked that the stove was off and the answering machine on, shlepped her suitcase down the stairs and she was on the road.

There wasn't much traffic on the highway and before Shayna could rewind her tape for the eighth time, she was pulling off the Belt Parkway onto Forest Avenue, and turning right toward the heart of Brooklyn, instead of left toward the ocean which she could already smell through the open car window. Forest Avenue was lined with apartment houses on the left and stores on the right: Waldbaums, McDonald's, Baskin and Robbins, Radio Shack, Bagel Heaven, Shoe Parade and Hello Gorgeous Beauty Parlor. Further down were split-level, two-family houses and a school yard where some kids were shooting hoops. Shayna stopped at a red light and watched the game. It looked more like monkey-in-the-middle than basketball, for two tall kids kept throwing the ball to each other over some poor short shlemiel who kept running back and forth between them. Every once in a while one of the tall kids would spin on his heels and sink the ball into the basket. Boys sure love to torment each other, Shayna thought, but the insistent honking of the car behind her prevented Shayna from expounding on her theory of male competition in sports.

"All right, all right, gimme a second, wouldja? Sheesh. Welcome to New York." Shayna floored the gas pedal and pulled over into the right lane, only to slam on her brakes a second later, as she pulled up to an eight story red brick building with some fenced in benches out front and a green awning over the glass door, announcing to the world in bright yellow letters: ROSENBAUM ESTATE NURSING HOME.

Shayna pulled into the parking lot, cut the motor and took off her sun glasses. The sun streaming in through the window made her sleepy and for a moment she considered crawling into the back seat for a nap, for anxious as she was to see Tzeydl, Shayna was also scared. "What if she doesn't recognize me?" she asked her reflection in the rear view mirror. "Hello Gorgeous," her reflection answered back. She got out of the car, slung her bag over her shoulder and smoothed down her skirt. Shayna always dressed up when she visited Tzyedl: it gave her one less thing to hock her chaynik about. "It's bad enough I don't got no husband and kids for her to kvell over," Shayna said aloud as she walked up the driveway, already reverting back to her Brooklyn accent. "At least I can give her some naches by looking like a mensch."

The glass door to Rosenbaum Estate swung open as Shayna approached it. "Sign in please," a security man said, pointing to a large spiral notebook on a small desk. Shayna filled in her name, her grandmother's name, the time and date, and then walked through another set of glass doors into a huge lobby. There was a large desk directly in front of her with a young woman behind it talking on the phone. Behind the desk was a gigantic TV screen with some soap opera on it, the volume turned up loud. To Shayna's right was a big fish tank full of bright orange and yellow tropical fish swimming in and out of greenish-gray leaves.

Beyond the fish tank stood a white piano. The lights were florescent, the plants were fake, and the shmaltzy wallpaper was half gold matté and half red velvet. The place kind of reminded Shayna of the borsht belt hotel her parents had shlepped her to in high school every summer vacation. Once she had even met Cousin Brucie, the radio deejay of "W-A-Beatle-C" and gotten his autograph.

Shayna took a few steps inside and stopped in her tracks, for this was certainly no fancy-shmancy upstate New York hotel full of middle-class Jewish families with their pale skin sticking out of Bermuda shorts and sundresses. This was clearly a nursing home. Along the lobby, as well as around the fishtank and in front of the TV screen were chairs, dozens of chairs, and on each chair sat an old man or an old woman, staring intently at Shayna, as though they were waiting for her to do something. She had a wild impulse to curtsy or burst into a song or a tap dance, but she just stood there, studying the faces before her. Right in front of her sat a bald man in a wheelchair; next to him was a woman with a steel walker placed in front of her, her beige pocketbook hanging from one of the metal bars along with a pink cardigan in case it should get cold. Most of the men wore button-down sweaters and ties; a few of them wore felt hats. The women wore skirts and blouses; one or two of them had on flowered housedresses. Shayna stood rooted to the spot, until a man came up to her, looked her up and down and then asked, "Do you know where I live?"

"Where you live?" Shayna asked blankly.

"Look on his bracelet," someone called from over by the fishtank. "On his left arm, he's got a bracelet there, with the number on it."

"Oh." Shayna took the man's left hand and pushed up his sleeve a little, revealing a hospital bracelet that said, MURRAY PERLMAN, ROOM 533.

"Room 533," Shayna said to him. "See, it says right here."

"Thank you," Murray Perlman said. "You like my sweater?" He pulled at the sides of his bright blue cardigan.

"It's very nice."

"My wife made it for me," he said proudly. "Goldeneh hands she had. Forty-six years ago she made it. Goldeneh hands, I'm telling you, goldeneh hands." He walked away mumbling.

Oy vey. Shayna blinked back tears as she searched the worn-looking faces in the lobby for her bubbe. Tzeydl was nowhere to be found, so Shayna went up to the front desk to ask.

"Tzeydl Zimmerman? She's on the third floor. Are you her granddaughter? Good, go on up." The woman pointed to the elevators at the far end of the lobby.

Shayna pressed the elevator button and immediately it opened. "Just a minute, just a minute." A woman in a yellow smock with the word VOLUNTEER emblazoned across the front of it pushed a man in a wheelchair out of the elevator. She set his brakes and went back to get several more people in wheelchairs. As Shayna waited, Murray Perlman approached her again. "Do you know where I live?" he timidly asked.

Finally the elevator emptied and Shayna got on, alongside an old man with a long gray beard, wearing a black beret at a jaunty angle. She pushed three, the man pressed four, and they both stepped back, looking up at the numbers over the door. Nothing happened.

"Nu, what's the story here?" Shayna asked.

The man shrugged. "Do I know? Until this elevator makes up its mind to move, a person could really get old." They waited a little longer. "Try pushing the door," the man said.

Pushing the door? Shayna pressed the edge of the door with the heel of her hand, forcing it to disappear into the wall for a minute and then slide out about half a foot.

"No, not like that." The man stepped forward as Shayna moved back. He straddled the doorway and bent over, giving the door a zetz with his behind. Then he stepped inside and the door instantly closed. "It's all in the tuchus," he said, and for the first time all morning, Shayna smiled.

The elevator stopped at the third floor and Shayna practically flew out of it, for there sitting in the hallway on a wooden chair, was at long last, her bubbe. "Bubbe, Bubbe!" Shayna cried, reaching out her arms. "I'm so glad to see you." She bent down to hug Tzeydl, tears streaming down both their cheeks.

"Mamela, I'm happy to see you, too." Tzeydl rose to her full height of four-feet-ten-inches in order to give Shayna a proper hug and a kiss on the cheek.

"Don't cry, don't cry, it ain't so bad." A woman with a thick Polish accent touched Shayna on the shoulder. "Believe me, it ain't so bad," she repeated. "You survive. I been here ten years already."

Ten years. Gevalt. Shayna stared over Tzeydl's shoulder at the woman's back as she got on to the elevator. The door closed, swallowing her up. Tzeydl removed a crumpled tissue from the sleeve of her light blue polyester blouse. "Here darling, blow your nose."

"Such a pretty granddaughter, oh my, such a pretty granddaughter. Just gorgeous." A woman in a pink cotton housedress came up to Shayna, stood very close and looked her square in the face. "A gorgeous girl she is, takeh, with a face like an angel. Lovely, just lovely."

"C'mon, Linda." Tzeydl took Shayna's arm. "Come into my room." She led Shayna down the hall.

"Such a beautiful girl, oy kinehora, are you gorgeous." Shayna's admirer followed them.

"Just ignore her, Linda," Tzeydl said. "They're all crazy in here."

"What's so crazy, Bubbe?" Shayna asked. "She's just stunned by the dazzling good looks that run in the family, that's all."

Tzeydl replied by rolling her eyes, pulling down one side of her mouth and turning over her left hand and pushing down, as if she was shoving something out of the way. This gesture-expression combo was one Shayna was very familiar with: it was the equivalent of a non-verbal oy and had just as many meanings; go away, you don't understand, woe is me, it's no use, go bother your own head, oh please. Shayna followed her grandmother down the hall, walking quickly to keep up with her. She seems the same as ever, she thought as they stopped in front of a nurse wheeling a cart full of orange juice cans and plastic cups.

49

"This is my granddaughter," Tzeydl said to the nurse, patting Shayna's shoulder. "And this is the nurse, my friend, she's a doll, this one, she's my only friend in here." Tzeydl touched the nurse's arm. "She's very nice, the only one I can talk to, the only one that makes me feel like a person." Tzeydl's voice broke and she started to cry.

"All right, Tzeydl, all right. Don't cry now. Your lovely granddaughter is here, you should be smiling."

"Thank God I have one thing left to smile about," Tzeydl said, turning back toward Shayna. "Ain't she beautiful?"

"A lovely granddaughter, such a lovely granddaughter, oy, I'm telling you, gorgeous she is, like a beauty queen." The woman in the pink housecoat had caught up to them.

"That's enough, Esther. Why don't you go down for lunch?" The nurse turned Esther around by the shoulders and pointed her back toward the elevator. She ambled off, still mumbling.

That's probably somebody's bubbe too, Shayna thought, swallowing hard to push back her tears. She took a deep breath and managed a smile. "Come, Bubbe, show me your room." She took Tzeydl's hand and almost passed out on the spot, for this was the first time in all her thirty years that Shayna had ever seen her grandmother without nail polish. It was like a stranger's hand was attached to the end of Tzeydl's arm. Shayna noticed too, that Tzeydl had no make-up on, and the only jewelry she wore was a hospital bracelet that said TZEYDL ZIMMERMAN ROOM 313. Shayna continued studying Tzeydl as they walked down the hall. She was wearing black polyester pants, a light blue blouse, an off-white, button-down sweater vest, and black patent leather, toe-less sling-backs with chunky two inch heels. She looks the same as ever, Shayna thought, only littler. It's not like she's lost weight, she's not skinnier, it's like she's a smaller version of herself. Like she's shrunk. A woman even shorter than Tzeydl walked by and waved at them. Goddess, I feel like a giant in here, Shayna thought as the woman passed, barely reaching her shoulder. Shayna looked down and almost passed out for the second time that day, for never before had she seen grey roots showing at the top of Tzeydl's dark brown hair. Things must be really bad if Bubbe hasn't gone to the beauty parlor, Shayna thought. For Bubbe to be seen with her roots showing is like me going out stark naked. She looks old, Shayna thought, pressing her lips together to fight back yet more tears. I mean, I know she's ninety-nine, but she never looked so old before.

"In here." Tzeydl turned into a room and switched on the light. "Here's my palace, my castle. Rosenbaum Estate, hoo-hah some estate." She crossed the room and sat down on the bed by the window. Shayna followed her and leaned her behind against the radiator, trying to take in the fact that this small room, with its two matching beds, bureaus and closets, divided by a sink and a hospital curtain was now her grandmother's home. She has absolutely no privacy, Shayna thought, as she heard the flush of a toilet nearby. She looked toward the other half of the room, which, she surmised by the labels on the bureau and closet, belonged to one Zelda Bernstein. Zelda had pictures of her children and grandchildren standing on her dresser and hanging over her bed. Tzeydl's side of the room was completely bare.

"That's my partner, you ain't met her yet." Tzeydl waved her hand in the direction of Zelda Bernstein's territory. "I don't know where she is, she's usually laying on the bed kvetching—this hurts her, that hurts her—believe me, she's no bargain, my partniker. She walks around half naked with her gatkes sticking out and she don't know if she's coming or going. I can't live like this, Linda, it just goes against me. It ain't in me to be one on top of the other like this." She held her hand up to her heart in a fist.

"I know, Bubbe, I know." Shayna sat down next to her and patted her arm.

"I shouldn't bother you with my tsouris, such a young girl you are, you should never know from such troubles. Golda Meir takeh shouldn't even know from such troubles." Tzeydl laughed and then started to cry. "But I have to tell somebody or else I'll... I'll bust. And who can I tell, strangers, that my own daughter put me in a home? Oy, I'm so ashamed I can't talk to nobody, Linda, nobody but you."

"It's all right, Bubbe, I'm not so young. I'm already thirty."

Tzeydl looked at her. "Go on. Thirty? I don't believe it. You don't look a day over twenty-five. Stand up and let me look on you, I ain't seen you in so many months, since I went down to Florida." Shayna stood up for Tzeydl's inspection. "Oh you look beautiful. That skirt fits you so nice, and the green blouse goes with the white skirt, gorgeous. And your hair, Linda, it looks so nice pulled back, we can see your face, kinehora, turn around, let me see the back." Shayna spun around. "Look how nice it stayed in, your hair looks so good, I can't get over it. Where'd you have it done?"

"I do my hair myself, Bubbe. You know that."

"You see, you look so nice now, Linda, you look like such a mensch, ooh, I shep such naches when I see you like this." Shayna turned back around, relieved to see Tzeydl was in fact smiling. "You used to dress like such a slob, with your hair in your face hanging, and those ripped up dungarees all the time, like a hippie, and now you look just gorgeous."

If only she knew, Shayna thought, that I only started wearing skirts again when I came out as a lesbian and blossomed into a femme. I could just imagine her if I was a butch: oy, mamela, why do you have to cut your hair so short, like a boy you look; would it kill you, God forbid, to put on a dress once in a while, you got a good figure—you're lucky you ain't too skinny—you're just right. What would she make of Luz, for example, Shayna wondered, as Tzeydl wet her finger and rubbed at a microscopic spot on Shayna's skirt. Oh no, Luz! That's what I forgot this morning. I was going to stop in and see Luz. Oh Goddess, I really blew it. She'll never ask me out again. Shayna looked around for a phone, but neither Tzeydl nor Zelda Bernstein had one. Maybe there was a pay phone downstairs, but how could she really talk here? I'll have to call her later, Shayna thought, feeling like a shmendrick.

"Sure," Tzeydl was still talking. "You look nice now. Pretty soon you'll meet a handsome fella..."

51

"Bubbe."

"All right, we'll talk about it later. You must be hungry, darling, you didn't eat no breakfast, right?" She wagged her finger at Shayna. "Come, we'll go down, it must be twelve o'clock already, no?"

"Bubbe, where's your watch?"

"My watch? I told you, your mother took it. Everything she's got; my watch, my wedding ring, my medal that I always wear." Tzeydl's hand flew up to her chest, where the gold pendant usually rested against her bosom. "She's got my money, my keys, my pocketbook, everything. Half a person I am since I been in here. Less than half. Come, let's go down." Tzeydl stood up, straightened out her vest and lowered her voice. "Linda, you gotta go into the toilet?"

Shayna smiled. Some things never changed. "No, Bubbe, I'm fine."

"You sure you don't have to pish? That was a long drive you took."

"I'm sure."

"It's right here." Tzeydl walked over to a wooden door, banged on it, then pushed it open. "Here's the toilet, if you need it. Four women share one toilet, have you ever heard of such a thing? Me and her," Tzeydl nodded toward her roommate's bed with disgust, "and two from the other side. And half of them are so crazy, they don't even bother to knock."

"Let's go eat, Bubbe. I'm fine."

"All right," Tzeydl said with a little shrug. She took a few steps and then stopped. "You got your bag, Linda? You can't leave anything laying around here, even your teeth they'll steal in the middle of the night."

"Bubbe, who would want your teeth?"

Tzeydl clenched her fist with impatience. "I'm telling you, Linda, they're all crazy in here. They don't know what they're doing. Come, you'll see what I'm talking about." She walked out of the room and turned left.

"The elevator's this way," Shayna said, touching Tzeydl's right shoulder.

"This way?" She turned around. "See, I'm getting crazy already, locked up with all these meshugenehs." Her chin started to tremble.

"No one said you were crazy, Bubbe. You just went the wrong way, that's all. I do it all the time."

"Your mother thinks I'm crazy, that's why she put me in here. Would a sane person live in half a room with a stranger when she's got a whole apartment standing empty? Does that make any sense to you?" Tzeydl jabbed the elevator button with her finger for emphasis. "How would you feel if they chupped you out of your apartment to live with strangers all of a sudden? Wouldn't you be mad?"

"Yes, Bubbe, I'd be mad. I'd be very mad."

"Sure." Tzeydl nodded her head, satisfied.

"Excuse me." Someone tapped Shayna on the shoulder and she turned around to see Esther, her not-so-secret admirer standing behind her. "Excuse me," Esther repeated. "Have you seen a girl, a very pretty girl, a granddaughter standing around here somewhere? Such a lovely girl she was, gorgeous, she was just standing here a minute ago."

Shayna's mouth fell open. "That was me."

Esther laughed. "You? What are you talking about? You? I'm talking about a granddaughter, oy, so pretty she was, with a face like an angel. I gotta find her." She turned and walked away.

"Nu, what did I tell you?" Tzeydl slapped Shayna lightly on the arm. "They put in the gezunt with the meshuguneh and the meshugeneh with the gezunt. It's no good here. I want to go home."

"I know you do, Bubbe." Shayna put her arm around Tzeydl and led her into the elevator. "I'll see what I can do."

"Do? What can you do, a young girl like you? I know you had nothing to do with this." Tzeydl pressed L for lobby and the door slid closed, opening a minute later downstairs. Tzeydl took Shayna by the hand into the dining room, which was filled to capacity. Round tables took up every inch of space, with five or six people around each one. Many of the people wore plastic bibs. Women in light pink uniforms bustled about, wheeling carts full of food in styrofoam bowls and paper plates. Even though there were over three hundred people in the room, Shayna was amazed at how quiet it was, like watching TV with the sound turned off. Why, you could practically hear a kichel drop.

Tzeydl led her to the back of the room. "This is my table. Sit. I'll go get another chair."

"No, Bubbe, you sit. I'll get it."

"Sit, sit, you're tired. You shlepped all the way here from God-knows-where already."

"Sit, sit." A woman at the table echoed Tzeydl, gesturing with half a piece of rye bread. "She'll get it for you. Sit."

"Okay, so I'll sit." Shayna sat down in the empty chair and smiled at the people around the table. Right next to her was a bald man with very thick glasses wearing a denim work shirt, and next to him, across from Shayna was a plump woman with blue-tinted hair, wearing a bright red dress with matching earrings. To the woman's right sat a thin man in a baseball cap, and next to him was a woman in a yellow flowered housedress, who was very busy taking food wrapped in napkins out of her pocketbook and piling it on the table.

Shayna rose as Tzeydl approached the table, dragging a chair behind her. "Sit, sit, I'm coming," Tzeydl called. She pulled the chair up next to Shayna and sat down.

"Here's your lunch, Bubbe." Shayna slid the paper placemat in front of her over to Tzeydl.

"Eat, eat, they'll bring me an extra setting." Tzeydl pushed the placemat, plastic utensils, napkin, tossed salad and carton of milk back to Shayna, keeping her hand on the placemat so Shayna couldn't push it back.

Shayna looked down at the salad which was 99% iceberg lettuce, garnished with one-sixteenth of a tomato, drenched in salad dressing that was probably equal parts mayonnaise, sugar and orange dye number two. "No, Bubbe, you eat it. I'll wait."

"Linda, don't be silly. I ate a big breakfast, you didn't eat nothing." Tzeydl tore open the plastic bag that held the utensils and handed Shayna a plastic fork.

"Eat, eat. Listen to your bubbe," the lady in red said to Shayna.

"Don't worry, nobody's gonna starve if you eat something. There's plenty for everyone. Eat," the man next to Shayna added.

"All right, I'll eat, I'll eat, if it'll make everyone so happy." Shayna picked up her fork and took a bite of salad. What the hell, she thought, trying not to make a face as she chewed. It won't kill me. It certainly hasn't hurt them. She looked around at Tzeydl's tablemates, who all looked quite healthy, even under the florescent lights. Shayna assumed they all followed the same basic diet Tzeydl did: lots of chicken and cottage cheese, fresh fruit, overcooked vegetables, mashed potatoes, Wonderbread, club soda, and of course coffee, with a piece of honeycake or babka thrown in, to make life sweet. Shayna picked at her lettuce, watching the woman in the housedress wipe the salad dressing off her tomato slice. When she was satisfied it was dry enough, she unzipped a compartment in her bag, dropped it in, and pulled out two Pepperidge Farm cookies, which she placed on the table.

"Please take your pocketbook off the table." Tzeydl had also been watching. "It ain't nice."

The woman stopped what she was doing, flashed her dark eyes at Tzeydl and snapped at her in Yiddish. Tzeydl answered just as loudly, and the woman yelled something else back.

"What'd she say, Bubbe?" Shayna asked.

"Never mind Mrs. Chocolata," the woman in red said. "You just eat."

The man in the baseball cap mouthed the word crazy at Shayna, shrugged his shoulders and went back to eating his salad. Reluctantly, Shayna did the same.

"What are they saying, Linda?" Tzeydl shmeered a piece of rye bread with butter and handed it to Shayna.

"Can't you hear them, Bubbe? Don't you have your hearing aid on?" Shayna turned to face Tzeydl, and raised her voice a little bit.

"I can't hear a thing, Linda. Here, eat some bread."

"No thank you."

"What do you mean, no thank you? C'mon, eat, eat, you got too skinny, you ain't on a diet. Eat."

Shayna took the piece of bread and tore it in half. "You got too skinny, too. We'll split it." She gave the bigger piece to Tzeydl, who promptly put it on Shayna's placemat and took the smaller piece for herself.

"I know I got too skinny," Tzeydl said, taking a bite of bread.

"Bubbe, how come you can hear me, but you can't hear them?" Shayna gestured toward the people at the table.

"You I'm used to, that's all. Here, the bread is dry, drink some milk."

"Bubbe, I don't like milk. You know that."

"Still you don't like milk? I never met anyone like you, even when you was a baby you wouldn't take no milk. Here." Tzeydl opened a small red and white carton and pushed it to Shayna. "Have a little milk, it wouldn't kill you."

"Is there any water?"

"Here's water." The man in the baseball cap pushed a styrofoam pitcher across the table.

"Thank you." Shayna poured some into a styrofoam cup. "I'll drink water, Bubbe, okay ?"

"Sure." Tzeydl shrugged. "What are you asking me for, it's my business what you put in your mouth?"

"Hey, table number seven, table number seven. We ain't got all day here." The man next to Shayna snapped his fingers and shouted at one of the women who was serving food.

"What's your big hurry, Manny, you got a date?" the woman in red asked. "What are you doing today, something special? Come up to my room."

"Your room? What for?"

The woman leaned toward Manny and said in a loud whisper. "For a little nookie, why not? You want to?"

"Sure, why not? It's Shabbas, it's a mitzvah."

"It's a mitzvah with a shiksa," the man in the baseball cap said.

It sure is, Shayna thought, looking down at her plate, listening, and trying to look like she wasn't.

The woman continued whispering loud enough for the whole table to hear. "Come to Minnie's room. Three o'clock. Du hearst?"

"Three o'clock." Manny nodded.

"No, wait a minute," Minnie said. "I changed my mind."

"Nu?" Manny said, "what happened?"

Minnie shrugged, and leaned toward Manny again, motioning for him to come closer. When their heads were almost touching, Minnie slapped him on the arm and said, "Sorry, Manny, I got my period." Then she chuckled, her ample body shaking up and down. Everyone smiled, except the woman in the house-dress, who was blotting bits of lettuce with her napkin, and Tzeydl, who was pulling at Shayna's sleeve, and asking, "What are they saying, Linda? I can't hear a thing."

"Never mind, Bubbe. They made a joke; it isn't important."

"Never mind, Bubbe," Minnie echoed. "Eat your soup." She pointed to the styrofoam bowl that had just been set down in front of her, along with an extra place setting.

"Thank you, darling," Tzeydl said to the woman who was serving them. "Can we have another one for my granddaughter?"

Oy gevalt, this I gotta eat, too? Shayna stared into the grey mush of her bowl, Campbell's Cream of Elephant jokes from her childhood reverberating in her mind.

"Umm, is that good," Tzeydl said, dabbing at a bit of soup on her chin. "Eat up, mamela, it shouldn't get cold."

Shayna took a bite of soup. I'll eat nothing but brown rice for a month when I get home, she vowed to herself. If I don't eat, she won't eat, and I don't like how tiny she got. As Shayna slurped her soup, a plate of cottage cheese, pineapple rings and a roll was set down in front of her.

"Here, Linda, take my roll. One ain't enough for you." Tzeydl was already rearranging Shayna's plate.

"No, Bubbe, you eat it. I already had the rye bread."

"I can't eat so much no more, Linda, my stomach shrunk down to nothing, eppes, I ain't got no appetite."

"Eat, Bubbe, eat," Minnie yelled from across the table. "You can hear me, Bubbe? You gotta eat."

Tzeydl shrugged and began to butter her roll. "Look how much weight I lost already. The food in that other place was terrible. All goyishe food it was, ham they had there, and who knows what. I couldn't eat a thing."

"What other place, Bubbe?"

"You know, that place they took me to. The first place."

"The hospital?"

"I don't know what it was. Oy, I'm so aggravated between this place and that place, I can't eat nothing." Tzeydl cut into a pineapple ring with the side of her fork and put a piece into her mouth. "But the food here is so good, it's a shame to waste it." She took a bite of cottage cheese. "Who can eat so much food?" Tzeydl mumbled, biting into her roll. "They give you so much, it's too much for one person, I can't finish it, I'm full up to here." She gestured to the top of her head with her fork and took a few more bites of pineapple. "I'm so full, I'm busting, but I don't want they should throw it out." Tzeydl tilted her plate to catch the last curds of cottage cheese on her fork.

"Sponge cake or applesauce? Coffee or tea?" A woman wheeled a dessert cart up to the table.

"Nothing, thank you." Shayna pushed her plate to the middle of the table, as everyone else had done.

"Take a piece of cake." Tzeydl turned her styrofoam cup rightside-up and poured a little milk into it. "Coffee, please. And two pieces of cake, for me and my granddaughter."

"Bubbe, please. I'm so full, I'm plotzing."

"Listen to her, the granddaughter's plotzing," Minnie said, genuinely impressed. "A yiddishe kop she got, this granddaughter."

"Full, what full? You didn't eat nothing," Tzeydl said. "We'll take it for later." She wrapped each piece of cake in a napkin.

"Here Linda, put these in your bag," Tzeydl whispered, handing the cake to Shayna under the table.

Minnie was putting a piece of sponge cake into her pocketbook as well. "Okie dokie, chimney okie." Minnie snapped her bag shut, scraped back her chair and stood up.

"See you later," Manny said, standing up as well. One by one, all the tables cleared out, until only Tzeydl, Shayna, and the clean up crew were left. Tzeydl sipped her coffee slowly, as a woman came up to them and cleaned off their table with one grand sweep of her arm.

"Are we in your way?" Shayna asked.

"No, no. Sit. You want more coffee?"

Tzeydl didn't respond. "You want more coffee?" Shayna repeated loudly. "Sure, why not?"

The woman went into the kitchen and came back with a fresh cup for Tzeydl. "This is your grandmother, no?" she asked Shayna. She started wiping the table with an orange shmate and then stopped. "Between you there is something special, yes? I can tell. My grandmother died last year. So close we was, like this." She held up two fingers pressed tightly together. "Before she died, she wouldn't let nobody but me take care of her. 'I want Tina,' she would say. 'Only Tina.'" Instead of wiping the table, Tina swiped at her eyes with her forearm. "Yous are lucky to still have each other. Sit as long as yous want, it's nice in here after lunch. No one will bother you, almost like in your own home. Sit, sit." Tina leaned over and scrubbed the table, making wide circles with her arm, until it shone. Then she moved away.

Shayna wiped her own eyes. "So, Bubbe, tell me what happened."

"Nu, I don't even know myself what happened." Tzeydl leaned toward Shayna. "I told you they wired the whole apartment. When I was in Florida they must have done it, the super got keys. I saw the wires, on the fire escape they were. I thought maybe I should go cut them down, but I ain't so young no more, takeh, I was afraid I shouldn't fall."

"Bubbe, those are the wires for the television. Those wires have been up since I was born."

"Linda, don't you think I know what I'm talking about? Didn't I live in that apartment for forty-eight years? Don't you think I would see wires if there were wires on my own fire escape?"

"Yes, Bubbe, but..."

"But nothing. You think I'm crazy too, just like your mother. She thinks I put the wires up myself. What, an electrician I am all of a sudden? What do I know from wires?" Tzeydl made her 'oh please' gesture with her hand. "Of course a child has to side with the mother, that's the way it goes. But you, Linda, I thought you had more sense. Of all people, I thought you would believe me." Tzeydl looked at Shayna and then turned away. "All right, the hell with all of yous."

Shayna's eyes filled with tears. I can't lose her, she thought, remembering what her father had said: *when we didn't believe her, she insisted we were in on it.* I need her, Shayna thought. And she needs me. "Bubbe." Shayna touched Tzeydl's arm. "Bubbe, I believe you. Of course I do. It's just hard for me to imagine who would do a thing like that."

"Who? You want to know who?" Tzeydl turned back around, shaking her fist. "The lousy super, that's who. They want me out so they can raise the rent, you know I only pay seventy-two dollars a month because of the rent control. A big place it is, three rooms and the bathroom, I bet they could get a hundred dollars a month for my apartment if they wanted."

"Oh at least," Shayna laughed.

"So, when I was in Florida, the super put in the wires to make me crazy. And he did something to your mother and father, too."

"What'd he do to them?"

"Do I know?" Tzeydl lifted her palms to the ceiling. "There's gotta be some reason a daughter chups a mother out from her house with two cops in the middle of the night. What, a crime I committed, they had me arrested? I'm telling you, the super did something to your mother. It just ain't like her."

"Bubbe." Shayna touched her arm again. "They said you yelled at them for seventeen hours."

"Yelled, who yelled? All right, maybe I said a few words, but that's all. For that they should take me from my own house? You should see the first place they took me to, Linda. That was no place like this." Tzeydl looked around the room. "That was like a jail or something. A hundred doctors made tests on me. 'Mrs. Zimmerman, pick up your right hand; Mrs. Zimmerman, pick up your left hand; Mrs. Zimmerman look at me, what color is my hair, what color is my eyes?' They took so much blood from me, they listened to my heart, they made me take off my blouse, they looked at me, all those strangers." She began crying softly. "So many men came to look and they only wanted I should take off the bottom, too, but that I wouldn't do for one million dollars. Not one million dollars." Tzeydl took out the napkin from lunch she had tucked into her sleeve and blew her nose.

I am going to murder my parents. I don't care what Pearl says, Shayna thought, taking the napkin from Tzeydl to blow her own nose. "Bubbe, the first place they took you to was a hospital. Didn't anybody tell you?"

"Nobody told me nothing. A hospital, a jail, I didn't know where I was."

"Weren't you ever in a hospital before?"

"A hospital? When should I be in a hospital? I was never sick."

"What about when Sylvia and Uncle Ira were born?"

"Them I had at home."

"Oh." *Poor Bubbe,* Shayna thought. "So what did they say after they did the tests?"

"They made all the tests and they said I was fine. Perfect, they said I was, they couldn't get over me. They all said they should only be as healthy as I am when they get to be my age." Tzeydl leaned back and crossed her legs.

"So then why didn't they take you home?"

"Why? Do I know why?" Tzeydl shook her head. "I stayed there a week, and they was making me sick, I told you, the food in there was terrible. I lost fifteen pounds, at least. It was a goyishe place, how could I stay there? So your mother and father came to get me, they don't say nothing, I think I'm going home and no, this is where they bring me."

"They didn't tell you they were taking you here?"

"They didn't tell me nothing."

I don't believe it, Shayna thought, but then again she did believe it, for these were the same two people who hadn't yet told Shayna that her grandmother was no longer in the hospital, but was in a nursing home.

"Vey iss mir, am I glad my mother ain't alive to see what became of me." Tzeydl was crying again. "All my life I worked and saved for my old age, and now look at me. Every week I put money away. If I made a nickel, two cents I'd spend, two cents I put in the bank and a penny I gave away to charity. And now a home I'm in. A home. I never would put my mother in a home. Never. Your mother is your best friend, Linda. Remember that. Sixty-three years my mother's been dead and I think about her everyday. Not a day passes that I don't miss her. Oy but for the first time in my life, I'm glad she ain't here."

Shayna waited as Tzeydl removed the ever present tissue from the cuff of her blouse and blew her nose.

"I never even had a childhood," she said, sobbing. "Since I was ten years old, I worked in the factory, you know that, I showed you the picture. I put my hair up on my head, I should look older, gorgeous hair I had just like you, mamela, only not so dark, mine had a little red. When the inspectors came, the girls used to hide me and when they left I would come out from the closet."

Shayna smiled, though she was fighting back tears. Out from the closets. Maybe I'll make a banner and get a bunch of Jewish dykes to march under it at gay pride next year.

"I didn't want it to be like that for your mother," Tzeydl went on. "I made her stay in school and I gave her singing lessons and dancing lessons and viola lessons. Whatever lessons she wanted. She was crazy over the viola, your mother. She used to practice in the house and all the neighbors would stick their heads out from the windows in the building to see who was making such beautiful music. So what does she want from me?" Tzeydl implored Shayna with a pleading look. "It ain't my money she wants, she ain't poor, your mother; your father is a rich man. I wasn't no bother to her, I washed every dish when I went to her house, I scrubbed every pot. Every crumb I swept from the floor. So why was she in such a hurry to get rid of me? The super, I don't know what he did to her, but a daughter don't turn like that on a mother."

Shayna put her arm around the back of Tzeydl's chair and stroked her shoulder, but Tzeydl shrugged her off. "All right, so that's how it is. I don't care. They got rid of me so fast, so now I'm rid of them, too." She patted her hands together and shook them off as if she was getting rid of some crumbs.

Shayna pushed back her chair. "Come, Bubbe, let's take a walk. It's nice out. Maybe some fresh air will make you feel better."

"A walk? Where we gonna go, I don't know this neighborhood. I'm telling you, it's like a jail in here, they won't let me out."

Shayna stood up. "You're with me, Bubbe, we can do whatever we want. We can go for a walk."

Tzeydl got up, too. "I'm telling you, rules they got here, like kindergarten." She took Shayna's arm. "Come, we'll sit in the lobby."

Tzeydl and Shayna walked through the dining room and found two empty chairs in the lobby by the fish tank. Tzeydl stared straight ahead of her, sighing every once in a while. Shayna looked down at the toes of her white flats and blinked a lot, trying not to cry.

"Hello, Tzeydl. How are you?" A young man in a white shirt and brown pants squatted down in front of them.

"How am I? How can I be? All right." She patted his arm.

59

"Are you Tzeydl's granddaughter?" The man addressed Shayna, who nodded, afraid she would cry if she spoke. The man extended his hand. "I'm Alan Meyerhoff, your grandmother's social worker. Come talk to me in my office." He stood up. "Have a nice visit with your granddaughter," Alan Meyerhoff said loudly. "She looks just like you."

Shayna stood up, too. "Listen, Bubbe, I'll be right back, okay?"

"You gotta go into the toilet? Come, we'll go upstairs." She half rose.

"No, Bubbe. I'm going into the office a minute, okay?"

Tzeydl looked from Shayna to Alan Meyerhoff, who was waiting for her. "All right. Go, go. I'll wait right here." She sat back in her seat as Shayna followed the social worker down the hall into his office.

As soon as the door closed behind them, Shayna burst into the tears she'd been holding back all afternoon.

"It's very difficult at first," Alan Meyerhoff said as he pulled out a chair in front of his desk for Shayna to sink into. He tactfully busied himself with some files on the other side of his desk, until Shayna stopped crying.

"It's so hard to see her in here," she said, taking some yellow tissues out of the box on the desk. "She isn't crazy. She has a home. Why is she in here?"

"You're Linda, right?" Alan Meyerhoff asked.

"Yeah, right." Shayna didn't bother filling him in on the details of her name change, for it seemed to belong to a different life of hers; a life she could barely remember, though she had in fact only left it less than twenty-four hours ago.

"Well Linda, it seems to me that your grandmother has been diagnosed with senile dementia and she really can't live on her own anymore. It's a miracle she stayed in her apartment as long as she did. She needs daily supervision and we have her on some medication that will make things easier for her."

"You're doping her up?" Shayna grabbed onto the edge of the desk to keep from either passing out or throwing something.

"Of course not. We have her on a very mild tranquilizer called Haldol. It's just so she can get some sleep at night." He spoke calmly, and Shayna wondered if he was on Haldol himself. "Don't worry. The nurse said she was refusing to take her pills, anyway, except for her heart pills, she recognizes those. She's been on those for a few years now, hasn't she?" He looked into one of his files and Shayna leaned back with a sigh. This is a nightmare, she thought. But at least Bubbe's not taking their stupid drugs. That's a good sign. "What's senile dementia?" she asked.

"It means, in very simple terms, that a part of your grandmother's brain has worn out, and she can't always distinguish fantasy from reality."

"My grandmother is not senile," Shayna stated flatly. "We've had perfectly normal conversations all day. She's just upset and a little confused, and who wouldn't be, in her situation? No one's told her what's going on or why she's here. I'd be confused, too."

Alan Meyerhoff sighed. "I understand how upset you are. But even if your grandmother was rational..."

"She is rational."

"Okay, let's give her the benefit of the doubt." He put down his file folder. "Her eyesight and her hearing are deteriorating. How old is she?" He consulted his magic file that seemed to have all the answers. "Ninety-nine. Don't you think it's time for her to be in a home?"

"Yeah. Her home." Shayna let out a long breath. "Look, her hearing is fine, she hears every word I say. And she's got glasses. Can't she go home and get some home health aids or something? There must be programs for people like her. I mean, after all, this is New York."

"That's really up to your parents."

Oh great, Shayna thought. That's just swell. Oh, why didn't I interfere years ago, when they first started talking about nursing homes? I should have looked into some options for her closer to me, or I should have moved in with her for a while.

Alan Meyerhoff interrupted Shayna's should-haves. "Your grandmother might be able to remain at home with twenty-four hour care, but I don't think she would tolerate having a stranger in her home. And besides, there's that business about the wires she keeps talking about."

"What do you think that is?" Shayna asked. "Other than this wire complex, she's perfectly fine."

Alan Meyerhoff shook his head. "The human brain is a mysterious thing. Who knows why? Only God." He rolled his eyes skyward. "Your grandmother is a lucky woman. She's had a long and happy life up until now, and she has a daughter and a son-in-law who only want what's best for her. It's a shame she's so angry at your mother. That's very typical, though, for a resident to pick one family member to vent all their frustrations on. I think, all in all, Rosenbaum Estate will be a very good place for your grandmother, if she can make the adjustment."

"And if she can't?" Shayna asked, half-fearful and half-hopeful.

"We'll just have to see." Allan Meyerhoff tapped the edge of Tzeydl's folder on his desk. "It would help if your parents came to visit, though, and brought her some of her things, so she wouldn't feel so abandoned. Pictures of the family, some clothes, make-up, whatever. How long will you be around?"

"I'm not sure yet. At least a week."

"Good. I'm sure having you around will lift her spirits. See if you can get her involved in some activities. There's Bingo, card parties, whatever."

"There is one thing." Shayna leaned forward and rested her elbow on the desk. "She likes to sit outside and talk to people, see what's going on. She says she's not allowed to go out."

"Of course she can go out. In fact, we encourage it. Take her to a movie, take her shopping, anything that will make her feel her life is normal."

Right. Normal. Shayna stood up. "Tell me one more thing. Do you ever recommend that a family not visit someone who's in here?"

"Never," Alan Meyerhoff said, as he also rose. "Even when residents are angry, and we've had some very unpleasant visits here, believe me, it's still better for the family to come."

"I see." Shayna slung her bag over her shoulder. "Can my grandmother go out by herself?"

"Usually when people first come in, they need a volunteer to go along, so they don't get lost or mixed up and try to go home. But she can sit out front on the benches."

And watch the world go by, Shayna thought, bitterly.

Alan Meyerhoff opened the door for her. "Come, I'll walk out with you," he said, letting her leave the office first. As they walked toward the lobby, Shayna concentrated on the beige rug, thinking, maybe this is all a dream. Maybe Bubbe won't be sitting by the fish tank at all, and I'll drive to her apartment and she'll be there, standing in the kitchen with her apron on, making knaydlech for Friday night. She'll finish cooking and we'll sit down in the living room with coffee and pound cake and watch Jenny Jones.

But no such luck. Tzeydl was sitting right where Shayna had left her, asleep with her head tilted back and her mouth open. "Let her sleep," Alan Meyerhoff whispered. "She must be exhausted. Last night was the first night she slept in her bed because you were coming, she didn't want to be tired. She needs her rest."

"Thanks." Shayna sat down next to Tzeydl and Alan Meyerhoff walked away.

As soon as he was gone, Tzeydl opened her eyes. "He's a nice fella, ain't he?" She half-turned to watch his back disappear down the hall. "And good-looking, too. He ain't married, Linda. I think he likes you."

"Oh, Bubbe."

"Don't 'oh Bubbe' me. A young girl like you shouldn't be alone. A stone is alone, not a person."

Shayna sighed. Now I know she's fine, she thought, folding her arms. If we didn't have our usual discussion about my sad state of affairs, or lack thereof, then I'd first start to worry . "I'm not alone, Bubbe. I have plenty of friends."

"What, all girls still? You call that friends? I never met anyone like you, Linda. It's time you should grow up and have both boyfriends and girlfriends."

Boyfriends, I'm not too interested in, Shayna thought, staring at a yellow fish swimming around in the tank. Girlfriends, on the other hand, sure, but one would be quite enough.

Tzeydl went on. "You used to dress like such a hippie, Linda, and now you look so gorgeous. Soon you'll meet the right fella, believe me."

"Bubbe, for the millionth time, you know I don't like men."

Tzeydl shrugged. "So, don't like. Who says you gotta like? Just get married, that's all."

"I don't want to get married," Shayna said slowly and clearly.

"Oy Linda, I was just like you, first going with this one, then going with that one. You gotta make up your mind, it's enough already, it's time to get married. And then you find someone that's kind, someone that treats you like a mensch, you know what I mean? And you say, all right, he ain't perfect, but I'll tell you something, darling, you ain't so perfect either." Tzeydl patted Shayna's arm. "You make do, you get used to each other. And in the end, if you're lucky, you love each other and you try to be happy. And that's all."

62

"I'm happy the way I am," Shayna said, dying to add the words, *as a lesbian*, but not having the chutzpah to.

"Happy? Who could be happy living alone, a young girl like you? Nobody to bring you a drink of water in the night, you got a thirst; nobody to bring you an Alka-Seltzer, something didn't go down so good. Linda," Tzeydl poked her on the arm. "I know what it's like to be alone, believe me, thirty-five years I been by myself, ever since grandpa died, and I don't want that for you."

Shayna took Tzeydl's hand. I don't want that either, she thought. I agree with you, Bubbe, Shayna wanted to say. There's just that slight problem of gender. Aloud she said, "I'm not alone, Bubbe. I got lots of friends."

"Friends, big deal, friends. Soon they'll get married and go off, you'll see."

"No they won't, Bubbe. They don't want to get married, either."

"Feh," Tzeydl said. "That's even worse. What kind of friends is that for you, meshugeneh girls that don't want to get married. You should make new friends."

Shayna shook her head. "Bubbe, stop criticizing me, all right?"

"Who's criticizing you? I ain't criticizing you, Linda, I'm just telling you your faults." She looked Shayna square in the face. "You're too sensitive, Linda. So, all right, if you're happy, I'm happy, too."

"I'm happy, Bubbe, really," Shayna said. "Look, I gotta go."

"So soon you're going? Nu, where you running?"

"To see Sylvia."

"You'll sleep by her?"

"No, I wanna sleep by you. Okay?"

"Sure, why not, you got keys. A whole apartment standing empty, somebody should use it." Tzeydl stood up. "You have to go into the toilet before you go? You ain't pished all day. Come, we'll go up."

"You sit, Bubbe. I can go myself." Shayna got up, too. "I'll take the stairs. Till that elevator comes, we could both turn a hundred."

"All right, go." Tzeydl nudged Shayna gently. "Wait, Linda, give me your pocketbook, it's heavy, why should you shlep it up two flights of steps?" She took Shayna's bag. "And go into the top drawer of my dresser there by the bed. An apple's in there, I saved it for you."

"You keep it, Bubbe. Maybe you'll be hungry later."

"Hungry? Who can eat with so much aggravation? Take it for the ride, you'll be hungry, do me a favor."

"All right, all right, I'll take it." Shayna walked through the lobby, past the elevators and offices and took the stairs up to the third floor. After she used the bathroom she opened Tzyedl's top drawer and found the apple, along with some cookies in a waxed paper bag and two pieces of rye bread wrapped in a napkin. She saved all this from yesterday, Shayna thought, gathering up the food. For me. Shayna remembered her visits to Tzeydl's house which seemed like forever ago, when she would leave to go back to New England with a bag of oranges, a baked chicken, half a challah, a jar of homemade applesauce, and enough knishes to feed the entire lesbian softball league. She still wants to do for me, Shayna thought, closing the drawer. I'm still her baby. She took a deep breath, waited for her misty eyes to clear, and went back downstairs.

"You found the apple?" Tzeydl stood up and handed Shayna her bag.

Shayna nodded. "Are these for me, too?" She held up the cookies and bread.

"Yeah, I forgot to tell you, I saved those from the lunch yesterday. You see how I'm forgetting things already?"

"Don't forget I'm coming tomorrow. For lunch, okay?"

"Fine. That I'll remember." Tzeydl took Shayna's arm and steered her toward the door. "Don't worry, I ain't running away," she called to the woman at the front desk. "I'm just saying goodbye to my granddaughter." Tzeydl took a few steps and stopped at the glass door. "Run. Where would I run?" she asked Shayna. "With these feet, eppes, you think, I could run?"

Shayna opened the door and signed herself out in the spiral notebook.

"That's how they know who's coming and going," Tzeydl said, peering over Shayna's shoulder. "Goodbye, darling. Be careful how you go."

"I love you, Bubbe." Shayna put her arms around Tzeydl and hugged her tight, burying her face in her hair to hide her tears.

"I love you too, darling. Oy, a laybn on dine kop. Thank you for visiting me." She pushed Shayna away. "Go, already, I don't want you should drive in the dark. And enough with the tears. Call me when you get there."

"I'll call you from Brooklyn."

"Okay, darling."

Shayna left the building, turning around once to see Tzeydl standing by the glass door. She waved, and Tzeydl blew her a kiss. Then she got into her car and started the motor. "Don't lose it now," Shayna said, looking up at her green-eyed friend in the rear view mirror. "You gotta go see your mother on Long Island and drive back to Brooklyn in rush hour traffic. Then I promise, I'll let you fall apart. Goddess, what a day. What a fucking day." She shifted into reverse, pulled out of her spot, and got back on Forest Avenue, heading for Vey Iss Mir.

Chapter Seven

Shayna stopped her car on her parents' suburban street and as soon as she cut the motor, there was no sound to be heard except the beating of her own heart. No cars honking, no kids yelling, no sea gulls calling, nothing. She looked out the windshield and studied the manicured lawns and shrubs, and the split-level, aluminum-sided houses that all looked exactly the same. I can't even remember the last time I was back here, she thought, taking a minute to breathe before she got out to face the music. She slouched down in the driver's seat, that old I've-got-wet-cement-instead-of-blood feeling coursing through her veins. Shayna had spent her Wonder Years in Brooklyn, and then her family had migrated to Long Island but Shayna had never gotten used to it, and escaped back to the 'old neighborhood' to use her parents' lingo, every chance she could get. She'd stay with her bubbe who always had time to take Shayna shopping, or go to a museum or an off-Broadway play. There was always something to do in the city: Chinatown, Little Italy and Central Park were only subway stops away, not to mention the boardwalk and the beach, which were a mere few steps out of Tzeydl's building. Long Island was a different story. "There's nothing to do," Shayna would moan to her mother on a Saturday morning. "I'm bored." "Go run around the block and see if it's raining," was her mother's stock reply. And that's about all there was to do, because if Shayna wanted to go anywhere, she had to wait for her mother to drive her there and her mother never had the time because she was always waiting for someone to show up: the gardener, the painter, the floor waxer, the plumber, the cleaning man, the UPS man, the gas man, the washing machine man. There was always something besides Shayna in need of her mother's attention. And Shayna, who of course had been Linda at the time, was forever in the way. She felt embarrassed in front of all these men who stared with open admiration at her body which seemed to be growing rounder and softer by the minute.

In Brooklyn, men stared at her too, and whistled or yelled things sometimes, but for some reason, Shayna knew how to handle herself on the street. When things happened in her own home, with men that were supposed to be working for her parents, she was totally at a loss. Like the time when she was fifteen, and the exterminator came into her room, found her sprawled belly-down on her bed, and gave her a friendly potch on the tuchus. Shayna felt like she, not he, had done something wrong, and she knew this was something she could never discuss with her mother. Instead she just made sure that from then on she stayed downstairs in the kitchen whenever the exterminator came to de-bug the house.

Why am I thinking about all this now? Shayna broke into her own thoughts. I've got to get in there and talk to Sylvia. She shook her head to clear it, got out of the car and rang the bell. Maybe she's not home, Shayna thought, knowing that she was by the sight of the green Chrysler in the driveway. She rang the bell again and heard her mother's footsteps clicking down the hall. She saw the cover of the peephole slide open and the red light of the burglar alarm go off before her mother opened the door. "Linda, what a surprise. What are you doing here?"

I've become an Avon Lady, Sylvia. What do you think? "Oh, I was just in the neighborhood, so I thought I'd stop by," Shayna said. "Mind if I come in?"

Mrs. Steinblatt stepped aside and let Shayna pass. She closed the door behind her, locked it, and reset the burglar alarm on the panel inside the hall closet before joining her daughter in the kitchen. Shayna slung her shoulder bag on the back of a kitchen chair and sat down. The first thing she saw was Tzeydl's pocketbook lying on its side on the table. It was white patent leather, with a double adjustable strap and five zippers leading to various compartments. The sight of the bag made Shayna furious, but she just took a deep breath. I have to remain calm, she reminded herself. I have a mission here. She watched her mother's back as she bustled about, putting up water for coffee and lighting her ever present cigarette. Shayna hated that her mother smoked, had hated it ever since she was a little girl. But her cute, "Mommy, I don't want you to die," tactics had been no more successful than her sarcastic adolescent, "One more nail in your coffin" remarks, though the latter did succeed in getting Shayna sent to her room without any supper. When Shayna had entered her health food stage, she would cook with a red bandanna tied around her nose and mouth, "to preserve my lungs," she'd self-righteously mumble to Mrs. Steinblatt, who would scream, "Get that shmate off your face, you look like a goniff, for God's sake."

Shayna sighed, and Mrs. Steinblatt turned. "Want some coffee?" she asked.

"Sylvia, you know I don't drink coffee."

"How should I know what you drink or don't drink? Sometimes a person changes over the years. All right, so you don't drink coffee; I'm sorry I asked." She turned back around and dumped a spoonful of Instant Maxwell House into a Garfield mug, poured the water in and brought it over to the table along with her cigarettes and an ashtray from Atlantic City shaped like a giant peanut.

This is just great, Shayna thought. We're off to a terrific start here. She picked up the *TV Guide* and pretended to leaf through it, sneaking glances at her mother, who was taking small sips of her steaming black coffee. "I'll take some orange juice if you have any," Shayna said, in an attempt to make peace.

Mrs. Steinblatt pointed with her head. "You know where the refrigerator is."

Shayna scraped back her chair, wondering how in the world she was going to bring up Tzeydl's situation when she couldn't even get a glass of OJ out of her mother without a snide remark to go along with it. True, I could have said, no thank you, when she asked if I wanted coffee, she thought, pouring some Tropicana she didn't want into a Welch's grape jelly jar with a picture of Fred

Flintstone on it. But all right, I'm not perfect, even Bubbe said so, so what does Sylvia want?

Shayna sat down at the table again, listening to the refrigerator hum and watching her mother who was staring into the black hole of her coffee. Shayna noticed that her mother was immaculately dressed in a short-sleeved pink and white sweater, matching pink pants and white shoes. Her hair and make-up, not to mention her nails, were perfect. Anyone else would have asked Mrs. Steinblatt if she was on her way out somewhere, but Shayna knew better. Her mother always looked perfect, even when she spent all day in the house, which she frequently did.

Shayna felt the silence between them closing in on her. She took a swig of juice and glanced at the digital clock on the microwave. Three-thirty-seven. I'll say something at twenty-to-four, Shayna decided. She cleared her throat, but before she could utter a word, her mother spoke.

"I know why you're here." Mrs. Steinblatt ground out her cigarette, picked up a deck of cards and started shuffling them. "I've talked to the doctor, the nurses and the social worker," she said, laying out seven piles of cards for a game of solitaire. "They all say your grandmother needs a good rest and as soon as they think we can see her, they'll give us a call." She started going through the cards three at a time, placing the aces up top, setting a red six on a black seven, and the Jack of Spades on the Queen of Hearts.

How can she keep such a straight face and lie to me like that? It's unbelievable. Shayna stared at her mother's hands as they sorted through the cards. I wonder what other untruths she's told me. Maybe she isn't even my real mother. When Shayna was a little girl, she liked to pretend she was adopted, and her real mother was a movie star like Natalie Wood or Sophia Loren, who would one day come rescue her. It wasn't hard to imagine, for Sylvia Steinblatt's hair was as straight as Shayna's was curly, her eyes were a dark brown to Shayna's green, and she was tall and nervously thin, unlike Shayna, who was short and zaftig. But needless to say, no one had ever come to claim her.

Shayna watched her mother play cards. She appeared calm, but Shayna knew she wasn't for she missed putting the four of diamonds on the five of clubs, and Sylvia Steinblatt never missed a thing.

"Sylvia, the four. On the five of clubs," Shayna said, pointing. This display of imperfection dissolved some of Shayna's hostility. Suddenly she didn't feel so angry any more. "I saw Bubbe today," she said softly.

Mrs. Steinblatt continued to play cards, as if she hadn't heard what Shayna had said. Shayna was about to repeat herself when she noticed a tear sliding down her mother's cheek. It hesitated for a moment on the thin point of her chin before dropping with a plop on the ten of spades. Shayna was stunned. This was even more shocking than her grandmother's unpainted nails and greying hair. Sylvia, who Shayna always said was allergic to having any type of feeling, never cried. Never. Not when Shayna's grandma Sarah had died; not when Shayna had fallen off her skateboard and broken both arms; not even when her dog Pooky had been run over by a Good Humor truck. Maybe the ceiling was leaking? Shayna looked up but the roof was still intact. Mrs. Steinblatt continued to play cards and Shayna stared down at Bill Cosby's face, smiling up at her from the cover of the *TV Guide*.

"Sylvia," Shayna began again. "I went to the nursing home this morning. Bubbe's miserable there. She wants to go back to the apartment."

Mrs. Steinblatt finished her game, piling all the cards on top of the four aces. She always wins, Shayna thought. How come she always wins? Mrs. Steinblatt combined all four piles into one and began to shuffle the deck again. "She can't go home, Linda and that's final. I don't want to discuss it."

For this I had to drive two hundred and fifty miles? Shayna felt tears starting and willed them back into her brain, or wherever it was they originated. She had cried so much lately she was amazed she had any tears left. Mrs. Steinblatt dealt herself another hand, and Shayna felt mass hysteria rising up from the tips of her toes. I am really going to lose it, she thought. She was shvitzing all over, and had to restrain herself from grabbing the cards in her mother's hand and flinging them into the air for a rousing game of fifty-two pick-up. Instead she said, incredibly calmly, "Sylvia, please put the cards down." And to her amazement, her mother did.

"Look," Shayna said. "I know I haven't been here in forever and this isn't the greatest time for a family reunion, but we have to discuss this. You can't just dump Bubbe in an institution and dope her up, like she doesn't have a life. Why can't she stay at home with a live-in nurse or something? Then she could have her things and be by the ocean, her friends could come see her..." Shayna's voice trailed off, for her mother was staring at her, her eyes brimming with tears. I've never seen her like this, Shayna thought, letting her own eyes fill as well. She watched tears fall from her mother's eyes, wondering why her mascara didn't run.

"Linda, do you really think I threw her in there just like that?" Mrs Steinblatt asked softly, "Don't you think I love my mother? Don't you think I want what's best for her?"

"Of course," Shayna said, almost reaching out to take her mother's hand, but deciding that was pushing it. "But what you think is best for her may not be what really is best."

Wrong words. Mrs.Steinblatt's eyes darkened, her lips tightened, and whatever brief tenderness that had passed between mother and daughter was instantly gone. "And I suppose you know what's best for my mother, Miss Know-It-All with the fancy-shmancy college education your father and I paid for? She hasn't been home in years and now all of a sudden she's back to tell us what to do." Shayna groaned. She hated when her mother referred to her as "she" and she knew her mother knew that she hated it.

Mrs. Steinblatt paused to light a cigarette, striking the match with deliberateness. "Your grandmother has always been miserable. She was miserable in the apartment, she was miserable in Florida and now she's miserable in the nursing home. So what else is new? That's why she's lived so long; she always has something to kvetch about." Mrs. Steinblatt took a drag on her cigarette. "I'll tell you a secret," she said, exhaling a cloud of blue smoke. "She ain't so miserable. I'm sure she told you that because she knew you'd tell me, and then I'd have one more thing to feel guilty about, which I need like a hole in the head. She's probably very happy she doesn't have to shop and cook and clean anymore. And if she is miserable, it's her own damn fault. She should stop complaining and make herself some friends. Nobody likes a kvetch. Believe me, she's better off where she is now, with people around and things to do. She was too much alone, your grandmother, she drove herself nuts."

"She isn't nuts!" Shayna slammed her hand down on the kitchen table. "She's just a little confused, which you can hardly blame her for. And angry, which you can't blame her for either."

"Did she tell you about the wires? Did she tell you the super was out to get her? Don't you think that's more serious than being a little confused?"

"Sylvia." Shayna rubbed her forehead, trying to ward off Exedrin Headache Number Ninety-nine. "Sylvia, she's just exaggerating a little. It's true the super wants to evict her; they've been trying to get her out of that apartment for years, so they can raise the rent. You know that's true. She didn't do anything really crazy, like crawl out on the fire escape and try and cut the wires. I'm sure I could get her over this wire thing and then with a live-in nurse she'd be fine."

"Oy, Linda." Mrs. Steinblatt groaned as she shifted her weight and crossed her legs.

"What's the matter?"

"My hip. It's nothing." Mrs. Steinblatt waved her hand in a gesture that echoed Tzeydl's. "Everything hurts me today; my hip, my stomach. I haven't been able to eat for a week." She took a last sip of coffee which Shayna hoped wasn't burning a hole in her empty belly. "Linda, I wanted to spare you all this, that's why we didn't want to tell you yet. We were waiting until she calmed down."

"From the drugs they have her on?"

"Linda, what they're giving her is very mild, it's like a tenth of a Valium. I wouldn't mind taking one myself. It's just to take the edge off, so she won't be so agitated."

"That edge is all she's got left!" Shayna shrieked, more than a little agitated, herself.

"Don't worry, the social worker called me this morning, she's not taking her pills anyway." Well, at least that story's consistent, Shayna thought. "He's gonna have them put it in her juice, in liquid form; maybe she won't notice. You see how paranoid she is, she won't take her pills; she thinks they're trying to poison her."

Shayna stared at her mother. "But they are trying to poison her."

"Oh, Linda, don't be so dramatic." Mrs. Steinblatt inhaled her cigarette and let two puffs of blue smoke stream out of her nostrils. "She cannot go back to that crummy apartment in that lousy neighborhood, nurse or no nurse. And believe me, your grandmother would never let a stranger into the house to cook and clean for her. And even if she did, you think she wouldn't hock her every five seconds, do it this way better, do it that way better? You think someone would be able to put up with your grandmother? No," Mrs. Steinblatt shook her head, "a saint like that hasn't been born yet."

"I know it would be hard for Bubbe, but I'm sure if we explained it to her, she'd accept it. It would certainly be better than being in a home."

"Linda." Mrs. Steinblatt used her cigarette, which was almost smoked down to the filter, to light a fresh one. "You cannot explain things to your grandmother. She is no longer capable of making her own decisions. Do you understand that? She is half in and half out of this world. Do you know she thinks we had her arrested?"

Shayna sat back in her chair and folded her arms. "And what would you think if two cops hauled you out of the house in the middle of the night?"

"Linda, we had no choice. What are we supposed to tell her? That she's losing her mind so we have to put her somewhere where they'll take care of her? She screamed for so many hours that night, it's a wonder she didn't have a heart attack."

"What'd she say?"

"Never mind what she said. The super this, the super that, the telephone, the wires." Ms. Steinblatt reached for the wooden napkin holder that was carved into the word *shalom*. Shayna pushed it closer and she took out a yellow napkin and blew her nose. "We only wanted to take her to a hospital, but no, she wouldn't go. We called a private ambulance, but she wouldn't go with them either, and they're not allowed to take someone against their will." Mrs. Steinblatt dabbed at her eyes. "So we didn't know what to do. Who else could we call?"

Hello, Shayna wanted to scream. There is a person sitting next to you here at your very own kitchen table, in case you didn't notice. Aloud she said, "You could have called me."

"You? What could you do from so far away?"

"I could have talked to her on the phone."

"Linda." Mrs. Steinblatt leaned forward. "I'm telling you, she screamed the whole night and then she locked herself in your room and sat on a chair against the door so if we forced our way in, we'd knock her over. Only once she opened the door, when the first ambulance came. She says to the driver, 'Ain't my blouse buttoned right? Don't my shoes match? Do I look like a crazy person to you?' So he looks at me like I'm the one that's crazy. And then he leaves and she starts screaming again. Until one o'clock in the morning this went on, we had to call the county ambulance. A man and a woman they sent, and they were as nice as they could be, under the circumstances. And when they took my mother away," Mrs. Steinblatt's voice broke, "she screamed bloody murder so the whole neighborhood should only know that her lousy daughter did such a terrible thing." Mrs. Steinblatt leaned back and stared at her daughter.

"So she had a fit." Now Shayna leaned forward and rested her elbows on the table. "It's over now. She acted perfectly normal today. We just have to figure out how to calm her down about these wires, and maybe hire a private nurse or something, and then she can go home."

"It's out of the question." Mrs. Steinblatt pressed her lips firmly together, sealing her emotions in tight as the zip-lock baggies she used to pack Shayna's cream cheese and jelly sandwiches in. Shayna knew that look well. It meant the discussion was over.

"All right," she said, pushing some crumbs together on the oil cloth that covered the table. It looked like her father had had an onion bagel for breakfast that morning. "But don't you think you should go visit her? I'm going back there tomorrow to bring her some things. She wants her pocketbook."

Both women's eyes travelled across the table to Tzeydl's white bag, which lay on its side like an overturned milk truck.

"The first thing she'll do is look for her keys and then she'll be mad that I took them," Mrs. Steinblatt said.

"Sylvia, don't you think she knows she doesn't have her keys whether or not she has her pocketbook? She needs her bag." Shayna reached for it and Mrs. Steinblatt slid it toward her. "And what about her watch and her wedding ring, and that necklace she always wears?"

"I don't know what to do." Shayna's mother ground out her forgotten cigarette. "I put them in a safety deposit box. They say you shouldn't leave them their valuables, they don't want to be responsible." She shook her head. "I never thought this would happen to us. If she fell and broke her hip, God forbid, you think I wouldn't have her up in your room in a minute with a private nurse? Why do you think we stayed in this house so long; I have nothing better to do than clean your empty room, and your father loves commuting over an hour every day into Manhattan? We were going to move to a smaller house closer to the city years ago—it would make things a lot easier on your father—but we never moved, just in case. And this is some just in case."

"What about a different nursing home?" Shayna asked, sensing her mother was thawing out just a little. "Maybe we could find her a place where she could have her own room and a little kitchenette or something. Maybe a place by the ocean; there must be a place in Brighton Beach. Then her friends could see her."

Mrs. Steinblatt shook her head again. "They say to take them out of their neighborhoods they shouldn't try to run back to their apartments." Shayna wondered if the *they* her mother was referring to was the staff of the nursing home, or the general, authoritative *they*, as in *they* say pastel colors are going to be very popular this fall. Though her mother's mind seemed to be made up, so what did it matter? "We were lucky to get her in there at all," Mrs. Steinblatt continued. "The place had a waiting list as long as your arm. But your father knew somebody who knew somebody…" (Translation: he bribed his way in, Shayna thought) "…so we lucked out. And believe me, this place ain't cheap."

"How much is it?" Shayna asked.

"None of your business," her mother replied. "It's a very nice place; it's clean, it's kosher, not that your grandmother's so religious, but the food is familiar to her, it's what she's used to. We'll manage."

"But what if you can't?"

"Calm yourself; your grandmother won't wind up on the street. As a matter of fact, she's on the list for a private room."

"She is?" Shayna's eyebrows rose. "Isn't that even more expensive?"

"Of course it's more expensive. Don't be so surprised. Don't you think we want her to be happy there even if it's gonna cost us an arm and a leg and half your father's paycheck? What can I tell you, Linda? I'm doing the best I can."

"I guess so." Shayna had to admit her mother wasn't exactly the Wicked Witch of the West. She was trying, but she wished her mother could see things her and Tzeydl's way.

Shayna got up. "I better go. I don't want to get caught in rush hour traffic."

"At this hour it's all going the other way. Don't you want to stay? I'm making pot roast. Your father will be home soon."

Shayna was about to say, "You know I don't eat red meat," but, remembering the coffee/orange juice disaster, changed her mind. "You know, I think I'd like to stay at Bubbe's tonight," she said, lifting her shoulder bag. "I'll look through her things and bring her some stuff she needs tomorrow."

Mrs. Steinblatt also stood. "Here, take a piece of fruit, you'll be hungry in the morning, I'm sure there's nothing left to eat in the house." She took some oranges out of a big wooden bowl on the counter. "Take some cottage cheese for breakfast," she said, opening the refrigerator. "I got a new one here, it's not even open yet. You want some bagels?" Mrs. Steinblatt turned around, the red and white cottage cheese container in her hand. "How long you gonna be there?"

"I don't know. It depends on Bubbe. Maybe a week."

"A week? Take a loaf of bread." Shayna watched her mother load up a shopping bag with the fruit, bagels, cottage cheese, a stick of butter, half a loaf of bread, some Swiss cheese and a container of orange juice.

"Sylvia, what do you think, the stores in Brighton Beach all went bankrupt?"

"So why should you shop there? Here the prices are cheaper." Mrs. Steinblatt added a few bananas to the bag. "Call me tomorrow and let me know how everything went. Maybe your father and I will come at the end of the week." She handed Shayna the bag. "Be careful how you go."

"Thanks, Sylvia. If anyone mugs me, at least they won't starve." She took the bag and put it down. "Wait a minute. I have to use the bathroom."

Shayna went upstairs, but instead of taking a right into the bathroom, she took a left into her childhood bedroom, for, being a reporter, she wanted to see the scene of the crime. Everything looked the same as it had when she was growing up, except that her twin beds with their pink bedspreads and her matching bureau and desk set all looked so tiny, much smaller than Shayna remembered. Shayna went over to her bookcase, wondering if she should take her Bobbsey Twins and Hardy Boys collection home. She looked at all the familiar tchotchkes on her bureau: a fat red candle with a swirly white design her parents would never let her light for fear she'd go off into a meditative trance and burn down the house from her hippie days; a pink and black speckled stone the size of her fist that she had carried down from a mountaintop somewhere in Vermont in an attempt to be more in touch with nature; and a small wooden lopsided duck Shayna had carved in her shop class. Shayna was proud that she had been the first female in the whole school to ever take shop. She had just signed up as L.P.

Steinblatt, and no one, including the computer, had questioned her.

Maybe I'll take this duck back with me, Shayna thought, moving to pick it up. After all, it did take a whole semester to make the thing. She picked the duck up from the edge of the dresser, and something shiny on the floor caught her eye. She squatted down and ran her hands around the edge of a cut-glass crystal bowl.

"Bubbe's bowl," Shayna whispered, lifting it up. The bowl was the size and shape of a large honeydew melon, standing on three delicate legs. Every inch of it was etched with flowers and leaves in a very fine design. The bowl had always sat on Tzeydl's coffee table and as a little girl, Shayna had never been allowed to touch it. "Look with your eyes, not with your hands," her mother would say sharply. If she was good, she was awarded a piece of candy from the bowl: a cherry lifesaver, a butterscotch sucking candy, or Shayna's favorite, a coffee nip. Shayna picked up the bowl and hugged it against her belly for a minute. This thing is solid, she thought, feeling comforted by the weight somehow, like having Tzimmy on her lap. Seeing the bowl in her old room made Shayna feel strange and sad, almost like Tzeydl had already died. She put the bowl back in its corner, and looked around.

She picked my room to lock herself up in, Shayna thought proudly. She felt safe here. Like she was with me. Shayna took one final look around and then went back downstairs. Her mother had shlepped everything out of the kitchen and was standing with it at the front door.

"Sylvia, why is Bubbe's good bowl in my room?" Shayna asked.

"So there should be one more thing in the house for me to dust." Mrs. Steinblatt handed Shayna her pocketbook.

"Sylvia."

"Linda, what do I know? Here." She handed her Tzeydl's pocketbook and the shopping bag. "Your grandmother was convinced the super was only going to steal it. She wouldn't budge from the apartment without it."

"Do you think I should take it to her?"

"What do I know? Ask her if she wants it. Meanwhile, it's safe upstairs."

"Okay." Shayna turned to go.

"Wait, I'll let you out. You have everything?"

"Everything but the kitchen sink."

Mrs. Steinblatt moved some coats in the hall closet around and reached in to disengage the alarm. "Tell your grandmother hello for me."

"Okay. Bye, Sylvia."

"Goodbye, sweetheart. Thank you."

"You're welcome," Shayna said automatically, though her brain was trying to sort out what her ears had just heard. My mother called me sweetheart and thanked me? I must be dreaming. She shlepped all her stuff to the car, got in, and was on the road again.

Chapter Eight

It was a miracle. A parking space on Brighton Seventh Street. Maybe the messiah had come after all. Shayna squeezed her little red Toyota between a big black Buick and a gold spray-painted van with a green plastic garbage bag taped to the driver's side, where the window should be. "Oh Goddess of the Parked Cars, please watch over Tandeleyeh the Toyota," Shayna prayed as she got out. She stood up, arched her aching back and took a deep breath. Ahh, that smell. The boardwalk was right in front of Shayna and beyond the boardwalk was the beach and beyond the beach was the ocean and that fresh salty air rushed to Shayna's nostrils like a long lost lover. "That's why I lived so long," Tzeydl often told Shayna. "Because I was always by the water. In Europe we lived on the ocean, here too, and even when I go down to Florida, only a few steps I am from the beach." Shayna loved the ocean too; the beach had been her backyard when she was a little girl. "You never wanted to come out of the water," her mother told her. "You would scream so, people would turn around to see what kind of parents would beat a little girl like that." Every night Shayna would look out her bedroom window, say, "Good-night, ocean," and blow the water a kiss. Shayna took another deep breath and then leaned into the car to get her things. She slung her pocketbook over one shoulder and Tzeydl's over the other, picked up her suitcase with her left hand and the bag of food with her right, slammed the car door with her hip, and headed up the street.

She turned the corner, soaking up the familiar sounds. To her right, Shayna could hear the waves rushing in and retreating back, sea gulls calling to each other, and the clicking of high heels as couples strolled down the boardwalk, arm in arm. In her left ear, Shayna heard the El rumbling overhead and screeching to a halt, cars honking, and a kid walking by with a boom box as big as Shayna's old camp trunk hoisted onto his shoulder. The sidewalks were lined with people sitting on folding chairs outside their apartment buildings gossiping in Russian, Yiddish and Polish. They all stopped their conversations to stare openly at Shayna, nod their heads at her, and then resume talking, about her no doubt, as soon as she passed.

Two women all bundled up with babushkas tied under their chins, sat on wooden folding chairs outside Tzeydl's apartment house. Shayna smiled at them, wondering if they knew her bubbe. Most of Tzeydl's friends had left the neighborhood; some had moved to Florida or to live with their children in New Jersey;

many of them had died. The new tenants were young Russian immigrants; in fact, the neighborhood was now referred to as Little Odessa. But Tzeydl wasn't very friendly with the newcomers. "They don't talk Jewish the same like I do," she explained to Shayna. "I can't understand a thing they say."

Shayna unlocked the door to the building, crossed the lobby and approached the elevator warily. And now, today's sixty-four-thousand dollar question: would the elevator do its thing, or would Shayna be stuck shlepping all this chazzeri up five flights of stairs? She pushed the button and immediately a whirring noise sounded. Another miracle.

Shayna walked down the fifth floor hallway, stopped in front of number five-fourteen and opened the three locks on the door. Before she went inside, she kissed the mezzuzah nailed at an angle in the door frame. Then she dragged all her things inside, closed the door, secured the three locks, switched on the foyer light and leaned her back against the door.

"Bubbe, I'm home," Shayna whispered. But there was no reply. Her knees gave way and she sank down onto her suitcase, her head in her hands. Breathe, Shayna, breathe, she reminded herself. The smell of Tzeydl's apartment instantly calmed her. It was the smell of chicken: half a century of baked chicken, boiled chicken, roasted chicken, broiled chicken, chicken liver, chicken cutlets, chicken fricassee. It was as if the walls had soaked up the smell like a sponge mopping up spilled chicken soup. Shayna closed her eyes and saw her family sitting at Tzeydl's small kitchen table on a Friday night, the candles lit, the wine and challah blessed. Tzeydl was standing by the stove with her back to the table and then she turned with her arms outstretched, cradling a plate of soup lovingly, like a brand new grandchild. She served Shayna's father first, her mother second, and Shayna last, and then she'd stand by the stove with her hands on her hips, waiting.

"It's delicious, Ma," Shayna's mother would say. "The knaydlech melt in your mouth," Shayna's father would add. Only then would Tzeydl untie her apron that said WORLD'S GREATEST BALABOOSTEH on it, serve herself a plate of soup and sit down to eat.

Shayna opened her eyes, got up and wandered into the kitchen. She put on the light, sat down at the formica table that was at least ten years older than she was, and looked around. Everything seemed the same: the clock on the wall, the toaster on the counter, a bag of potatoes and a bunch of onions hanging in a wire basket, the Shabbas candlesticks on the table. Shayna looked up: was that Tzeydl's footsteps in the living room she just heard, or her wishful ears playing tricks on her? Her eyes returned to the kitchen table, and took in a half-filled coffee cup with greyish milk floating on the top, an empty orange juice glass, a plate with toast crumbs scattered across it and a knife, sticky with butter. Shayna knew her grandmother would never leave a dirty dish in the sink, let alone on the kitchen table. No, Tzeydl wasn't home, wasn't coming home, and hadn't been home in a long time.

A car horn sounded and Shayna went over to the kitchen window and looked down into the street. There was hardly anyone sitting outside now; it was dark except for the beams from the headlights of the car whose horn had just sounded. Shayna could see into the apartment directly across from Tzeydl's, just like an old Alfred Hitchcock movie. A man was sitting at a table in his undershirt, drinking a beer and reading the newspaper. Shayna closed the curtain and stuck her finger into the soil of the two plants on the windowsill. Both dry as bones.

Shayna filled the saucepan on the stove with water and dumped it into the plants. One pot had half-inch shoots just starting to poke up from the soil. "I wonder if these are oranges or grapefruits," Shayna said, for whenever Tzeydl came back from Florida, she would bring a big bag of citrus fruit to have for breakfast. She'd spit the seeds into her hand, throw them in a pot of dirt, and up they'd come, like magic. The other plant had been on the windowsill ever since Shayna could remember. It had thin striped leaves over a foot tall, pointing from the soil straight up to the ceiling. Tzeydl loved that plant, and washed its leaves with a half-water/half-milk solution to keep them shiny.

"Here, bubbeleh, you must be thirsty, take a nice long drink," she'd say, whenever she watered that plant.

"Who takes care of your plant when you're in Florida?" Shayna once asked her.

"Nobody. Nobody goes into my apartment when I'm away. You know that."

"But how can it live with no water for six months, Bubbe?"

Tzeydl shrugged. "It waits for me. Nu, I'll tell you something. When you don't got no food you live on water, when you don't got no water you live on air, and when you don't got no air, you live on hope. And that's all."

That was the closest Tzeydl had ever come to talking about her childhood, though Shayna had asked her about it many times. What was it like in Russia, Bubbe, what was it like at Ellis Island, wasn't it strange to hear English for the first time? She'd even brought along a tape recorder once, for a Woman's Studies Oral Herstory Project, but Tzyedl wouldn't even let her turn it on. "What are you doing, writing a story about me, my picture they'll put in the paper?"

"No, Bubbe," Shayna said, "it's for school."

"For school?" Tzeydl asked. "What kind of cockamammy school is that? They should be teaching you something important, not sending you here to hock me with your tin can. I'm an ordinary woman, Linda, with a husband and two children and three grandchildren, who should only grow up and get married, God willing, I should live so long. Now put that thing away and eat some soup."

So Shayna had to piece together the story of Tzeydl's life from bits and pieces she heard here and there. Like the time Shayna took her to the doctor, and he had the nerve to tell her she should lose a little weight, it would be better for her heart. "Pardon me, doctor," Tzeydl had said. "I ain't no doctor, but I know a thing or two, a few years I lived. Better you should be a little too fat than a little too skinny, just in case you should get sick, God forbid, you need a little extra meat on your bones, like a little extra money in the bank. Plenty skinny I was when I was a young maidl, believe me. Ask me what I ate."

The doctor complied. "What did you eat?"

"Oy, what I ate, don't ask. Grass I ate, and I was grateful to get that. You was born in this country, doctor, you don't know what the Jews in Europe went through. I didn't starve for so many years to go in my old age on a diet. Come Linda," and she'd taken Shayna's arm. "Thank you very much."

They left with Tzeydl still murmuring, "What kind of doctor is that, to put an old lady like me on a diet? What, a beauty contest he thinks I'm entering all of a sudden, or maybe for a bikini at my age I'm going shopping?"

Shayna sighed, absently stroking the leaves of Tzeydl's plant. "Goddess, I can't even breathe without thinking about her," Shayna said aloud. "Everything has a story. I bet you have some good ones." Shayna addressed Tzeydl's plant. "You've been here for at least thirty years. What did she do all day? Did she talk to you about my grandpa? Did she talk to you about me? Oh never mind, I didn't bring my tape recorder anyway."

Shayna picked off a dead leaf and crumpled it in her hand. "Maybe I'll take you to the nursing home to see her. Brighten up the place a little. It sure could use a little life." Shayna poured some more water into the plant's soil and then went into the living room. She turned on the light and flopped into a chair. Here too everything looked the same: the deep purple couch with black fringe and the springs falling through; the coffee table with its ashtray of green blown glass and the ceramic candy dish shaped like an open hand; and the two easy chairs with doilies on the arms and back, facing each other like two old women enjoying each other's conversation. And of course there were pictures everywhere: standing on top of the television and the end tables, hanging on the walls and taped to the mirror over the couch. Shayna gave herself a walking tour of the family photos: there was Uncle Ira in his uniform just home from the war; there were Shayna's parents on their wedding day, her mother's face flushed and unworried, her father with a full head of wavy light brown hair. On the television set were two pictures of Shayna's cousin Sam: in one he was at his Bar Mitzvah in a yarmalke and tallis, and in the other he stood in shorts and a T-shirt, proudly holding a bunch of bananas they had grown on his kibbutz. Next to Sam was a picture of his sister, Shayna's cousin Abbie, with her daughter Melinda, Tzeydl's brand new great-grandchild. And of course there were pictures of Shayna everywhere: in diapers holding a pail and shovel on the beach; in a playsuit with her front tooth missing; at her high school graduation in a cap and gown with straight hair she had ironed; on top of some mountain she had climbed on vacation in Maine one year; and sitting in her present living room with Tzimmy on her lap. Obviously Shayna was Tzeydl's favorite, even though she hadn't done anything spectacular like spend a year in Israel or produce a great-grandchild. Still, a tochter's tochter is special, as Tzeydl would say. Shayna continued her walking tour, heading for Tzeydl's bedroom. The small double bed with its whiter-than-white bedspread beckoned to her, and she threw herself down, rolled over and stared at the ceiling. Sylvia was right, there were cracks in the ceiling; the one right over the bed was shaped like a draydl. So what, Shayna thought, that should be her biggest problem. Better the whole ceiling should crumble like a piece of matzo and fall on her head in her own house than move her into a home. A nursing home. Shayna's eyes filled and the tears came raining down.

"Bubbe, I want you. I want my Bubbe." Shayna turned on her belly and buried her face in one of Tzeydl's pillows. "Bubbe, come home. I need you." Shayna sobbed for a long time, crying herself into a much needed sleep.

A half hour later, a ringing jarred Shayna awake. She sat up, fumbling for the alarm clock, but it wasn't on the night table where it usually was, nor was the night table there either. Shayna blinked. "Oh, I'm at Bubbe's." She got out of bed and went into the living room to answer the phone, which sounded like it was screaming. "Hello?"

"Hi, is this Shayna?" a voice boomed.

"Wait a minute." Shayna held the phone away from her ear and adjusted a little dial on the receiver which controlled the volume. The phone was a special instrument for the hearing impaired that Shayna's mother had gotten Tzeydl a year ago. "Hello?"

"Hi, Shayna. This is Luz."

Luz! Shayna's hand flew up to her hair which was all farpotshket from sleeping on it, but then she remembered that Luz couldn't see her over the phone. "Hi Luz," Shayna said, feeling calmer. "How'd you get this number?"

"From Pearl. I called to see what time I should pick you up tomorrow and she was there feeding your cat. We had a nice little chitchat."

"I bet you did." Shayna said a quick prayer that Pearl hadn't told Luz too many of her secrets. "So, well, I guess you know I'm in New York then."

"Yeah, Pearl said you were visiting your grandma."

Shayna didn't know why, but the word *grandma*, coming out of Luz's mouth made her sad enough to start crying again. "I'm sorry, Luz," Shayna said with a sniff. "I'm having a pretty sad day."

"What's the matter?"

"Wait a minute, I'm all fahshnotzed."

"What?"

Shayna looked around for a box of tissues but didn't see any. "Hold on a sec," she said to Luz. She went into the bathroom where the toilet was running, and blew her nose on some TP, wondering why her bubbe, who always had a million tissues tucked away in her pocketbook or rolled up in her sleeve, never had a box of them in the house. "I'm back."

"So, is your grandma sick?"

"Well, that's a matter of opinion."

"What do you mean?"

"It's a long story." Shayna sat down on the purple couch and started playing with the black fringe hanging from the arm, the way she used to play with the strings of her father's tallis when she sat next to him during the High Holy Days at shul. "She's not exactly sick, but I wouldn't call her well, either. She just moved into a nursing home, and I'm kinda helping her out."

"So, will you be back tomorrow night for our date?"

"No." Silence on the other end of the phone. Shit. "Luz, I'm really sorry." Shayna started to play with a blue rhinestone earring she found on the coffee table. "My grandmother needs me. She's ninety-nine years old and I'm the only one in the family that's really close to her." The word grandmother sounded strange to Shayna's ears, but she felt too shy to say *bubbe* to Luz. More silence. Shayna tried again. "She's been on her own for ninety-nine years, doing perfectly fine, and now all of a sudden, she's sharing a room with a stranger and eating lousy food with plastic silverware and she can't even go for a walk by herself…" More silence. Oy, I don't need this right now, Shayna thought, opening and closing the clasp of Tzeydl's earring with a crisp snap. I've got enough to worry about. "Look, I'll take a raincheck, okay?"

"Sure."

Shayna rolled her eyes. "I'll call you when I get back, all right?"

"Sure," Luz said again, with even less enthusiasm.

Swell, Shayna thought. Either she's even shyer than I thought, she has phone-o-phobia, or she hates my guts. This is a great way to start a relationship. If we are starting a relationship, that is. Oy. Shayna frowned. I need this right now like a hole in the head, and to top it all off, I'm beginning to sound like Sylvia.

Luz broke the silence. "I saw Wilma walking up Main Street today and I thought of you."

"That's a nice thing to say to a Jewish girl."

"Hunh?"

"We don't eat pork. And besides, I don't know if I like the fact that a pig reminds you of me." Shayna was startled by the harshness of her voice. It had been a long day. "Never mind, Luz. I'm sorry."

"Maybe this isn't going to work," Luz said slowly. "I've been trying to get up the nerve to ask you out for months and then I finally did and now…"

"You've been thinking about asking me out for months?" Shayna was surprised. "Why? What took you so long?" Shayna was in her reporter mode now, all set to get the facts; the earring she was futzing with already posed like a pen on a notepad.

"I've had my eye on you ever since last August at the Softball Ball, but you were with someone else."

Shayna groaned. "Don't remind me." Her affair with that particular someone else had been what had prompted Shayna to take a vow of celibacy, so she could sort out what she wanted and with whom.

"I'm kind of shy, you know," Luz continued. "So I had to wait until I was sure you were really unattached before I made my move. And then this friend of mine kept trying to talk me out of it."

"What friend?" Shayna demanded. "Is my reputation that bad?"

Luz laughed. "No, no, it had nothing to do with you."

"What?" Shayna cocked her head. "I don't get it."

"I have this friend Alicia, she used to live around here, did you ever know her? Alicia Melendez."

"I don't think so."

"Well, she went to school up here and then she moved to New York to be around more Puerto Ricans. And she thinks I should have a Puerto Rican girlfriend."

"Oh." Shayna didn't know what to say. Somehow it was okay for her to want

79

a Jewish girlfriend, but it didn't feel very good when the tables were turned.

"Alicia and I have been arguing about it for years. I tell her people are people and what's most important is what's inside a person's heart, no matter where they come from."

"And what does she say to that?" Shayna asked, holding her breath.

"She says if I really loved myself, I'd want to be with one of my own people. And I say, if you really love yourself, you're free to be with whoever you want."

"Does Alicia have a Puerto Rican girlfriend?" Shayna asked.

"Oh yeah." Luz chuckled. "I always tease her because they fight all the time. I tell her, 'Alicia, if you didn't have such a hot-tempered Puerto Rican femme, you wouldn't be sleeping on the couch every other night.' I don't really believe that of course," Luz hastened to add. "I just say it to make her mad."

"And does it make her mad?"

"Yep, and then she says to me, 'Just wait until you have a girlfriend.' But I don't buy it. I've never been a separatist."

"But," Shayna was thinking out loud now, "don't you think couples from different cultures have a lot of issues to work out?"

"Sure," Luz said. "But two women from the same culture would have issues to work out, too. Just different issues. All couples have problems, Shayna, it doesn't matter if they're from the same culture or not. What matters is that they love each other and respect each other and learn how to work things out."

We're talking about relationships, Shayna thought, a mixture of excitement and nervousness swirling through her veins. "I've had Jewish girlfriends and non-Jewish girlfriends," she said to Luz. "I went out with a Jewish woman once who wouldn't celebrate any of the holidays with me because she thought they were too patriarchal. So we fought about that constantly. And then," Shayna continued her stroll down memory lane, "I went out with this woman who wasn't Jewish and she wanted to study Hebrew so she could go to shul with me and we fought about that. So I guess you're right," Shayna concluded in her usual optimistic fashion, "no matter who you wind up with, there's always something to fight about."

"Exactly." Luz agreed. "But why didn't you want your girlfriend to learn Hebrew?"

"I guess her heart was in the right place," Shayna said. "But it just made me uncomfortable."

"Maybe you felt like I used to feel whenever I heard a white woman chattering away in Spanish."

"How was that?"

"Stupid, mostly. And jealous. And like I wasn't a good enough Puerto Rican because I didn't know my own language."

"And you don't feel that way anymore?"

"I'll always be a little sad that I don't speak Spanish," Luz said. "But there's no use putting myself down about it. I yam what I yam," she said in perfect Popeye dialect.

Shayna laughed. "So what did finally convince you to ask me out?" she asked.

"My dazzling good looks, my magnetic personality, my hourglass figure?" There was nothing like knowing a handsome woman was attracted to her to make Shayna feel a little cocky, or rather cunty.

"Actually, I think it was your modesty."

Two points. "No, really, Luz."

"I don't know, it just felt like the right time. So I took a chance and I thought maybe you'd be willing to take a chance, too." Luz's voice trembled and Shayna wondered if she was going to cry. There was nothing like a teary-eyed butch to melt the ice around Shayna's heart. "I'm just disappointed, Shayna. I thought maybe you were the one, but I guess not. I'll get over it."

"No you won't."

"Oh yeah? You really think I'll pine away for you the rest of my life?"

"No." Shayna put Tzeydl's earring down. "I mean, I'll make it up to you. I promise. We'll have a fabulous date as soon as I get back."

"You want to?"

"Yeah." Shayna paused. "Listen, I'm sorry I snapped at you about the pig. I had a tough day and I guess I'm a little touchy, that's all. I wasn't really insulted. Wilma's kind of cute."

"Not as cute as you."

"You think so?" Shayna smiled. "Well, I do try."

"You don't have to try."

That did it. Shayna was sold. "Luz, did you really want to ask me out for months?"

"Yeah."

"Well, I'm very flattered."

"You are?"

"Yeah. Believe me, I'd rather be kicking up my heels with you on the dance floor than eating fishsticks and overcooked string beans at my grandma's nursing home tomorrow night."

"Nursing homes are tough. My mother and father both died in one, only two weeks apart. I'll come with you to see her sometime, if you don't want to go alone."

"You will?" Shayna lay back against the couch and put her feet up on the coffee table. "That's really sweet of you. I bet Bubbe would like you."

"Is bubbe Hebrew for grandmother?"

"No, it's Yiddish. How do you say it in Spanish?"

"I don't know, I left Puerto Rico when I was kind of little and I don't remember much Spanish. Oh, except for one word."

"What?"

"Linda. It means beautiful."

"Really?" Shayna took her legs down and leaned forward. "That's my name. I didn't know it meant beautiful."

"I thought your name was Shayna."

"It is." She picked up the earring again and traced an S shape with it. "See, my parents named me Linda, but then when I came out I wanted to choose my own name and I wanted something that sounded more Jewish, so I picked Shayna. And guess what, Luz?"

"What?"

"Shayna means beautiful in Yiddish. I didn't know Linda meant beautiful, too. What do you think that means?"

"Obviously," Luz said, "you're very beautiful."

Good answer. Shayna was smiling so broadly now, she could barely speak, but she managed. "Did you ever try to learn Spanish?"

"Once I tried taking a class at the university, but I wasn't too good at it."

"I tried to learn Yiddish once, but it felt really weird to be learning my grandma's language in a classroom. I just pick up phrases here and there from Bubbe." Shayna lay back against the arm of the couch and swung her legs up. "Hey," she said softly. "Maybe we're not so different after all."

"You think?" Luz sounded hopeful. "When will you be back?"

"I don't know. In a week, probably." Little butterflies started flitting around Shayna's stomach. "Luz, are you going to take some other girl to the dance?"

"Well," Luz paused. "How would you feel if I did?"

Fine, Shayna thought. No problem. After all, I should play the field myself. Why should I settle for the first sweet butch that comes along? Go ahead, take two girls, see if I care. Aloud she said, "I'd be jealous."

"You would?"

"Yeah. I know it isn't politically correct, I mean I don't own you or anything, but—"

"Never mind," Luz said. "It's music to my ears." She paused. "Wanna be monogamous?"

"Monogamous? We haven't even been out on a date yet."

"Well, I mean, let's date monogamously. I won't take anyone to the dance, and you don't fall in love with anyone in New York, okay?"

"Okay." Shayna wondered how she could be celibate and monogamous at the same time, but she supposed she would figure it out.

"I might go myself," Luz went on. "It is a chem-free dance and they only happen once in a while. Would that be okay?"

"Just don't slow dance with anybody. Especially a femme."

"Yes, dear."

Shayna was satisfied. "Luz, when did your parents die?"

"About five years ago."

"Were they very old?"

"My mother was seventy-two and my father was seventy-eight."

Mere children compared to Bubbe, Shayna thought. "What did they die of?"

"My mother died from diabetes complications, and my father died of a broken heart."

"You mean a heart attack?"

"No," Luz's voice grew shaky. "My parents were like those couples you read about in the newspaper, you know, childhood sweethearts, happily married for over fifty years, and then when one dies, the other one dies right after because they can't stand to be apart."

"Wow, no wonder you believe in marriage," Shayna said. "But how did you stand it? Bubbe's nursing home is so awful. And both of them at once."

"Well, it wasn't easy. My mother was pretty sick or I would have never put her in a nursing home. And my father, well, he wasn't sick really, but he wasn't strong enough to take care of her and of course he wanted to be right by her side. He used to complain to me about the twin beds in their room." Luz laughed. "I visited them every single day. Touching them helped a lot, like if I could feel them, I knew they were still there. And every time I left I said, 'I love you,' in case they died in the night, it would be the last thing I ever said to them. They were both pretty frail at the end." Luz sighed deeply. "It was terrible to lose them both at once. It's still not easy for me to talk about."

"At least Bubbe's not sick," Shayna said, half to herself.

"You're lucky she's in such good health," Luz said. "And speaking of health," Luz went on, "you gotta take care of yourself. You gotta eat good and get enough sleep…"

Shayna laughed. "You sound just like Bubbe."

"Us old women are wise. You should listen to us."

"Oh yeah? How old are you?"

"Forty-one. How old are you?"

"Thirty."

"Am I too old for you?"

"No. Am I too young for you?"

"No."

Silence. Well that's settled, Shayna thought, rolling on to her side and sticking her feet under the couch's cushions. "Well, I better let you go, Luz. This is probably costing you a small fortune. Oh shit!"

"What's the matter?"

"Hang on." Shayna picked up the phone book from the bottom shelf of the coffee table, took aim, and smashed it down on the the rug. Then she cautiously turned the phone book over, revealing an upside-down, flattened cockroach, with one leg still wiggling in the air.

"Sorry," Shayna said into the phone.

"What was it?"

"Nothing. Just a roach."

"A roach? Shayna, are you sure you'll be all right there?"

"Sure, I'll be fine. This is New York, the roaches are very friendly."

"Did you lock the door?"

"With all three locks."

"Don't let anyone in. And don't talk to strangers."

"Luz, you're kind of a stranger."

"That's different. I'm worried about you."

"I'm a big girl. I can take care of myself." As soon as the words were out of her mouth, Shayna didn't feel very big at all. "Bubbe says it's time someone else besides her should worry about me for a change," she said softly.

"Your bubbe's right. She sounds pretty smart." Shayna started to cry. "What's the matter?" Luz asked. "Did I say something wrong?"

"No," Shayna sobbed. "Everyone's been calling her crazy and she's not crazy, she is smart." Shayna took a deep breath and sighed. "I wish you were here. I've never been here by myself before."

"Are you scared?"

"No," Shayna said in a small voice. "I just wish I had someone to tuck me in, that's all."

"How about taking a hot bath?"

"No, the water's probably brown from the pipes."

"I wish I was there to take care of you." Luz's voice was soothing. "Call me any time, my phone's right by my bed."

"Okay."

"And don't forget we agreed."

"Don't you forget." Shayna's voice got a little more life to it. "I'm not the one going to a dance."

"Well, I'm not the one roaming around the streets of the city that never sleeps."

"Okay. Bye, Luz."

"Bye, bubbeleh." She pronounced it more like *boobaleh*.

Shayna smiled. "Hey, where'd you learn that?"

"Oh, I don't know. A little birdie told me."

A little faygeleh named Pearl, no doubt. "Well, I better let you go."

"I guess." It was pretty clear that neither of them wanted to hang up the phone.

"We'll count to three," Shayna said. "One…two…two and a half…three." She waited for a click that didn't come. "Hey, you didn't hang up."

"You didn't either."

"You first."

"No, you."

"No, you."

"You."

"I thought forty-one year olds were supposed to be mature."

"Who told you that?"

"I don't remember. Is it true?"

"Not really," Luz said. "You're only as old as you feel."

"How old do you feel?"

"About sixteen. What about you?"

"Five," Shayna said softly.

"Shayna, maybe you should call your grandma and say goodnight to her. Would that make you feel better?"

"Yeah."

"Well, call her, okay? And call me back if you want."

"Okay."

"Ready?"

"Set…"

"Go." Shayna pushed the button down on the phone, released it and dialed the nursing home's number.

"Rosenbaum Estate. Good evening."

"May I speak to the third floor?"

"Who do you want?"

"Tzeydl Zimmerman."

"Just a minute. I'll page her."

Shayna sat up. "She won't hear the page, she can't hear it. Just give me the third…" But Shayna was talking to a tinny version of "Raindrops Keep Falling On My Head." After a minute the woman came back on the phone. "I'm sorry, Miss. She doesn't answer."

"That's Ms.," Shayna snapped. "And I was trying to tell you I know she won't answer the page. She won't even hear it. Please just give me the third floor."

"Hold on." More muzak. This time it was "Do You Know The Way To San Jose."

"Third floor."

"May I speak to Tzeydl Zimmerman, please?"

"Tzeydl Zimmerman?"

Goddess, they don't even know who she is. "Yes, Tzeydl Zimmerman. She just got there about a week ago."

"Oh yes. I'm sorry, Miss, I'm giving out medication right now. Can you call back tomorrow?"

"No, I can't call back tomorrow. I need to speak to her now."

"I'm sorry, but I can't leave my cart."

This didn't sound like the same nurse Tzeydl had introduced Shayna to that morning. This must be the evening shift. "Isn't there anyone else up there?" Shayna asked.

"No, Miss, there isn't."

Shayna's chin quivered. "Listen, I gotta speak to her tonight or she won't sleep. She'll think I got killed in a car accident or something."

"You'll have to call tomorrow, Miss. I'm very sorry."

"You're not sorry at all," Shayna shouted. "If you were sorry, you'd go find her. How would you like it if you couldn't speak to your grandmother?" Silence. Shayna lowered her voice. "Listen, can you at least give her a message for me? Tell her Linda got home safe."

"Who are you looking for again?"

"Tzeydl. Tzeydl Zimmerman. Don't you even know who's up there, for Goddess' sake? I'll wait right here until you give her the message so you can tell me what she says." But Shayna could wait until they paved the beach and drained the ocean, for the woman had already hung up.

Shayna hung up too and sat motionless on the couch. "I'm sorry," she said to the woman even though she couldn't hear her. "I just want Bubbe. Bubbe," she called out to the empty apartment. "I'm home. I'm safe." She got up, went into the kitchen and emptied the shopping bag of food her mother had given her into the refrigerator. Then she walked through the apartment shutting off the lights, until she came to the bedroom. Shayna stepped out of her clothes, folded them neatly and put them on an extra kitchen chair Tzeydl kept by the bed. She opened the third drawer of her dresser and picked out a pink flowered nightgown, the one she always wore when she slept by Tzeydl. The nightgown was soft and worn, like Tzeydl's skin and spotless too, which Shayna never could understand, since she handwashed it. And though Tzeydl never ironed anything either, her clothes were completely wrinkle-free.

Shayna opened the top drawer of Tzeydl's dresser and the five year old inside her who was feeling so sad only a minute ago, now gasped with delight, for this drawer held Tzeydl's collection of costume jewelry. Nestled in little white boxes filled with cotton, or hidden in tiny felt drawstring bags, were dozens of earrings, bracelets, pins, necklaces, sweater clips, anklets and rings, made of rhinestones, plastic, glass, wood, sequins, and fake gold and silver. Shayna took a green rhinestone brooch shaped like a snowflake and pinned it onto her nightgown. Then she found a pair of fake diamond earrings to pinch onto her earlobes. A strand of pearls with a rhinestone clasp went around her neck. A gold anklet with two adjoining hearts circled her left leg. A charm bracelet with a tiny pair of scissors and a miniature baby carriage jumped onto her wrist. A cloisonne necklace. A pin shaped like a poodle with emerald eyes. A ring of plastic beads with a gold elastic band. Another rhinestone necklace with stones shaped like tear drops. Shayna put on as much jewelry as her body could hold, and then looked at herself in the mirror. "Am I pretty, Bubbe?" Shayna asked. "Am I as pretty as you?"

On top of the dresser were bottles of perfume. Shayna unscrewed the top of a bottle shaped like a small violin and dabbed her wrist with it. She uncapped another bottle and sprayed the nape of her neck. Then she opened the second drawer of Tzeydl's dresser and oohed with delight, for here were Tzeydl's evening bags: a purple satin bag with a gold chain handle; a black patent leather clutch; a small purse stitched with hundreds of pearls; a black beaded bag; a pink leather purse; a gold lamé pocketbook. Shayna opened each one to find a crumpled tissue, a book of matches from the Concord Hotel, lipstick, a card that said TABLE NUMBER EIGHT, and two copper pennies that had turned green. She took the purple bag and put the rest back in the drawer. Then she went over to the closet and took a pair of silver high heels out of Tzeydl's shoebag. They fit perfectly.

"Look at me, Bubbe. Don't I look pretty? Just like you." Shayna clomped into the bathroom to put on some face powder and a touch of lipstick. She studied herself in the medicine cabinet's mirror. "I'm pretty, right, Bubbe? You're proud of me, right?" Shayna whispered to her own reflection, who stared at her blankly, offering no reply. She went back into the bedroom and slowly removed the jewelry—she shouldn't roll over and stick herself with a pin in the middle of the night, God forbid—and put everything back in Tzeydl's drawer. She stepped out of Tzeydl's shoes and pulled back the white bedspread. "I want to sleep on your side, Bubbe," Shayna whispered, climbing into bed. She pulled the covers up, curled herself into a tight ball, and after yet more tears, finally slept.

Chapter Nine

As soon as Shayna woke up the next morning, she called the nursing home and got through to Tzeydl, thank the Goddess. "Hi Bubbe, it's Linda."

"Hello darling. Where are you?"

"I'm by you, Bubbe. I tried to call last night, but I couldn't get through."

"I know. She told me."

"The nurse told you?" Shayna was surprised.

"Yeah, when she brought me in the orange juice, but I didn't drink it, it smelled funny, eppes. You know they ain't trying to force me to take no pills no more, I think they're putting something in the juice."

Well, it didn't take her long to figure that one out. "Don't drink it if it smells funny, Bubbe."

"Don't worry. I didn't drink nothing but tap water. I said to the nurse she should taste it, see if it's a little off maybe, but she wouldn't touch it, Linda. So that's how I knew. Anyway, she told me somebody wanted to talk to me, so of course I knew it was you, who else is calling me?" She paused. "Everything all right there?"

"Everything's fine, except I can't get the toilet to stop running."

"The toilet?" Tzeydl sighed. "I know. The super came in to fix it and he only made it worse. I'm telling you, they hate me like poison there, so bad they want me out of that apartment."

Shayna tried to change the subject. "How'd you sleep?"

"Sleep? All right." Shayna knew Tzeydl had punctuated the "all right" with a shrug. "Never mind me, enough about me already. What about you, darling? Did you sleep good?"

"Like a baby."

"Did you eat some breakfast?"

"No, Bubbe, you know I never eat breakfast."

"Linda, breakfast you gotta have. Some orange juice, a little coffee at least."

Shayna ran her fingers through her hair. "I'll get something down on the avenue, okay?"

"That's right, there's no food in the house anyway."

"Sylvia gave me a care package." Shayna glanced around the apartment. "Bubbe, what do you want me to bring you? I'll pack a suitcase, I'll bring you some clothes, some pictures..."

"Don't bring me no valise." Tzeydl's voice grew shrill. "Don't take out nothing from the apartment. I ain't spending the rest of my life in here. I'll die first. Just bring me one or two blouses. And a couple pairs of pants. And some bloomers I need, and some stockings. And some shoes."

"Which shoes?" Shayna walked over to the closet, stretching the phone cord to its limit, and stared at the shoebag hanging on the inside of the door.

"Which shoes? Do I know which shoes? If I was there, I could pick out for myself which shoes I want, which blouses I want. Here, what can I do, my hands are tied. Why did she do this to me, your mother? What got into her? Why can't I come pick out a few things for myself, Linda? Why?"

Shayna could hear that she was crying. "Bubbe, you want me to bring you here this afternoon? After lunch we can come."

"It's no good, Linda, I'm telling you. You'll get in trouble with your mother."

"Bubbe, Sylvia won't know."

"Believe me, Linda, a mother knows. It's no good."

Shayna sighed. Well, at least she had tried. "You want me to bring you some pictures of me? I'll take the one of me and my cat that's on the wall. You remember."

"I don't know what to do."

Shayna didn't know what to do either. Choices, give her some choices, she thought, so she won't feel so helpless. So she'll feel like she has some control over her life. Yeah, right. Listen to me, Shayna the social worker. "You want me to bring you your plant, Bubbe? The one on the windowsill?"

"No, Linda, you take it. Take whatever you want."

"Bubbe, I don't want to take your things."

"I can't have anything in here, Linda, don't you understand?" Tzeydl's voice was nearing hysteria. "They're all mixed up here; they'll steal you blind. These are not normal people they threw me in with, I'm telling you."

"I know, Bubbe, I know."

"Sure." Acknowledgement of her situation seemed to calm Tzeydl. Her voice softened. "You take home my plant, Linda, better it should be by you, it'll have what to drink. And go into my dresser; in the bottom drawer there, under my sheets and towels is some silverware I was saving for your wedding present, but all right, take it already. And take," Tzeydl's voice broke, "take my candlesticks."

Tears came to Shayna's eyes. "Your candlesticks, Bubbe? Are you sure?"

"Of course I'm sure. Who else should get my candlesticks? Pick yourself out something nice from my top drawer there, a pair of earrings, a pin, a pocketbook. I ain't going out dancing no more, that's for sure. A young girl like you should look nice to go out."

"Okay, Bubbe." Shayna let the tears slide down her cheeks, her chin, her neck. "Listen, I'm just gonna get dressed and pack up a few things. I'll be there as soon as I can, okay?"

"Don't forget to eat some breakfast."

"I won't."

"I mean it, Linda. I ain't running nowhere. Whenever you'll come, you'll come."

Shayna went into Tzeydl's bedroom and pulled out the big brown suitcase she kept under the bed. She packed a few pairs of polyester pants with elastic waistbands; a couple of polyester blouses; two button-down, knitted vests and a light blue cardigan in case it should get cold; five pairs of bloomers; three brassieres; a few unopened packages of knee-high stockings and two pairs of shoes, one brown and one white, both with inch-and-a-half heels. From the living room she took her high school graduation picture and her most recent picture, and Tzeydl's photograph album that was stored under the coffee table; from the hall closet, Shayna took a light jacket. She carried everything back into the bedroom and then remembered to look in Tzeydl's bottom drawer. Under some crisp, clean, impossibly white sheets, she found four rectangular cardboard boxes. She opened the top box to find twelve silver-plated knives. "Look at this." Shayna held one up to the light and studied her small reflection in it. The other boxes held twelve forks, twelve teaspoons, and twelve soup spoons. "All these years she's been saving this for me," Shayna said, closing up the boxes. She brought them into the kitchen and placed them on the table next to Tzeydl's candlesticks. "I'm not ready to take you yet." She addressed the silverware through her tears. "I'm not ready yet. Not yet." She wiped her eyes and opened the curtain, letting what little sun that could creep down between the buildings bathe Tzeydl's plant in light. Shayna got washed and dressed and spritzed on some of Tzeydl's perfume. She opened Tzeydl's top drawer and moved some things around. "Her pearls she might want," Shayna murmured, "and maybe a pair of earrings." For herself, Shayna picked out a pretty wild-looking black and white beaded necklace, to jazz up the plain black jumpsuit she was wearing. Finally she was ready.

Let Tandeleyeh the Toyota be in one piece, Shayna prayed as she lugged the suitcase and her and Tzeydl's pocketbooks up the street. It was a quiet Saturday morning, warm, but not yet hot. Shayna held her breath as she approached Brighton Seventh Street, but she needn't have feared, for there was her little red Toyota, glinting in the sunlight, perfectly intact. Shayna got into the car and pulled out, which was easier said than done, as the two cars in front of her and behind her had packed her in tight as a piece of gefilte fish in a jar.

She turned up the street and stopped in front of that famous Brooklyn landmark, Mrs. Stahl's Knishes. "Maybe Bubbe would like a knish," Shayna said aloud, knowing that was only a flimsy excuse to hide the fact that she wanted one herself. There was something about eating a kasha knish from Mrs. Stahl's that always soothed Shayna's nerves. It had always been her and Tzeydl's special treat, even when she was a little girl. They'd buy two knishes and then stroll along the boardwalk noshing until they were full, and then throw the rest to the seagulls. Even nowadays when Shayna felt a little blue, she'd cook up a batch of kasha and immediately feel better because her kitchen smelled like home.

As Shayna pushed open the door a little bell tinkled overhead. Even though it was only ten in the morning, an old man with his sleeves rolled up, wearing a dirty white apron was already taking a big tray of steaming knishes out of the oven, using two white dishtowels as potholders. "Be right with ya," he called over his shoulder. Shayna waited until he put down the tray, wiped his sweaty bald head with a handkerchief from his back pocket, and walked over to the cash register. "Hello, Miss," he said. "Has anyone ever told you, you're a very pretty girl?"

Shayna pretended to ponder the question, raising a finger to her chin. "No," she said, "can you believe it? No one's ever told me that in my entire life. You're the first one. Mazel tov."

Now it was the man's turn to ponder Shayna's reply. "You're kidding, right?" he chuckled. "You're a smart girl, too, not only pretty. You live around here?"

"No, my bubbe lives here. Around the corner. At least she used to. Now she's in a nursing home."

"Oy-oy-oy-oy-oy. That's terrible. Oy, what a shame. But that's the way it goes." He looked down at Shayna's left hand. "You married?"

"No, not yet." Shayna couldn't believe the words that had just come out of her mouth. First of all, she hadn't bothered to correct this guy when he called her Miss instead of Ms., and now she wasn't even going to give him her how-dare-you-presume-I'm-heterosexual shpeel. "Are you married?" Shayna asked, not so much because she cared, but because she wanted equal footing in the conversation.

"Forty-five years this month," the man said proudly, leaning his forearms on top of the cash register. A dreamy look came into his eyes. "I met my wife April fifth, nineteen-forty-seven and two months later, we was married."

"Two months later?" Shayna's eyebrows rose.

"Yep." The man chuckled again. "I took her out and on our second date I proposed."

"Wow," Shayna said, "love at first sight."

"Yep." The man nodded. "She wanted to be a June bride, but we didn't want to wait a whole year, we had shplikes in tuchus, you know what that means?"

Shayna nodded. "Ants in your pants."

The man chuckled. "So we eloped. And boy was her mother mad. Wow!"

"But how did you know she was the right one?" Shayna wasn't just pretending interest now.

"I just knew. Right here I knew." He pointed to his heart. "And I haven't regretted nothing. Not one single minute."

"That's great." Shayna unzipped her bag and took out her wallet. "Let me have…" she stepped back to read the huge menu hanging over the cash register, next to a sign that said, 'Count your blessings, not your calories.' "Give me two kasha and two potato."

The man wrapped each knish in waxed paper, put them in a cardboard box and tied the box up with red and white string he pulled from a spool hanging from the ceiling. "Something else you want? I got some nice hammentaschen, fresh it is, I just made it this morning."

"No thanks." Shayna handed the man six dollars.

"Take, take. You gotta have something sweet to make up for all the bitterness in this life." He rang up the sale and then slid open the glass display case for a piece of hammentaschen. "Go on, take. On the house."

The whole world only wants to feed me, Shayna thought, taking the pastry. "Thank you." She took a bite and then delivered the ultimate compliment. " Almost as good as my bubbe's. Delicious."

"Next year you'll get married," the knish man called to Shayna's back as she headed out the door. She turned around and he smiled. "Next year, I'm telling you. Don't ask me how I know. I just know. Right here I can feel it." He pointed to his heart.

"From your mouth to God's ears," Shayna said, pointing to the ceiling and leaving the store. She noshed on the hammentaschen and pulled up to the nursing home's parking lot at exactly eleven o'clock. She wrote her name into the sign-in book and took the elevator up to the third floor, where she found Tzeydl sitting in the same chair as yesterday, waiting. Already they were falling into a routine.

"Linda, oy, what are you shlepping there, vey iss mir, so heavy it is, you shouldn't hurt your back."

"It's not so heavy, Bubbe, I'm a strong woman." Shayna bent down to give Tzeydl a kiss. "Come, let's bring everything to your room. Here's your pocketbook."

"My bag you brought? Oy, Linda, a labyn on dine kop. Only you could do it, you're my lucky charm." Tzeydl opened her bag and started rummaging around. "Where's my keys? I ain't got no keys, eppes, your mother don't need my keys, she got her own set. I could have her arrested for that, takeh, she stole from me the keys."

"Come on Bubbe, let's get this stuff out of the hall." Shayna reached for the suitcase but Tzeydl pushed her hand away and lifted it herself. "It's too heavy for you, Linda, so much work you did for me already, packing and shlepping. What else you got there, knishes?"

Shayna held up the box. "Yeah, from Mrs. Stahl's, I got us a treat."

"Where am I gonna keep knishes? I ain't got no icebox. Why'd you throw away your money?" Tzeydl was making slow but steady progress down the hall.

"Bubbe, please let me take the suitcase." Shayna reached for the handle.

"Linda, don't be silly, I'm strong as a horse. All the doctors in that other place there said so. One doctor, a young fella, only wanted I should invite him to my hundredth birthday party."

"So, you going to?"

"Why, you interested?" Tzeydl stopped in her tracks, but Shayna shook her head. They continued walking. "What, a party you think I'm gonna have to celebrate that I lived too long? That's what your mother thinks." Tzeydl intercepted Shayna's protest before it left her mouth. "I'm telling you, the super convinced her, I'm sure. Well, what can I say, for some reason God still wants me here on this earth, so here I am." She pushed open the door to her room. "The only party I'm waiting for is your wedding. I'll dance at your wedding, and then I'll die happy."

Next year, Shayna thought, heaving the suitcase onto the bed. According to the knish man, anyway. "That's why I'm never getting married, Bubbe," she said, "so you can live forever." Shayna put the box of knishes on the dresser.

Tzeydl made her 'oh please' gesture with one hand while she tugged at the suitcase's zipper with the other. "Plenty long I've lived, Linda, believe me. Don't be silly, mamela, you should get married already. What'd you bring me, pictures?"

"Yeah, I brought some pictures of me, so you shouldn't forget what I look like." Shayna stood a picture of herself on Tzeydl's dresser.

"Who could forget such a shayneh punim?" Tzeydl turned from the suitcase and pinched Shayna's cheeks with her two hands, laughing out loud. "Like an angel you are to do all this for me." She kissed Shayna's forehead three times. "Who else would have done it? Only you."

"Here're some more pictures." Shayna reached into the suitcase and handed Tzeydl her photo album.

Tzeydl opened it and turned to a picture of herself at sixteen, curly hair cascading down her back. "Look how young I was," Tzeydl mused. "Who would have thought such a terrible thing would happen to me, that my own daughter would lose her mind and put me in a home." Tzeydl turned the page to a brown photograph of a stern-looking woman with jet black hair parted in the middle and pulled severely back. "Oy, mine mameh." Tzeydl stared at the picture, tears coming to her eyes. "That's your great-grandma, Linda; it's better she ain't alive to see all this." Tzeydl closed the album. "Take this away."

"I'll put it in your drawer, okay, Bubbe?"

"No, not in the drawer. From the drawer they steal everything. Already I lost a pair of stockings that nice nurse gave me."

Shayna sighed. "What about the closet then?" She walked across the room to the two matching closets on the wall near the door. "This one is locked, Bubbe. It must be your roommate's." She tried the other one. "Look, this is empty. it must be yours."

Tzeydl came over to inspect the closet. "That looks all right," she said, "but I ain't got no key."

"I'll go ask the nurse about it, okay?"

"Sure. You're the boss."

Shayna left the room and came back in a few minutes with a key. "Let's see." She fit the key into the lock and turned it. "Look, Bubbe, up and down is open, across is locked. See?"

"Let me try it." Tzeydl opened and closed the closet a few times. "That's good."

"Here, I'll put the pictures up on this shelf, and we'll hang up your clothes, all right?" Shayna walked back and forth from bed to closet, carrying Tzeydl's things. "You want these in the closet, too?" She held up a pair of panties.

"Everything put in the closet. My bloomers they'll steal yet, too."

"All right." Shayna put Tzeydl's undergarments on the closet shelf. "I brought you your pearls, Bubbe, and a pair of earrings."

"My pearls you brought me? For what do I need my pearls? Maybe you should keep them." Tzeydl looked at the necklace in Shayna's hand. "And earrings I can't wear no more on account of the ear aid."

"Here, you wear the pearls." Shayna looped the necklace around Tzeydl's neck. "I'll keep the earrings." She put them in her pocket. "Here's your key. Where do you want to keep it?"

"The key to the closet? In my bag, I guess. Wait, Linda, do me a favor. Open up the closet and put this away." Tzeydl carefully took off the same sweater-vest she had worn yesterday and folded it neatly. "So warm it is in here, like an oven they keep it, and every night I only fight with my partnicker there, we should open up the window, get a little fresh air. But no, she says, she don't wanna catch cold. So a whole night I lay here shvitzing, did you ever see anything like it, that a person should live like this?" Tzeydl watched Shayna futzing at the closet, trying to untangle a hanger. "All right," Tzeydl went on, "if I have to live in a home, that's one thing, but to share such a small room with a stranger? A television I can't have, she'll fight with me it's too loud; a phone I can't have, she'll holler on me about the ringing. Cut off from the whole world I am, like a prisoner." Tzeydl pushed her suitcase under the bed and sat down, smoothing out the bedspread.

"What if you got your own room, Bubbe? Sylvia said you're on the waiting list. Would that make it a little better?"

"It couldn't be no worse, that's for sure." Tzeydl surveyed the room with a look of utter disgust. "What'd you do with my key already, I shouldn't lose it."

"Here, take it. Where's your bag?"

"My bag? Over there, by the knishes."

Shayna got up and brought the pocketbook across the room. "What do you have in here, Bubbe? This thing weighs at least five pounds. You can't shlep this around all day."

Tzeydl shrugged. "What do I know what I got in there? Take a look."

Shayna unzipped the first compartment. "Here's your change purse; you have any money?" She opened it. "Fifteen dollars you have. You need more?"

"Fifteen dollars? Linda, take five dollars. For gas money."

"Bubbe, I have money. Keep it."

"Take it, Linda, what do I need money for? I ain't going shopping. Just a few singles I need to tip the girls there, the nurses, that's all."

"All right I'll take five dollars." She took a bill and folded it in half.

Tzeydl touched her arm. "What do you got there, a one? Take five dollars, Linda, let me give you a little gelt. I got plenty money, a rich lady I am, believe me. Where's my bank book, I'll show you."

"That's okay. I believe you." Tzeydl took the bag and started sifting through her things. "There's my numbers book, we can call your Uncle Ira later, he should only know what happened to his own mother. There's my reading glasses, my seeing glasses, my batteries for the ear aid, nu, where's my bank book?"

"Let me look." Shayna took back the bag and unzipped another compartment. "What are all these papers? You need to save all this?" She started organizing. "This is a Chanukah card from me. You wanna keep this?" She held up a card with a picture of a draydl on it.

"What's that, from you?" Tzeydl studied the card. "I want that. From you I keep everything."

"What's this?" Shayna held up a postcard of a sunset and read the back. "This is from Sylvia, from when they went to the Bahamas last year. You want it?"

Tzeydl shrugged. "I don't care."

Shayna put it back in the bag, in case of a reconciliation, which wasn't likely. "Here's a picture of Abbie and Melinda. You want that." Shayna knew a picture of a granddaughter, not to mention a great-granddaughter, was more precious to Tzeydl than gold. "What's this?" She unfolded a dry, brown piece of paper.

"That I need. That's from when they turned on the gas in the apartment. Five dollars I paid them, keep that paper, I get interest on that, I'm sure."

"September first, nineteen-forty-four," Shayna read out loud. "Okay, I'm putting it back." She searched through a roll of cherry lifesavers, a comb, Tzeydl's address book and change purse, pictures of the grandchildren, a tiny sewing kit just in case, a roll of stamps, a pocket mirror, used and unused tissues, loose change, pens, two tubes of lipstick, a compact, a plastic rain bonnet, a package of saltine crackers, emery boards, matches and five packets of sweet'n' low, but there was no bank book to be found.

"Never mind," Tzeydl said, taking the bag from Shayna. "I'm sure your mother has it. Everything she got, my keys, my watch, my medal. It's a lousy life, but you gotta smile, right? Maybe I got some lipstick in here?" She pulled out a tube of bright red lipstick and pried open her compact. "For who am I putting on lipstick, nu, I ask you?" Tzeydl held the compact up, looked in the mirror and gasped. "Vey iss mir, this is my face? In two weeks so old I got?" Her lips trembled and she started to cry. "Look what they done to me, Linda, look at my eyes, so red they are from crying. I don't even recognize myself no more, such an old woman I look like." She put the mirror down and looked at Shayna, who wanted to say, it's all right, Bubbe, you are an old woman, but knew better.

"You look fine, Bubbe, you look the same as ever."

Tzeydl peered at the mirror again. "The same, she says. Look at me, look at my hair. I look like a regular vildeh chaya."

"We'll get your hair done, Bubbe, okay? Don't worry. You look beautiful to me." She took the compact from Tzeydl and put it back in her pocketbook. "Look, I'm putting your key in your change purse, okay? Don't forget." She zipped the bag shut and stood up. "Come, it's almost twelve o'clock, let's go down for lunch." She picked up the box of knishes.

Tzeydl hooked her bag over her arm and patted her hair. "I can't get over it. In this mirror I don't look so bad." She stood in front of the mirror over the sink. "This mirror is maybe too far away." She gave her hair one last pat and then surrendered to her reflection. "All right, come, Linda, you must be starving." She took Shayna's arm and steered her to the elevator.

When the door opened, a nurse looked up from her clipboard. "Going up," she said.

Tzeydl stepped inside. "Come, Linda, we'll go up, then we'll come down. If we wait till the next one comes, the lunch will be over." They rode in silence to the tenth floor. When the nurse got out, Shayna caught a glimpse of the hallway, which was lined with people in wheelchairs, each one wearing a full-length plastic bib. One woman, leaning all the way over to the right, as if she was tumbling out of her chair, moaned, "I want to go home. I want to go home." The man next to her groaned softly and the smell of excrement drifted into the elevator.

Tzeydl averted her eyes and didn't speak again until the elevator door closed. "I can't live like this the rest of my life. Did you see that? Did you smell that? Feh. Such sick people, so mixed up they are, where do I shine in here? Where, I ask you?"

"Bubbe, it's not their fault they're so sick," Shayna said, feeling a little sick herself. Thank the Goddess Bubbe's not like that, Shayna thought as the door opened. I don't think I could take it. She followed Tzeydl into the dining room, holding back not the first and certainly not the last of the day's tears.

Today there was an extra place set for Shayna. "Hello Bubbe, hello Granddaughter," Minnie called from across the table, her mouth full of pumpernickel bread. "A very fancy-shmancy lunch we got today: chicken cacciatore."

Tzeydl looked at Shayna. "What did she say?"

"Chicken cacciatore." Shayna repeated loudly.

"Chicken cockamammy," Manny said, sitting down next to Minnie.

"Don't worry, Bubbe. It's chicken, we'll like it." Shayna slung her shoulder bag over the back of her chair and Tzeydl put her pocketbook on her lap.

The man with the baseball cap sat down and smiled at Shayna. "You're dining with us again? That's nice," he said, his face full of pleasure.

The woman who only spoke Yiddish and seemed to carry an entire delicatessen in her bag sat down as well. Today she took out a piece of babka, some gefilte fish wrapped in a napkin, and a Baby Ruth bar.

"Whatta ya got there, Mrs. Chocolata?" Minnie leaned forward with interest, but the woman ignored her.

"I like your shawl," Shayna said to Minnie, pointing.

"This shawl you like?" Minnie looked down at the maroon fringed shawl she was wearing over a navy blue dress, and adjusted it across her bosom. "Oy, I'll tell you something. This shawl is so old," she lowered her voice to a whisper everyone could hear, "I was a virgin when I first bought this shawl." She leaned back with a laugh and slapped Manny lightly on the arm.

"Here, Linda." Tzeydl had shmeered some margarine on a piece of bread, but before Shayna could say, "No, Bubbe, you eat it," she was distracted by two loud voices at the next table.

"Sadie Malinski, that's my name. I sit at table number eight. You're at table number nine. Over there." A woman with short silver hair stood at the table, pointing.

The woman Sadie was addressing didn't look up. "You was moved yesterday. I sit here now."

Everyone at Tzeydl's table craned their necks to see what was going on.

"Sadie Malinski, room 424." She stuck her hospital bracelet in the other woman's face, her shrill voice piercing the dining room's silence. "This is a fourth floor table. You're on the fifth. You don't belong here."

The woman in Sadie's place continued eating her salad calmly, as Sadie got more and more agitated. Her face turned red and her whole body started to shake. Quickly she reached across the table, grabbed a styrofoam pitcher of water and threw it in the woman's face. "Gey aveck, gey aveck from my place," she screamed.

The other woman jumped up and grabbed a fistful of Sadie's hair. "You gey aveck," she screamed back. "Oy, if only my husband was alive, he'd make a latke out of you!"

The two women struggled and the Yiddish-speaking woman at Tzeydl's table jumped up, too. "Essen tummult, essen tummult!" she screamed, wringing her hands, in either glee or dismay, it was hard to tell.

"You see what goes on here, I'm telling you." Minnie gestured with a piece of green pepper on her fork. Shayna half-rose out of her seat, about to go over and help when Alan Meyerhoff arrived upon the scene, thank God.

"Never mind, Linda, you just eat." Tzeydl hadn't missed a mouthful. "One is crazier than the other. Just ignore them."

"Oy, look at me. In all the excitement, some dressing I dropped on my shawl." Minnie took a tissue from her sleeve, spit on it and dabbed at the spot.

"Don't worry. Whatever you eat looks good on you," Manny said, wiping his mouth with a napkin. "Nu, where's the chicken?"

The food arrived. "Go ahead and eat. You like chicken." Tzeydl pointed to Shayna's plate.

"I think I'll just have a knish, Bubbe." Shayna cut the red and white string with her plastic knife and opened the box.

"A knish? Who eats just a knish for lunch? What kind of lunch is that, a knish?" Tzeydl put her fork down and held out her hand. "Give me that. You never know when a piece of string could come in handy."

"Knishes she got there? Let's see." Minnie leaned over her plate. "You got kasha?"

"I got kasha and potato. You want some?"

"Cut me a piece of kasha." Minnie held up her plate. "Thank you very much."

Shayna gave the other half to Manny and cut a potato knish in two even pieces. "Take a piece of knish," she said to the man in the baseball cap.

"Thank you."

"Bubbe, ask her in Jewish does she want a knish." Shayna tilted her head toward the woman on the other side of Tzeydl.

Tzeydl made a face. "Never mind her, she's got what to eat."

"Bubbe, don't be rude. Ask her."

Tzeydl leaned over, making it clear by the look on her face that she was only doing this for Shayna's sake. "Vilstu a knish?" she asked. The woman stared at Tzeydl for a full minute and then went back to her babka without a word.

Tzeydl threw Shayna an I-told-you-so look.

"Never mind," Shayna said. "What do you want, kasha or potato?"

"You eat, Linda. I got plenty here."

"There's two left, Bubbe. Who can eat two knishes for lunch?"

"So, you'll take one home."

"Such delicious knishes, all the way from Brighton Beach you brought them?" Minnie read the printing on the box. "How much were they?"

"A dollar fifty each."

"A dollar fifty?" Minnie repeated. "You see that." She poked Manny on the arm. "A big spender this granddaughter is. She ain't no miser." Minnie turned to Shayna. "Granddaughter, you got a car?"

"Yeah, Minnie, why?"

"After lunch you'll take me shopping maybe? I need a new bag." Minnie swiveled around in her seat and took her pocketbook off the back of her chair. "This one the strap is no good, see, the one strap is good, the other got a rip there. After lunch we'll go," Minnie raised her voice, "okay, Bubbe?"

"Sure, why not?" Shayna was surprised. She expected Tzeydl to say "Don't bother with her, she's a meshugeneh like everyone else in here," or something like that. Well, this will be an adventure. Shayna took a bite of knish, savoring the pleasure of eating her childhood treat next to Tzeydl, who sipped her coffee quietly.

When they finished eating, they walked out of the dining room and found Minnie waiting for them in a chair by the fishtank. "You need a sweater, Linda? Go upstairs and get from my closet."

"No, Bubbe, I'm fine. You need one?"

"Me? No, I'm all right."

"It's plenty warm out." Minnie, of course, had to throw in her opinion about the weather. "I was sitting in the sun before, it's nice."

The three of them crossed the lobby and Shayna pushed open the glass door. "Wait, wait." Minnie pulled Shayna over to the front desk. "Over here. You gotta sign us out. You can't fight city hall."

"All right." Shayna picked up a pen. "Minnie, what's your last name?"

"Lieberman. Minnie Lieberman. I before E."

Shayna wrote down Minnie Lieberman and Tzeydl Zimmerman. Under DESTINATION she wrote shopping. Under EXPECTED TIME OF RETURN she wanted to write never, but decided instead to be a good girl and write down three o'clock.

They stepped outside into the warm June air. "Come," Shayna said, "my car's down there." She linked arms with Tzeydl and Minnie and they slowly made their way down the long driveway, with Shayna towering above the two old women.

"Linda, this is your car? Such a gorgeous car you got, how shiny it is." Tzeydl ran her hand along the door.

"You never saw this car before?" Shayna opened the door, pushed the driver's seat forward and went to help Minnie into the back but she waved her off.

97

"Minnie's fine. Oy." She dropped herself onto the back seat. "Go help the bubbe."

Shayna went around to the other side of the car and unlocked it. "I don't need no help," Tzeydl said. She bent down, sat herself in the front seat and swiveled her legs inside. "Don't put your hands there." She leaned out of the car for the door handle. "I'm closing the door."

"Everybody set?" Shayna got into the driver's seat and started the car. "We're off." She turned her head to back out, and caught a glimpse of Minnie in the back seat, her legs out in front of her, too short to touch the floor, and her bag in her lap. She was staring out the window, already enjoying the ride. "Minnie, you know the neighborhood?" Shayna asked. "Where we gonna buy your bag?"

"Take a right. A right take." Minnie pointed out the window. "On the next block they got beautiful bags, a whole store full they got."

"Maybe you need a new bag, Linda?" Tzeydl asked, hopefully.

"No thanks, Bubbe. I got a bag." Shayna kept her eyes on the street, looking for a parking spot. "Here, here." Minnie utzed herself forward to tap Shayna on the shoulder. "Here's the store with the bags."

"Hang on, Minnie. I gotta park the car." On the next block, Shayna found a space. They got out of the car and once more, arm in arm, ambled up the street until they came to the pocketbook store. "Such beautiful bags," Tzeydl mumbled, looking at the window display.

"A white one I need. For the summer." Minnie pulled open the door.

"My white one I use all year round. They're wearing white now winter too," Tzeydl said. She followed Minnie in, looking over her shoulder to make sure Shayna, who wouldn't miss this for the world, was coming, too.

The store was empty, except for a young woman reading a book behind the counter.

"Hello." She smiled as they came in.

"Hello, darling, how are you? My friend here needs a bag." Tzeydl was quick to show the saleswoman who was in charge of this excursion. "A white one she wants, you know for the summer."

"White bags are over there." The woman pointed to a rack of white pocketbooks across the store. They went over, and all three of them immediately started looking at the price tags. I wonder how much money she has, Shayna thought, perusing the bags. The cheapest one here is twenty-five bucks. Shayna moved aside as Minnie took down an enormous white bag from overhead, almost knocking Shayna unconscious in the process.

"This is some bag." Minnie unzipped one of four huge compartments and rustled the tissue paper inside.

"I don't like that bag, Minnie. The buckle is too big for you, it ain't flattering." Tzeydl shook her head in disapproval. "What do you need such a big bag for? Here, this one is nicer." She handed Minnie a smaller version of the same bag.

"This one you like?" Minnie took the bag and handed the one Tzeydl had rejected to Shayna to hang back up.

"Yeah, this is nice, see it's got two departments and a zipper inside for your change purse." Tzeydl opened the bag and gave Minnie a guided tour of it. "And look what a nice strap it has," Tzeydl continued. "Here's a buckle, you can make it bigger, you can make it smaller, any way you like so it hangs on you nice."

"That's good." Minnie futzed with the strap a little, adjusting its length. "You sure you like it?"

"Would I let you buy a pocketbook I didn't like?" Tzeydl asked Minnie, as if she'd known her for a hundred years. "Of course I like it, it looks very nice on you. It's a smart bag, you'll get a lot of good use out of it."

"Okie dokie." Minnie brought the bag up to the register, with Tzeydl following close behind, to continue supervising no doubt, and Shayna bringing up the rear.

"How much is this bag?" Tzeydl asked the saleswoman.

The woman put down her book and reached over the counter to turn the price tag toward her. "Thirty-six dollars."

"Twenty-six dollars? Really?" Tzeydl raised her eyebrows and nodded her head. "That's a very good price."

"No, Bubbe, she said…" But Tzeydl poked Shayna with her elbow. "Shah, Linda. Minnie, you got twenty-six dollars?"

"That's thirty-six dollars." The saleswoman spoke a little louder.

"Thirty-six dollars? Go on, for such a small bag like that?" Tzeydl sounded shocked. "Twenty-six she'll give you. We're from Rosenbaum Estate, plenty business we'll send you, believe me." Tzeydl held the new bag, while Minnie searched for her wallet in the old one. "Senior discount she gets, okay darling? Twenty-six dollars."

"I'll take thirty."

"All right, thirty dollars, but no tax." Tzeydl of course had to have the last word on the deal. She turned to Minnie again. "You got thirty dollars? That's a lot of gelt."

"I got, I got." Minnie finally found her wallet and took three tens out of it. "Here." She gave the money to Tzeydl, who counted it out, before handing it over. "Thank you darling. Now do me a favor and cut off the tag. And this we don't need either." She took the tissue paper out of the pocketbook, piled it on the counter, and handed the new bag to Minnie.

"Ready to go?" Shayna steered Tzeydl and Minnie out of the store and down the street into the car.

"So, you like my bag?" Minnie asked from the back seat, holding up her pocketbook.

"Sure I like it. It's a beautiful bag, use it in good health." Tzeydl turned around to see. "Wait a minute." She opened her own bag, found her change purse and took out two quarters. "A little good luck money you gotta have. You can't buy a new pocketbook with no good luck money."

Minnie leaned forward and took the coins. "Thank you very much."

"We're home—I mean back." Shayna had truly forgotten, for one brief happy moment that they were headed back to Rosenbaum Estate, rather than

Brighton Tenth Street. She parked the car, helped Minnie and Tzeydl out of it, and brought them back into the nursing home. They sat down by the fish tank and again inspected the pocketbook.

"You're a good girl." Minnie patted Shayna's arm. "A good girl and a good granddaughter, kinehora." She held her bag up to a thin woman who was slowly coming toward them with a walker. "Selma, you like my bag? I just got it. Today I bought it."

"It's a beautiful bag. Here." Selma opened her pocketbook, which hung by its strap on her walker. "Here's some good luck money, you should use it in good health."

"A new pocketbook? Very nice. The granddaughter took you?" Another woman came up to see Minnie's bag.

"A strap it's got, see, you can make it bigger or smaller." Minnie gave a little demonstration.

"Look at that. Very nice." A third woman came up to them. Then a fourth. One by one, all the women in the lobby and even a few men came to pay their respects to Minnie's new bag, each one of them dropping in a few coins for luck. Shayna felt her eyes grow moist for the millionth time in the last two days. "C'mon, Bubbe, let's go upstairs." Shayna stood up.

"You gotta pish?" Tzeydl whispered loudly.

"No, I'm just tired."

"Sure you're tired, all this work you're doing for me, shlepping my things from the apartment, putting them away upstairs, taking me and her shopping. Come, you'll take a rest." Tzeydl took Shayna by the arm over to the elevator.

"So, maybe you'll make friends with Minnie," Shayna said as they waited for the elevator. "She seems nice."

"Nice?" Tzeydl half turned and looked over her shoulder to where Minnie and her pocketbook were still holding court. "I don't know, she's mixed up too. You think she's in here on account of her good looks? Everyone that's in here, there's something wrong with. All right, we did her a favor, maybe sometime I'll need something, she'll do for me, too. We'll see." The elevator opened and they got on. "Ten years she's been here already, Minnie. Her own room she got, with a television, a little ice box…" Tzeydl's voice trailed off.

"What if you had your own room, Bubbe? Would that make it a little better?"

Tzeydl shrugged. "I don't care." They got out on the third floor. "Come, maybe it's time to eat something. At three o'clock they give us a little snack. Something to drink we get, and a piece of cake, some cookies, maybe a little ice cream. Come, we'll see what's doing." Tzeydl took Shayna's arm and led her to the nurse's station. "Excuse me, darling," she said to the nurse, "can we have a little drink? My granddaughter is very thirsty."

"I'm all right, Bubbe."

"I was just coming out with the cart." The nurse wheeled a cart of plastic cups, cans of juice, ice cream and sponge cake out into the hall. "Tzeydl Zimmerman, right? Here's your juice." She picked up an already poured cup and handed it to Tzeydl who sniffed at it suspiciously.

"Here Linda, taste this." Tzeydl offered her juice to Shayna.

"No, here's some for you." The nurse quickly poured some OJ from the can into a cup for Shayna.

"I'll take some of that, too," Tzeydl said.

"But you have some juice already."

"This juice I don't want. Feh." She put it back on the cart. The nurse looked at Shayna, who refused to meet her eye. "Here, Bubbe, drink mine," Shayna said, handing Tzeydl her cup. "The nurse will pour me a fresh one." The nurse put the juice Tzeydl wouldn't drink on the bottom shelf of the cart and gave Shayna another cup of juice. "Would you like some sponge cake?" she asked.

"Cake? What else you got there? Ice cream?" Tzeydl picked up a dixie cup. "We'll take two of those."

"No, Tzeydl, you don't get ice cream. You get sponge cake."

"What are you talking about? I can have ice cream. I ain't sick."

"I know you're not sick." The nurse consulted a clipboard hanging by a string off the side of the cart. "The dietician has it right here. Sponge cake. No ice cream."

"Since when are you the boss that tells me what to eat?" Tzeydl's voice was rising. "I ain't got no diabetes. There's nothing wrong with me."

"Bubbe, let's just have juice and cake. I don't want ice cream anyway." Shayna touched Tzeydl on the arm.

"If I wanted the cake, I'd eat the cake. There's no reason for it. See, they're trying to make me crazy in here; they're trying to make me think I'm sick." Tzeydl watched as the other people on her floor came up to the cart to get their snack, including Minnie, who arrived on the elevator with her new pocketbook, and her old one, dangling from both arms. "Look at Minnie. She's much bigger than me and she gets ice cream. Is that right?"

Minnie turned, a dixie cup in her hand. "Minnie's solid," she said, patting her belly. "Solid mahogany."

"C'mon, Bubbe. I'll take you out for ice cream," Shayna said. "I saw a Baskins and Robbins near the pocketbook store."

"So why should we pay for it? Here we get it for nothing." Tzeydl turned back to the nurse. "Please, darling, don't embarrass me in front of my ainekal no more. Give us a little ice cream. I don't got diabetes, I promise." The nurse once again tried to catch Shayna's eye, and then shrugged. "All right, take it. I don't have time for an argument."

"Thank you, darling. Come, Linda." Tzeydl led Shayna down the hall to her room, carrying the two cups of ice cream.

"Since when do you like ice cream so much?" Shayna sat down on the bed next to Tzeydl and took the open dixie cup she offered.

"What?" Tzeydl was busy tearing the paper off a little wooden spoon.

"I said I didn't know you liked ice cream so much." Shayna took the spoon and started to eat.

"The ice cream? What do I care about the ice cream?" Tzeydl took one bite of her snack and then put it on the bed between them. "Here, you finish it. I don't want no more."

"Bubbe, you eat it." Shayna picked up the ice cream and tried to give it back to Tzeydl, who wouldn't even look at it. "Why'd you make such a fuss then, if you didn't want it?"

"Linda, use your head." Tzeydl wiped her mouth with a tissue. "I didn't care nothing about the ice cream. They got some nerve, first putting my pills in the juice, and then telling me what I should eat, what I shouldn't eat. These nurses are all mixed up, too, they ain't even real nurses."

"Of course they're real nurses."

Tzeydl made a face. "C'mon, Linda. A real nurse works in a real office with patients and a doctor. These nurses are just learners; they're just practicing. A real nurse ain't gonna waste her time on old people. You see that nurse was all mixed up, diabetes she thinks I have."

Shayna finished her ice cream, knowing it was useless to argue. "Well, at least you showed them what was what."

"Linda, listen to me. You gotta fight for what you want here. Me, what little rights I have left, I'm gonna fight for. Everything they give you with an argument, the juice, the snack. Don't you see, it's not the ice cream I care about, it's that somebody else should tell me what to eat."

"You're right, Bubbe." Shayna got up to throw out the ice cream and there was a knock on the door. "Yes?"

She turned to see a nurse standing in the doorway. "Hello." She stepped inside with a white towel draped over her arm. "Tzeydl, it's time for your bath."

"What'd she say?" Tzeydl asked Shayna.

Uh-oh. Shayna could smell another fight brewing. "She said it's time for your bath," Shayna said loudly, knowing that Tzeydl had heard exactly what the nurse had said.

"My bath?" Tzeydl asked, as if she'd never heard of such a thing. "I don't need no bath."

"It'll only take fifteen minutes," the nurse said, taking a few more steps into the room.

"Bubbe, I'll take a rest on the bed while you have your bath, okay?"

"I don't need no bath," Tzeydl repeated, this time to Shayna and the nurse. "Who takes a bath at three o'clock in the afternoon? A bath you take in the morning before you get dressed, or a bath you take in the evening before you get into bed. Only a meshugeneh takes a bath in the middle of the afternoon." She looked up at the nurse. "I ain't crazy yet. Go. I ain't taking no bath now. You ain't supposed to force me, I know the rules."

"Can't she have her bath in the morning?" Shayna asked the nurse. "She always takes a bath first thing in the morning at home."

The nurse shrugged and flipped the towel over her shoulder. "I don't make the schedule."

"Well, who can we talk to about it?"

"Never mind. I'll let it go for today." The nurse, who Shayna suspected had been warned by the nurse with the snack cart, left the room.

Tzeydl shook her head. "You see, you have to show them you still got half a brain left in your head, or they'll take advantage. They wanna bathe you when it's good for them, not when it's good for you. Oy, this is some life, I'm telling you." Tzeydl stood up, ready to fight the next imminent battle, no doubt. Shayna, on the other hand, lay back on Tzeydl's pillow and put her feet up in a state of total exhaustion.

"Here, take off your shoes, I'll give a little rub on your feet." Tzeydl sat on the edge of the bed and lifted Shayna's right foot onto her lap.

"Let me rub your feet, Bubbe."

"Shah. Go to sleep, mamela." Tzeydl slipped off Shayna's shoes. "Take a little rest. Gey shlufen."

"Sing me a song, Bubbe." The five year old inside Shayna had this strange new habit of popping out at the most unexpected moment. "Sing the one about the little goat."

Tzeydl stopped massaging Shayna's feet and started singing "Rozhinkes Mit Mandlem:" "In dem bays hamik-dosh…," her body swaying back and forth. Shayna didn't remember exactly what the words meant, something about raisins and almonds and a little white goat, but it didn't matter for the lullaby worked like magic, and even before Tzeydl could sing, "Shluf-zhe yideleh shluf," Shayna was fast asleep.

Chapter Ten

Early Sunday morning, Shayna walked along the sand at the water's edge, dangling her black flats over her shoulder. When she had woken up an hour before, Shayna had opened the bedroom window for a little fresh air and the lulling sound of the waves in the distance had beckoned her down to the beach. I've been so upset about Bubbe, Shayna thought, walking quickly through the lobby, I forgot the ocean was only half a block away. Now she let it wash over her ankles and feet as she strolled along, following a flock of gulls. It was so peaceful on the empty beach, it was hard to believe that New York City with all its meshugas was right behind Shayna. She stopped walking and stood with her hands on her hips, looking out at the water and breathing deeply.

A wet, glistening shell caught Shayna's eye and she squatted down to pick it up. I'll bring this to Bubbe for her room, she thought, sticking it in her pocket. She'll like that. She took a few more steps and then turned around, heading back for her grandmother's apartment building.

Shayna sat on the boardwalk steps to clean off her feet and put her shoes back on, for she didn't want to expose her bare soles to the Brooklyn sidewalks and catch Goddess-knows-what. Also, she needed to look presentable because last night when Shayna had called Tzeydl to say goodnight, Tzeydl had asked her to do her a favor. "Go by Tillie, my neighbor down the hall and tell her where I am. So many days I been gone already, I'm sure she's worried what happened to me, takeh." Tzeydl wasn't sure what number apartment was Tillie's, but she told Shayna to just ask anyone. "Everyone knows Tillie. Tillie Scolnick. Just ask anybody in the elevator."

No one was sitting outside the building when Shayna approached it. She went inside and pressed the elevator button, hoping someone would come along. Her hope was answered in the form of an old woman in a tan coat with a fake leopard print collar, walking with a cane.

"Did you push the button?" she asked Shayna. "Oy, I hope it ain't gonna break down this morning. Me and my friend here," she lifted her cane and shook it, "we don't got the strength to climb up five flights of stairs. My friend," she repeated, making a face and shaking the cane again. "My gift from God."

Shayna pressed the button again and asked the woman, "Do you know which apartment Tillie lives in by any chance? Tillie Scolnick?"

"Tillie?" The woman's hand flew to her chest. "That's me." She stared at

Shayna. "Who are you?"

"I'm Linda, Tzeydl's granddaughter."

Tillie started again. "Tzeydl? My Tzeydl? How's your grandmother, darling, I've been worried so. Come." She pointed at the elevator which had just arrived. "Come by me, I'll make you some coffee, we'll talk. Did you eat breakfast?"

"No, I just took a walk on the beach." Shayna followed Tillie's tiny frame into the elevator.

"By yourself you went to the beach?" Tillie pressed five and stepped back. "You shouldn't walk by yourself on the beach, darling, stay on the avenue. There's all kinds of meshugenehs in this neighborhood now, I'm telling you."

The door opened on the fifth floor and Tillie led the way to her apartment, which was at the opposite end of the hall from Tzeydl's. She unlocked her three locks, pushed the door open and looked over her shoulder at Shayna. "Every night when she wasn't gone in Florida, your grandmother and I would come up from the boardwalk together and I would stand here and watch to make sure she got in all right. If you stretch your neck just so, you can see." Shayna leaned back and caught a glimpse of Tzeydl's doorway, wondering what Tillie would have done if Tzeydl hadn't gotten in all right. She didn't ask.

Shayna followed Tillie into her kitchen. She had already hung up her coat and was busy futzing around. "Sit, sit, I'll make a light under the water." She pulled out a yellow vinyl chair for Shayna and hung her cane on the back of the other chair. Tillie's kitchen was small, just like Tzeydl's, and Shayna had to scoot her chair all the way in so Tillie could get by her. She opened the refrigerator for a jar of prune juice. "Here, start with this," she said, pouring a glass for Shayna. Tillie moved slowly, but Shayna knew offering to help would just insult her. "You want toast? Rice Krispies? Have a banana with the cereal. A little mandelbrot, too, I made yesterday, what's bad?" As she spoke, Tillie emptied the entire contents of her kitchen cabinets onto the table. "Eat, eat, a young girl like you shouldn't be so thin." She stopped, with a butter dish in her hand, eyeing Shayna critically. "What's the matter, you don't know how to cook? You're skinny as a rail."

The tea kettle whistled, just as Shayna opened her mouth to reply. Tillie turned the water off and reached up into the cabinet. "Postum I drink," she said, holding a jar out to show Shayna. "So many years I been drinking it, I call it coffee already, I can't tell the difference."

"That's fine. I don't drink coffee anyway," Shayna said, slicing a banana into her bowl.

"That's right. Coffee ain't good for you." Tillie put a teaspoon of Postum into two cups and poured in the hot water. "A smart girl you are, just like your grandmother says. Ooh does she love you darling, she talks about you all the time. Every story you wrote that you send her from the newspaper, she saves in the kitchen drawer. So nu, tell me, darling," Tillie finally sat down, "how's your grandmother?"

"Well," Shayna paused, listening to the snap-crackle-pop of her cereal. She knew Tzeydl would want her to tell Tillie everything was fine, she shouldn't worry, but she just couldn't. "I'll be honest with you, Tillie, you're a good friend of Bubbe's. You know she wouldn't want you to worry, but she's really unhappy in the nursing home. She wants to come back to the apartment, but my parents won't let her."

Tillie nodded, stirring some milk into her Postum. "A home they took her to? Oy." She continued stirring her drink, long after the milk had mixed in and the granules of Postum had dissolved. "To go into a home is a terrible thing. It's not so easy here for me either, I'm telling you, with my leg and the shopping, the cooking, the cleaning, but still, this is my home, these are my things." She waved her hand around the room. "I got a girl that comes in, from one o'clock to five o'clock everyday she comes. I said to your grandmother, 'Tzeydl,' I says, 'why don't you get a girl too, you wouldn't have to shlep the groceries all the way up from the avenue, even with the cart it's too much already.' But she says to me, 'Tillie, what do I need a girl for everyday? Two days a week is enough.'" Tillie leaned forward and put her hand on Shayna's arm. "Now who's gonna come in two days a week, I ask you? Then the same girl's gotta find a different job for the other three days and it's too much. I tried to explain that to your grandmother, but she wouldn't listen. You know how she is when she makes up her mind. So now she's in a home, vey iss mir." Tillie sat back with a sigh. "Eat some mandel-brot," she said, pushing a plate toward Shayna.

"Thanks." Shayna picked up a pastry, not knowing quite what to say. Not to worry though, for Tillie had a lot on her mind.

"I love your grandmother, darling, don't get me wrong," she said, folding her hands on the table. "We used to play cards together every night since Jack died, and that was a good eight years ago." Tillie sighed again. "Better than a husband she was, your grandmother, a husband is always on top of you, but a girlfriend comes, she plays a little cards, she eats a little cake, and then she goes home so you can be by yourself."

Not exactly my idea of the ideal girlfriend, Shayna thought, as Tillie went on.

"But this year, eppes, something was different when she came back from Florida. Something just wasn't right."

"What do you mean?" Shayna wiped her face with her napkin and pushed her food away, wondering how, after such a big breakfast she would manage to eat lunch with Tzeydl in just a few hours.

"She wasn't herself." Tillie stared out the window as she spoke. "And then she started in with the phone, something was wrong with the phone, I should come in and listen, and look at the wires the super put up. 'What wires?' I says to her. Those wires have been up for forty years, darling, they're for the television."

"I know."

"Well, your grandmother just wouldn't listen to me. And then, that day when she says to your mother on the phone, 'Sylvia, don't come, they'll kill you,' I says to her, 'Tzeydl, what are you talking about? Who's gonna kill Sylvia? Who?' And then your father came and that's the last I saw of her."

"Well, I don't know what all that was about," Shayna said. "But she's okay now, and she wants to come home."

"I wish she would. I miss your grandmother, darling. You know, you look exactly like her. I'm telling you, your grandmother was some gorgeous girl when she was young." Tillie's gaze left the window and fell upon Shayna. "All the old people are gone, the building now is all young ones. They speak a different Jewish; I can't understand them. Maybe I should go into a home, too, I'd have who to talk to. But this is my house." Tillie looked around the kitchen, taking in the pots on the stove, the needlepoint flowers on the wall, the plant on the windowsill in a big ceramic pot. "How can I leave my home?"

Shayna didn't know what to say. Besides all the food she'd just eaten, she felt full of life's sadness. "You wanna give her a call, Tillie?" Shayna asked. "I'm sure Bubbe would love to hear from you."

"Sure, I'll say a few words. You got the number?"

"Right here." Shayna tapped the side of her head. "I'll write it down for you."

"Come, the phone's in here." Tillie got up a little shakily and reached for her cane with a scowl. "My partniker. Who asked for you?" She shook her cane at the ceiling. "It's a rotten life, but you gotta make the best of it. Come." She motioned for Shayna to follow her into the living room, which as Shayna might have predicted, was chock full of pictures: weddings, Bar Mitzvahs, graduations and family portraits adorned every available space on the coffee tables and walls.

"Here, sit down." Tillie lowered herself onto a white couch and patted the seat beside her. "There's the phone." Shayna sat down, dialed the nursing home and spoke to the receptionist and the third floor nurse. "They went to look for her," she said, handing the phone to Tillie. "Here, you talk to her. She'll be surprised."

Tillie waited. "Hello? Hello, Tzeydl? This is Tillie, Tillie from Brighton Beach, Tillie from your floor." She paused, listening intently. "Yeah, I bumped into her on the elevator, ain't that something? And she says to me, 'Do you know Tillie?' And I says to her, 'I'm Tillie.' I'm telling you, it's such a strange thing, out of all the people in the whole building, she asks do I know Tillie."

She listened again, nodding her head. Shayna watched for a minute, and then leaned back against the couch, shutting her eyes. Well, that's it, Shayna thought, hearing nothing but an occasional "un-huh." Tillie's gotten her last word in. I'm sure Bubbe will tell her the whole gantzeh megillah. Goddess, I'm exhausted and it isn't even ten o'clock yet.

"Listen, Tzeydl," Tillie had to interrupt Tzeydl, no doubt for the sake of her phone bill. "You gotta take whatever God hands you. You got what to eat, you got where to sleep, what can you do? Things are bad all over. I got troubles with my leg, the elevator don't work so good, by us everything's the same, the roaches, the lousy super." Tillie paused. "Oh yes, she's a lovely girl." Shayna smiled. Tzeydl was probably in no mood to hear Tillie's kvetching, so she'd cut her off with her granddaughter's merits. "Maybe next time she's here she'll meet my Richie. Don't worry, Tzeydl, I miss you too, but you gotta make the best of it. At our age we're lucky to be alive. Yes," Tillie nodded, "she ate a good breakfast. Sure, anytime, your granddaughter is always welcome, you don't have to thank me. Now try to make the best of it, Tzeydl. All right. Do you want to talk to her?"

Shayna opened her eyes. "Just tell her I'll see her at twelve o'clock."

Tillie relayed the message and hung up the phone. "You'll write down the number for me, darling, I'll call once in a while. She sounded eppes a little funny."

"What do you mean, funny?"

Tillie handed Shayna a pen and a small pad of paper she kept by the phone. "Here, lean on this." She picked up a thick photo album from the table and shrugged. "I don't know. Maybe she's just tired." She reached for the pad and studied the number Shayna had written down. "Thank you, darling. Are you in a hurry?" Shayna shook her head. "Look, here's my family." She opened the album and pointed out her mother, her father, eight brothers and sisters, all dead. She must be so lonely, Shayna thought, watching Tillie flip backwards through the album. "And this is me, at my wedding." She pointed with a shiny red nail.

"You were a beautiful bride." Shayna stared at the picture, tracing Tillie's veil with her finger. It suddenly occurred to her that she had never seen a picture of Tzeydl as a bride.

"I'll tell you something," Tillie said, staring at the open album on her lap. "Sometimes in the morning when I'm by myself, I look at my pictures, I talk to my husband, to my mother, and I have a good cry. Then I wash my face, I put on a little lipstick, and I go down to the boardwalk because," Tillie slapped the album shut, "when you cry you cry all alone, but when you smile the whole world smiles with you, just like the song. And that's the way it is."

Shayna didn't say anything for a minute. I feel like I'm taking a course in Sadness 101, she thought. Not depression. Sadness. The genuine pure sadness of getting old. But if you don't get old, you die, and that's sad, too. Obviously, there was no way around it. Maybe that was the lesson. Shayna stood up. "I better go, Tillie, Bubbe'll be waiting for me. Let me do the dishes for you."

"Don't be silly, darling, what's there to wash? Two cups and a bowl." She hoisted herself up with her cane. "Take some mandelbrot, for your grandmother take, she always liked my mandelbrot." Tillie wrapped some pieces up in tin foil. "Give Tzeydl my regards, darling, and come again for breakfast. For supper, too, if you want. Why should you spend your money on the avenue?"

"Thanks." Shayna left the apartment and heard Tillie call "zei gezunt" to her back. She turned and called "zei gezunt" to Tillie, her eyes brimming with tears. Shayna walked down the hallway, unlocked Tzeydl's door, and turned to wave to Tillie, whom she knew would be standing in the hallway, watching to make sure she got in safe.

Shayna put the mandelbrot in the refrigerator and sat down at Tzeydl's kitchen table. It was too early to leave yet, only a little after ten. I suppose I could just sit here and digest, Shayna thought, feeling her full belly. Or take a nap. She headed for the bedroom but was stopped in her tracks by the ringing of the phone. Uh-oh, what if it's Sylvia, Shayna thought. I'm in no mood to talk to her. But then again, what if it's Luz? Shayna decided the risk was well worth it, and snatched up the phone. "Hello?"

"Mrs. Bubbelinski?"

"Pearl!" Shayna flopped down on the couch with a big smile on her face. "Goddess, you're a sound for sore ears! How's by you?"

"Fine, Shayna. How's by you?"

"Oy, don't even ask."

"That good, huh? Well, tell me."

"No, you talk to me a little first, Mrs. Mamelinski. I haven't talked to a dyke in two days." All of a sudden Shayna felt homesick. "How was the dance? Was she there?"

"Who?"

"Pearl!"

"Of course Luz was there. Every dyke on the planet was there," Pearl added a pout to her voice, "except my best friend."

"Oh, Pearl, you wouldn't have even noticed me. Who'd you go with anyway, Bobbi or Joan?"

"As a matter of fact, neither. I went with Deb."

"Deb?" Shayna's voice and eyebrows shot up. "Not Deb Samuels, the fabulous redhead you've had a crush on since March?"

"The very one," Pearl said in a dreamy voice.

"How'd you manage that?"

"Oh, I have my womanly ways."

"You sure do," Shayna said, feeling a bissl sorry for herself. "Goddess, here I am stuck in the heart of Brooklyn, of all places, and every butch this side of the Wailing Wall is after my best friend's tuchus."

Pearl laughed. "I wish. But don't worry, Shayna, you have nothing to fear. Don't you want to hear about Luz?"

"Don't change the subject, Pearl. Did you sleep with her?"

"None of your beeswax. Now, do you want to hear about Luz or not?"

Shayna thought for a minute. "Yes, if she held up the wall with her back all night, no if she slow-danced with anyone."

"As a matter of fact, she worked the refreshment table the entire evening."

Shayna's face lit up. "You mean, she didn't dance one dance the whole night?"

"Not one."

"Not even when you and Deb went into the bathroom to smooch?"

"How'd you find out about that?"

"Ah-ha! So it's true." Shayna imagined Pearl's face turning red. "I know what none-of-your-beeswax means." Shayna started playing with the phone cord, wrapping it around her pinky. "So, where is she now?"

"In the shower."

"What was she wearing?"

"Oh, she looked great!" Pearl's voice took on that moony tone again. "She had on these really tight turquoise pants and a black T-shirt she cut the sleeves off of, and she put silver glitter in her hair..."

"That's weird. That doesn't sound like Luz at all."

"Luz? Who's talking about Luz? I'm talking about Deb."

"Deb? Who cares what Deb was wearing? I'm talking about Luz."

"I care what Deb was wearing." Pearl's verbal pout was back.

"Oh, Pearlie, c'mon. Anyway, you only care about what Deb was wearing under what she was wearing."

"Oh, like you're not dying to discover the glory under Luz's short sleeve white shirt and black pants?"

"Is that what she wore?" Shayna was delighted. "She's so traditional. I bet she looked adorable." Shayna sighed. "Tell me, Mrs. Mamelinski, is there life after Brooklyn? I feel like I've been here forever."

"How's it going?"

"Oy, I don't even know where to start."

"Well, how's your bubbe?"

"Miserable. She wants to come home." Shayna recounted the last few days' events to Pearl. "I'm so worn out, Pearl, and she has more and more energy. Yesterday, I wound up taking a nap at the nursing home. I mean, who's thirty years old here, and who's ninety-nine?" Shayna shook her head. "After supper last night—and the food is from hunger, believe me—they had some entertainment, so I took her down. She didn't want to go, but she said she'd go for my sake, I should have a good time."

"So, what happened?"

"Oy, what a disaster." Shayna covered her forehead with the palm of her hand. "This woman comes out dressed to the nines in silver: an oversized silver sweatshirt, a silver peasant skirt, silver sequin shoes. She's with this bald guy in a suit, who has one of those keyboards with built in percussion, you know what I mean, you press a button and instant samba?"

"Like Bar Mitzvah music?"

"Exactly. So the woman starts telling these really tasteless Jewish jokes which I won't even bother repeating, and then she starts to sing, and I swear Pearl, her voice was worse than Edith Bunker's."

Pearl laughed. "Did your bubbe like her at least?"

"Oh, Goddess," Shayna groaned. "We were sitting up front, you know, so Bubbe could hear, and right in the middle of 'Alexander's Ragtime Band,' Bubbe turns to me and says, 'Linda, why is she shrieking like that? Turn down my ear aid, it's like a fire engine screaming in my head.' And of course she says this really ly loud, but the woman keeps on singing. And then the volunteers start clapping their hands and dancing with the Alzheimer patients, and Bubbe can't stand that, she thinks they treat them like two year olds, which they do, actually. And then everyone got ice cream and some of the people had to be fed and that got Bubbe going about how can she live like this, where does she shine in with such sick people, and meanwhile everyone's screaming at her, shah already, because they're singing, "Tumbalalaika," and I'm crying because you know how I get when they start in with the Yiddish. Oy, Pearl, no wonder I'm all wiped out."

"Wow, that sounds like quite a scene."

"It was, believe me." Shayna rubbed the middle of her forehead in little circles. "When we got upstairs, Bubbe asked me to talk some sense into my mother. Every night she begs me to convince Sylvia to take her back here. That she'll cut down the wires and everything will be okay."

"Do you think about taking her yourself?"

"Of course I think about it. I think about it every five seconds. But she wouldn't come with me, she doesn't want Sylvia to get mad at me. It's really weird, Pearl. She's not mad at me at all. Only at Sylvia."

"Well, you didn't do anything wrong."

"I know, but I'm at her house. I have her keys."

"So, have you talked to your mother?"

Shayna rubbed her forehead. "Nope. She hasn't even visited Bubbe yet."

"You're kidding."

"Nope." Shayna recalled the conversation she'd had with her mother last night after she'd dragged herself back to Brighton Beach. "Sylvia, come see Bubbe tomorrow. Meet me there at twelve o'clock, we'll have lunch."

"No, Linda, I'm really not ready yet."

"Sylvia, you gotta go see her. I can't stay here forever."

"While you're there, Linda, she's happy, she got company. After you go home, we'll see. Besides," Mrs. Steinblatt pointed out, "too many visitors is no good. She's not going to adjust to the place with you there so much. She won't talk to the other people there, or go down for the activities while you're around."

"Sylvia, what are you saying here?" Shayna wanted to make sure she was catching her mother's drift. "You're saying I shouldn't visit Bubbe?"

"Linda, she has to adjust to the place."

Adjust was obviously the key word here. You adjust the TV antenna and the picture clears. You adjust the buckle on the pocketbook so the strap becomes longer or shorter. You adjust the setting on the microwave so your frozen pizza doesn't burn. You adjust your grandmother so she won't make a fuss about the fact that her life's been stolen right out from under her. Shayna had started crying tears of rage, but she choked them down, damned if she'd let Sylvia know. "I'll stop visiting Bubbe when she tells me to," Shayna had sputtered. "Who would you want to spend the last few years of your life with, Sylvia, strangers or your own grandchildren?" There had been silence on the other end of the phone, and Shayna realized, too late of course, that her mother didn't need to be reminded at that particular moment in time, of her grandchildren-less state, due to the fact that her only daughter was a lesbian. Or so she believed, being completely unaware of the turkey baster baby boom sweeping the lesbian community. "Not only do you stick the knife in my heart, Linda," Mrs. Steinblatt said quietly, "but you have to twist it a few times too, it shouldn't be a total loss."

Shayna cried again as she repeated the conversation. "I can't help it, Pearl," she said, sniffling. "I cry all the time now, in the nursing home, in the car, in Bubbe's apartment. Everything's so sad, and it's like time is running out." Shayna wiped her nose with the back of her hand.

"Come home, Mrs. Bubbelinski, you need a little rest. Come, I'll make you blintzes, not as good as your bubbe's of course," Pearl had to admit, "but still. You need a shoulder to cry on, Shayna…"

"And you've got some shoulders there, Pearl."

"No, I mean it, Shayna. Doctor's orders. I'll make you some chicken soup…"

"Oy, not you, too, Pearl."

"What?"

"The whole city of New York only wants to feed me. Bubbe, Sylvia, the knish man, Bubbe's neighbor down the hall…"

Pearl laughed. "Can we help it if we all love you? So come home, Shayna. I'll feed you, I'll rub your back…"

It sounded like heaven. "Maybe I should come home, Pearl, just to recharge myself. I can always come back in a day or two; my job doesn't start for a few more weeks. Bubbe would understand. She knows I have a life." All of a sudden though, Shayna wasn't so sure. "Pearl, do I have a life?"

"Of course you do." Pearl spoke in a soothing tone. "I miss you, Tzimmy misses you, your faithful readers miss you…"

"What if I forgot how to write?" Shayna moaned. She rubbed her thumb along the inside of her third finger against her writing callus, relieved that it was still there.

"Of course you didn't forget how to write, Shayna. Oh, hey, I almost forgot to tell you. Guess who was on the front page of the paper yesterday?"

Shayna wasn't in a guessing mood. "I don't know. Who?"

"Wilma."

"Wilma who?"

"Wilma the pig."

"I've been outscooped!" Shayna slapped her hand down on the arm of Tzeydl's couch. "Shit. I wanted to write that story."

"She's a great pig, Shayna, she goes to dog obedience school and everything. I'll save this for you."

Shayna shook her head. "Well, it just goes to show you; my old journalism teacher was right. He said that if you want to sell your newspaper, put animals or children on the front page, the younger the better. Hey," Shayna jumped up. "Guess what else he said?"

"What?"

Shayna started pacing. "He said you have to be tough to be a reporter. You have to do whatever it takes to get a good story. Even, and I quote," Shayna raised a finger in the air, "kidnap your own grandmother."

"Shayna, you wouldn't."

"Why not?" Shayna continued to pace around Tzeydl's living room, holding the telephone wire away from her, like the singer from last night's microphone cord. "Don't you think it's a sign, like a prophecy or something?"

"No, I do not," Pearl said. "Shayna, darling, promise me you won't do anything foolish."

"Pearl, when have I ever done anything foolish? Don't answer that. Look, I gotta go."

"Well, call me anytime, okay? Love you."

"I love you, too. Kiss all the girls for me. Except Luz."

"Okay. Bye."

"Bye." Shayna hung up the phone and continued to pace. "I could do it," she said to the empty apartment. "I could fix up the living room real cozy with some

112

of her pictures, her tchotchkes, yeah." All of a sudden, Shayna was in a big hurry to see Tzeydl. "I better call her first, to see if she wants me to bring her anything," she said, thinking out loud now. "Maybe I'll go home today, fix my place up and then come back for her. Maybe she'll need a little time to get used to the idea, she's been jerked around so much lately. Or maybe I should take her right away. I don't know, let me call her." Shayna sat down on the couch again and dialed, going through all the appropriate channels until she got Tzeydl on the phone. "Hi, Bubbe."

"Hello, darling. You still by Tillie?"

"No, I'm by you." Shayna pressed the phone closer to her ear. Tillie was right, she did sound a little funny, like her voice was out of focus. "Are you okay, Bubbe?"

"Yeah, sure, I'm fine."

"You're not sick?"

"No, I ain't sick."

Shayna was puzzled. "Bubbe, are you drunk?"

Tzeydl laughed. "Yeah, sure, you know me, hoo-hah, what a groyseh shikker I am. No, Linda, I know what it is. I don't got my teeth in."

Shayna laughed too, but then stopped abruptly, because Tzeydl had begun to cry. "Oy, Linda, what went on here last night was terrible, just terrible. Oy, what went on here, don't ask."

"What happened?" Shayna knew "don't ask" really meant ask.

"Tillie, I was too ashamed to tell, but you, all right, I'm sorry to bother you with my troubles, too, but who else takeh, do I have to tell?"

"It's okay, Bubbe. Tell me what happened."

"One of the really mixed up ones, a true meshugeneh, takeh, I'm telling you, she came down to our floor, naked she was, not a stitch of clothing on her, can you imagine such a thing, and she pished right in the hall there. And then she comes into my room, Linda, my room," Tzeydl repeated, "and she lays herself down on my bed. I was just opening the closet to get out a clean towel. So she says to me, 'Go home,' so mixed up she is, like she was in her own house and I was breaking in, like a goniff." Tzeydl moaned something in Yiddish Shayna couldn't understand. "So I tell her this is my room, upstairs she belongs, I go to show her on the bracelet they make us wear, you know with the room number, and she starts hitting me and kicking me so, oy, don't ask. She gave me such a zetz in the punim, would you believe she knocked my teeth right out of my head."

Shayna let out a deep sigh. "Bubbe, that's awful. Then what happened?"

"Then I opened my mouth and such a gershray I gave, I'm surprised your mother didn't hear me all the way on Long Island. A hundred nurses came running and they took her away."

Shayna rubbed both her eyes with one hand. "So what's gonna be with your teeth?"

"My teeth? What do I care about my teeth?" Tzeydl asked. "I can't eat nothing in here anyway, so much aggravation I got. My teeth they'll fix, they ain't even broken really, the nurse just took them away to clean." Tzeydl sighed. "Now on top of everything else, I gotta be afraid to go to sleep, some meshugeneh from upstairs shouldn't come down and give me a bang on the head in the middle of the night."

"Bubbe, let me talk to the nurse, okay?" Shayna was squeezing the phone so tightly her knuckles were white. "I'll be there for lunch, okay? Tell the nurse I want to talk to her. Twelve o'clock I'll come."

"I can't live like this." Tzeydl was crying again. "I'm going to die in here."

"No you're not," Shayna said firmly. "Get the nurse, okay, Bubbe?"

"All right, darling. See you at twelve o'clock."

Shayna waited until the nurse picked up the phone.

"Hello, third floor."

"Are you the nurse up there?" Shayna asked.

"Yes."

"And what is your name, please?"

"Mrs. Albert."

"Well, Mrs. Albert, this is Shayna P. Steinblatt, Tzeydl Zimmerman's granddaughter." Shayna tried to keep the rage out of her voice and sound calmly authoritative. "Can you please tell me exactly what happened to my grandmother last night?"

"Oh, yes, I believe there was an incident," Mrs. Albert said. "Let me see. The night nurse must have filled out a report. You can look at it when you come in, you're coming for lunch, right? Your grandmother's fine, really. Her teeth weren't damaged at all."

"Fine?" Shayna shrieked, her patience flying out the window. "She's terrified to go to sleep at night. You call that fine?"

"There's no reason to get excited. She'll forget all about it in a few days. We try our best, but sometimes these things happen to them."

"Well, your best isn't good enough." Shayna stomped her foot. "She's not just one of *them*. To you she's just an old lady, but she has a life. She's my grandmother."

"I understand," Mrs. Albert said. "Everything will be just fine. We'll take good care of your grandmother." Her tone of voice sounded remarkably like a nursery school teacher's. "It's very difficult, I know, but don't worry. Your grandmother's in good hands. She'll be fine, I'm sure."

"Don't be so sure." Shayna spat out the word *sure* like a piece of apple caught in her teeth. Then she stopped herself. "Listen, you're probably right. I'm sorry I've been so rude. I've had a rough couple of days and on top of everything else, I think I have PMS."

"It's quite all right," Mrs. Albert continued in her nauseatingly pleasant, voice. "Would you like to speak to your grandmother again?"

"No, just tell her I'll be there at twelve o'clock."

"All right. Goodbye."

"Bye." Shayna placed the receiver back on its cradle and stood up, her hands planted firmly on her hips. "Sorry Pearl, that does it. Bubbe and I are packing up our sorrows and we're coming home."

Chapter Eleven

Shayna drove back to the nursing home feeling better than she had all week. She'd packed up everything she thought was important to Tzeydl: her jewelry, her clothes, her soup pot, pictures of the family, the plant on her windowsill, the silverware Tzeydl had given to her, her candlesticks. It'll be great living with Bubbe, Shayna thought as she sped down the Belt Parkway for what she hoped was the last time. Instead of the cars in front of her, Shayna saw herself and Tzeydl rolling knaydlech in their hands, the chicken soup boiling on the stove; lighting the candles in Tzeydl's candlesticks for Shabbas; and sitting side by side in shul, swaying to the chazzen's deep, melodic voice. Not that I go to shul now, Shayna reminded herself as she passed the sign for her exit and put her blinker on. But if Bubbe wants to go to shul, we'll go to shul. She turned up Forest Avenue with visions of grandmother/granddaughter domestic bliss dancing a hora in her head: she would tuck Tzeydl in on the fold-out couch in the living room every night, and then fall asleep in her own bed, comforted by the sound of Tzeydl's snores, muffled by the closed door between them.

"Hi, Bubbe." Shayna had run up the back steps, three at a time, too impatient to wait for the elevator today.

"Hello, darling. Ready for lunch? You must be starving." Tzeydl was on her feet in an instant. Today she was wearing black polyester pants, a white blouse dotted with blue and black diamonds, and her black toe-less high-heeled slingbacks.

"I'm not so hungry. I ate by Tillie, remember?" Shayna kissed Tzeydl's cheek, which was soft as a rose petal. "Hey, you got your hair done. It looks nice." Shayna stepped back to admire Tzeydl's new do. Her hair had been washed and touched up so it was once again light brown all over, the way Shayna remembered, and it was set in tight little curls all over her head. "They did your nails, too, Bubbe?" Shayna took Tzeydl's hand. "Nice, Bubbe, I like the color."

"Yeah, you like it?" Tzeydl shrugged. "I told the girl to make it a soft pink, not a hollering pink, not like I holler." She shrugged again and patted the side of her head with the heel of her hand. "She did a good job?"

"Yeah, Bubbe, you look gorgeous."

Tzeydl rolled her eyes. "Gorgeous, she says, for who am I looking gorgeous, Prince Charming is gonna come on his horse and shlep me outta here? Well, all right, you gotta put on a face, if only for yourself." She eyed Shayna who squirmed, knowing what was coming next. "Now you, Linda, you should wear a little lipstick, a little something on your eyes wouldn't kill you either. At your age, you gotta think about these things, all the boys are looking at you."

"I doubt it, Bubbe. Let me see your teeth."

"My teeth? Look, they're all right." Tzeydl pulled back her lips so Shayna could see. "They gave me the royal treatment today, I'm telling you. The nurse gave me back my teeth, she took me down and showed me where the beauty parlor is, they took me to a foot doctor, he should cut my toenails, everything they got right downstairs, you can get your hair done too, if you want. Maybe we can go now. What time is it?" Tzeydl automatically looked at her left wrist for the gold watch that wasn't there.

"It's ten after twelve, Bubbe," Shayna said quickly. "Look, there's a clock right over the elevator." It was a large white clock with big black numbers and a second hand that jumped every second from one black mark to the next, the kind of clock Shayna remembered from elementary school.

"Come, we're late, they must be serving already." Tzeydl pulled Shayna toward the elevator.

"Let's go out for a change, Bubbe. I'm sick of the food here." Shayna pressed the elevator button.

"Out you wanna go? Why should we go out, here they give us the food for nothing, it's already paid for."

"I got money, Bubbe. It's a beautiful day, I want to be outside a little."

"Where we gonna go? I don't know the neighborhood."

"I passed a deli on the way, let's go there. C'mon, it's a couple blocks, we'll take the car." Shayna's idea was to get Tzeydl out in the world a little, and then present her plan for The Great Escape.

The elevator came, they got on, and Tzeydl pressed L for lobby. "I look all right like this to go out?" She turned toward Shayna and patted the side of her head again.

"You look beautiful, Bubbe."

"Beautiful, gorgeous, she calls me, oy, I'm telling you Linda, you're a Linda and a half." Tzeydl came forward with her two hands outstretched, her pocketbook sliding down toward her elbow, and pinched both of Shayna's cheeks. "Oy, shayneh maideleh, you're the beauty, you're the gorgeous one, you should only get married and have beautiful children just like you."

"Bubbe." Shayna stepped out of the elevator and stopped. She loved when Tzeydl called her shayneh but hated the message that always accompanied it.

"Don't 'Bubbe' me," Tzeydl said.

"Then don't start with me."

"I ain't starting nothing. I'm just telling you something for your own good."

"But Bubbe…"

"Excuse me." Shayna turned around, slightly annoyed and slightly relieved that Murray Perlman was interrupting their conversation with that dazed look on his face. "Do you know where I live?"

Tzeydl turned away in disgust while Shayna pointed out the room number on Murray Perlman's bracelet and admired his sweater made by his wife of the goldeneh hands. Murray ambled off and Shayna turned back to Tzeydl. "C'mon, let's go."

"Now you're in such a hurry? What are you hungry?" Tzeydl took Shayna's arm. "I knew you was hungry, you're too skinny, mamela, didn't Tillie feed you good?"

"Oh, sure." Shayna led Tzeydl through the empty lobby, not bothering to sign her out, since after all, she wasn't coming back. Not if Shayna could help it anyway. "She gave me juice and cereal, toast, a banana..." Shayna's voice trailed off and she didn't say anything for a minute, puzzled by the look of dismay on Tzeydl's face. Then she got it. "Well, of course she didn't feed me as good as you would have. I mean it was only cereal from a box and it was kind of stale actually, and the toast was burnt a little..."

Tzeydl nodded. "If only I was back in the apartment, pancakes I would have made you, you remember how you used to love my pancakes, darling? How do you like that, my own granddaughter I can't even feed, to a stranger she's gotta go for breakfast."

"Bubbe, Tillie is hardly a stranger. Come." Shayna opened the glass door. "You want to wait here and I'll go get the car?"

Tzeydl hesitated in the doorway. "Maybe we should eat here, it's too windy out, I'm afraid you shouldn't catch cold."

"It's eighty degrees out there, Bubbe, it's June already." Tzeydl peered out at the world and the look of fear on her face almost killed Shayna. These past few weeks have really been too much for her, she thought sadly. "C'mon, Bubbe. We'll walk down to the car together, okay?"

Tzeydl lifted one shoulder, her palm raised to the ceiling. "All right, if you wanna go out, we'll go out." They walked down the driveway arm in arm to Shayna's car. "Be careful, Linda, they drive here very fast," Tzeydl said as they pulled out.

"Bubbe, I know how to drive." Shayna alternated between feeling comforted and annoyed at being treated like a child. She took a right, drove two blocks to a shopping center and parked the car.

"We're here already?" Tzeydl peered suspiciously out the windshield.

"Yeah, I told you it wasn't far. Come." Shayna got out and walked around the car to help Tzeydl, but by the time she got there, Tzeydl had already slammed the car door and was standing with both hands on her hips, studying the restaurant.

"Goldman's Deli," She read the big gold letters over the door and looked through the window at some hot dogs and chickens turning on a spit. "Looks all right." She headed for the door with Shayna, but before they got there, the door swung open, held in place by a long, hairy arm. "Hello, ladies," the owner of the arm said as they stepped inside. "Two for lunch? Right this way." Shayna and Tzeydl sat down and were immediately presented with menus the size of the Sunday *New York Times,* along with a basket of onion rolls, a bowl of coleslaw and a plate of half-sour pickles. Only in New York, Shayna thought, watching their waiter set up the table, do they shtup you up to your kishkes before you even order anything. She opened her menu and began to drool just from reading the selections: latkes, knishes, kasha varnishkes, borsht, stuffed derma, gefilte fish, chopped liver. Maybe she could manage to squeeze in a bite or two, despite Tillie's amazon-size breakfast. "What are you going to have, Bubbe?"

But Tzeydl wasn't reading her menu. "Look at this. Real silverware." She picked up her fork and examined it closely like some rare and wondrous artifact from another civilization. "I haven't picked up a real fork in weeks. I forgot how to eat already." Tzeydl took some coleslaw onto her plate, spilling a little bit on the table, and put some on Shayna's plate too. "Here, Linda, it's delicious," she said, even though she hadn't yet taken a bite.

"Thanks." Shayna opened Tzeydl's menu and handed it to her. "What do you want for lunch? Look, there's appetizers, soup, sandwiches..."

But Tzeydl still wasn't paying attention. "I'm too excited, Linda. You order for me. Take whatever you want."

"I don't know what you want to eat, Bubbe. What are you so excited about?"

"This." She waved her fork, dripping with coleslaw around the restaurant. Three teenage girls in baseball jackets had just come in and were sitting at the next table cracking their gum and smoking. At the table behind them sat a young mother, her baby parked in a stroller beside her, chewing on a bagel that was practically bigger than he was. "I never thought I would be out of there, sitting in a restaurant with normal people, healthy people. How should I know what I want to eat, I can't even think straight."

Shayna followed Tzeydl's gaze around the restaurant. It sure was a relief to be out of Rosenbaum Estate. "How about a sandwich and some soup? You like soup." Shayna cringed at her own words, remembering all the times she had gone out with her parents and was told what she liked to eat. "This young lady," her father would say, pointing at his daughter, "will have the fried chicken. You like chicken, Linda." It was a statement, not a question. "And this young lady," Sol Steinblatt would say, pointing at his wife, "will have the broiled salmon."

"So what'll it be, ladies?" The waiter was back with a pad in one hand and a pencil in the other.

Shayna leaned toward Tzeydl. "What do you want, Bubbe?"

"I don't know, Linda." She turned to the waiter. "What's good?"

"I don't know. What's bad?" he asked with a smile and a shrug.

Shayna smiled, too. "Want some soup, Bubbe?"

"Sure, a plate of soup is good."

"Okay, we'll have two chicken soups with knaydlech," Shayna said, opening her menu again. "And, let's see. Want to split a sandwich, Bubbe?"

"Sure, why not? Soup and a sandwich, that's a good lunch."

"All right. And a turkey sandwich on rye, mayo, no mustard." She shut her menu.

"Very good." The waiter nodded. "Something to drink?"

Tzeydl looked at Shayna blankly. "What do you want to drink, Bubbe? You want coffee?"

"Yeah, sure. Of course we gotta have coffee."

"One coffee, and I'll just drink water."

"Fine." The waiter stuck the pencil behind his ear, reached across the table for the menus and went to make their sandwich.

"Maybe you should get a whole sandwich, Linda, half ain't enough for you." Tzeydl leaned forward and touched Shayna's arm, as if they were discussing a very intimate matter.

"I'm not that hungry, Bubbe. It'll be plenty. I'm full already." She pointed to her plate that showed evidence of the coleslaw, half-sour pickle and onion roll she had eaten while reading the menu. "Look, here's our soup." In the wink of an eye, the waiter was back.

"It's too late to change our order?" Tzeydl asked him.

"What, the soup you don't want?" He made a move to pick up the two steaming bowls he had just set down.

"No, the soup leave, but bring me a corned beef sandwich. On rye bread make it, with a little mustard."

"So you want corned beef and no turkey?"

"No, bring the turkey for her," Tzeydl pointed across the table, "and the corned beef bring for me. Maybe you want a knish too, Linda? You like a knish."

It was like a contest to see who could better feed who. "No, Bubbe, soup and a sandwich is plenty."

The waiter left again and Shayna and Tzeydl started slurping their soup. "Such a small knaydl," Tzeydl mused, lifting a matzo ball up with her spoon. "In our deli, a shissl of soup would have four, maybe five knaydlech, each one big like a baseball. A plate of soup would make a whole meal."

"What deli?" Shayna asked, blowing on her soup.

"The deli in Brooklyn, you know Grandpa and I had a deli."

"No, I didn't know." Shayna raised her voice a little, for the baby two tables away had just started crying. "I knew Grandpa's family had a deli, that's where you met him, right?"

"Sure, I met him at the deli, everybody went to Zimmerman's Deli, right on Eldridge Street it was, on the Lower East Side, next to Delancy. Sure, it was a much sweller place than this." Tzeydl put down her spoon and slowly opened her napkin, using her newly polished thumbnail to separate the sections, before tucking it into the collar of her blouse to make a bib so she shouldn't spill soup on herself. "First I met your grandpa's brother at the deli, Charlie his name was, and we went out once, maybe two times, I don't remember." Shayna stopped eating and listened intently, for she was much hungrier for stories about Tzeydl's life than she was even for chicken soup.

"So one morning I'm sitting out on the stoop, it was a very sunny day, I remember, and your grandpa's standing on the corner with another fella and the fella points to me and he says, 'Ain't that the girl your brother Charlie goes with?' And your grandpa takes a look and he says, 'Yeah, but he ain't gonna marry her.' So they call me over and I ask them what are they doing out so early, a Sunday morning it was. Your grandpa says he has to go buy some, what do you call them, some cuff buttons to hold his shirt together." Tzeydl pinched her sleeve together at the wrist. "So I says to him, 'I got some, I'll sew them for you, a minute it'll take.' Your grandpa says no and I says yes, and it goes like that until finally he says all right, but for a thank you he wants I should go dancing with him Saturday night." Tzeydl interrupted herself to take a bite of soup. "Ooh, is that good," she said, savoring the chicken soup along with the memory.

"So did you go out with him?" Shayna asked, knowing the answer, for after all, the man did become her grandfather.

"Of course I went out with him, but I made the friend come too, it should look nice."

Shayna didn't quite understand Tzeydl's logic. "What do you mean?"

"I mean," Tzeydl put her spoon down and leaned forward again, "how does that look for a girl to go first with one brother and then with the other? Your grandpa said so what, Charlie didn't own me, but still, we went out all three of us so it looked like all friends. We went to Coney Island and oh boy, what a swell time we had. I only danced with your grandpa, mamela, he was some dancer, all night long we danced, and the friend just sat at the table."

Shayna watched Tzeydl wipe her chin with her napkin, remembering how she would dance until the very last song at all the family affairs: Sam's Bar Mitzvah, Abbie's wedding, Sol and Sylvia's twenty-fifth anniversary party. Long after everyone else, too full of wine and honeycake had kicked off their shoes and plotzed at their assigned tables, or snuck off into the ladies lounge for a nap, Tzeydl would be out there on the dance floor with some young fella, doing the hora, the alley cat, the cha-cha-cha.

"All the girls only wanted your grandpa to take them dancing," Tzeydl went on, finishing her knaydl, "but after that first date, he only had eyes for me. And Charlie never got over it. Never. The day he got married, he pulls me aside and he says, 'Tzeydl, it ain't too late, I could still change my mind.' And I was married to your grandpa already, have you ever in your life heard of such a thing?"

"How come I never saw pictures of your wedding?" Shayna asked, also finishing her soup. As if on cue, their sandwiches and Tzeydl's coffee arrived.

"Oy, some beautiful bride I was, gorgeous like a movie queen. The boss from the factory made my veil himself, you know the lace factory where I worked since I was ten years old. With his own two hands he made it." Tzeydl looked down at her plate. "Gottinyu, such a big sandwich I got here, who can eat so much meat?" She lifted the bread off her sandwich and took out half the corned beef, piling it on the edge of her plate. "Take some corned beef, Linda."

"No thanks, Bubbe, I'm up to my elbows in turkey."

"All right." Tzeydl closed up her sandwich again. "You know all the girls from the factory chipped in together and bought for me the cut-glass bowl, you know my bowl, Linda, from on top of my coffee table. It's at your mother's house now, I want you should have it, you'll like it, it's from all the girls."

Does she or doesn't she know I'm a dyke, Shayna wondered, trying to work a caraway seed out from between her teeth with her tongue. When Tzeydl talked like that, Shayna really wasn't sure.

Tzeydl wiped her eyes with a used tissue she produced out of nowhere and continued. "The girls saved their pennies, for weeks without coffee they all went, you know cut-glass was very expensive in those days. I made the big boss himself drive me, all the way from Manhattan to Brighton Beach he drove, no one should steal from me the bowl on the train. Everything else later they stole, but the cut-glass was from the girls, it was special, it was important to me, so I hid it good under the pillows at the bottom of the closet."

"Who stole everything? What did they steal from you?"

"Who, do I know who? They watch, they read the papers, they find out who's getting married, they look up where you live, they watch, they wait, they follow you, they'd steal from you the hair on top of your head if you ain't careful." Tzeydl fumbled with the small container of non-dairy creamer that the waiter had brought with her coffee and Shayna resisted the temptation to help her. That's why Bubbe made such a fuss about who should take home all the presents after Abbie's wedding, Shayna thought, remembering how hysterical Tzeydl had been, insisting that someone other than the bride and groom take home "the loot" as her cousin Sam so crassly put it.

"They took all your presents, Bubbe?"

"Everything they took, even my veil, such a beautiful veil it was." Tzeydl finally got the creamer open and dumped it into her coffee. "After the wedding we brought everything back to the house and we changed our clothes to go to the restaurant. And when we got back from the party, everything was gone, the presents, my gown, even your grandpa's rented suit. So that's why there was no pictures." Shayna had forgotten her original question by now, but Tzeydl hadn't. "We was gonna get all dressed up the next day, we had an appointment with a photographer and everything. In those days we couldn't take the pictures at the wedding, the rabbi wouldn't allow it. And of course we couldn't take no pictures the day before, it's bad luck for the groom to see the bride. So, all right, we had bad luck anyway." Tzeydl took a sip of her coffee and shrugged. "Listen," she said, "that wasn't the worst thing to happen to me in my life. Thank God at least I knew to hide the cut-glass bowl. I'm telling you, I surely would have killed myself if they got that, too. I can't explain it, such a feeling I got from that bowl, that they all went without their coffee so I should have something fine. I don't know, it just gave me a feeling in my heart." She pointed to her chest with her finger.

Because it was from all the girls, Shayna thought, pushing her plate aside. Full didn't even begin to describe the feeling in her belly. Bubbe understands how women love each other and take care of each other. If only she could take it one step further. Shayna watched Tzeydl dab once more at her eyes. "Maybe I should bring your crystal bowl here for you," Shayna said, forgetting for the moment her plan to take Tzeydl away from all this.

"Here? Linda, what are you talking about? One of the crazy ones will steal it in five minutes, such meshugenehs I'm living with, so mixed up they are, they don't know whether they're coming or going. No," Tzeydl shook her head, "you take it."

"Okay, Bubbe, I'll get it next time I visit Sylvia." Which, Shayna thought, will probably be some time late in the 21st Century.

"Finished, ladies?" The waiter was back to clear their table.

"What'd he say, Linda, do we want dessert?"

"No, Bubbe, he wants to know if we're finished."

"Dessert you want?" the waiter asked. "I got some nice babka I just took out from the oven. I'll wrap these." He cleared their plates, both of which still held half a sandwich.

"Take a piece of cake, Linda."

"Bubbe, I'm so full, I can't move."

"You sure?" Shayna nodded. "All right, wrap up the sandwiches then. And this too." Tzeydl pushed the bowls of coleslaw and pickles toward the end of the table. When the waiter was gone, Tzeydl leaned forward and pushed the basket of onion rolls toward Shayna. "Put these in your bag," she whispered. "You'll be hungry later, you'll need something to nosh, it's a long trip."

"Bubbe," Shayna pushed the basket back, "if I'm hungry, I'll stop for something. Who says I'm going home today anyway?"

"Ain't you gotta work tomorrow, Linda? Tomorrow's Monday."

"No, Bubbe, I'm on vacation. I got a whole month off until summer school starts."

"Oh, you got vacation," Tzeydl said. "Such a vacation you had, listening to an old woman kvetch for three days. Why'd you waste your vacation on me?"

"I didn't waste my vacation on you. I love coming to see you." Shayna hated when Tzeydl talked like that. She fumbled in her pocketbook, looking for her wallet.

"Take the money from my bag, Linda. You ain't got enough money."

"Don't worry, Bubbe, I'm loaded." Shayna handed a twenty to the waiter, who had just returned to their table with a brown paper bag and their check.

"Thank you ladies, come again. A real pleasure to serve you."

"Everything was very good," Tzeydl said, patting the waiter's arm. Shayna hoped he realized how hard won the Tzeydl Zimmerman seal of approval was. "I had a deli, too. Years ago it was, her mother used to sit on my lap behind the counter and sell hot dogs for a nickel."

"I thought grandpa pressed pants," Shayna said, standing up and grabbing her and Tzeydl's purses.

"Sure he was a presser, but in the back of his head, a dream he had, a dream to open his own store and be his own boss, just like his father." Tzeydl pushed herself back from the table and stood up. "Everybody's gotta have a dream, right? A dream that things should be better. So every night we would plan it out, how the food should be cooked, how the tables should look, everything."

"So, what happened?" the waiter asked.

"So one day we opened up the store, then we worked like dogs for five years and lost everything. But oh boy, what a swell time we had, right?"

"Right." The waiter smiled. "You're okay," he proclaimed to Tzeydl, moving a chair so she could get by. "Zei gezunt, and come again, alevei." He handed

Shayna their doggie bag, followed them to the front of the deli and opened the door.

"Where we going now, Linda?" Tzeydl asked as Shayna pulled out of the parking space.

"Let's go sit by the ocean a little bit. It's right over there, there's a pier right near the highway." Shayna pointed with her finger. "It's early yet, not even two o'clock."

"Sure, why not? By the water's nice." Shayna was glad to see Tzeydl had some of her spunk back. She drove down the street and turned into a parking lot that looked out over the water. A sidewalk dotted with benches went around the perimeter of the lot. There were some grassy areas with picnic tables as well, a few of them shaded by trees, and a concession stand at the far end.

They got out of the car and as soon as Tzeydl was on her feet, she froze in her tracks, gasped and clutched at her heart.

"Bubbe, what is it?" Shayna ran around to the other side of the car, petrified.

"Oh, that's my friend, the ocean, oh I haven't been by the water in weeks. Smell the air, darling, that's my smell, ain't it wonderful?" She took in a deep breath.

Thank the Goddess she's all right, Shayna thought, even if I just lost a good ten years off my life. She took Tzeydl's hand. "C'mon, Bubbe, there's some benches over there, let's go sit down."

Shayna led Tzeydl across the parking lot, around a few greasy looking puddles, piles of dog poop and bits of broken glass toward a bench facing the water. A flock of pigeons flew overhead and Tzeydl stopped again. "You know, one time I was driving somewheres with your Uncle Ira and a whole flock of birds, maybe two hundred of them there was; they all flew over the car and they made, all at the same time. I ain't kidding you, I swear, it was like somebody closed a curtain over the windshield, such a mess they made, and inside it got so dark, pitch black it was, like night. Your Uncle Ira had to pull over and scrape it off with, you know, with a scraper like to clear off ice."

Shayna laughed. "The things you remember," she said, helping Tzeydl step up on the curb and sit down on a bench. Shayna sat down beside her and they were quiet for a while, watching a man in front of them unload his fishing tackle and throw his line into the water. Then a little girl rode by on the sidewalk, her pink two wheeler supported by training wheels. "Hello, darling," Tzeydl called, waving her hand. "That's some beautiful bicycle you got there."

The little girl stopped, straddling the bike. "It's my birthday present. Wanna see how fast I can go?" She sped away, not waiting for a reply.

"The sun is so warm here," Tzeydl said, lifting her face up to it. "The doctor says I shouldn't go out in the sun, it's no good for my skin he says, but what does he know? All my life I sat in the sun by the water and it ain't killed me yet."

"It does feel good." Shayna turned sideways on the bench so she could face Tzeydl. She watched her soak up the sun as if she was soaking up life itself, the pleasure as plain as the nose on her face. Shayna hated to interrupt her reverie, but now was as good a time as any, she supposed. "Bubbe," Shayna said softly, in

123

case Tzeydl had fallen asleep, "how would you like to come home and live with me?"

"What are you crazy?" Tzeydl's eyes flew open. "How could I come live with you?"

"Simple," Shayna said. "We just get in the car and go. I got plenty of room; there's a fold-out bed in my living room and everything. Why should you stay here and hate it, when you could come live by me?"

"Why? Because you're talking like a meshugeneh, that's why." Tzeydl patted Shayna's arm. "I know you only want to help me, darling, but how can an old woman like me live with a young girl like you? You got friends, a boyfriend you'll get someday, I should only live so long, God willing, I shouldn't be in the way. A young man don't want a wife that comes with an old woman as part of the bargain."

"Bubbe, you wouldn't be in the way, and I'm not getting a boyfriend."

"All right, a boyfriend, a girlfriend, whatever you want, you can't be alone your whole life already, somebody you gotta get, and it ain't right I should be in the way of it."

Shayna's jaw dropped. "Bubbe," she said slowly, "did you just say what I think you just said?"

Tzeydl shrugged. "Listen, you think they didn't have girls like you in my time? You think maybe you invented it, you think you're the first one? I'll tell you something." Tzeydl poked Shayna on the arm and from the intensity of the poke, Shayna knew what she was about to hear was very important. "When your Uncle Ira married the shiksa, you think I was happy about it? You think I didn't wanna throw myself in front of the subway? So many years we suffered on account of we was Jews, first in Europe and then here, and in Russia still, Jews are suffering yet, and my Ira wants to marry an Italian girl? He says to me, 'Mameh,' he says, 'if you want I shouldn't marry her, I wouldn't marry her.' So nu, what could I do? I should say to him, 'No, tateleh, you shouldn't marry her,' and have my son be mad on me the rest of my life?" Tzeydl leaned forward and looked at Shayna. "And besides, he was just home from the war and believe me, I was so glad to see him with his two arms and his two legs and his head all in one piece on top of his shoulders, I didn't care who he married, so happy I was just to have him home already.

"So he brings her to the house and of course she's a very nice girl, your Aunt Maria; my Ira wouldn't go with just anybody. So what could I say to him? Here," Tzeydl pointed to her heart, "is more important than here." She pointed to her head. "And such a nice family she had, too. At the wedding her mother comes up to me and she says, 'Mrs. Zimmerman, now we're machatunim.' You know what that word means, machatunim?" Shayna shook her head. "It means now we're related because our children got married to each other. She went and learned that word special for me, maybe she went to see a rabbi, I don't know. So you see," Tzeydl sat back against the bench, "you don't have to be Jewish to be a mensch. If you love somebody and they love you, that's what's important."

"Even two girls?" Shayna asked tentatively.

"Sure, you can have a girlfriend, but a boyfriend you gotta have too. And then a husband and then children. You can't be happy without a family and that's why I ain't coming home with you."

I knew it, Shayna thought, looking down at her hands. I shouldn't have pressed my luck. I should have accepted the inch and not pushed for the mile. "Look Bubbe," Shayna said aloud. "For the millionth, billionth time, I am not going to marry a man. So if that's the only reason you're not coming home with me, just forget it."

"Oy, Linda, you think only you know what's best for you. I'm telling you this because I'm your bubbe, because I love you, I've lived a long time, I know a thing or two. The old and the young don't mix so good, like oil and water they are. God wants me here with the meshugenehs for some reason. Why, I don't know, that's God's business, He don't consult me for my opinions, eppes, so what can I do? All right, the really crazy one, the naked one that gave me a zetz in my teeth, her they gave a private nurse to be with all the time, she ain't gonna bother me no more. Listen," Tzeydl spoke softer now, almost like she was talking to herself. "First God wanted me to leave Europe, so I came, I didn't ask no questions." She looked out over the water, as if she could see across time and space to a little village that Shayna didn't even know the name of. "And now God wants me to leave Brighton Beach and be here. So there's nothing to do but be happy we have each other and that we had a nice day together. My mother, your great-grandmother used to say to me, whether you're one or a hundred-and-one, it don't matter, all you got is today."

Shayna looked out over the water too, tears falling from her eyes, enough takeh to fill an ocean. "But Bubbe, you're so unhappy. How can I leave you here?"

"Happy? At my age I'm walking, I'm talking, on top of everything else you want I should be happy, too? Don't cry no more, mamela." Tzeydl untucked a tissue from her sleeve and handed it to Shayna. "Listen darling, how would it look for me to come live by you, how would your mother feel, her own mother goes to live by the granddaughter, not by the daughter?"

"I don't care how she feels." Shayna was wailing shamelessly now.

"Shah, Linda. Your mother would be ashamed, it's enough already you two don't get along so good, I don't want you should fight on my account. I never understood why you and your mother never got along. Yous was always fighting about this, about that…" Tzeydl shook her head. "Your mother is your best friend, Linda, remember that. Believe me, when I lost my mother, takeh, I lost everything."

Yeah, right, Shayna thought, searching her tissue for a clean spot. With a best friend like Sylvia, who needs enemies?

"Listen," Tzeydl said, poking Shayna again. "You think I don't know how it is? Your mother and I disagreed plenty when she was growing up, believe me, but I always loved her. Even now, even after the super made her crazy and she called the cops to arrest me and take me here, still I love her. I could call the police myself and have her arrested for what she done, stealing from me my keys, but I don't want she should get in trouble. I'm a mother, you think I could do that to my own daughter? You think I couldn't go home if I wanted to, Linda? You think I couldn't take my keys out from your bag when you go into the toilet, and hop on a bus and go? I thought about it, Linda, believe me, but I don't wanna make no trouble for your mother. Maybe she's right, maybe I am takeh meshugeneh, the meshugeneh mameh, that's me." Tzeydl laughed. "That's how much I love your mother, and believe me, that's how much your mother loves you."

Shayna looked out at the water again, watching the sun glinting on the little waves. I can't believe she's not coming home with me, she thought miserably. I just can't believe it.

"It ain't so bad," Tzeydl said, as if she was reading Shayna's thoughts. "I survived plenty worse, believe me."

I should be comforting her, Shayna thought, sniffling. I'm the one that gets to go home to my life and she's stuck here. "I'll miss you, Bubbe."

"Oy, a laybn on dine kop, I'll miss you, too. You'll come again soon and visit me darling, all right?"

"Yeah." Shayna leaned forward and rested her cheek on Tzeydl's shoulder. Reality, hard as the rock in Shayna's stomach, was setting in. Tzeydl really lived at Rosenbaum Estate and there was nothing Shayna could do about it. Nothing. She sat still for a few minutes, with Tzeydl stroking her hair away from her face; then Tzeydl sat Shayna up and gently pushed her away.

"Come, we should go. But wait, first I got for you a present." Tzeydl unzipped her pocketbook and moved the contents around, looking for something.

"What is it?" Shayna sat up and wiped her eyes.

"Here. Now shah." Tzeydl pulled out one of her eyeglass cases, turned it upside-down and shook out her glasses. She stuck her hand inside and pulled out a large heart-shaped gold locket on the end of a chain and held it out to Shayna.

"That's for me?" Shayna took the locket and turned it over in her hand. It was beautifully etched with two elaborate S's.

"I got that locket when I was twelve years old, my sister Libye gave it to me, oh was she glad to see me. You know all my brothers and sisters came over first, I was the baby, I stayed behind with my mother until there was money for us to come, too, and in the meantime my father died already." Tzeydl stared at the locket in Shayna's hand. "That locket is eighty-seven years old, darling, that's like I'm cutting out my own heart and giving it to you."

"Does it open?" Shayna pried the locket until the two halves sprung apart. "Oh, look," she cried. "Is that you and Grandpa?"

Tzeydl took the locket and held it toward the sun. "That's when I first met your grandpa. My God, look how young we look." Shayna looked over her shoulder at the worn photograph of a round-faced young woman with dark hair smiling into the eyes of a lean, handsome man. "Wear it in good health, mamela." Tzeydl snapped the locket shut and handed it back to Shayna.

"S.S." Shayna read out loud, tracing the curvy letters with her finger. "The second S is for Shiplitsky, that's your maiden name, right?" Tzeydl nodded. "But what's the first S for?"

"That S is for Sally, my American name. You know, when we got off the boat they gave all of us new names, our old names was no good, too much work it was for their mouths, you know, the officers there. And Libye, she was here a few years already, she wanted to be American. Libby, we should call her, she said, and me she always called Sally. All right, what do I care what she called me, she loved me so much, my sister, a solid gold locket she gave me, like a real American girl, she only wanted me to be. You like it?"

"It's beautiful, Bubbe," Shayna said. "And it's perfect because my initials are S. S. too; Shayna Steinblatt. Isn't that amazing? They changed your name to sound less Jewish and I changed my name to sound more Jewish." Shayna felt like a little piece of history had just been healed. "Everyone calls me Shayna now except you, Sylvia and Sol. What do you think about that?"

"Of course they should call you shayneh, such a shayneh maideleh you are, takeh. Put on the locket, let's see how it looks."

"Okay." Shayna didn't have the energy to try to further explain. "Oh look, there's a knot." She tried to untangle the delicate chain.

Tzeydl laughed. "You know what that reminds me of? Years ago, they used to give the groom, maybe even they gave the bride sometimes, I don't remember, anyway, they gave him a piece of knotted up string to straighten out the night before the wedding, it should take his mind off it, he shouldn't be so nervous." Tzeydl watched Shayna work at the chain. "You got it?"

Shayna held the locket up to her throat and reached behind to fasten the chain. "How's that?"

"Oh does that look beautiful. Beautiful." Tzeydl smiled with pleasure.

"Thank you, Bubbe. I'll wear it everyday and think about you." Shayna touched the heart around her neck. "Oh guess what, I have a present for you, too."

"A present? What do I need with a present, I don't need nothing. Come." Tzeydl stood up. "It's time to go."

"Wait, Bubbe. It's nothing big." Shayna reached into her pocket and held out the shell. "It's from the beach near your house."

"From Brighton Beach you brought it?" Tzeydl took the shell and examined it, turning it over in her hand. "On my dresser I'll put it, right next to your picture. Thank you, darling." Tzeydl bent down to kiss Shayna's cheek. "Come."

Shayna reluctantly got up and took Tzeydl's arm, slowly leading her back to the car, though to an onlooker, it wouldn't be so crystal clear who was leading whom. They drove back to the nursing home and Shayna parked out front in the EMERGENCY ONLY/PASSENGERS LOADING AND UNLOADING space right near the door. She put on her blinkers and walked Tzeydl to the curb.

"You gotta pish before you go?" Tzeydl asked.

Shayna smiled. "No, Bubbe."

"You got the sandwiches, that'll be enough for you for the ride home?"

"Yes Bubbe, it's plenty." Shayna bent down to kiss Tzeydl, and clung to her for a minute. Tzeydl kissed her cheek three times and then pushed her away.

"Go already, I don't want you should drive in the dark." Tzeydl's voice cracked with tears.

"Okay, Bubbe. I love you." Shayna gave her one last hug.

"I love you, too. You know I love you."

Shayna got into the car and rolled down the window. "Bye, Bubbe," she said, turning on the ignition.

"Just a minute, just a minute." A woman in a blue dress dotted with little white flowers, white gloves, and a white pillbox hat with a small veil attached to it dashed out of the nursing home, almost knocking Tzeydl over. "Are you the Jewish chauffeur?" she asked, leaning into Shayna's car.

"Excuse me?" Shayna asked.

"What are you talking about? That's my granddaughter," Tzeydl said, coming back toward the car.

The woman took a step back, adjusting her hat. "I'm waiting for the Jewish chauffeur. On Shabbas he's coming, he told me. On Shabbas he'll take me to see my boyfriend."

"What are you talking about? You ain't got no boyfriend." Tzeydl looked the woman up and down, her face full of disapproval.

"My boyfriend is waiting for me," the woman said, one finger pointing up to the sky. "The Jewish chauffeur is coming on Shabbas. On Shabbas," she repeated.

"Well, today's only Sunday," Shayna said. "You got a whole week to wait. And," she patted the side of her car, "I hope the Jewish chauffeur has a nicer car than this."

"Maybe that's him." The woman pointed to a sleek black car that was pulling into the driveway and headed over to investigate.

"Maybe she meant the shofar, not the chauffeur," Shayna said, shifting the car into first. "Someday, isn't the final blast of the shofar supposed to summon all the Jews to heaven?"

Tzeydl shrugged. "What do I know, they're all crazy in here, what can I tell you." She leaned into the car and kissed Shayna. "Call me when you get home, Linda, so I shouldn't worry." She stepped back onto the curb and waved. Shayna drove forward to the back of the parking lot, turned the car around and stopped in front of the nursing home again.

"Bye, Bubbe," she called.

"Bye, darling." Tzeydl came forward again. "Listen, Linda, don't worry about me so much, I'll be all right. You're young, you're healthy, that's the most important thing. Go home and be happy," Tzeydl backed away from the car, "and eat a good supper."

"Okay, Bubbe, you be happy too. I'll call you." Shayna eased out into the street, turning once to wave to Tzeydl, who waved back, the white shell from Brighton Beach still grasped tightly in her hand.

Chapter Twelve

Home. There's no place like home. There's no place like home. There's no place…Shayna rubbed her eyes with her fists and propped herself up on her elbows to look around. Tzimmy was curled next to her on the extra pillow and heavy grey clouds hovered in the sky outside the window. One of the clouds was shaped like a fat matzo ball being held up by a spoon. Shayna stared at it, indeed feeling like Dorothy from the *Wizard of Oz* for she had certainly returned from as equally a bizarre trip. New York was just as weird as the Emerald City, full of people who were somewhat familiar and somewhat strange at the same time.

"But you weren't there," Shayna said, stroking Tzimmy between the ears to elicit a purr. "Bubbe was there, but she wasn't in her apartment; Sylvia was there, but she was crying; the apartment was there but it was empty…" Shayna's voice trailed off as she stared out the window. Maybe it was a dream after all. Maybe she would dial her bubbe's number this afternoon and Tzeydl would pick up the phone and kvetch about how much her feet hurt from shlepping the groceries all the way up from the avenue. Shayna lay back on the pillow and shut her eyes. Just as Tzeydl's face appeared in technicolor on the big screen behind her eyelids, Tzimmy crawled up her chest and started pawing the chain around her neck.

"Ow! Tzimmes Steinblatt, retract this instant!" Shayna reached for Tzimmy's paw, complete with offending claws, and realized what she knew but didn't want to know all along: it wasn't a dream after all, for there around her neck was Tzeydl's gold locket, smooth and cold against her skin.

"Oy vey." Shayna sighed and rolled onto her belly. Tzimmy readjusted herself along Shayna's spine. Rain began to fall and Shayna listened to the drops splashing against the window, her breathing deepening. Just as she was falling back asleep, she thought she heard thunder rumbling in the distance. She put Tzimmy's pillow over her head, but the thunder grew louder anyway. And more insistent, for as Shayna sat up, she realized it wasn't thunder at all, but a knock at the door.

"Okay, I'm coming, I'm coming. I'm coming!" Shayna yelled as if she was announcing to the world at large she was having a 9.5 orgasm on the Richter scale (she should be so lucky) instead of dragging herself out of bed to answer the door. "It better not be a Jehovah's witness," she said to Tzimmy, as she tied her red silk robe firmly about her waist, for besides Tzeydl's locket, Shayna wasn't wearing a thing.

"Who is it?" Shayna asked, not opening the door, for having just spent a few days in New York she was still feeling suspicious.

"Delivery for Shayna Steinblatt," a deep, muffled voice called. Strange, Shayna thought, I'm not expecting anything. She made sure her robe was securely fastened before she opened the door and gasped, for there were a dozen long-stemmed peach roses, all wrapped up in lavender paper lying on the porch.

"Wow." Shayna bent down to pick them up, closed her eyes and inhaled deeply, almost drowning in their sweet fragrance.

"Like 'em?"

Shayna's eyes flew open. "Luz," she cried, as none other bounded up the steps. "What are you doing here?"

Luz shrugged. "Delivering roses."

"But what's the occasion?"

"You're the occasion."

"Oh." Shayna felt a warm flush overtake her face. "You disguised your voice, didn't you? Very tricky."

"That was my Jimmy Stewart imitation," Luz said. "Wanna hear Mae West?"

"Sure."

"You gonna invite me in to peel you a grape, sweetheart, or do I have to strut my stuff out here for the entire neighborhood?" She put one hand on her waist, the other behind her head, and shifted hips from side to side.

Shayna laughed. "Wow, Jimmy Stewart and Mae West chipped in to buy me a dozen roses."

"Hey," Luz's voice was back to normal, "don't I get any credit?"

"Oh, they're from you?" Shayna asked, surprised.

"Of course they're from me." Luz feigned indignation.

"Wow, that's even better. The handsomest butch in town sent me a dozen roses."

Now it was Luz's turn to blush. "That's more like it," she said. " Can I come in for a minute?"

"Sure." Shayna stepped inside.

"Unless now's not a good time. I mean, if I'm interrupting anything…"

Shayna watched Luz's blush deepen. "Oh no, not at all. Luz, did you think…hey, don't you remember our agreement?"

"Sure I remember, but there's only one reason a beautiful woman is still in her bathrobe at one in the afternoon."

"Oh Goddess, is it one o'clock?" Shayna backed into the kitchen with Luz cautiously following. "I guess I didn't realize how wiped out I was." She lay the roses on the table and scooped up Tzimmy who had finally utzed herself out of bed as well. "Nobody here but us chickens," Shayna said, holding up Tzimmy under her armpits, or in this case paw pits. "This is Luz, Tzimmy. Check her out. Let me know if she passes inspection." Tzimmy arched her neck and moved her head forward to sniff Luz's face. When she got to her mouth, she closed her eyes, lay back her ears and licked Luz's lips.

"Hey, Ms. Chutzpah." Shayna whisked Tzimmy away and set her down on the kitchen floor. "Didn't your mother ever teach you to ask permission before you kiss a girl?" Shayna scratched the base of Tzimmy's tail and then slowly straightened up, her eyes taking in the tips of Luz's high-topped sneakers, her tight jeans, her white T-shirt and finally her dark eyes.

"Hi," Shayna mumbled.

"Hi." Luz reached up and tucked a stray strand of hair behind Shayna's left ear. It promptly boinged right out again. "Welcome home." She opened her arms and Shayna melted into them. She lay her head on Luz's chest and let Luz stroke her hair, listening to the pounding of her heart. Shayna sighed deeply, and Luz held her tight. "It's okay now, Shayna," Luz whispered. "It's okay. You're home."

There's no place like home, Shayna thought again, letting out another sigh. She does feel like home. She feels safe. I feel safe with her. She relaxed her body even more against Luz's and just as she felt herself floating away to Ecstacyland, something pulled at her robe.

"Tzimmy!" Shayna looked down at two green eyes, innocent as her own, which wasn't very. "Excuse me, but is somebody jealous?" Shayna bent down and picked up the cat.

"Uh-oh, is she the jealous type?" Luz rubbed Tzimmy between the ears. "Hello, kitty. Don't be jealous. Your mama's got plenty of love. I ain't gonna steal none away from you. Okay? That's right. That's it." Luz had found Tzimmy's G-spot, the white dot of fur on her chest about two inches below her chin, and was now rubbing it with her fingers in small, even circles. Tzimmy stretched her neck up, exposing the entire area for Luz to explore, purring loudly and spreading her toes in pure, unadulterated bliss.

"Hey, that's enough." Shayna whisked Tzimmy away again. "Now I'm jealous. I mean, she never lets anyone do that but me."

"Looks like I'm gonna have my hands full around here," Luz said, staring down at her empty palms.

"You think so?" Shayna stared at Luz's hands too. "Want to hear your fortune?"

"Sure."

Shayna lifted Luz's right hand. "This line," she said, tickling the length of Luz's palm, "means you're going to live a long, happy life. And this line," she ran her finger up another crease, "means you're going to meet the woman of your dreams when you're forty-one years old." She looked up. "That'll be fifty dollars, please."

"Would dinner and dancing do instead?" Luz cupped Shayna's hand between her own and started stroking her fingers.

"For you? Sure." Shayna took Luz's hand and shook it, cementing the deal. "When?"

"How about Saturday night? I'll pick you up at eight."

"You'll pick me up? You mean I don't have to drive?"

"Not unless you really want to."

"Want to? I hate driving. I mean, I love being driven."

"Finally, a real femme. I didn't think there were any left." Luz smiled broadly. "Hey, you got any coffee? This is my lunch hour, I usually get a cup."

Uh-oh, a coffee drinker. Shayna's balloon of bliss burst. Maybe we are too different after all. Her wild imagination, which had already started planning which college their children would go to, was suddenly interrupted by Tzeydl's voice; *So she drinks coffee and you don't. That should be your biggest problem.* Shayna smiled and moved toward her kitchen cabinet. "I don't drink coffee, but I have all kinds of herbal teas and maybe there's some decaf." She opened one of the cabinets.

"No coffee? Are you gonna make me eat brown and green food and shlep me to pot luck dinners?" Luz came up behind Shayna, encircling her waist with both arms and peered over her shoulder at her stash. "Oh my God, do you really eat this stuff?" she asked, staring at the packages of seaweed, miso, organic almond butter and rice cakes right before her very eyes.

Shayna shut the cabinet door and turned around. "Are you going to make me eat Wonderbread and Skippy peanut butter and shlep me to McDonalds for whoppers? And anyway," she put her hands on Luz's shoulders, "who taught you how to shlep?"

Luz moved her hands along Shayna's back, sending silky shivers up and down her spine. "I'm a professional shlepper, I shlep flowers around all day. And besides," her hands came to stop at Shayna's waist, "didn't anyone ever tell you, you don't get whoppers at McDonalds? You get them at Burger King. At McDonalds you get Big Macs."

"Oh, right." Shayna stared into Luz's dark eyes for a long moment, feeling the bottom of her stomach drop. If she kisses me, I'll die, Shayna thought, tempted to untie her robe and let it slide down her body to land in liquid folds around her ankles then and there. But maybe that would be a little too dramatic, she thought. Maybe I should just use telepathic communication. She concentrated hard on Luz's eyes: *kiss me, kiss me, kiss me.*

"You're very pretty," Luz said, tucking that same strand of unruly hair back behind Shayna's ear. "All them curls." Her eyes wandered over the various nooks and crannies of Shayna's wild and wooly head.

"Well, now you know what I look like in the morning," Shayna said, letting out a great big yawn.

"Not bad, not bad." Luz stepped back to give Shayna an exaggerated once over. "When do I get to see what you look like at night?"

"Saturday at eight," Shayna yawned again, "if I can keep my eyes open, that is."

"You better rest up today," Luz said, putting her arm across Shayna's shoulders. "You had a rough weekend. Maybe you should take a hot bath and relax. I'll put your roses in a vase for you."

"Oh, that's okay. I'll do it." Shayna looked for a vase and her eyes fell on three droopy orange tulips stuck in a mayonnaise jar she hadn't even noticed. "Oh, Pearl must have brought these," Shayna said. "Too bad they're all fallen over like that." She lifted one flower, then let it go and watched it flop its tired head over, almost brushing the table. "Oh well, guess those have had it."

"Wait," Luz said. "Got a penny?"

"A penny?"

"Never mind." Luz fished in her pockets, found one and moved the tulips gently so she could drop the penny into the water. "They'll stand up straight," she looked at her watch, "by the time my lunch hour's up. But that's a pretty sorry looking vase."

"Oh right, a vase." Shayna opened a cabinet to continue her search. "Look, here's some food that isn't brown or green. Think fast." She tossed a baggy of dried apricots to Luz and continued poking around. Pushing aside a jar of millet, she said, "I don't think I have a vase."

"No vase?" Luz was shocked. "What do you do with all the bouquets you get from your millions of secret admirers?"

"Oh, I just fill the bathtub with them." Shayna turned around with an old wine carafe in her hand. "This will have to do, I guess." She went over to the sink and filled the carafe with water, jammed the flowers into it, and stepped aside. "There," she said, "how's that?"

"Pitiful." Luz shook her head. "You got some scissors?"

"Yeah, in my study." Shayna padded through the apartment on bare feet. "Here." Luz had taken the roses out of the carafe-turned-vase and set them on the table. She stood one up next to the make-shift vase and studied it with one eye closed like a painter. Luz took the scissors, cut the bottom of the rose and placed it into the carafe. She stood up another rose, eyeballed and trimmed it, and did the same thing ten more times. Then she arranged the greens and the baby's breath so that the roses were delicately peeking out between the small white flowers. Shayna watched, fascinated. She does everything with such care, she thought, as Luz swept the small stem ends into the palm of her hand and tossed them into the garbage can beside the sink. This woman is serious.

"How's that?" Luz stepped up behind Shayna to admire her work, then leaned forward to shift one of the roses a little to the left.

"Perfect," Shayna said. "A work of art."

"Well, a beautiful woman deserves beautiful things." Luz looked from the roses to Shayna.

"You're sure not stingy with the compliments, are you?" Shayna put her hands on her hips and looked squarely at Luz. "You like me, don't you?"

"Yes, I do."

"And you're not shy about letting me know it, either."

"Why should I be?" Luz took both Shayna's hands in her own. "Life's too short to play games, don't you know that?"

Shayna nodded, not saying anything, but hearing Tzeydl's voice echo in her mind again: *you ain't getting any younger, darling. Whether you're one or a hundred and one, it don't matter, all you got is today.* She squeezed Luz's hands tightly to keep the tears from leaking out of the corners of her eyes. "Yeah, life is short," she whispered, leaning her head on Luz's chest again.

"Poor Shayna." Luz stroked her cheek. It felt so natural to be standing in her kitchen with Luz like this, to share some of the burden she'd been carrying all alone. Shayna sighed and then tensed a little as a wave of insecurity washed over her. "Luz, do you treat all your girls like this?"

"All my girls are standing right here in this kitchen."

"I was wondering why it was so crowded in here." Shayna, whose mush cup was running over, eased the delicious tension between them with a joke, knowing that if she didn't, Luz's lunch hour would extend to days, weeks, years even. Shayna stepped away and arched her back in a slow, sensuous stretch.

"I better let you rest." Luz looked at Shayna's cat clock on the wall. "I gotta get back to the store anyway. So, pick you up Saturday at eight?"

"Saturday at eight," Shayna repeated, walking Luz to the door.

"Give us another hug." Luz took Shayna in her arms again.

"How many of us are there?" Shayna mumbled into Luz's shirt.

"Just two. Just me and you."

"Just me and you," Shayna echoed sleepily. Maybe this was really a dream and reality was back at Rosenbaum Estate. How could such misery and such happiness exist at the same time? I'll worry about it later, Shayna decided, for if this was a dream, she definitely didn't want to be woken up, especially since Luz's face was descending towards hers in slow motion, for the kiss Shayna had been waiting all her life for, or so it seemed. Just as their lips were a breath apart, Shayna heard someone fumbling with her lock and then a loud knocking.

"What is this, Grand Central Station?" Shayna reluctantly moved away from Luz and pulled open the door to find Pearl at the top of the stairs, down on one bent knee. As soon as the door opened, Pearl spread her arms wide and burst into song: "Hello, Shayna, well hello, Shayna, it's so nice to have you back where you belong." She strutted into the kitchen, still singing: "You're looking swell, Shayna, I can tell, Shayna..." Pearl interrupted her act, seeing Luz, as well as Shayna staring at her. "I can tell, Shayna..." she faltered. "Whoops, I can tell Shayna isn't exactly thrilled to see me at this particular moment in time. Oh well, that's show biz." Pearl smiled an apology at Shayna, whose joy was spread all over her face in an ear to ear grin. Luz was smiling, too, but looking down at the floor, shyly.

"Well, umm, guess I'll go see a man about a dog. Or a woman about a pig. Or something." Pearl opened the door that had just shut behind her and backed out, as Tzimmy dashed by her.

"Wait, Pearl, it isn't what you think."

"I gotta go anyway." Luz kissed Shayna's forehead. "See you Saturday."

"Eight o'clock." Shayna stroked Luz's upper arm and then she was out the door and Pearl was in. "Is the coast clear?" Pearl whispered loudly, before practically jumping into Shayna's arms. "Yay! You're back! Yippee! Yabba-dabba-doo!" Pearl put two fingers in her mouth and let out a loud whistle. "Shayna's back, Shayna's back, sis-boom-bah! Alka seltzer, alka seltzer, rah-rah-rah!" Pearl ran around the kitchen shaking imaginary pompoms, and then gave Shayna a big hug. "Welcome home, Mrs. Bubbelinski."

Shayna's smile widened, which she didn't think was humanly possible, but it was so wonderful to be loved so enthusiastically. "Hello Mrs. Mamelinski. How's by you?"

"By me?" Pearl shrugged. "By me, never mind, it's not so important. How's by you is the question of the moment. Nu?" Pearl folded her arms and raised one eyebrow. "What was that woman doing slinking out of your apartment in the middle of the afternoon, leaving you in your bathrobe with a shmechle on your punim the size of New Jersey?" Pearl pointed at Shayna's smile, which was indeed stretched to the limit.

"She brought me flowers," Shayna said, pointing to the table.

"Wow." Pearl walked over to the table to smell the roses.

"Don't be so impressed. She owns at a flower store; I'm sure she got them wholesale."

"Hey, the best things in life are half off, remember?"

"I came, I saw, I did a little shopping. Want some breakfast?"

"Breakfast?" Pearl sat down at the table. "It's almost two o'clock." She studied the flowers. "My three tulips sure look pitiful next to a dozen roses," she grumbled. "Hey, yesterday they kind of plotzed over. How'd you get them to stand up so straight?"

"Look!" Shayna stared in disbelief at the tulips, which were pointing straight up to the ceiling, like three sentries at absolute attention. "Luz dropped a penny into the water. Look at that. She knows magic."

"Magic my tuchus. She's just got a few tricks up her sleeve, that's all. Must be something to do with the copper. I'm glad she decided on the peach roses instead of the white," Pearl mumbled, still admiring the flowers.

"Hey." Shayna stopped mid-way to the refrigerator. "Did she consult you?"

"Well…"

"I wondered how she knew I was back." Shayna tapped her foot. "Pretty tricky, Mrs. Mamelinski."

"Well I didn't tell her you'd be home today for sure, Mrs. Bubbelinski. I told her I just had a feeling from our last phone call…" Pearl reached out and touched a rose petal. "Wow, a dozen roses and you haven't even done it yet. For a shy girl, eppes, she ain't so shy."

"Yeah." Shayna, having surveyed the contents of the refrigerator in half a second, came back to the table. "I got a few goodies in here," she said, lifting her pocketbook off the back of a kitchen chair where she had hung it last night. "Let's see. We got an epl here, if you still got your teeth; a few cookies in case you need something to nosh; a slice of rye bread wrapped up, it shouldn't go bad, a few sandwiches, it shouldn't be a total loss…" As Shayna spoke, she placed each item on the table.

Pearl shook her head, laughing. "They didn't want you to starve, I see."

Shayna closed her pocketbook and smiled. "There's more. That's just what Bubbe snitched from the nursing home. Sylvia packed me up a care package, too. Oh, here it is." She picked up a shopping bag from the floor. "Look at this: oranges, bread, Stella D'Oro cookies—"

"Stella D'oro?" Pearl dove for the bag. "Give me those!" She tore open the package and started munching away. "Oma used to have three Stella D'Oro cookies every afternoon with her coffee when she watched the Mike Douglas show. When she went into the nursing home, she told everyone Stella was leaving her half her fortune, such a good customer all her life she was. Everyday she'd check the mail: anything from Stella? She wanted to take me to Israel with the money."

"That's sweet." Shayna set some knishes and Tillie's mandelbrot in front of Pearl. "Here, ess a bissl. Want some tea with that?"

"Sure, what's bad?" Pearl took another cookie and closed up the package. "So nu, tell me everything. How's your bubbe? Are you in love? What's that you got around your neck, Fort Knox?"

"This is bubbe's locket." Shayna turned on the kettle and reached up to feel the locket around her neck. "Look, S.S. for Sally, her American name, and Shiplitsky, her maiden name. Her initials are the same as mine."

"So, are you going to put Luz's picture in it?" Pearl asked, stepping over to the cabinet. "You got any peppermint tea?"

"I don't know. I think so." Shayna answered Pearl's questions in the order they were asked. She got out two grey mugs that had elephant heads on the sides, their trunks curved into handles. "Bubbe kind of gave us her blessing."

"She did? You told her about Luz?" Pearl took out a box of peppermint tea along with some rice cakes and almond butter.

"Well, not exactly." Shayna poured the tea and brought it over to the table. "She told me all about my Uncle Ira and the shiksa he married, and she said you don't have to be Jewish to be a mensch."

"Well, that's true." Pearl brought two plates and a knife over to the table. "Here, Shayna, have a little nosh."

Shayna dribbled some honey from a plastic bear into her tea. "I don't know. I guess it really doesn't matter if my lover's Jewish or not. Bubbe doesn't care. She says the most important thing is that you love each other. And Luz says the same thing, too."

"You talked to Luz about her not being Jewish?" Pearl held out her hand for the honey bear.

"No," Shayna said. "We talked more about me not being Puerto Rican."

"And how did it feel to have the shoe on the other foot?"

"Kind of scary," Shayna admitted. "But Luz doesn't think it matters as long as we love and respect each other. I guess she's right, but still..."

"What?"

"I don't know." Shayna tried to find words for the aching in her heart. "I don't know," she repeated. "I just imagined me and my girlfriend lighting candles on a Friday night and celebrating the holidays..."

"But Shayna, you could still do that. You can share your culture with Luz and she can share her culture with you."

"You think so?"

"Sure, why not?"

"I don't know." She stirred her tea. "I guess I wanted a Jewish girlfriend so I would feel more Jewish."

"But Shayna, you're one of the most Jewish-identified women I know."

"Yeah, but I never went to Hebrew School or got Bat Mitzvahed or anything."

"So?" Pearl reached for the bag of rice cakes and opened it. "Do you want to be more religious?"

"No." Shayna made a face. "I don't know, I can't explain it, Pearl. It's like, remember when I tried to take Yiddish at the university and that didn't work out, and then I talked to the rabbi about having an adult Bat Mitzvah and then that didn't feel right either, and then I thought about having a daughter and raising her really Jewish..." Shayna's voice trailed off.

"You know, Shayna," Pearl was smoothing some almond butter onto a rice cake, making swirls with her knife. "It sounds to me like you're looking outside yourself for something, some validation maybe, that you're a good enough Jew. It's not what you know," she pointed to her head with the knife, "it's how you live your life. It's what's in here." She pointed to her heart, careful not to get almond butter on her shirt.

Shayna sighed deeply. "That's what Bubbe says."

"Then it must be true." Pearl put the rice cake on a plate and passed it to Shayna.

"I guess you're right," Shayna said slowly, as if she was still trying to figure it out. "I'll probably always be a little sad about it, just like Luz will always be a little sad that she doesn't speak Spanish."

"You want my opinion, Mrs. Bubbelinski?"

Shayna smiled. "Do I have a choice, Mrs. Mamelinski?"

"No." Pearl took a swallow of tea. "I think you're sad about your bubbe getting old, not about Luz not being a Jew. A little transference in my professional, fifty-minute-hour opinion. And," Pearl picked up her rice cake and pointed at Shayna with it. "Whether you marry a Jewish girl or not isn't going to make your bubbe live any longer than she's supposed to anyway."

"It's not?" The five year old inside Shayna started to whimper. "It's so sad to see her so miserable, Pearl. How can I let myself be happy?" Shayna broke off a small piece of rice cake and traced a B for bubbe in her almond butter.

"Shayna, how in the world will your unhappiness help your bubbe?"

"I don't know. Misery loves company, I guess." She shmushed the rice cake crumb into the almond butter. "You know how it is, Pearl, surpassing the mother and all that feminist theory stuff. How can I be falling head over heels in love, while Bubbe's stuck in some Goddess-awful nursing home? I tried to get her to come home with me, I packed up a bunch of her stuff and everything, but she wouldn't budge. She said she didn't want to get in my way and be a burden." Shayna's eyes filled. "Oh," she brushed her tears with the back of her hand, "I thought I finished crying in New York."

"I'll get you a tissue." Pearl hopped up and got Shayna a few squares of toilet paper from the bathroom.

"What's the matter, you don't got any rolled up in your sleeve? Thanks." She blew her nose and waited a minute, playing with the soggy piece of TP in her hand. "So, you really think it's okay if I go out with a shiksa?"

Pearl pondered the issue. "Well, I think it would be more okay if you stopped calling her a shiksa. It ain't nice, if you know what I mean." She paused. "I think the best present you could give your bubbe would be to do whatever makes you happy. If she really loves you, that's what she wants."

"I think she really loves me," Shayna said, meaning both Tzeydl and Luz, for even though it was a little early to tell, wasn't the proof in the long-stemmed roses? "We're going dancing Saturday night, Pearl. What'll I wear? Do you think I should trim my hair? Maybe I better bleach my mustache." Now that she had the go ahead, Shayna felt free to be her old lovable, neurotic, compulsive-obsessive self.

"Thatta girl. There's the old Shayna I know and love." Pearl finished her rice cake, stood up, and brought her knife, plate and cup over to the sink.

"Leaving so soon?" Shayna asked. "Don't you want to stay and play with me?"

"Can't." Pearl ran some water over the dishes. "I'm meeting Deb at three."

"Ah, Deb." Shayna picked at a rice cake crumb. "What happened to Bobbi and Joan?"

"Nothing happened to them. That's what nonmonogamy is all about." Pearl shut the water. "Hey, Shayna," she said, wiping her hands on a dish towel that had pink flamingoes wandering all over it. "Isn't it strange that I'm the one who never thought about it, and all three of my lovers are Jewish?"

"Truth is stranger than fiction." Shayna recited the old adage she frequently quoted to her writing students.

"Ain't that the truth?" Pearl leaned down and kissed Shayna's cheek. "You going to be all right here by yourself? What are you doing today?"

"I don't know." Shayna shrugged.

"Well, just rest, okay? Don't start a million new projects or anything. Doctor's orders."

"I thought doctors didn't make house calls any more."

"Well, this one does." Pearl opened the door. "You want me to bring Tzimmy in for you?"

"No, leave her out. I'm going to take a bath."

"Good girl." Pearl patted Shayna's keppeleh. "And eat something."

"I'll eat, I'll eat. Call me later."

"Okay." Pearl bounded down the steps, turned, and bounded back up. "Here's your key. Your door sticks a bissl."

"I know. Thanks. See ya." Shayna waved as Pearl ran down the steps, and then quietly shut the door.

Chapter Thirteen

Saturday evening found one exhausted Shayna P. Steinblatt plotzed on her couch with Tzimmy beside her, staring out the window in a daze. Keeping busy would be an understatement in describing the way she had spent her week. Not only had she written over a dozen top-notch query letters to various publications for articles she'd been storing in the hard disk of her mind all semester, and gone over her lesson plans for the four summer school courses she'd soon be teaching, but, going on Shayna's new, age-old theory that life is short—too short to live in a pig pen, unless your name is Wilma of course—she had decided to clean, really clean her apartment, which now shone and sparkled from the corners of its newly polished clutterless wooden floors, all the way up to its cobweb-free ceiling. Shayna didn't know if she'd busied herself into oblivion to escape her nervousness over her date with Luz or her grief about her bubbe. Probably both, not to mention her anger at her parents, who still wouldn't listen to reason.

"I better perk up, Tzimmy," Shayna said to her constant companion. "It's six-thirty already, only an hour and a half before the Big Date. I better call Bubbe and get dressed."

She dialed the number and waited for the third floor nurse to get Tzeydl.

"Hello?"

"Hi Bubbe, it's Linda."

"Hello darling, how's by you?"

"Fine, Bubbe. How's by you?"

"By me, oy, by me it's terrible. A woman died in her sleep last night. A young woman she was, only seventy-four years old."

"That's really sad, Bubbe."

"My best friend she was," Tzeydl said, her voice cracking. "The only one in here I could really talk to. Oy, do I miss her already. She's the only one that made me feel like a person." Shayna was puzzled. Unless things had remarkably changed in the last five days, as far as she knew, Tzyedl hadn't made any friends at Rosenbaum Estate. "What was her name, Bubbe?"

"Her name? Her name was…" Tzeydl paused. "I don't remember her name, but you know who I'm talking about, the one that was always dressed so nice with gloves and a hat with that netting over her face…"

"Oh yeah, the one who was talking about the Jewish chauffeur and her boyfriend?" Shayna couldn't resist. "The one you said was crazy?"

"Shah Linda, don't insult the dead. Friday night it happened. Last night it was, right after supper. She went upstairs; she said she didn't feel so good. She ate at the table right next to us."

"I remember."

"All right, I thought maybe she ate too much, I don't know, a good supper it was: chicken we had, and challah, you know we always have challah for Friday night, and soup and honeycake. So maybe she got a bad stomach, I thought, let her go lie down, but who would imagine she would go upstairs and die?"

"She said the Jewish chauffeur was coming on Shabbas," Shayna mused. "Maybe she knew."

"So you know your friend there, what's-his-name, the social worker?"

"Alan Meyerhoff?"

"Yeah, him. You know the one, the good-looking fella that ain't married?" Shayna waited, refusing to give Tzeydl the acknowledgement she was hoping for. "So after breakfast today he comes upstairs and he asks do I want her room. A beautiful room she had all by herself, with a nice big window and two closets."

"Hey, Bubbe, that would be great, don't you think? We could fix it up real nice with a telephone for you and a TV…" Shayna was busily interior decorating already, but Tzeydl cut her off. "I don't know what to do, Linda." Her voice sounded depressed.

"But Bubbe," Shayna was puzzled again. "I thought that's what you wanted. Then you wouldn't have to fight with your roommate about opening the window at night…"

Tzeydl interrupted her again. "Linda, if I go in by myself, surely your mother will forget about me altogether. I'll never go home. This way, I got a partniker in the room, if I scream and holler loud enough, maybe she'll complain to the manager, or the Mrs. Manager, I don't know who's in charge here. If I make enough trouble, takeh, maybe they'll throw me out on the street and I can go home."

Oy Bubbe, Shayna thought with a sigh, what can I tell you? If you get thrown out of there, Sylvia and Sol will just find another place for you. They'll never let you go home again. But how can I take away your hope? Hating herself and the words she felt forced to say, Shayna spoke. "I think you should take it, Bubbe. You'll be by yourself like you're used to. You'll be happier."

"Happy? Who could be happy in a place like this? Happy people got their own apartments, they shop, they cook, they clean, they go out. Why can't I go home, Linda? What did I do that was so terrible? What does your mother want from me?"

Shayna shut her eyes for a minute, as if that would shut out the pain in Tzeydl's voice. She felt like a traitor, consorting with the enemy. Should she keep feeding Tzeydl's futile hope that one day she would be able to go home, or join ranks with Sol and Sylvia, in their also futile attempt to get Tzeydl to adjust to life in a nursing home? For the first time, Shayna fully grasped the meaning of the phrase, stuck between a rock and a hard place. Oy was she stuck.

"Why don't you take it in the meantime, Bubbe, just for a temporary solution, until we can figure something better out?" There. That was a reasonable compromise.

"I don't know what to do," Tzeydl said again. "I want you should see it first, Linda, you know better than me what's good. If you think I should take it, I'll take it."

"But Bubbe, I can't come down until Saturday." Shayna scanned the week-at-a-glance calendar page in her mind. She had an acupuncture appointment, a couple of interviews for an article she was working on, and a lunch meeting with her summer school supervisor, all of which she supposed she could cancel, but the thought of turning around and heading right back to New York at this moment in time, even to see her bubbe, was as appealing as jumping off the Brooklyn Bridge.

"All right, so come Saturday. I ain't going nowheres."

"Will they hold the room for you?"

"What do I know?" Tzeydl asked. "I don't care."

Oy vey. Shayna would much rather hear rage in Tzeydl's voice than this total apathy. "Let me talk to the nurse, Bubbe. I'll ask her."

"The nurse you want? Hold on."

Shayna heard Tzeydl's footsteps growing softer through the receiver as she walked down the hall to the nursing station. Tears rose in her eyes like always when she talked to Tzeydl, but she forced them down, trying to keep up the appearance of being an adult even though at the moment she felt like a child. Not just any child. A granddaughter. Tzeydl's granddaughter. But for how much longer? Shayna dared not ponder that question, and luckily she didn't have to, for just then someone got on the line. "Hello?"

"Hi, Bubbe, did you find the nurse?"

"No, that man is coming, you know from the office. He was up here on the floor."

"Oh, okay."

"Just a minute."

Shayna heard Tzeydl say, "Talk to my granddaughter," before handing over the phone.

"Hello, Linda, this is Alan Meyerhoff."

"Hi. My grandmother tells me there's a single room on the floor. Could you possibly hold it for her until Saturday? She wants me to see it."

"Well, to tell you the truth," Alan Meyerhoff said, "your grandmother is third on the waiting list for a single room. Some of these people have been waiting a lot longer than she has." Shayna's heart sank. "However," Alan Meyerhoff's voice and Shayna's heart rose, "sometimes, if it's in the best interest of the entire floor to give someone a single room, someone who is having a particularly difficult adjustment, we will make an exception. And your grandmother and her roommate have been fighting every night, waking up half the residents on the floor."

You go, Bubbe, Shayna thought, her lips curving into a smile. I guess you're right, sometimes it does pay to scream and holler and carry on until you get what you want. "So you'll hold the the room for her?"

"That's not a problem; the woman was a private patient, the room's paid up until the end of the month. You're lucky she wasn't Medicaid."

"I'll be there Saturday. Thank you." Shayna was glad she was speaking to Alan Meyerhoff over the phone rather than in person, for she had an overwhelming desire to bow down in front of him in a full body prostration and kiss his feet. "Can I speak to my grandmother again?"

"Hold on. She's right here."

"Hello?"

"Bubbe, they'll hold it until Saturday."

"So you'll come?"

"Yeah. I'll see you on Saturday for lunch. Okay?"

"Fine."

"I love you, Bubbe."

"I love you too, darling. More than the sky. Bye-bye."

"Bye." Shayna hung up the phone and looked at the clock. Five after seven! "Tzimmy, c'mon." She dashed into her bedroom and pulled open a dresser drawer. "What should I wear? Oh Goddess, why didn't I decide yesterday? Well, maybe I do work best under pressure." She lifted a gold lammé top up by its spaghetti straps and turned to face the mirror, holding it in front of her. "Nice," she said to her reflection, "but maybe a little too much." Shayna studied herself. "I definitely want to look sexy," she thought out loud, "but not sleazy. Not on our first date anyway."

She put the top back in the drawer, folding it neatly, as per her new regime. "How about this? You can't go wrong with basic black." She picked up a black strapless button-up bodice. "Well, it is kind of slutty, but I'll dress it up a little. Yeah, with black pants and heels, and my green earrings and green necklace, I'll look like a good, old-fashioned elegant slut. Perfect." As Shayna spoke, she gathered her outfit together and laid it on the bed. She sat down next to her clothes, unscrewed a bottle of pink nail polish and began doing her nails.

"Want me to do your claws?" Shayna asked Tzimmy who had just jumped up onto the bed. She showed the cat her nails, but Tzimmy was not impressed. In fact she was rather repulsed by the smell and walked to the far end of Shayna's pillow where she curled up for forty winks. "I hope Bubbe gets her own room," Shayna said, waving her hands around so her nails would dry faster. "I wonder if it'll cost more? Probably. What if it's twice as much? What if Sol can't afford it?" Shayna had no idea what her father's income was, for money, along with sex and practically every other topic besides food, the weather and the condition of one's bowel movements, was a taboo subject in the Steinblatt household.

Shayna felt the tip of her thumbnail with her lip to see if it was dry. It was. She finished getting dressed, brushed her hair, pulled it back with a rhinestone clip, let it loose, pulled it back and let it loose again and then she was finally ready. A good thing, too, because it was almost eight o'clock. She walked into the living room, catching a sight of her reflection in the newly polished glass of a framed poster on the wall. "Hello gorgeous," Shayna called to her reflection at the same moment there was a knock at the door.

"Coming." Shayna dashed through the apartment and then stopped, for after all, she didn't want to look too eager. She waited for another knock, then opened the door. "Hi." A big grin spread over Shayna's face, blowing her attempt to appear cool.

"Hello." Luz stepped inside and brought her right arm out from behind her back in one smooth motion, presenting Shayna with a solitary long-stemmed red rose. "For me?" She took the rose and smelled it. "Luz Maria Borges, you're spoiling me rotten."

"About time somebody did." Luz shoved her now empty hands into her pockets.

"You're right. It is about time." Shayna looked up from the rose and into Luz's eyes, whereupon her kishkes dropped down to her feet. "I'll put this in some water." Shayna moved about the kitchen, trying to regain her composure.

"Here, let me do that." Luz took the same old wine carafe from Shayna and filled it with water. Then, keeping the water running, she took a sharp knife from the dish drain, held the rose under the faucet and trimmed its stem. "Always cut flowers under running water," she said, putting the rose in the carafe. "They last longer. There." She set the flower on the table and they both stepped back to admire it. Then, as if on cue, they turned to admire each other.

"You look pretty," Luz said, running a finger down the length of Shayna's arm.

"Thanks. You look nice, too. Hey, we match."

"You can't go wrong with basic black," they both said in unison, and then laughed. Luz was wearing a short-sleeved black shirt that had been ironed within an inch of its life, and black chinos with creases in them sharp as razor blades.

Luz offered her arm. "Ready?"

"Sure. Where we going?"

"My house. I made us a little treat." They left Shayna's house and started down the stairs.

"You made dinner? Why didn't you tell me?" Shayna stopped at the sidewalk. "I would have brought something." Like an overnight bag stuffed with my black nightgown and a pair of edible underwear.

"This is my treat." Luz unlocked the passenger side and opened the door. She helped Shayna inside and then went around to the driver's side. As soon as she slid behind the wheel and turned on the motor, loud Spanish music filled the car. Luz lowered the volume and pulled out into the street.

"Ooh, I like this music." Shayna took the liberty of turning the volume back up a little. "Who is this?"

"Magda Lake, one of the best merengue singers around."

"Is merengue a kind of dance?"

"Yep," Luz said. "As a matter of fact, it's known as the dance of love." After a long, pregnant pause, she added, "I'll teach you how to do it sometime."

Shayna tried not to let her smile take over her entire face. "I'll bet you're a great dancer," she said to Luz.

"Yeah, I was born dancing. It's in my blood." Luz took a right turn. "I drove my mama crazy, always singing and dancing around the house. I had to have the radio on at all times. Too bad they hadn't invented walkmans yet." She moved her body to the music and Shayna felt a warm glow start in her belly and move upward and downward at the same time. She watched Luz, her head turned slightly to the side, except of course when Luz took her eyes off the road to glance at Shayna, who would immediately snap her head forward to gaze out the window or look down at her nails until she felt Luz was once again paying attention to her driving. Then Shayna would turn her head slightly to the side again.

"This is it." Luz pulled into her driveway and cut the engine. "All out." Shayna got out and followed Luz to the door. "Age before beauty," Luz said, pushing the door open. She entered the house and flicked on a light. "Ta-da!"

"Wow." Shayna stepped into a kitchen and came face to face with a beautifully set table, complete with lace tablecloth, flowers, candles and champagne.

"You sit here," Luz pointed, "and dinner will be served in a minute."

"Don't I get a tour?" Shayna asked, looking around the kitchen. To her left were two huge windows with a stunning array of hanging plants adorning them: spider plants, Swedish ivies, philodendrons, an asparagus fern, even a wandering Jew.

"Oh sure." Luz turned from the stove and took Shayna's arm. "This is the kitchen. This," she led Shayna through a doorway, "is the living room."

Shayna glanced around and walked over to a huge framed collage of photographs: beach scenes, a church, women in bright costumes with flowers in their hair, a ship, and splashes of flowers.

"That's Puerto Rico," Luz said, standing beside Shayna.

"Did you take these?" Shayna asked, moving closer to admire the photos.

"Yeah, I was there about five years ago."

"These are really good, Luz."

"Yeah, well, it's kind of a hobby of mine," Luz said, studying the pictures, too. "I don't develop them or have a fancy camera or anything. I just snap."

"Have you been doing it long?" Shayna turned from admiring the pictures to admire Luz.

"Yeah, I started about ten years ago."

I should have known, Shayna thought, going back to the photos. This one doesn't do anything for less than a decade. "I've always liked photography."

"I love it," Luz agreed. "There's something about making time stand still...you know, you see something a certain way and then you can freeze that moment forever..." Luz turned to Shayna and took her hand. "I can't explain it. It's kind of like watching a flower bud, then bloom and then die. Each minute has its own beauty, and that's what I try and capture on film before that minute fades into the next and the next and the next..." Luz looked down. "Don't get me started. I don't want to bore you."

"Oh no." Shayna looked at Luz trying to meet her gaze. "I'd love to see more of your photos."

"Next time," Luz said, and Shayna smiled broadly, secure now that there would be a next time. They smiled at each other for a long minute and then Luz led Shayna out of the living room.

"This is your basic bathroom," Luz said, continuing Shayna's exclusive tour. "And this is the bedroom." Shayna looked in and felt her knees go weak at the sight of Luz's double bed which she was tempted to fling herself onto, her arms and legs open wide. Instead, she walked back through the living room, glancing at Luz's photos once more, and into the kitchen.

"Sit down." Luz pulled out a chair for Shayna and then went over to the stove. She put two platters on the table: one held a roasted chicken, the other rice and beans. Half the rice was white and half the rice was brown, a detail that didn't escape Shayna's appreciative notice.

"What's that?" Shayna pointed to a small glass jar with a lid on it between the candlesticks as Luz reached for the champagne.

"That's sand from Puerto Rico. Watch out." Luz pointed the bottle away from Shayna, turned her head sideways and popped the cork. "Quick, quick." Luz turned back to the table and poured champagne into a crystal glass. The bubbles rose to the top of the rim, threatening to overflow. "Put your finger on the edge," Luz said. Shayna did so, and the bubbles retreated.

"How does that work?" Shayna touched the rim of Luz's glass as well.

"Magic." Luz put down the champagne bottle, picked up a book of matches and lit the two white candles on the table. Then she turned off the overhead light, sat down and picked up her glass. "To the beautiful Shayna."

Shayna smiled, feeling her cheeks turn rosy even before her first sip. "And to the chef." She clinked Luz's glass.

"To us." Luz raised her glass to her lips and sipped her champagne. Shayna did the same. "Help yourself." Luz gestured with her glass before setting it down.

"Is this what they eat in Puerto Rico?" Shayna asked, spooning some brown rice and beans onto her plate.

"It's what I ate when I was a little girl." Luz cut a piece of chicken.

"When did you move here?"

"When I was about three and a half. Do you want light meat or dark?"

"I'll take light." Shayna held up her plate and Luz dropped two slices of chicken onto it.

"Once we came here, my mama didn't cook rice and beans so much. She wanted me to be American so she fed me hamburgers and hot dogs and peanut butter and jelly sandwiches." Luz spread her napkin on her lap.

"Why do you think she did that?" Shayna took a bite of chicken. "This is delicious."

Luz shrugged. "I don't know. So I'd fit in better, I guess."

Shayna stopped, mid-chew. A familiar light bulb suddenly clicked on over her head as she recognized it: assimilation. So the Jews hadn't cornered the market on it. "So, when did you say you went back?"

"Oh, about five years ago. After my parents died."

"Did you like it?" Goddess, what a dumb question. Shayna stuffed another forkful of beans into her mouth before another idiotic remark could leak out of it.

"I loved it. Everyone looked just like me. Except I couldn't understand them at first, because they all assumed I spoke Spanish. I had a great time though. Puerto Ricans are the warmest, friendliest people in the world."

"Do you still have family there?"

"No." Luz took a sip of champagne. "My mama was pretty old when she had me, and then when we came here, we pretty much lost touch with everyone on the island. Maybe I have some relatives there, but it's been so long, I wouldn't know how to find them."

"Did your parents speak Spanish at home?"

"Only when they didn't want me to understand what they were saying."

This all sounded very familiar. "You know," Shayna said slowly, "it's not so different from my family. I mean, it is and it isn't. I may still have distant relatives in Europe, or they may have been killed. I'll never know. And my parents spoke Yiddish in the house when they didn't want me to understand what they were saying. I only know little phrases." She was quiet for a minute. "Ever think about moving back to Puerto Rico or to New York like your friend Alicia?"

"Not really," Luz said. "When I was in my twenties, I went through this whole thing about reclaiming my heritage. First I got mad at my parents for never teaching me Spanish and for saying things like, 'You're lucky you have such light skin, you look like a real American.'"

Shayna's eyebrows rose. "They said that to you?"

Luz nodded. "All the time. And they were really proud that I didn't have an accent. They meant well, though, I can't blame them. They just didn't want me getting teased or beat up for being different. Anyway, then I tried to take a Spanish class at the university but I told you, that didn't work out; I've never been good in school. So then I tried going to some support groups but that was kind of a disaster."

Shayna smiled. "You don't exactly seem like the support group type."

Luz poured the last of the champagne into their glasses. "No, groups make me kind of nervous, but I thought I'd give it a try. First I went to a Women Of Color group, but everyone there was Black, so they had really different issues than me. They were nice to me and everything and they really wanted me to stay, but I just didn't feel like I belonged. I mean, look at my skin." She extended her arm toward Shayna who matched her forearm to it.

"We're almost the same color," Shayna said, feeling her flesh grow hot at the touch of Luz's skin.

"Exactly," said Luz. "So then I found a Latina group, but I didn't feel like I belonged there either because everyone in the group spoke Spanish."

"Wouldn't they speak English for you?" Shayna took a sip from her glass.

"I never asked them to." Luz wiped a drop of champagne from Shayna's chin with the edge of her hand. "I mean, that's what they have to do every day of their lives—speak English instead of Spanish—so I wasn't going to ask them to do that in their support group on account of me. How could I?" Luz lifted her palms toward the ceiling. "I wish I could just inject Spanish into my veins or something."

"I know what you mean," Shayna said. "I wish I could take a Yiddish pill."

Luz took a bite of her chicken. "Food and music," she said, putting down her fork. "That's what I know best about my culture. And what's in here of course." She thumped her chest.

"But maybe if you moved back to Puerto Rico, you'd learn Spanish," Shayna said, leaning forward. "I'm sure if you heard it everyday, you'd pick it up."

Luz laughed. "Now you sound just like Alicia. Don't try to fix me, Shayna. I'm happy with my life. I've made peace with who I am. I've got my food, my music, a few friends, and what's inside my heart, which is the most important thing. Oh, and there's some great Puerto Rican festivals in Boston I go to every year. Maybe you'll come with me sometime."

"I'd love to."

"Someday I'd like to go back to Puerto Rico for another visit," Luz said, looking up at Shayna. "Maybe I'll take you with me." She paused. "If you were to go back home, where would you go?"

Shayna sighed. "Nowhere. There's nothing left. I mean, there's Israel, and I'd love to go there someday, but it's not really Bubbe's home." Her eyes filled and she took a deep breath. Stop it, she scolded herself. I refuse to be sad on my date.

"Well then, we'll have to make you a new home," Luz said, taking a final sip of champagne. "Want some more food?"

"No thanks." Shayna pushed her plate away, for her belly was full of beans and butterflies.

"Want some tea then?"

Shayna smiled. "You remembered I don't drink coffee."

"Yep. I got some herbal tea right here." She got up to open the cupboard and then stopped. "Oh, no. Look."

"What's the matter?"

"I forgot about these." Luz brought a big metal bowl over to the table. In it, soaking in water, were what looked to be three fat bananas. They reminded Shayna of whales. "Soggy bananas?" She raised her eyebrows at Luz.

"No, plantains. They were supposed to be the appetizer." She poked one with her finger. "I guess I got so excited that you were finally really here and everything, I forgot all about them." She sounded crushed.

"Can't we have them for dessert?" Shayna asked.

"Well, I guess so. But it isn't the same."

"I won't know the difference. I've never had them before."

"You've never had plantains?" Luz's face lit up. "Then we gotta have 'em." She cleared their plates off the table and set down a wooden cutting board.

Shayna just sat back, continuing to let Luz spoil her rotten. "Why are they soaking in water?" she asked.

"It's salt water. It draws out the bitterness." Luz got a knife and started slicing the plantains in broad slanted sections. "This is how my mama used to make them, before we came here." She brought the slices to the stove, dropped a big gob of butter into a frying pan and waited for the butter to melt. "Some people fry 'em up, then mash 'em and fry 'em again," she said, sliding the plantain slices off the cutting board into the pan, "but I just fry 'em once." The butter sizzled and a delicious aroma filled the kitchen.

When they were done, Luz brought the fried plantains over to the table in a bowl and sat down. She picked up a slice and blew on it. "Open your mouth." Shayna complied and Luz set the fruit on her tongue.

"Umm." Shayna swallowed and opened her mouth again. "I want more."

Luz laughed. "You like it?"

"Yeah, it's so sweet."

"Sweets for the sweet." Luz fed Shayna another piece.

"You have some." Shayna picked up a slice of plantain and offered it to Luz, who nibbled on Shayna's fingers before taking the food into her mouth.

"Delicious," Luz said, smacking her lips. "More, please."

"More plantain?"

"No. More you." Luz leaned forward and took Shayna's hand, kissing each finger and then the center of her palm. Shayna's toes began to curl inside her not-so-sensible shoes. I've just discovered a new erogenous zone, she thought, as Luz licked the crevice where her thumb met her palm. Shayna pulled her hand back and Luz followed it. When she looked up, Shayna smiled. "C'mere," she whispered. Luz leaned over, brushed Shayna's hair away from her face and pulled her close until they were only a kiss apart. Shayna shut her eyes and the distance between them melted away as their lips met softly. They teased each other with small smooches before Shayna opened her mouth and welcomed Luz's tongue.

"Oh Shayna," Luz breathed, leaning her cheek against Shayna's so that her mouth was against Shayna's ear. "Be my girl."

"Yes." Shayna closed her eyes again and moved her lips across Luz's face to meet her mouth once more. They kissed for another long delicious minute and then Luz held Shayna close, stroking her back with the flat of her hand. Shayna rested her head on Luz's shoulder, breathing deeply and feeling like something precious held between Luz's strong arms. Again a feeling of safety washed over her. A feeling of home.

"Ready to go dancing?" Luz leaned back to look into Shayna's eyes.

"Sure." Shayna smiled. "But I can't guarantee my feet will touch the floor."

Luz smiled too. "C'mon." She stood and held out her hand.

Shayna rose and glanced at the table. "What about the dishes?"

"What about 'em?" Luz leaned over and blew out the candles. "Come." She led Shayna out the door and back into the car.

"Where are we going, Wilma and Betty's?" Shayna asked, admiring the shape of Luz's closely cropped head as she looked over her shoulder to back out of the driveway.

"Yeah." Luz glanced at Shayna. "I wanted to take you somewhere else, where everyone and her mother wouldn't be asking you to dance, but there's no other girls' bar around for fifty miles." She ran her finger down Shayna's cheek. "Is it okay I want you all to myself?"

"It's more than okay." Shayna settled back in her seat, cloaked in happiness.

Luz turned down Grove Street and pulled into a parking lot. Shayna scanned the cars to see if she recognized any. None looked familiar, though they were covered with the usual bumper stickers: I'D RATHER BE PACKING, and MY OTHER CAR IS A BROOM.

Luz parked and they walked through the lot into the bar. Shayna stood a little to the side as Luz paid their way in. The bar was dark and smoky, with two bigger than life cardboard cut-outs hanging over the dance floor: one of Betty Rubble and one of Wilma Flintstone. Though Shayna always thought of her as Wilma Flint-Stone-Butch, for she was dressed in a leather cap, leather jacket and tight jeans. Betty was the femme, complete with a low cut tiger-striped mini dress, high heels and pearls. A local dyke artist had made them years ago, when the bar had first opened, and so far, much to everyone's relief, no big wig from Hollywood had gotten wind of it and slapped them with a law suit.

"C'mon." Luz took Shayna by the hand and led her over to the bar. "Want something to drink?"

This is a real date, Shayna thought dreamily, as her eyes adjusted to the bar's dim light. Dinner, dancing, romancing. I'm in heaven.

"Shayna?"

"Oh, no thanks. The champagne's still bubbling around in my brain. I'm not a big drinker."

"Want some seltzer then?"

"No thanks."

"Listen, the deejay's a friend of mine. Let me go say hello for a minute and then I'm yours for the night, I promise. Okay?"

"Sure."

"You'll be all right by yourself?"

Shayna smiled. "Well, if I'm not, I'm sure I'll be able to find some handsome butch to lend me a hand."

"I'll only be half a minute." Luz disappeared into the crowd of women out on the dance floor.

Shayna leaned her elbows back against the bar, trying to look like a tough femme, and watched the dancers. There seemed to be a of women from out of town at the bar tonight, because there were lots of faces Shayna didn't recognize. Faces and bodies. Shayna moved her feet to the music, her eyes drinking in all those hips, all those asses, all those beautiful women moving to the song. She could feel the bass line of the music pumping through the huge speakers into her own body, as if the whole bar was throbbing with the same heart beat.

In less than a minute, as promised, Luz was back. "Wanna dance?"

"Sure."

Luz led Shayna out onto the dance floor. She moved gracefully and as Shayna watched Luz's body, pretending not to of course, she saw that Luz was indeed born dancing. She moved in that smooth, subtle way that only butches could move, and it drove Shayna wild. Luz, on the other hand, made no secret of the fact that she was watching Shayna's body. Watching and admiring.

"I asked for a song," Luz said loudly over the music. "I think she's gonna play it next."

"Did you ask for a slow one?" Shayna shook her finger at Luz and kept dancing.

"Not quite." The music changed and a fast latin beat came on. "This is a merengue." Luz moved her body to the beat. "Wanna try it?"

"Wait a minute. How come the deejay just happens to have a merengue tape with her?"

Luz smiled. "Because her girlfriend just happens to be getting a dozen roses delivered to her door Monday morning. C'mon." She held out her arms.

"What do I do?"

Luz put her right hand around Shayna's waist and with her left hand she took Shayna's right, holding it up to shoulder height. "Now, move your hips to the beat. See?"

Shayna moved her hips in time with Luz's. "Like this?"

"Just your hips. Your shoulders should stay still. See? Hip, hip, hip, hip…" She counted the beat.

"Like this?" Shayna squared her shoulders, trying to keep her upper body still.

"That's it. Just your hips." Luz steered Shayna around the floor.

"What about my tuchus?" Shayna yelled over the music. "It's attached."

"What?"

"Never mind." Shayna smiled into Luz's eyes. Who needs aerobics, she thought as Luz twirled her around. Jane Fonda should try this. "I'm exhausted," Shayna mumbled as the song came to an end.

"Wanna rest?" Luz asked.

The music changed again and a slow song came on. "Not on your life." Shayna looked at Luz who opened up her arms and folded Shayna into them. They held each other close until the song ended and then danced a few more fast ones.

"Had enough?" Luz asked as Shayna let out a yawn.

"I think so. I'm kind of tired. And not used to champagne."

"Well, you'll have to get used to it. We're gonna have a lot to celebrate." They left the bar for Luz's car.

"Oh yeah? Like what?"

"Like…like I don't know. Like next Saturday night."

"What's next Saturday night?"

Luz unlocked the car. "Next Saturday night is our one week anniversary. I'd say that calls for another bottle of champagne." She leaned down and kissed the space between Shayna's neck and shoulder which was shining in the moonlight like a glow-in-the-dark star stuck on the ceiling over a child's bed.

Shayna beamed. Being spoiled rotten was wonderful. Then a thought flew across her mind like a comet. "Oh, I can't, Luz. I have to go to New York next weekend. To see my grandmother."

"So? They don't have any champagne in New York?"

"What do you mean?"

"I mean I'll go with you."

"You will?" Shayna reached up and hugged Luz around the neck. "You mean it?"

"Of course I mean it. It would be my pleasure."

"Don't be so sure. You haven't met my family yet."

Luz looked down into Shayna's sparkling green eyes. "Well, if they're anything like you…"

Shayna interrupted. "They're not. Well, my grandmother is, and you probably won't meet anyone else. You sure you want to come?"

"Sure I'm sure. I can bring my camera and take some pictures of the two of you."

"I don't think so." Shayna shook her head. "Bubbe's not too keen on being preserved for posterity. She almost threw my tape recorder out the window when I tried to interview her once."

"Never mind then," Luz said. "I'll just come. If you want me to."

"I want you to."

"Then it's settled. Shall I take you home?"

"Kiss me first." Luz kissed Shayna deeply, then helped her into the car and drove her home, leaving her at her front door with plenty to sweet-dream about.

Chapter Fourteen

"Do you think your grandmother will mind that I'm Puerto Rican?" Luz asked, taking her eyes away from the New York traffic for a split second to glance at Shayna.

"Are you kidding? That should be our biggest worry. Our exit is the one after this." Shayna pointed out the window with a shiny, red, politically incorrect fingernail. She had gotten all dolled up to go to New York, for Bubbe's sake, she'd insisted to Pearl, who'd come over early that morning to pick up the key for Tzimmy duty. "What do you think, I was born yesterday?" Pearl asked, admiring Shayna's nails which matched her red summer dress with little red buttons going all the way down the back. "Your bubbe, you don't have to impress. But Luz…"

Not that Shayna had to impress Luz either. They'd spent every night together that week: going out to dinner, catching a movie, hanging out at Shayna's kitchen table or on Luz's living room couch for hours and hours, talking about everything: growing up (they'd both been only children); coming out (Luz had never been anything but a lesbian); the scar on the back of Shayna's hand from frying matzo brei one Pesach; the diamond ring on Luz's pinky that had been her mother's engagement ring. And they'd talked about their past relationships: Shayna told Luz that this time she'd decided to wait for someone to pursue her, since she'd always been the one to chase: and Luz told Shayna that this time she'd decided to go after what she wanted, instead of going out with whoever happened to ask her. Well, there wasn't much left to say after that, and what do two lesbians who are falling in love do to fill a lull in the conversation? They smooch of course. Long lovely luscious luxurious lusty kissing that lasted for hours.

"She's a perfect gentleman, you should pardon the expression," Shayna said to Pearl as she snapped her suitcase shut. "Or, to be more politically correct, gentledyke."

"That's good," Pearl said, "because you sure ain't no lady. I can't believe you haven't even gone to second base with her yet."

"Pearl, this is not about S-E-X," Shayna said, making one final check of her apartment, which by some miracle had remained clean all week. "This is much deeper than that. I mean we talk for hours about everything. You know how it is when you meet someone and it's like you've known her forever?"

Pearl responded by folding her arms across her chest, tapping her foot and raising one eyebrow.

Shayna smiled. "Listen, Pearl, what can I say? I'm smitten. She's everything I've always wanted to be but was afraid of."

Pearl squinted her eyes, puzzled. "You've always wanted to be a butch working in a flower shop?"

Shayna shook her head. "No. You know, the way she's so settled. The way she makes a commitment to things. She's owned the same store for thirteen years, and she's been into photography for ten years and—"

"She does photography?" Pearl asked. "I didn't know that."

"You see?" Shayna dragged her suitcase into the kitchen with Pearl following. "That's what I mean. She's not an egomaniac like some people we know who have to have their bylines in the newspaper at least once a week or they think their life is over. She's really shy about it. You know, still waters run deep?"

"And opposites attract?"

"Exactly." Shayna looked at Pearl who evidently was still not convinced. "Oh Pearl, I can't explain it. She just has such a gentle spirit. Even Tzimmy took to her in two seconds flat and you know how fussy she is." Shayna got a moony look in her eye. "She's so kind to animals and plants and me... She just feels like home. You know."

"I know all right." Pearl shook her head. "Only lesbians. We mate for life in five minutes flat and then it takes us years to get out of it."

"Some of us do mate for life," Shayna said. "You know, the swan theory."

"No, I'm more familiar with the sitting duck theory." Pearl fit Shayna's key onto her key ring. "Hey, here comes your bird of paradise now." And Luz walked in the door with yet another long-stemmed rose, pink this time, to match the shirt she was wearing.

"Ooh, only real butches wear pink," Shayna cooed.

Luz let out a two-note whistle. "Look at this gorgeous lady in red." She bent down to give Shayna a kiss on the mouth.

"You two are nauseating. I'm outta here." Pearl left, muttering something about puppy love, and now here Shayna was, hours later, about to introduce the two most important women in her life to each other. Shayna instantly felt guilty as the lesbian thought-police invaded her brain. What do you mean, the two most important? Already in two weeks your girlfriend is more important to you than your best friend of five years? All right, all right, Luz isn't more important than Pearl, she's just differently important, Shayna thought. Oh the hell with being politically correct—I'm in love, in love! Shayna wanted to stick her head out the window and shout it into the traffic, but cautious of inhaling all that carbon monoxide, she restrained herself and simply said to Luz, "This is our exit."

Luz put on her blinker. "Which way off the ramp?"

"Right."

Luz left the highway and made a right onto Forest Avenue. "Does your grandma know?" she asked, looking at Shayna as they waited at a red light.

"Know what?" Shayna looked into Luz's dark eyes and felt her insides go all mushy, like a jar of Mott's applesauce. She wondered what Tzeydl would think of Luz. She told her over the phone that she was bringing her girlfriend, but girlfriend in Tzeydl's book was different than girlfriend in Shayna's.

"Know that we're girlfriends."

"Oh that." Shayna smiled broadly, her face stretching out like a piece of silly putty. Of course she knew what Luz meant; she just wanted to hear her say it.

Luz reached for Shayna's hand and planted it firmly on her thigh. "Be my girl, Shayna."

"I am your girl, Luz." Shayna squeezed Luz's leg. "Bubbe knows I'm not interested in boys, but I've never said the L-word to her. I don't think she even knows what it means. Did you ever tell your mother?"

"I didn't have to tell her. She figured it out. Mothers are pretty smart."

"Some mothers. Pull into this driveway." They had just passed the awning of Rosenbaum Estate. Luz turned, pulled into a space and cut the motor. She turned and took Shayna's hand. "You ready?"

But Shayna was still deep in thought. "I've thought about telling Bubbe, I mean really telling her, but I guess I never had much of a reason before."

Luz hesitated. "Before what?" she asked softly.

"Before you." Shayna squeezed Luz's hand. "I've been hinting around to her for almost ten years now, and sometimes I think she gets it, she'll say it doesn't matter, and then in the next sentence she'll ask me when I'm getting married."

"Well, you don't have to tell her."

"But I want to." Shayna stroked Luz's fingers. "It makes this huge distance between us, and I hate that. And besides, she worries all the time about me being alone. She even says the only reason she's still alive is because she's waiting to dance at my wedding."

"So? We can invite her."

"She's too old to travel that far. What?" Shayna stared at Luz. "What did you say?"

"I said," Luz raised Shayna's hand to her lips and kissed it, "Shayna will you marry me?"

"Luz, are you kidding?" Shayna looked at Luz and knew at once that she wasn't. She was serious. Dead serious. She wants to marry me, Shayna thought, her eyes watering. This is our second date. Just like the knish man. But I didn't think things like this happened any more. It's the nineties, for Goddess' sakes. Oy vey, I'm plotzing. Shayna stared at Luz, who quietly waited for a reply, and Shayna was sure she had never seen anyone look so beautiful and trusting and brave and vulnerable before. She just handed me her life, Shayna thought, as a tear rolled down her cheek. She used Luz's finger to wipe it away so Luz could feel how moved Shayna was. This is what I've always wanted, Shayna thought, but I never thought there was another dyke on the planet who wanted it, too.

"Well?" Luz asked softly, after an eternity of two minutes had passed. "I know it's kind of soon, but I made up my mind that my next relationship would be IT. I know I'm ready to settle down and I know I'll never find anyone else as wonderful as you. I want a relationship like my parents had. They were as close to a storybook romance as you could get."

Luz squeezed Shayna's hand. "I mean, I know we don't know each other that well, and I'm sure we'll have a problem or two, I mean no relationship's perfect, but I just know we'll work things out. I can feel it." Luz stopped for a minute and stroked Shayna's arm with the tips of her fingers. "I'll take good care of you, Shayna," she said softly. "I'll love you and cherish you and keep you safe...."

"You got a ring?" Shayna asked with a wicked smile.

"A ring?" Luz patted her shirt pockets and searched inside her pants pockets, pretending to look for one. Then she pulled the diamond ring she always wore off her pinky. "Here."

"Luz, you can't give me that. That's your mother's engagement ring."

"That's what I like. Bossing me around already." Luz chuckled and slipped the ring onto the fourth finger of Shayna's right hand. "What's mine is yours, Shayna. We're getting married."

"It's beautiful." Shayna admired her hand, glad she had taken the time to do her nails that morning and then looked at Luz. "Are you sure?"

"Sure I'm sure. Are you?"

"Yeah. I hate to admit it, but this is what I've always wanted."

"Why do you hate to admit it?"

"Oh, you know. Not that many lesbians believe in marriage."

"Luckily, not that many lesbians are sitting in this car." Luz peered into the back seat.

"How many are there?" Shayna asked.

"Just two. Just me and you."

"Just me and you." Shayna smiled and leaned forward to kiss Luz. "Thank you."

"For what?" Luz asked, holding Shayna close.

"For the ring. For asking me to marry you. For coming with me to see Bubbe."

"You're welcome." Luz stroked Shayna's hair.

"What would your mother think?" Shayna flattened her hand against Luz's shoulder to admire the ring. The tiny diamond glinted in the sun.

"Oh, she'd be tickled, I'm sure." Luz pulled away gently, so she, too could see the ring. "She got it from her mother, because when they got engaged my father was too poor to buy my mother a ring. Right before she died she took it off her finger and gave it to me. She said even though it looked like I was never gonna get married, I should have it anyway. I have her wedding ring, too."

"We're getting married! I want to tell Bubbe." Shayna put her hand on the car door.

"Now don't do anything rash," Luz said, unlocking her side.

"Oh, you should talk! You just proposed to a woman you barely know."

"Oh I know her all right," Luz said, placing Shayna's hand against her pink shirt, right over her heart. "I know right here. You ready now?"

"I guess so." In all the excitement of being proposed to, (being proposed to!) Shayna had almost forgotten where they were and why. "I don't know how I'm going to keep this a secret from Bubbe, though." She picked up her pocketbook, got out of the car and waited as Luz bent down to check her reflection in the rearview mirror. "Bubbe's never met anyone with a buzz cut before."

"Buzz cut? It's not that short."

"Yes it is."

Luz pocketed her comb and took Shayna's arm. "Don't you like it?"

Butches were always so fussy about their hair. "I adore it. Don't worry. Bubbe will love you."

They entered the nursing home and Shayna scanned the faces of the people sitting in the lobby. "Hello, granddaughter," Minnie waved from across the room. "Go on up. She's upstairs. She's waiting for you."

"Thanks, Minnie." Shayna led Luz over to the elevator and pressed the button, keeping an eye out for Murray Perlman, but he didn't seem to be around.

"Hello, maidl." A woman in white pants and an orange sweater stopped her walker next to Shayna. "You know what that means, maidl? That's French for young girl." Shayna smiled and explained the joke to Luz as the woman walked away and the elevator opened. They got out on the third floor and there was Tzeydl, waiting on the wooden chair outside the TV room.

"Girls, here I am." Tzeydl waved to Shayna and Luz. "Hello, darling. How was the driving, all right?"

"Luz drove, Bubbe. This is my girlfriend, Luz, remember I told you on the phone she was coming?"

"Of course I remember. Hello Luz, it's a pleasure to meet you." Tzeydl patted Luz's arm. "Oh, I'm so glad yous are finally here already, all morning I been waiting." Tzeydl looked from Luz to Shayna. "Oh, Linda, you look so gorgeous, that dress is beautiful on you. Turn around, let me see the back." Shayna pirouetted for Tzeydl's inspection. "Ain't that cute, with all those little buttons. And the locket looks gorgeous on you. Like it was made for you. And you got your nails done, too. Let me see." Shayna extended her left hand for Tzeydl to admire. She peered at Shayna's nails and then lifted her other hand. "What do you got on your finger there, a diamond? An engagement ring it looks like, I should only live so long."

"Luz gave it to me, Bubbe," Shayna said, bursting with excitement, but trying to keep a cap on it. I should have known, she thought. Bubbe never misses a thing.

"Yeah?" Tzeydl looked at Luz with a bit more interest. "You got a rich girlfriend? That's nice."

"Show us your new room, Bubbe," Shayna said, picking Tzeydl's pocketbook off the chair. "Here, take your bag."

"The room? The room can wait. First we gotta eat something. I know you didn't have no breakfast, Linda." Tzeydl shook her finger at Shayna.

"Bubbe, you know I never eat in the morning."

"Nu," Tzeydl took Luz's arm and started down the hall. "Did you ever in your whole life meet someone who didn't eat no breakfast? She leaves the house with nothing in her stomach, like a car that ain't got no gas. Coffee, a little juice, something you gotta have to start the morning."

"I tell her the same thing." Luz nodded her head. "I never leave the house

156

without at least a cup of coffee."

"Of course. You're a smart girl." Tzeydl threw Shayna a look over her shoulder and then turned back to Luz. "You married?"

"No."

Tzeydl looked at Shayna again. "Another one of your meshugeneh girlfriends that don't like boys either?" Shayna didn't respond; Tzeydl shrugged her shoulders. "All right, never mind. Whatever you want."

They got to Tzeydl's room and she motioned for them to sit on the bed. "I'm sorry," Tzeydl said to Luz, "you'll have to excuse me." She opened up the top drawer of her dresser and pulled out two American cheese sandwiches, two cartons of milk, some crackers and a few hard boiled eggs. "I ain't the hostess with the most-est no more," she said, spreading her arms wide, "but I do the best I can."

"Bubbe, we can go out," Shayna said, surveying the sad little feast. "You don't have to feed us."

"Shah, Linda, sit down and eat something. I had them make it special for us; we couldn't all three crowd around my table. I have to live with these people," she explained to Luz. "I don't want to make anybody upset that I'm taking up too much room." She went over to the sink and got some paper towels to use as plates.

"This is fine," Luz said, already upwrapping a sandwich. "It was very thoughtful of you to get lunch for us."

"My fancy dining room." Tzeydl gave each of them a paper towel and spread the food on the bed. "If you had met me before, when I was a person, I would have made you a real lunch." She handed Shayna an egg. "Blintzes, latkes, gefilte fish, oy, some cook I was. My chopped liver you could die for. Did Linda tell you I owned a deli?"

"No." Luz extended half a sandwich to Tzeydl. "Aren't you going to eat something?"

"Me? No, I'm too aggravated to eat nothing. You girls eat. I had a deli with Linda's grandpa for five years. Before that I worked in a lace factory. Such beautiful lace I made, fine, like a spider web." Tzeydl turned to Shayna. "Drink some milk, Linda." She opened a carton of milk and pushed it to Shayna.

"You know I don't like milk, Bubbe," Shayna said, her mouth full of Wonderbread and American cheese.

"Did you ever?" Tzeydl asked Luz.

"No, never," Luz agreed with a smile.

"I'll have water, Bubbe. You got a cup?"

"By the sink there's some paper cups." Tzeydl turned back to Luz. "So one day when I was still at the lace factory I decided I needed more money. So I made up a story, I says to the boss, I got an offer for another job for more money, but I'll stay by him if he gives me the same money as the other boss. So you know what he says to me?" Tzeydl paused for dramatic effect, and to wait for Shayna to stop running the water. "He says to me I make enough money for a girl."

"Did you quit?" Luz asked.

"Did I quit?" Tzeydl placed her hands on her hips and stood up taller. "I took the lace I was holding in my hands and I threw it in his face. Ooh, was I mad." She shook her hands in the air and Shayna could see she was still mad. "I said I was gonna walk out right then and there, so he says to me, 'No, wait, I like your spunk, I'll give you a raise.' So he gives me a little more money, not as much as the other boss I made up, but I says all right and after that we was very good friends. He even made me my veil for my wedding."

"You never told me that story, Bubbe," Shayna said, washing down her sandwich with water.

"I never told you. You think you invented women's rights?" Tzeydl addressed Luz once more. "My whole life I worked like a dog. Volunteer work, too."

"What kind of volunteer work did you do?" Luz asked.

"I belonged to a club. You remember my club, Linda."

"The Ethel Rothman Aid Society," Shayna dutifully recited.

"Years ago," Tzeydl moved closer to Luz to explain, "we would have card parties at the club, or some entertainment, you know, something for the people to do. And the money we raised from selling the tickets, sometimes a raffle we had, the money we would give to the poor Jews who just came from Europe with nothing. I remember one girl, from Poland she came, and only one leg she had. She couldn't work, of course. You know in those days it was different, not like now. We gave her money every month for a long, long time. And then one day," Tzeydl raised a finger, "she sent us back the check with a note. She met a fella, they was getting married, she didn't need the money no more. So we cashed the check and bought her silver candlesticks for her wedding."

"And Bubbe has a necklace, too, from the club," Shayna added.

"A medal they gave me, fourteen karat gold it was, for selling the most tickets and making the most money. I was so proud from that medal, every day of my life I wore it, every day, until I came here. Now her mother has it, I'm sure." Tzeydl pointed to Shayna. "All right, what do I care? You can't wear no fourteen karat gold in here anyway, they'll steal it right off your neck. I don't got my watch, my wedding ring, my medal, nothing."

Luz and Shayna finished eating. "Thank you for lunch." Luz got up to throw away her paper towel and milk carton. "Is this the bathroom?" She pointed to a wooden door.

"Wait, wait a minute." Tzeydl crossed the room and pounded on the door with her fist. "Four women share one bathroom, can you imagine that a person has to live like this? Anybody in there?" She gave the door one more good zetz, just in case. "All right, go ahead. But be careful, there's another door on that side, for the next room, make sure it's closed." Tzeydl held the door open for Luz.

"Thanks."

Tzeydl pulled the door closed and then came to sit by Shayna. "You want a piece of fruit, Linda? An apple I got from yesterday, I can't eat it on account of my teeth."

"No, Bubbe, I'm not hungry."

"So, you're not hungry. Who has to be hungry to eat a piece of fruit?"

Shayna took Tzeydl's hand. "You like my girlfriend, Bubbe?"

"Sure, she's very nice, darling." Tzeydl lowered her voice. "But maybe she's a little old for you?"

"She's not so old. She's only forty-one." Shayna looked into Tzeydl's eyes. Did she mean what she was saying in the way Shayna hoped that she did?

"Is she Jewish?" Tzeydl whispered.

"No, Bubbe."

Tzeydl shrugged. "So all right, never mind. Listen, there are good Jews and bad Jews and good goys and bad goys. People are people. Shah now." At the sound of the toilet flushing, Tzeydl released Shayna's hand.

"Let's see your new room, Bubbe." Shayna stood up. "Where is it?"

"Down the hall, it is. Take your bag." Tzeydl took Luz's arm and led her down the hallway, with Shayna following. "If it was my house, she could leave her bag, you could take off your shoes, make yourself comfortable. But here," Tzeydl rolled her eyes, "don't ask."

They stopped in front of room three-twenty-six and Tzeydl opened the door. "So, nu, what do you think?"

"Not bad, Bubbe, not bad," Shayna said cheerfully, as she entered the room and looked around. The room depressed her immediately but she didn't want Tzeydl to know that. It's better than sharing a room, I guess, Shayna thought, but I'm still going to try to get her out of here. She crossed the tiny room that had a bed and bureau just like Tzeydl's other room, as well as a sink, two little closets, and a small table and chair.

"How's the bed?" Shayna went over to test it, but Tzeydl stopped her.

"Linda, don't sit down on there, the woman died in her sleep, feh! Don't you sit on that bed."

"Okay, okay. Look, you got a nice view." Shayna walked over to the window. "Check this out, Bubbe. You can see the street."

"The light is good, no? I can see all right by the fenster, you know, by the window there. And look at these closets." Tzeydl opened the closet doors. "Look how big they are."

"There's a lot of room in there," Luz said, standing behind Tzeydl to see.

"And look, I only gotta share the bathroom with one woman." Tzeydl opened the door to the bathroom and continued conducting a walking tour of the room. "The carpet is brand new, Linda, a month ago they put it in, that fella told me. So what do you think, girls? You think I should take it?"

Shayna felt torn. She knew she had to convince Tzeydl to take it, but it was sure hard to work up the necessary enthusiasm. She stared at the new carpet, which was a mixture of blues and greens, soothing colors, Shayna supposed. "It would be better than sharing a room, Bubbe, don't you think? We'll get you a telephone so you won't have to talk out in the hall anymore, and a TV…"

"I don't know." Tzeydl crossed the room and looked out the window. "I'm afraid I shouldn't be lonely."

"Bubbe, there's people all over the place. If you get lonely, you can just walk down the hall to the TV room. Or call me."

"I don't know," Tzeydl said again. "Remember what I told you on the phone? My partnicker is plenty mad on me, I'm telling you. Maybe if I stay with her and holler and carry on a little more, the big boss will kick me out and send me home." Shayna looked across the room at Luz, silently asking for help.

Luz rose brilliantly to the occasion. "I like this room much better than the other one. We can get you some nice curtains for the window, and a bedspread to match. We'll fix it up however you want it."

"Curtains I don't like. I like those, what do you call it, those strips going across flat, you know, like lokshen."

Now it was Luz's turn to look at Shayna for help.

"Noodles," Shayna translated. "You mean venetian blinds, Bubbe?"

"Yeah, that's right. Blinds are smarter, more modern, don't you think?"

"Sure, if that's what you want."

"Want, she says, what I want is to go home, but who has what they want anymore?" Tzeydl looked first at Shayna and then at Luz. "When you're old, you gotta do what they tell you, and that's that."

Shayna sighed. "Bubbe, I'll talk to Sylvia, I'll see what I can do."

"Sylvia she calls her mother, did you ever?" Tzeydl shook her head. "I talked to her yesterday, Linda, did I tell you?"

"No. Did she call you?"

"Yeah, yesterday she called me, in the afternoon, right after I hung up with you. Two minutes she stayed on the phone, a very busy person she is, her mother," Tzeydl explained to Luz. "I says to her, 'Sylvia, why am I in here, what did I do, why can't I go home?' but she says we'll talk about it another time, she just called to see how I am. How I am? How can I be in a place like this? All right, I don't wanna bother you girls with my troubles, but I gotta get it off my chest, takeh. My daughter I can't talk to, she don't wanna know nothing, but her," Tzeydl pointed at Shayna. "People are always talking to her. Her you can tell everything. She's got such a gorgeous face, no? A nice Jewish face, you can see on it when she's happy, when she's sad, when she's mad, that's the way we Jews are."

"Who are you talking about?" The door pushed open and Minnie stuck her head in. "Oh, you was talking about the granddaughter. The advertising was so good, I had to come see for myself what the product was."

"You know Minnie, right Linda? And this is Luz, her friend."

"Nice to meet you. Very nice." Minnie came into the room and sat down on the only chair, next to the little table. "So, you like the room? You gonna take it, Bubbe?" Minnie raised her voice for Tzeydl's benefit. "It's a very nice room, just like mine it is; you should take it. Then they'll fix it up nice for you. I got everything: a TV, an ice box. It's nice, by yourself, no one to bother you. You wanna come to my room and see?"

"Go ahead, girls," Tzeydl said. "I'm gonna go into the toilet."

"We'll be right back, Bubbe."

Shayna and Luz followed Minnie down the hall. "See, two doors down from your bubbe I am. Here, this is my dresser, from my old apartment this is, and this little table too, ain't that nice?" Minnie picked up a framed photo and handed it to Shayna. "And this is my husband, may he rest in peace, this is our wedding picture."

"You were a beautiful bride." Shayna handed the picture to Luz and picked up another photo, this one of a young boy in a yarmalke and tallis. "Who's this?"

"Oy, my son that is. Twenty-eight years old he was when he got sick. Oy oy oy." Minnie took the picture from Shayna and sat down on the edge of her bed with it. "The fever he got, it was going around. One night he calls me and he says, 'Ma, I'm sick.' By the time I got to the hospital he was dead. Dead, just like that." Minnie clapped her hands sharply. "When the doctor came into the waiting room and in his hands he had my Stanley's glasses, I'm telling you, I opened my mouth and such a scream I gave, I'm sure God in heaven must have heard me himself. So what did God do? Nothing." Minnie raised one hand to the ceiling, the other one still clutching the photo. "What a feeling that was, I'm telling you, to put my son in the ground next to my husband, in my place, where I should go." Minnie's eyes filled with tears. "Oy, they had to hold me back, I shouldn't jump in, too."

Shayna and Luz were quiet for a moment as Minnie wiped her eyes. The silence was interrupted by the sound of Tzeydl's voice drifting down the hall. "Linda? Linda, where are you?"

"We have to go, Minnie. Your room is very nice. I'm sorry about your son." Shayna patted Minnie's hand and looked at the picture in her lap again.

"He was such a good boy, a smart boy, an accountant he was, a whole row of numbers he could add up in a second. Why God did such a thing to Minnie, first my husband, then my son, I can't tell you. For a mother to lose a child, oy, Gottinyu, vey iss mir."

"We'll see you later, Minnie."

"Bye." Luz put Minnie's wedding picture back on her table.

"Go, go take care of your bubbe. You're a good girl and she appreciates it, she talks about you all the time. Go." Minnie shooed them out of the room.

"You're crying." Luz stroked Shayna's shoulder. "Your grandma's right, people do tell you everything."

"It's my job to get people to talk. I'm a reporter." Shayna checked her pockets for a tissue.

"Here." Luz reached into her back pocket for a hanky. "It's not your job, Shayna. It's your heart."

"Girls." Tzeydl poked her head out of the room. "Let's go tell the nurse I'm taking the room. They have to move my things."

"I'll go tell them," Shayna said.

"You? You're tired. I'll go. Watch your bag." Tzeydl marched out of the room, her own pocketbook dangling off her arm.

"Bubbe," Shayna called.

Luz steered Shayna into the room. "Let her go Shayna. She needs to show you she isn't helpless."

"Helpless? That'll be the day." Shayna almost sat down on the bed, and then remembered not to. "Do you like my bubbe?"

"Like her? She's great. Now I know what I have to look forward to. Someday you're gonna be one hell of an old lady."

"Someday? Try next week. I'm exhausted." Shayna lay her head on Luz's shoulder.

"She sure does have a lot of energy." Luz touched Shayna's cheek. "Think she likes me?"

"Of course she likes you. I was getting jealous, the way she kept taking your arm."

Luz laughed. "I never had a grandma, you know."

"Well you got one now, and here she comes." Shayna picked her head up at the sound of Tzeydl's voice. "Right this way. Right here." Tzeydl entered the room, followed by two men, carrying a bed. "Leave that one in and take this one out. I don't want her bed." The men did as they were told.

"Those are the painters, they're fixing a room down the hall; I borrowed them," Tzeydl explained to Shayna. "The nurse asked them to help. She's coming with my things." And sure enough, a minute later, a nurse appeared with a big plastic bag full of Tzeydl's clothes, toiletries, pictures, and whatever else she had managed to put by for herself.

"Hello." The nurse put the bag down on Tzeydl's bed.

"Hi," Shayna said. "I can put everything away. Thanks."

"You don't do nothing. You're tired," Tzeydl said to Shayna. "You take a rest, I'll put everything away later. A whole night I sit with nothing to do, I got plenty time. And I want they should wipe out the closets and the drawers first."

"I can wipe them out, Bubbe."

"You sit still and take a rest. She's so stubborn," Tzeydl said to Luz, fishing.

Luz caught the bait. "I know. She never lets herself take it easy."

"Hey, thanks a lot." Shayna folded her arms, but Luz's smile undid her anger. "Let's go shopping, Bubbe. We'll make a list of what you need for your new room."

"Shopping? Why should we go shopping?" Tzeydl asked, sitting down on the bed and resting her arm on the plastic bag that held her things. "You need something? All right, come, we'll go."

"No, I don't need anything, Bubbe. Let's go shopping for you."

"For me?" Tzeydl had half risen at the thought of buying something nice for Shayna, but now sunk back down on the bed. "Why should I go shopping, so many things I have at home: beautiful skirts and blouses; so many shoes, ones with big heels, ones with little heels; my fur coat your grandpa gave me; so much jewelry, so many pocketbooks. Why should I go shopping?"

"Well then, tell me what I should bring you from home, Bubbe. I'll make a list." Shayna sat down on the bed next to Tzeydl and pulled her ever present notebook out of her shoulderbag.

"Don't bring me nothing, I ain't gonna live here the rest of my life."

Three steps forward, two steps back, Shayna thought. Well, at least she took the room. "All right." She flipped her notebook closed. "I won't bring you anything."

"Wait, my clock I need."

Shayna re-opened her notebook. "Which clock? The bedroom clock or the kitchen clock?"

"The clock from the kitchen. That clock keeps such good time." Tzeydl leaned forward to address Luz, who had sat down in the chair across the room. "And I can read it good, too, white it is with big black numbers. I got it from the bank when Linda was a little girl, she don't remember, but they used to give you things, prizes like, for opening a new account. Toasters they gave you, and frying pans, all kinds of things. I didn't take nothing, but when I saw this clock I said, oh, this I need. So I went up to the teller there, and I says to her, 'Mrs. Teller, you can give me a clock?' And she says to me no, a new account I have to open. I ask you, is that fair, ten years I had my money in that bank already and I got nothing, and a new customer walks in one day and gets a clock?" She looked at Shayna and Luz, neither of whom could argue with her logic. "So I says to her, listen, I says, I'll take all my money out from the bank and put it back in with a new account and it'll be more work for you and more work for me, so do us both a favor and give me the clock."

Luz laughed. "Did she give it to you?"

"Right off the wall she took it." Tzeydl turned to Shayna. "See, your old bubbe ain't so dumb after all."

"I never said you were dumb, Bubbe. What else should I bring you?"

"Bring me my lamp, the big white lamp from the living room. My eyes got so bad since I been in here, at night I can't see a thing, like I'm half blind. And bring me my radio, the one by the bed. At night, I can't sleep, I like to listen to a program." Tzeydl watched Shayna write it all down. "That's all. I can't think no more, Linda. Use your judgment. Bring whatever you think I need."

"Okay, Bubbe. You want me to bring up what I got in the car?"

"No, first I want they should wipe out the room. Bring everything tomorrow."

"Okay."

"Maybe you should go now, Linda, you shouldn't drive in the dark."

Shayna furrowed her brow. "Bubbe, it's not dark. It won't be dark for hours."

"Really? Ain't it almost time for supper?"

"I don't think so. Luz," Shayna's voice had a worried edge, "what time is it?"

Luz looked at her watch. "It's three-thirty."

"It's only three-thirty," Shayna repeated to Tzeydl.

"Ain't that funny," Tzeydl said, "it got so dark all of a sudden, like a cloud went right over my eyes."

"It is a cloudy day," Luz said gently, even though it wasn't. Shayna blinked her a kiss with moist eyes.

"Go girls, go take a walk on the beach, so nice it is in Brighton by the water, you shouldn't spend your whole weekend in the house with an old woman." Tzeydl laughed. "In the house, listen to me. I forgot for a minute my bad luck. See, she's like medicine to me, she makes me forget my troubles." Tzeydl patted

Shayna's arm.

"But Bubbe," Shayna took Tzeydl's hand, "we came to see you."

"So, me you saw, what's there to see? Go, take your friend to the beach, me you'll see again tomorrow."

"Come with us, Bubbe."

"Linda, don't talk crazy, you know I can't go from here."

"Why not, Bubbe? We got a car, we'll go and we'll bring you back."

"Linda, you know why not. I don't want you should get in trouble with your mother." Tzeydl's voice was firm.

"She wouldn't know." Shayna's voice, on the other hand, was a thin whine. "Bubbe."

"Don't 'bubbe' me. Mothers know everything, believe me. Go, I have plenty work to do here, all my things I gotta put away, a blouse from yesterday I wanna wash out."

"I'll help you."

"Linda, do me a favor, mamela, go enjoy yourself, that would be the biggest help." Tzeydl stood up and was out the door, walking toward the elevator. "Come tomorrow and we'll spend the day, all right?"

"Okay, if you're sure you don't want me to help."

"Go." Tzeydl kissed Shayna as the elevator door opened. "Goodbye, darling."

"Bye, Bubbe. I love you."

"I love you, too. Goodbye, Luz." Tzeydl stood in the hallway waving until the elevator door closed.

Chapter Fifteen

Luz and Shayna sat at Tzeydl's kitchen table in their pajamas, the morning sun somehow finding its way down between the apartment buildings to filter in through the tiny fifth floor window. Luz was sipping coffee and Shayna was drinking the orange juice Luz had made her buy down on the avenue yesterday after they had taken a walk on the beach and eaten supper at a corner deli.

"My first cup of coffee made by my wife." Luz took a sip. "Delicious."

Shayna laughed. "Listen, wife, when do you want to get married?"

"I don't know, wife. How about next June?"

"Next June?" Shayna's eyebrows shot up. "That's a year from now."

"Well, if you think that's too soon, we could wait two years."

"Two years!" Shayna's eyebrows rose even higher. "I was thinking six months at the outside."

Luz warmed her hands around her coffee. "Well, a year would give us time to figure out the details. We want to do it up really big, don't we?"

"Are you kidding? It'll be the social event of the season."

"And," Luz continued, "a year will give us time to get to know each other better. My mother told me not to marry anyone until we'd had at least four fights."

"Oh yeah?" Shayna looked at Luz. "What do you think we'll fight about? Our cultural differences, our religious differences…"

"You're still worried about that, aren't you?" Luz patted Shayna's hand. "I bet we'll fight about really stupid things. Like whose turn it is to take out the garbage."

"Or do the dishes."

"Or walk the dog."

"Or make the bed."

"Still," Shayna's forehead started to crease, "things are bound to come up."

Luz took another swallow of coffee. "Like what?"

"Like…like the C-word."

"What's the C-word?"

"Christmas." Shayna said the word distinctly, adding an exaggerated hiss to the end of each syllable.

"Christmas?" Luz put her cup down. "I'm sure we'll figure out how to celebrate it," She looked at Shayna and quickly added, "or not celebrate it when the time comes."

"Maybe we should talk about it now," Shayna said, pushing her orange juice away. "So we'll have a game plan for next December."

"Drink that," Luz said, pushing the OJ back. "Shayna, it's only the beginning of June. I can't think about next week, let alone December."

Shayna stared into her glass. "But what if we can't work it out?"

Luz lifted Shayna's chin with her finger. "Are you really going to worry about that now?"

Shayna smiled in spite of herself. It did seem rather silly. "Well, maybe not," she said. "But that's what we Jews do, you know. We worry. We've been doing it for five-thousand years; we're very good at it."

"Not me," Luz chuckled. "I take things as they come. You know, the mañana theory of life."

"I guess."

"Hey." Luz took Shayna's hand. "We'll work it out, I promise. Can't we just wait a few months to talk about it? This is our honeymoon phase, you know."

"Okay." Shayna gave in, but only for an instant. Then she said, "But Luz, what if we live together and you want a Christmas tree? I don't know if I could deal with that."

"Shayna, if I want a tree and you don't, we'll talk about it and work out a compromise, that's all."

"You mean like have half a tree?"

"Exactly. Now drink your juice."

Shayna took another sip and made a face. "Luz, what do you think about having a Jewish wedding?"

Luz traced the rim of her cup with her index finger. "Well, what do you do?"

"Oh, it's really fun. You stand under a huppa, that's a wedding canopy; and the rabbi blesses the wine and you take vows and exchange rings and sign a ketuba, that's a marriage contract; and then you break a glass and everyone cries and yells mazel tov! and then you eat and dance." Shayna picked up her orange juice and downed it in one gulp. "L'chiam." She toasted the air.

"What does that mean?"

"To life."

"Why do you break a glass?"

"Because," Shayna paused, trying to remember. "Because even in our happiest moments, we're supposed to remember the saddest moment, the destruction of our temple. And because once the glass is broken it can never be like it was before, and once we're married we can never be like we were either. It's permanent. Kind of like Humpty Dumpty. And one more thing." Shayna searched the depths of her brain. "Oh, I know. However many pieces the glass breaks into is how many years of happiness we'll have together."

"The pressure's on." Luz picked up Shayna's orange juice glass and felt the weight of it in her palm. "Do I get to break it?"

"Sure. You wrap it up in a cloth," Shayna got up, took a dish towel off the back of her chair and wound it around the glass in Luz's hand. "Then you smash it." She put the glass down on the linoleum floor and stepped away from it. "Want to practice?"

"You can't break that glass, Shayna. That belongs to your grandma."

"It's only an old shrimp cocktail jar. Go on. Step on it."

Luz looked at the floor. "I don't know. What if I hurt my foot?"

"You gotta put your shoes on, silly rabbit."

"Okay, wait a minute." Luz disappeared into the bedroom and came back out wearing her black Reeboks, which looked to Shayna awfully cute with her blue-striped pajamas.

"Ready?"

"You sure about this?" Luz still looked doubtful, but Shayna nodded. "Hold my hand then." Shayna took Luz's hand, counted to three, and cheered as Luz's foot came down and smashed the glass into a billion smithereens.

"Mazel tov, mazel tov!" Shayna threw her arms around Luz and gave her a kiss.

"How are we going to find a rabbi to marry us?" Luz sat back at the table and Shayna perched on her lap.

"Well, the thing is, you don't need a real rabbi to have a real Jewish wedding." Shayna who had often wondered about it herself, had finally done some recent research. "You just need someone who knows what they're doing. I'm sure we can find a nice Jewish dyke who knows the traditions. And we can make some up. Like we can write our own vows."

Luz frowned. "I don't know. Maybe you should write them. After all, you're the writer in this family."

Family. Before that very moment Shayna hadn't cared much for the word, but now it took on a whole new meaning. "We'll do it together. And you can be in charge of the flowers."

Luz smiled and swept the room with her hand. "Roses everywhere. And a big bouquet for my girl."

"Can we really have a Jewish wedding?" Shayna leaned back to look at Luz, her eyes shining.

"It's really important to you, isn't it?" Luz asked.

"Yeah, it is." Shayna paused. "But we could combine it. You know, we can do something from your tradition, too."

"Don't furrow that pretty forehead." Luz smoothed Shayna's brow with two fingers. "I was raised Catholic but it doesn't mean anything to me. I haven't been to church in about twenty years."

"Then why do you celebrate Christmas?"

"That's different. That was never a religious holiday for me, it was more like a family holiday."

"Well, isn't there something Puerto Rican we can do at our wedding?"

"We'll dance a merengue or two," Luz said. "And can we have some Puerto Rican food, like plantains?"

"Of course we can."

"I know." Luz moved Shayna's hair behind one shoulder. "We'll have a

167

Jewish wedding and a Puerto Rican honeymoon. How's that?"

"Yeah!" Shayna threw her arms around Luz and gave her a big kiss on the cheek. "Yes, yes. Can we really go to Puerto Rico? Really?"

"Sure, why not? You'll love it there. Pure white beaches, blue ocean, blue sky, old San Juan..." Luz got a faraway look in her eye. "We'll see some great shows, we'll take walks, we'll hear coqui..."

"Who's Coqui?"

"Ah, coqui." Luz sighed with pleasure. "Coqui is a little frog that only lives in Puerto Rico. Coqui's about this big," Luz held her thumb and forefinger about an inch apart, "but the song of coqui is this big." She spread her arms as far as they could go.

"What does coqui sound like?"

Luz closed her eyes, as though she was listening. "I can't describe it, you'll just have to hear. Coqui sounds very beautiful and very loud. You think a coqui is right next to you," Luz pointed to her feet, "and you look down, but there's nothing there. Then you hear another coqui coming from over there." She pointed across the room.

"Does coqui sound like a bullfrog?"

"Oh no." Luz shook her head. "Coqui doesn't sound like anything else. Coqui is unique, just like the Puerto Rican people. The first time I went back to the island and heard coqui," Luz sighed again, "I knew I was home. Coqui only lives in Puerto Rico, nowhere else. In fact, a few years ago, I read that a scientist took some coquis to Germany to study them, but they wouldn't sing for him. Not a peep."

"Poor coquis. They must have been homesick." Shayna took Luz's arm and wrapped it around her. "What happened to them?"

"I don't know," Luz said. "Maybe the scientist brought them back, or maybe they died."

"That would be awful." Shayna stroked Luz's arm. "He should never have taken them away from Puerto Rico." She thought for a moment and then asked softly, "Do you wish you had never left the island, too?"

"Oh no, that's different. My parents brought me here."

"Why?"

Luz shrugged. "For better opportunities, I guess. You know, everyone on the island was pretty poor back then, and my father had an easier time finding work up here. And anyway," Luz gave Shayna a squeeze, "if I hadn't left the island, I'd never have met you."

"Will you show me where you were born?"

"I'll show you everything. We'll have a great time."

"Wow, Puerto Rico. I'll have to get a new bathing suit."

"Maybe two." Luz squeezed Shayna again. "Maybe seven, one for every day of the week."

"Oh, Luz." Shayna put her feet up on the chair and curled into her wife-to-be. "I'm so happy. But I'm so sad, too."

Luz stroked Shayna's cheek. "Sad about your grandma?"

Shayna nodded and looked down at the floor. Her gaze fell on the broken glass wrapped in the dish towel. "It's kind of like that." She pointed, her chin trembling. "Even in our happiest moments, we remember our saddest. There's even a Yiddish expression: ' in every tear a laugh; in every laugh a tear.'" She sighed and looked up at Luz. "Are you sure you want to marry me? I'm quite a handful."

"Lucky I got two then." Luz held up her hands. "These big enough?"

Shayna matched her hands to Luz's. "Look, a perfect fit. Well, at least you won't get bored."

"Bored? Nah, I'm never bored." Luz clasped both of Shayna's hands.

"But maybe after, oh, I don't know, five, ten years, you'll want someone new."

"You're talking to someone who's had the same job for thirteen years, the same apartment for twelve…" Luz looked into Shayna's eyes. "Did you ever hear that zen saying: if you do something once and it bores you, do it twice. If it still bores you, do it four times. If it still bores you, do it eight times, sixteen times, thirty-two times, sixty-four times. Sooner or later," Luz shook a finger at Shayna, "you'll begin to find it very interesting." She took Shayna's hand again. "It's the same with a person. The more you know them, the more interesting and exciting they are." She hesitated. "But maybe you'll get bored with me. I mean I go to work, I come home…"

"You study zen."

"Oh no." Luz laughed. "I just read that somewhere once and it stuck because I liked it. My life's really not too exciting. Maybe you'll get bored."

"I won't." Shayna rested back against Luz. "That's what I like about you. You're so stable, so content with things. I wish I could be more like that."

"Yep, I'm pretty happy all right. Especially now that I found my dream girl." Luz leaned forward to take another sip of lukewarm coffee.

"But are you sure?" Shayna took the cup from Luz and set it back on the table.

"Yep." Luz took Shayna's hand and started playing with the ring on her finger. "I've been keeping my eye on you for a while now. You need me, Shayna. You need me to love you and take care of you and bring you flowers and make you laugh…"

Shayna certainly couldn't argue with that. "But Luz, what do you need?"

Luz didn't miss a beat. "I need to love you and take care of you and bring you flowers and make you laugh…"

"No, really Luz."

"What do I need?" Luz looked up at the ceiling, searching for the answer. "I'm a pretty simple person, Shayna. I need someone I can love and someone who'll love me for who I am. Throw in a steady job, a place to live, some food on the table, and the rest is gravy."

Shayna shook her head, smiling. "Luz Maria Borges, where have you been all my life?"

"Just hanging around, waiting for the time to be right."

"Uh-oh. Speaking of time," Shayna glanced up at Tzeydl's clock. "I bet Bubbe's waiting for us. We better get going."

"But it's only ten o'clock."

"I know." Shayna arched her back and lifted her arms overhead in a delicious stretch. "But I gotta pack up some things for her and we gotta take showers, and maybe we'll have time to say hello to Tillie. Would that be okay?"

"Sure. You're in charge of this trip. Whatever you say, ma'am."

"Luz, I'll do the same for you someday, you know that, don't you?" Shayna was starting to have a little trouble needing so much attention. "I'll love you and take care of you and bring you flowers and make you laugh, too."

"I know you will. I'm sure in the next fifty years or so, my turn will come."

"Luz, you're the greatest." Shayna burrowed into Luz's neck and kissed it. "I feel like we're married already."

"Well, I broke the glass and you have your ring. Doesn't that make it official?"

"Official enough for me." Shayna looked at her ring and smiled. "We'd better get ready. C'mon." She hopped off Luz's lap. "Oh wait. Will you look at Bubbe's plant?" She walked over to the windowsill.

Luz came over to inspect the leaves. "That's a grandma's needles."

"Really? That's what it's called?"

"Well, it's really a sansevieria, but no one calls it that. It has lots of nicknames: grandma's needles, snake plant. This is in pretty good shape."

"Does it need water?"

Luz stuck a finger into the soil. "No, this seems all right. It should be on the dry side. You don't want to make the dirt soggy."

"C'mon, you can take the first shower." Shayna took Luz by the hand into Tzeydl's bedroom and got her two white towels from the dresser. "Here. Now what did Bubbe want from the bedroom?"

"Her radio, I think."

"Oh yeah." Shayna walked around the bed to Tzeydl's night table where she usually kept her radio, but it wasn't there. "That's funny. This is where she always keeps it," Shayna said, thinking out loud. "I don't remember seeing it last time either." She scanned the room with her eyes. "Luz, you didn't happen to see a radio, did you?"

"No." Luz was taking a clean white shirt out of her suitcase. "Did you check the living room?"

"No, it wouldn't be in there. She listens to it at night, when she can't sleep. Maybe it's under the bed." Shayna didn't find the radio, but she did find two small suitcases, which were exactly what she needed. Shayna started going through Tzeydl's drawers, and just as she was refolding a pink blouse, she heard the shower start and the phone ring. She went into the living room, hoping it was Pearl calling with a friendly hello and not Tzeydl with another disaster.

"Hello?"

"Hello, Linda."

"Oh, hi Sylvia." What a surprise, though not necessarily a pleasant one.

"How'd you know I was here?"

"I talked to your grandmother Friday, she told me you were coming to see her. How's the apartment, all right?"

"Fine." Except for one minor detail: the chief occupant of the apartment wasn't in it.

"How's your grandmother?"

"She's depressed. She wants to come home."

"Linda, that's out of the question. Don't even start with me. How's the new room? Does she like it?"

"It's okay." Shayna heard Luz singing "The Bells Are Ringing For Me And My Gal" in the shower and was momentarily distracted by the pounding of her heart.

"The social worker called this morning, and he said she took it. I'm glad, maybe she'll like it better there." Mrs. Steinblatt sighed. "She better like it, it ain't cheap to be in a room by yourself, believe me. Does she need anything?"

"Why, are you coming to see her?"

"I was planning on it; we were going to come today, but after she yelled at me and carried on over the phone for twenty minutes, I changed my mind. I'm not gonna sit in traffic for an hour just for that. My nerves can't take it."

Goddess forbid we should talk about our feelings, Shayna thought. "Bubbe said you only stayed on the phone for two minutes. Anyway, she's upset."

"So, she has to upset me, too? If she's upset, let her be upset on her own time. Your father works hard all week, he doesn't have to spend his Sunday listening to my mother complain. If she wants visitors, your grandmother, she's gonna have to learn to be a little pleasant."

Shayna shook her head. It was useless. The way Sylvia was talking, you'd think Bubbe was two years old, instead of ninety-nine. "Sylvia, do you know where her radio is?"

"Look on her night table."

"I looked there already."

"It's not there? Look under the bed, then. Who knows, maybe she started hiding things, you know she was getting a little crazy up there."

"Don't say that! Bubbe is not crazy." Shayna slammed her hand down on the arm of the couch, causing the black fringe to jump.

"Linda, let's not talk about it, we'll only get upset, all right?" Shayna heard the click of her mother's lighter as she lit a cigarette. "So tell me, what's new?"

Shayna shook her head again. There it was, the old let's-change-the-subject trick. Sometimes Shayna felt like a television set: if Sylvia didn't like what was on, she just picked up the remote control, pressed a button, and voila! the channel changed. What else was new? Nothing really, besides the fact that Shayna had just gotten engaged to be married.

What the hell. "I just started dating someone. Her name is Luz."

"How's the weather in the city? It's very hot here, Linda, so if you sit outside with your grandmother, make sure she stays out of the sun."

Obviously Mrs. Steinblatt didn't like that program either. When in doubt, switch to the weather channel. But Shayna felt stubborn today. "Sylvia, did you hear what I just said?"

"Yes, I heard you." Shayna could hear her mother exhaling, and imagined two blue-grey tunnels of smoke streaming out of Sylvia's nostrils.

"Well, you could have fooled me."

"Linda, what do you want from me?"

Oy, Sylvia, Sylvia, Sylvia, Shayna thought. Didn't you ever read Dr. Spock? Must I be the one to give you a crash course in Parenting 101? Aloud she said, "Just pretend you're interested, okay? Ask me where she's from, what kind of work she does, you know, the same questions you would ask if I was dating a man."

"Linda, if you were dating a man, believe me, I'd be so happy, I wouldn't care where he was from or what kind of work he did. We'd take him sight unseen."

Well, I set myself up good for that one. Shayna heard Luz turn off the shower. Now she was singing, "Going to the Chapel of Love."

"Sylvia, we can't talk about Bubbe, and we can't talk about my life. You asked me what was new and I told you. Now you pick something to talk about."

"Linda, I didn't call to have an argument with you. I just called to say hello and see how everything is."

"Sylvia, you have to start caring about my life more." Because soon Bubbe won't be around to, Shayna thought, and to her horror, she began to cry. "I don't even feel like I have a mother," Shayna sniffed. "You never tell me you love me. You don't even like me and you hate my life." Shayna waited for her mother to take the ball she had just pitched her and smack it over the fence with the reassurance that of course she didn't hate her. You're my daughter, of course I love you, Shayna waited to hear, but unfortunately, Sylvia struck out by remaining silent, while Shayna cried harder. The louder she sobbed, the quieter the other end of the phone became.

Finally Shayna's tears subsided and Mrs. Steinblatt spoke. "Are you through?" she asked.

"No!" Shayna started crying again, muffling her face with one of Tzeydl's throw pillows so Luz wouldn't hear. "Sylvia, I'm a lesbian. You have to accept that. It's been over a decade and it's not going away." She paused, and then threw in the clincher. "Bubbe accepts it. She really likes Luz."

"What? Linda Steinblatt, you did not tell your grandmother." It was a statement, not a question.

"Yes I did." Shayna wasn't sure if she was lying or not. After all, she had told Tzeydl over a thousand times that she wasn't interested in men, and she had introduced Luz as her girlfriend.

"You have some nerve, Linda. It's bad enough that you ever told me, I don't have enough to worry about, but how dare you tell your grandmother? She has plenty of tsouris, believe me, this she needs like a loch in kop."

This whole conversation I need like a hole in the head, Shayna thought. "Like you really care what Bubbe needs," she yelled into the phone. Luz opened the bathroom door and took a few hesitant steps into the living room. "If you care so

172

much about what Bubbe needs, why don't you hire some day nurses or something, and let her go home?"

"Linda, this is getting us nowhere. I'll talk to you another time when you're not so upset. Goodbye, dear."

"And I'll talk to you another time when you're not so...so...so like a brick wall. Goodbye, dear." Shayna slammed down the phone, a moot gesture, since her mother had already hung up.

Luz came into the room and sat down next to Shayna. "What happened?"

"Oh, nothing. Just Sylvia tuning me out for a change. You'd think after all this time she'd get over herself already and realize her daughter has a life." Shayna stood up, the frustration coursing through her veins propelling her to pace around the room. "She just can't deal with anything. She won't talk to me, she won't talk to Bubbe." Shayna stopped in front of the TV set and picked up a framed picture of herself and Tzeydl, taken twenty-eight years ago. They were at the beach, and Tzeydl was holding her two year old granddaughter up to the camera like a prize. Tzeydl looked so different then, so much bigger; and Shayna looked different too, so much smaller. They were both so much older now and getting older every minute. All of a sudden Shayna felt like Dorothy from the *Wizard of Oz* again, only this time she was trapped in the Wicked Witch of the West's castle, and the sand in the hourglass was quickly running out.

"Luz," Shayna came whimpering across the room. "I'm afraid Bubbe's going to die soon and then I won't have anyone."

Luz took Shayna into her arms. "You'll have me."

"I know. Thank the Goddess for her impeccable sense of timing." Shayna smiled through her tears. "I just wish someone in my family besides Bubbe really loved me."

"Has it always been like this between you and your family?" Luz asked, stroking Shayna's hair. "I mean how you don't get along with your mother and stuff."

"Always. My first word was no." Shayna smiled proudly, in spite of herself. "My mother and I just don't connect; I was always closer to Bubbe. I could talk to her about almost anything. And I could talk to Sylvia about almost nothing."

"What about your father?"

"He's your basic absent father type." Shayna sighed. "He was always at work and he thinks family stuff is for women."

"We'll make a new family," Luz said, kissing the top of Shayna's head. "I really love you."

"I know. I love you, too. But I can't just forget about them."

"I know, Shayna. I just forget how it is sometimes, because I don't have parents anymore."

Shayna brushed Luz's cheek with the back of her hand. "You must miss them."

"I miss them a lot." Luz covered Shayna's hand with her own. "My mother adored me. She used to say I was the light of her life."

"Not my mother." Shayna sighed. "I can't talk to her about anything. I don't even know why I brought anything up. I should have just given her a stupid weather report. That's all she wants to hear anyway. But Goddess, I'm getting married, and I can't even tell my own mother."

Luz took Shayna over to the couch and sat her on her lap. "So, does this mean we're not gonna invite her?"

"Invite who, Sylvia? Are you kidding? Do you want to have a good time at your own wedding or what?" Shayna folded her hands. "How can I invite her when she can't even tell me she loves me?"

Luz didn't have an answer. "Maybe you should just think about your grand-ma. She loves you. Are we going to invite her?"

"I don't know if I'm ready to tell her yet; she's got a lot on her mind at the moment. But it's hard. I've never kept such a big secret from her before."

"Yes you have. She doesn't know you're a lesbian," Luz pointed out.

"I know. It's a problem." Shayna shook her head. "I've got to tell her, but I'm scared."

"There's lots of time to think about it." Luz tickled Shayna's bare arm with one of her long dark curls. "Maybe things will change between you and your mother. You never know. And maybe you'll be ready to tell your grandmother sometime soon."

"It's such a big risk, though." Shayna absently stroked her arm where Luz had just tickled it. "She loves me so much and she's so proud of me. I'd hate to lose that."

"I can't imagine her rejecting you. Aren't you her pride and joy?"

"I'll say." Shayna gestured toward the kitchen. "She saves everything I send her: my newspaper articles, cards for her birthday, Chanukah, Rosh Hashannah... It's all in the Shayna P. Steinblatt Memorial Drawer over by the sink. Want to see?"

"Sure. Do we have time?"

"I guess not. I better get dressed." Shayna got off Luz's lap. "Will you unplug that light for me?" She pointed to a big white lamp on an end table.

"Sure." While Shayna got dressed and finished packing Tzeydl's things, Luz unplugged the lamp, took down Tzeydl's clock and cleaned up the kitchen.

"Let's go say hi to Tillie before we go." Shayna came out to the living room wearing white pants and a green and white striped top. "Do I look okay?"

Luz looked up. "Cute as a button."

"Button...button...let's take Bubbe her sewing kit." Shayna got a huge round tin out of Tzeydl's closet and opened it. The first thing she found was a jumbled ball of red yarn. "Here, take this," she said, handing it to Luz.

"What do we need this for? It's full of knots."

"Trust me. You'll need it in a year. Or if you won't need it, I will." Shayna rummaged through the sewing box. "See, she's got her tape measure here, and needles and all kinds of thread. Look at this." Shayna pulled out a hand-made red pin cushion in the shape of a crooked heart. "I made this for her in third grade. And this is her button collection. I used to play with it when I was a little girl." Shayna opened a small square box of buttons and ran her fingers through them.

Luz put Tzeydl's sewing box next to the other things they were taking. "Ready to go, honey?"

"Yeah, let me get the keys." Shayna went to get her shoulder bag and then stopped. "Wait a minute. Did you call me honey?"

"Yeah, I guess I did." Luz seemed surprised. "Can I?"

"You bet." Shayna felt all warm inside. She got her keys from her bag, locked Tzeydl's door behind them, and led Luz down the hall to Tillie's apartment. Shayna knocked but there was no answer, so she waited a moment and knocked again. Finally, the door next to Tillie's opened cautiously and an old woman with blue tinted hair peeked out of her doorway. "Hi," Shayna said, turning toward the woman. "Do you know where Tillie is?"

The woman was suspicious. "Tillie you want? Who are you?"

"I'm Linda, Tzeydl's granddaughter. You know, Tzeydl from down the hall."

Instantly the woman's voice softened. "Sure I know Tzeydl, and you too, mamela, I remember you from when you was a little girl. Listen, Tillie ain't home, she went to stay by her son in Jersey."

"What happened?" Shayna asked. "Did she get sick?"

The woman lowered her voice to a whisper. "Mugged she got, poor Tillie. They tried to take her pocketbook and run up the steps to the El with it. But Tillie held on so tight, they took instead the arm right out from her shoulder. Dislocated."

"That's terrible."

"I'm telling you, this is some neighborhood." The woman still spoke in a stage whisper from her doorway. "Years ago it wasn't so bad, there was a cop here, an Irish girl she was, with hair red like fire. She took such a shine to your grandma, like a shiddach it was. Well, you know your grandma, darling," the woman laughed, "she could charm the wallpaper off the walls when she wanted to. So friendly she was," the woman addressed Luz, "we used to call her the Ambassador of Brighton Beach.

"Your grandma," the woman turned back to Shayna, "made sure that cop knew everyone in the building, she should watch out for us, make sure we was all safe. But they took her away from the neighborhood, they don't care." The woman shook her head. "They're after the Jews again, I'm telling you, it ain't safe to walk out your own front door. You girls be careful. Don't talk to no strangers." And with that last warning, the woman retreated, closing the door and locking it behind her.

Luz put her arm around Shayna and led her back down the hall. "You all right?" she asked.

Shayna nodded her head yes, and then shook it no. "Poor Tillie," she said as she unlocked the three locks on Tzeydl's door. "Last time I saw her, she told me not to walk on the beach by myself, it was too dangerous, I should stay on the avenue. So she stayed on the avenue," Shayna pushed open the door, "and look what happened to her." She walked into the apartment and stood next to the pile of suitcases in the middle of the living room floor. "We better get going."

"Want to wait here while I get the car?"

"No, I'll come with you. You can't leave the car on the street with stuff in it."

They both took a suitcase down to the lobby. Shayna waited with the bags inside the glass doorway, while Luz went to get the car, watching people walk by the building and thinking about Tillie. What if it had been Tzeydl that had gotten mugged instead? "Bubbe's a survivor," Shayna said out loud. "Nobody could go after Bubbe's pocketbook and live to tell about it."

The next thought that crossed Shayna's mind made her blood run cold: what if the guy had had a knife or a gun? Tears came to Shayna's eyes as she imagined the grisly scene. And for the first time, even though the thought almost killed her, Shayna considered the possibility that maybe, just maybe, her mother had done the right thing after all.

"Maybe," Shayna said out loud, "but still, she shouldn't have lied to her. It wasn't right to tell her they were going home and then bring her to Rosenbaum Estate. She should have talked it over with her and let her pick out a place and pack up her things. *Linda,* Shayna heard her mother's voice echoing in the hallway, *your grandmother is not rational. We could not discuss anything with her.*

Shayna blew against the glass door and started making little dots in her breath with her finger. Who would be rational in Tzeydl's situation? No one. She's ninety-nine years old, she doesn't have to be rational, Shayna thought. She's earned it. So what if she screamed and hollered? She has every right to. You can't kidnap someone and put them away just to avoid dealing with their feelings. And they could have called me, Shayna blew onto the glass again and made a heart with her and Luz's initials inside. *You,* Shayna could just hear Sylvia's voice, *you would be worse than her. That's all I need, my hysterical daughter along with my hysterical mother waking up the entire neighborhood at one o'clock in the morning. I'd like to knock both your heads together, knock some sense into both of you.* Shayna's thoughts were interrupted by the welcome sight of Luz's car pulling up to the building with a little toot. She grabbed the suitcases she was waiting with and ran outside. "Taxi," she called. "Rosenbaum Estate, please. And step on it."

"Yes, ma'am." Luz got out of the car and opened the trunk. Shayna handed her the suitcases and looked up, her mouth open in mock surprise.

"You know," she said, "you won't believe this, but you look exactly like my wife."

"Is that so?" Luz slammed the trunk. "Well, as a matter of fact, you look just like my wife. Small world, huh?" She grinned at Shayna and held out her hand. "Give me the keys and I'll go up and get the rest of it."

"Okay, look. This one's for the bottom lock, this is for the middle, and this is for the top." Shayna displayed Tzeydl's keys. "The bottom one you turn to the left; the middle one, I'm not sure..." Shayna turned the key in the air and then caught sight of Luz and stopped. "Luz Maria Borges, are you listening to me?"

Luz laughed. "I'm listening, all right, but I didn't hear a word you said."

Shayna put her hands on her hips. "And why not?"

"Too busy admiring you."

"Oh." She couldn't exactly get mad over that.

"Give 'em. I'll figure it out."

Shayna stood guard at the car and after Luz made a few trips upstairs they were off to the nursing home. When they got there, they brought some of Tzeydl's things up to her new room.

"Hello girls." Tzeydl kissed Shayna's cheek. "What do you got there, so heavy it is, you shouldn't hurt your back."

"We brought what you wanted, Bubbe. Here, I'll put the lamp on that table. Let me see if there's a plug."

"I'll go down for the rest of the stuff," Luz said to Shayna, who was bent in half, searching for an outlet.

"There." She straightened up and snapped on the lamp. "Look you got plenty of light." Shayna heaved one of the suitcases she'd packed for Tzeydl onto the bed and unzipped it. "Look what I brought you."

"Clothes I don't care about," Tzeydl didn't even glance at the suitcase. "Where's the clock?"

"Right here." Shayna pointed to the clock that Luz had lain on Tzeydl's dresser. "You want me to hang it up?"

"The clock, yeah, I need someone good and strong to help me hang the clock."

Shayna was immediately insulted. "So what do I look like, chopped liver?"

"You? Don't you do nothing. There's workers here, they'll come tomorrow and fix up everything, tomorrow's Monday, no? And that social worker, your friend there, what's-his-name, I gotta talk to him, make sure everything's kosher." She laughed. "Listen to me, kosher. So religious I am all of a sudden in my old age, I gotta make sure everything's kosher? Come, here's your friend, let's go down for lunch."

"Good idea." Shayna got up.

"Take your bag, Linda, they'll steal the sheytl off a woman's head, I'm telling you." Tzeydl turned to look at Luz. "You ain't got no bag?"

"No." Luz looked at Shayna. "What's a sheytl?"

"A wig. When a Jewish woman gets married, she cuts off all her hair and wears a wig. Don't worry." Shayna laughed at the look of horror on Luz's face. "I'm not that observant."

Shayna hooked one arm through Luz's and one arm through Tzeydl's. "You used to keep kosher, didn't you, Bubbe?"

"Sure, I kept kosher. When your mother was a little girl, if I wasn't home and she wanted something to eat, she'd go by the neighbors with a plate and ask, 'Is this a milkhig plate? Is this a fleishig plate?'" Tzeydl laughed at the memory as they started down the hall.

"When did you stop keeping kosher?" Shayna asked, for she didn't remember Tzeydl having two separate sets of dishes, one for dairy and one for meat.

"When your grandpa died. Then it was enough already. Whether a person keeps kosher or a person doesn't keep kosher don't make them Jewish," Tzeydl said. "What matters is what's in their heart." She pointed to her chest and then punched the elevator button. "I hope it's a good lunch today, you girls must be hungry."

"Let's go out, Bubbe, it's a beautiful day."

"Out you wanna go? Yeah, you're right, there's three of us; there won't be no room by the table."

They got on the elevator and made their way downstairs, through the lobby and out the front door, stopping at a fenced in area to investigate the commotion that was going on there.

"A petting zoo they brought us," Minnie was standing on the edge of a small crowd. "Look, all baby animals there are. Go see."

"You wanna see, Bubbe?" Shayna led her through the crowd. Some volunteers had set up a circle of fence and inside were a bunch of baby animals: a few chicks, a duck, two rabbits, a tiny goat and to Shayna's surprise and delight, even a baby pig.

"Look how they all get along," Tzeydl said, peering over the fence. "All different types and they get along better than people."

"See that pig, Bubbe?" Shayna pointed. "There's a woman in my town who has a pig named Wilma. She keeps it in the house like a pet."

"Go on, a pig in the house? Really?" Tzeydl turned from the animals to Shayna. "Feh. Well, all right, some people treat a pig better than they treat their own mother."

Well, so much for the activities serving as a distraction. Shayna thought. Aloud she said, "C'mon, Bubbe, let's go eat."

Shayna and Luz steered Tzeydl down the driveway into Luz's car.

"Where to?" Luz asked, turning the ignition.

"Let's go sit by the water, want to, Bubbe?"

"Sure, by the water's nice. Wait, ain't you girls hungry? What about the lunch?"

"There's a concession stand there. I'm sure they sell hot dogs and stuff," Shayna said, hoping "stuff" included something she could eat.

"Hot dogs? That would be good. I didn't eat a hot dog for a whole month, since I been in there."

"That way." Shayna pointed out the window, directing Luz. "Then go all the way down until you come to a big parking lot."

When they got there, Shayna pointed to a cluster of trees. "Park over there. We should sit in the shade."

Shayna hopped out of the car and pushed her seat forward so Tzeydl could get out of the back. "Here, take my hand, Bubbe."

Tzeydl waved her away. "I'm coming, I'm coming. If I don't get out today, I'll get out tomorrow. Watch out. Don't put your hand there, I'm closing the door." She slammed the door shut and they made their way over to a shaded bench that faced the water. Most people were sitting in the sun, glad for a chance to warm their bones. Four men sat on folding chairs around a card table playing pinochle, and two women sat on the next bench with a baby carriage between them. A steady stream of people happened by, eating ice cream cones, pushing strollers, pulling or being pulled by dogs.

"Ah, this is good," Tzeydl said. "This is life."

"Remember we came here last time?" Shayna and Tzeydl sat down on the bench, their pocketbooks on their laps.

"I wish I had a camera," Luz said, holding up her hands and pretending to click.

"Sit down, Luz. There's plenty room." Tzeydl patted the bench.

"I'll go get lunch. What do you want?"

"Here, take the money from me." Tzeydl unzipped her bag and handed her change purse to Shayna. "Here, Linda, take out the money."

"We have money, Bubbe."

"This is my treat. Here." She handed the change purse to Luz instead. "Take whatever you need, I got plenty money. Friday I went down to the social worker there, your mother made me an account with him, whenever I want he'll give me money. My banker he is now, maybe they'll give me another clock yet." She laughed.

Luz took the change purse. "You want a hot dog?"

"Bring one for me and two for her." She pointed to Shayna. "And take whatever you want for yourself. Don't be shy."

"Bubbe," Shayna interrupted. "You know I don't eat hot dogs."

"Nu?" Tzeydl asked Luz. "She didn't eat no chicken either, for a long time she didn't eat it. 'I don't eat meat,'" Tzeydl said, mimicking Shayna perfectly. Luz laughed. "I says to her, chicken ain't meat, it's Jewish, so then she started eating chicken again." Tzeydl turned to Shayna. "Was I right?"

"Sort of." Shayna didn't feel like going into the whole megillah of working her way back to eating only organically raised chickens that weren't shot up with hormones and kept in cages the size of shoeboxes. "Just bring me some french fries or something."

"Okay. Dogs and fries coming right up." Shayna and Tzeydl watched Luz walk off, one hand in her pocket, the other swinging Tzeydl's change purse.

Shayna let out a deep sigh of contentment that was interrupted by a poke of Tzeydl's finger.

"Look, ain't she cute?" The finger that had just poked now pointed to a little girl in a pink playsuit who was squatting down, throwing bread crumbs to a bunch of pigeons.

"Yeah, she's cute." Shayna wasn't too enthusiastic, for she knew what was coming next.

"What's the matter with you?"

"Nothing's the matter with me. I'm just not wild about babies, that's all."

"Everyone loves babies. Look, look." A young man, presumably the little girl's father picked her up and hoisted her onto his shoulders. The two were joined by a young woman, the wife/mother no doubt, and the three of them walked off into the sunset to live happily ever after. "You see," Tzeydl said, "a mother, a father and a baby. Ain't that nice?"

Shayna looked at her hands and said nothing, prompting Tzeydl to ask, "Linda, kinehora, what's wrong with you?"

"Nothing is wrong with me," Shayna stated. "That's just not what I want."

Tzeydl shook her head. "So stubborn you are, just like a mule. You want you should be alone your whole life, in your old age with no children to take care of you?"

"Bubbe," Shayna said. "I'm not alone. I have Luz."

"Sure a girlfriend is nice in the meantime, but then you gotta get married."

I am getting married, Shayna wanted to scream. Tzeydl had just given her the perfect opening, but the question was, did Shayna have the chutzpah to take it?

"Bubbe," Shayna looked at Tzeydl intently. "Bubbe, Luz and I love each other."

"That's good." Tzeydl was watching a young man stroll by with a Doberman pinscher on a leash. "But soon she'll go away and get married, you'll see, and then what will be? Linda, I don't want you should be alone. Believe me, I know what it's like to be by yourself. More than thirty years I been lonely, and I don't want that for you."

Shayna decided to try the logical approach. "Bubbe, you got married and you were still alone for over thirty years, so what's the point?"

"Linda." Tzeydl turned toward Shayna and put her hand on her arm. "Don't be foolish like your old bubbe. I should have married again but I was stubborn, just like you. Did I know I would live so long, eppes? When your grandpa died, I thought my life was finished."

Shayna's heart pounded loudly as she took the plunge. "Bubbe, Luz isn't going to run out on me. We're going to live together." At least Shayna assumed so, since after all, they were getting married, and that's what most married people did.

"So, that's all right. You can have a roommate. That's good, to have someone help out with the rent."

This was going nowhere. "Bubbe, we sleep in the same bed." Another assumption, but after all, they had slept side by side in Tzeydl's bed last night.

"Sure, that's all right. When my mother took in a boarder, we slept together in the same bed, too."

How blatant do I have to be? Bubbe, we touch each other, Bubbe, we kiss each other, Bubbe, we take off each other's clothes, Bubbe, we... Shayna looked down at her lap, feeling a slow blush crawl up her neck and spread over her cheeks, at just the thought of having sex with Luz, which she also assumed was part of getting married. Shayna stared at her hand, feeling Tzeydl's eyes on her. Her diamond ring broke the sunlight into a prism and she could see the tiniest rainbow refracted in the stone.

"Bubbe, see my ring?" Shayna held up her hand. "This is an engagement ring. From Luz. We're getting married."

Tzeydl looked from the ring to Shayna's eyes. "Linda, don't even talk like that."

"It's true."

"Feh. Puh, puh, puh." Tzeydl leaned over the side of the bench and spit three times. "Linda, what are you, crazy? You're ruining your life."

Shayna's voice rose. "I am not ruining my life."

"Linda now you listen to me." Tzeydl gripped Shayna's arm. "I didn't wanna tell you this, but I'm an old lady, I only got a few days left to live. Don't spoil them for me, let me enjoy myself."

Shayna almost laughed. "Bubbe, c'mon."

"Shah shtill, Linda. Just tell me what I want to hear. Tell me what you're writing for the newspapers, what you're teaching in the school—"

"Bubbe." Shayna sat back and stared out over the water. "I can't tell you only what you want to hear. I have to tell you what's important to me."

"What's important is to get married," Tzeydl poked Shayna's arm yet again for emphasis, "and to have a family."

"I am getting married and I will have a family. A different kind of family, that's all."

"Two girls? That ain't a real family." Tzeydl pointed to another young couple strolling by, their son between them, swinging a baseball bat. "See that: a mother, a father, a son. That's how it's supposed to be."

What is this, Shayna thought, het family on parade? I wish Luz would get back already. Well, what did you expect? Did you expect her to say mazel tov and kiss your cheek and tell you she would get to your wedding even if she had to crawl there on her hands and knees? "Bubbe, it's not the same for everyone." Shayna tried to explain again. "I'm very happy with Luz. I love her."

Tzeydl patted Shayna's knee. "Listen, darling. I saw a show on the television. There was a man who had gone with a man and now he was married in the right way, with a baby and everything."

"I don't believe you."

"It's true, I'm telling you. A whole bunch of them was on, boys that went with boys, girls that went with girls, and now they was all normal. In the afternoon it was on."

Oh, great. Thanks a lot, Oprah. "Well, I don't care, Bubbe. I've been with women for over ten years now, and I'm not going to change."

"Oh, you." Tzeydl waved her hand at Shayna in disgust. "You think you know everything, some big macher you are, hoo-hah, you know better than everybody else what's right."

"Bubbe, don't be mean to me."

Tzeydl softened her voice. "Look, mamela, I'm only telling you this because I love you. Believe me, you'll regret this later on, when it's too late. You should get married now, while you're young, and you should have a family."

"I'm marrying Luz," Shayna said, relieved to see her in the distance walking towards them with a cardboard box full of food.

"Listen, Linda, I'm only telling you this for your own good. If I didn't love you, I wouldn't say nothing." Tzeydl poked Shayna's arm, which Shayna feared would become black and blue if this conversation went on much longer.

"You don't love me, Bubbe. You only love who you want me to be, not who I really am."

"Don't talk crazy, Linda. Of course I love you."

"You do not."

"Shah now." Tzeydl, having caught sight of Luz, waved to her and then turned back to Shayna to have the final word. "Enough with the talking already. We don't see things the same way today, eppes; we're like a Jew and a goy."

Shayna shook her head and moved over, so Luz could put the food down on the bench.

"There was a huge line," Luz said. "Sorry it took so long. Here's your purse."

"Thank you." Tzeydl put her change purse back in her bag. "What did you get?"

"There's hot dogs and french fries and a grilled cheese sandwich."

Oy, more white bread and American cheese? Oh, what the hell, what do I care? Shayna took the sandwich Luz offered and tried to push the lump in her throat down with food.

"Oh, is that good." Tzeydl bit into her hot dog with relish. "We used to sell hot dogs at the deli for a nickel," Tzeydl said to Luz. "Her mother used to sit on my lap and drop the coins into the register." Tzeydl took another bite and extended the hot dog to Shayna. "Taste this, Linda, it's so good."

Shayna shook her head, trying hard not to scowl and Tzeydl laughed. "From my own mouth I'm feeding her, like a bird. Years ago," she still addressed Luz, "when we came over on the boat, there was hardly any food. My mother didn't eat nothing, not one drop. Every bit of food she got went into my mouth. You see what a mother's love is?" she asked, turning back to Shayna, who, not being in the mood for Tzeydl's your-mother-is-your-best-friend shpeel, didn't reply. Tzeydl shook her head and turned back to Luz. "What kind of work do you do?" she asked her, much to Shayna's surprise.

"I own a flower shop," Luz said. "I take care of the flowers and I make deliveries. My specialty is roses."

"Yeah, really? That sounds interesting." Tzeydl popped the last bite of her hot dog into her mouth and picked up a straw. She bit the end off the wrapper and slowly peeled the paper away, using the edge of her thumbnail. Shayna watched the process, which would have taken her about half a second, but took Tzeydl almost a full minute. Shayna knew better than to try to help and besides, she was afraid if she opened her mouth she might start to cry.

"I'd like a job like that." Tzeydl gave the straw to Shayna and handed her a soda. "Here, drink something."

"I brought two cokes and a seltzer," Luz said, opening the top of one of the plastic cups. "This one's for you."

"Thanks." Shayna switched sodas with Luz, falling more in love by the second.

"Sure," Tzeydl went on, unwrapping another straw. "It's good to get out, sometimes in the store, sometimes in the car. You must make pretty good money if you can afford a diamond ring."

Shayna perked up her ears, a smile almost replacing her frown. So she's checking her out, Shayna thought, to see if she can take good care of me. "Luz is a photographer, too," Shayna said, her pride in Luz dissolving the lump in her throat.

"Oh yeah, pictures you take?" Tzeydl was duly impressed. "Linda writes for the newspapers," Tzeydl told Luz, in case she didn't know. "You can take the pictures, like a team you'll be."

Shayna smiled. "She doesn't take those kind of pictures, Bubbe."

"So, pictures are pictures." Tzeydl looked at Luz. "Nu, why didn't you bring your camera, our picture you could have taken? Me, all right, I ain't no beauty queen, but Linda would make a nice picture."

"I'll bring it next time," Luz said, flashing an I-told-you-so look at Shayna, who shrugged and took a sip of seltzer.

"Let me see that ring." Tzeydl lifted Shayna's hand up to her face for a closer inspection. "A diamond only gets more valuable over the years," Tzeydl said, "even a little one. Oy, so much jewelry I got at home; rings, bracelets, necklaces. You wait," she said to Shayna, unwrapping straw number three. "Soon everything will be yours. Diamonds I got too, in a safety deposit box. You'll see, a whole jewelry store you'll have." Tzeydl laughed and then turned to Luz. "Don't worry, she's gonna be a very rich lady."

"Bubbe," Shayna broke in. "I couldn't find your radio. I looked all over the apartment. It wasn't by the bed."

"No?" Tzeydl put her straw in the last cup of soda and took a long drink. "That lousy super must have it. I'm sure of it."

"No one has it, Bubbe. It must have just gotten lost."

"Lost, how could it get lost? You think it just got up by itself and walked away? Linda," Tzeydl leaned forward. "The super went in, he got keys to all the apartments, he took my things, he put up the wires. They wired my apartment," Tzeydl explained to Luz, " and they cut off my telephone."

"Bubbe, I'm sure the super didn't steal your radio."

"Who then, Linda?"

"I don't know, Bubbe, maybe I took it."

"You? You didn't take nothing. I'm telling you, something fishy is going on up there."

"Oh Bubbe." Shayna sighed and looked at Luz helplessly. I give up, Shayna thought. There's no use trying to convince her. Shayna decided to try the Sylvia Steinblatt change-the-subject approach. "Let's go buy you a new radio, Bubbe. What do you think of that? There's a Radio Shack on the way back, I remember we passed it. Let's go see what they got."

"All right, sure. A radio I need." Tzeydl unzipped her bag and dropped the extra unused napkins from their lunch into it. "At that…that estate there, they all go to bed at seven o'clock. A whole night I sit, listening, listening, listening. A person could go off their mind."

"Come." Shayna took Tzeydl's arm and led her back to the car.

Luz found the Radio Shack, and double-parked in front of it. "Here, I'll just run in," she said, shutting off the motor. "I'll leave the keys, in case you have to move it."

"You need money?" Shayna asked.

"No, take from me," Tzeydl called from the back seat.

"I'm loaded," Luz said. "Be right back." Shayna felt warm with pleasure, as she watched Luz saunter up to the store. She's a real mensch, she thought dreamily. She acts like we're married already.

Ten minutes later, Luz was back with a big bag she handed to Shayna. "Your radio, madame."

"Oh, great." Shayna swiveled in her seat and held up the bag. "Look, Bubbe, we got it."

"Really? You girls are like magic, I'm telling you. I don't know what I'd do without you."

"How much?" Shayna whispered, as Luz steered into the traffic.

"Later," Luz whispered back. Shayna smiled, and boldly rested her hand on Luz's knee.

Back upstairs in Tzeydl's room, Shayna plugged in the radio and put it on the table next to Tzeydl's lamp. "Look, Bubbe, it's a clock radio."

"The clock I don't need, I got the other clock." Tzeydl pointed to the kitchen clock lying on its side on top of the bureau like something wounded. It still said eleven-fifteen.

"Okay, forget the clock. Sit down, I'll show you how it works." Tzeydl sat down on the chair and leaned forward as Shayna explained. "See this black switch on top here? This says on and this says off." She moved the button to the right and heard some static. "Wait a minute, let's find a station. Look, this knob here changes the programs." Shayna tuned in the news. "Now, this is the volume," she pointed to another knob and made the newscaster's voice louder. "Okay?" She shut it off. "Now you try it."

"This one here?" Tzeydl pushed the switch to the left and nothing happened. She looked up at Shayna.

"Let me see." She pushed the button to the right and the newscaster's voice filled the room again. "You have to push it to the right. See, this is off," Shayna clicked the radio off. "And this is on. This," she clicked the switch all the way to the left, "is for the alarm, if you want to wake up to music." She shut the radio off. "Try it again."

Tzeydl fiddled with the radio, sometimes getting it to work and sometimes not. "Linda, maybe you should take it home. It's too hard for me." Tzeydl pushed the radio away and sat back.

"Bubbe, it's easy. Forget about the alarm. Look, this is off, this is on. Simple."

"Take it, Linda. My radio at home I was used to. This is too modern for me." Tzeydl waved her hand at the radio, dismissing it.

"We'll get you a different one then. An easier one."

"That was the simplest one they had," Luz said from across the room.

"It's not too modern, Bubbe." Shayna's voice had gotten louder. "Look all you have to do is turn it on. What could be simpler?"

But Tzeydl wouldn't even look at it. "I don't want it no more. You take it."

"But we bought it for you!" Shayna stamped her foot. "You have to take it."

"Shayna, you're shouting." Luz crossed the room to stand by her side.

Shayna stopped yelling and started pleading. "Bubbe, please. Please take it,

184

Bubbe." Please be able to learn new things, her mind echoed. Please don't get old. Please don't die. She turned away so Luz and Tzeydl wouldn't see her tears.

"Take it away, Linda. I'm too old for new things, takeh. You take it."

"Okay." Shayna gave up and unplugged it. I suppose we can return it on the way home, she thought. "We better go, Bubbe."

"That's right. I don't want you should drive in the dark." Tzeydl got up and took them downstairs.

"I'll get the car," Luz said down in the lobby. "You two wait here."

"You need money for gas?" Tzeydl asked, pulling the door closed behind Luz. "Here, take from my change purse."

"That's okay, Bubbe."

"Wait, I'll go in the dining room there, and get you some fruit. You'll be hungry, it's a long trip."

"You don't have to, Bubbe. We'll be fine." A familiar tap scattered across Shayna's shoulder. She turned around to see, guess who? Murray Perlman. "Hi, Murray." She automatically lifted his arm before he could even ask the question. "You're in room 533. See, it's on your bracelet, right here. That's a very nice sweater you got on. Your wife, takeh, had goldeneh hands." Murray Perlman walked away satisfied.

Tzeydl turned to look after him. "You see what I have to live with the rest of my life?" she asked Shayna. "Look, look at that." Tzeydl pointed across the lobby. "For supper they're lining up already, and it ain't even four o'clock. For over an hour they stand and wait. Oy, the first time I saw that, I says to myself, what is this, back on the bread line I'm standing?" Tzeydl turned and rested her arm against the glass door. "Here's Luz."

Luz pulled open the door. "Ready?"

Shayna's chin quivered. She was never ready to leave her bubbe. "Goodbye, Bubbe." She bent down to kiss Tzeydl. "I love you."

"I love you, too. Goodbye, darling." Tzeydl pulled Shayna toward her and kissed her three times on the cheek. " Call me when you get home, I shouldn't worry."

"I'm a good driver," Luz said. "You don't have to worry."

"I don't have to worry?" Tzeydl looked at Luz like she was from another planet. "Don't worry, she says. Someone's gotta worry. Who's gonna worry if I don't worry?"

"It's her job to worry," Shayna explained.

"Goodbye, Luz, it was very nice to meet you." Tzeydl gave Luz a hug and a kiss on the cheek, too. "Thank you for spending your whole weekend with such an old lady. I hope I didn't spoil it."

"You didn't spoil it. I had a great time."

"Bye, Bubbe." Shayna gave Tzeydl another kiss, reluctant as always to go, not even daring to think the question that was always on her mind: what if this was the last time she would ever see her?

Luz opened the door, and just as Shayna stepped through it, Tzeydl called her back. "Girls." Obviously she had one more thing to say. "Listen, be careful how you go. And take good care on each other." She took Shayna's hand, placed it on top of Luz's and held it there. "You should both live and be well and be good friends, for a long, long time."

"Oh, Bubbe." Shayna's eyes filled with tears as she opened her arms to embrace Tzeydl, but she waved her off.

"Just go," Tzeydl said, turning her back, but not fast enough to hide the fact that she was crying, too.

Chapter Sixteen

"Who the hell can that be?" Shayna padded on bare feet into the living room and snatched up the phone. "Hello?"

"Collect call from Tzeydl Zimmerman. Do you accept the charges?"

"Yes." Shayna sank down onto the couch, bracing herself for the latest catastrophe.

"Hello?"

"Hi, Bubbe, it's me."

"Oh, thank God. A whole night I didn't sleep, I been waiting to talk to you."

"What's the matter?" Shayna hadn't slept the whole night either, but for a very different reason than Tzeydl. She'd been up until about five a.m. enjoying the exquisite body of her betrothed, who now lay blissfully asleep in the very bed that Shayna had just unhappily torn herself away from.

"I was thinking all night about yesterday, about what we was talking about."

"What were we talking about?" Shayna searched her brain in vain, for it was only eight o'clock, and even under the best of circumstances (which these were, come to think of it) she was not a morning person, whether she had three or a hundred and three hours of sleep.

"We was talking about you and your girlfriend there. I know why you didn't call last night. You was mad on me."

Shayna smacked herself lightly on the forehead. You shmendrick, she scolded herself. You forgot to call Bubbe and tell her you got home safe. "I'm sorry, Bubbe. There was a lot of traffic and then Luz took me out for supper and then…" Shayna stopped herself from giving out further details about the night's activities just in the nick of time.

"Well, I don't blame you for being mad. But listen, Linda, don't be in such a hurry all the time, a little patience you gotta have. Everything can't be one-two-three. I'm an old lady, I can't change overnight. You gotta give me time to get used to it."

As Tzeydl was talking, Luz came into the living room and draped Shayna's red silk robe around her shoulders. "It's Bubbe," Shayna whispered, cupping her hand over the mouthpiece. "She's fine. Go back to sleep." Luz kissed the top of Shayna's head and drifted back to the bedroom like a dream.

"I wasn't mad, Bubbe, I just forgot, that's all."

"Forget? You never forget. I had like a weight on my chest pressing down all night, Linda, to think you was mad on me. Listen, darling, I didn't mean no harm, but with you I have to say what's on my heart, you know that. With your mother it's different, but you and me, we're cut from the same cloth, you know what I mean?"

"Yeah, Bubbe, I know."

"I would have called you earlier but I had to wait for the nurse to help me with the call."

Thank the Goddess for small favors. Shayna lay back on the couch and motioned for Tzimmy to join her. But Tzimmy was miffed, due to the fact that Shayna, for some mysterious reason, now preferred Luz's smooth body in bed beside her, instead of Tzimmy's furry one. Consequently, Tzimmy was not handing out any favors this morning. She sniffed the tips of Shayna's fingers, then abruptly turned her back, sat down, and began vigorously cleaning her left front paw. "So, is everything all right now, Bubbe?"

"All right? I been lying here like a lox all night, thinking how I insulted you, how can everything be all right? You shouldn't be so sensitive, Linda, I was just telling you my opinion."

"But sometimes your opinion hurts my feelings."

"Sometimes what you say hurts me too, Linda, believe me. When you said I didn't love you, that was worse than if somebody stuck a knife right through my heart. Don't ever say that, Linda." Tzeydl's voice broke. "You know you'll always be my Linda, I don't care who you sleep with. You could sleep with a dog and I would still love you."

Hmm. There was a kind thought in there somewhere, but Shayna wasn't sure she could find it. "So, what are you trying to tell me, Bubbe?"

"I'm telling you, I was just expressing my opinion, that's all. I wasn't telling you to change it."

"You weren't?" Shayna sat back up to make sure she was wide awake and hearing correctly.

"Of course I'd be happier if you got married the other way, but, all right, if you're happy, I'm happy too."

"Really Bubbe?" Shayna's eyes filled, with tears of joy this time, for once in her life.

"Sure, as long as you ain't alone. That's the most important thing. And your health. As long as you're healthy. So tell me, Linda, are you gonna have children?"

"What?" Now Shayna was sure she was dreaming.

"Sure, why not? You could adopt a baby. There's plenty children that need a good home."

"We haven't really talked about it yet." Shayna was nonchalant, as if this was a perfectly normal conversation to be having with her grandmother.

"You should talk about it soon, Linda, children are very important. And don't be mad on me no more, alright, darling? I ain't got so much time left, we gotta make the most of it."

"I love you, Bubbe," Shayna said, some sad tears joining the happy ones trickling down her face.

"I love you, too, darling. You should take a rest today, you just got back from a long trip. Did you eat breakfast yet?"

"Not yet."

"What did you have for supper last night?"

"Chinese food. Luz took me out."

"That's right, after such a long trip you should go out, you're too tired to first start cooking. So go back to sleep, mamela. I'm sorry I called so early, but I had to call you, first thing. You know I don't stand on ceremony. If I want to call, I call, even if you're mad on me. And you should do the same. With me and with your mother."

"Okay, Bubbe."

"What's gonna be with the family when I'm gone?" Tzeydl asked. "Family is the most important thing, Linda, your new family and your old family, too. You should call your mother, darling. Don't be mad on her on my account."

"All right, Bubbe." Of course Tzeydl had to get a little lecture in, it shouldn't be a total loss, but nothing in the whole world could ruin this phone call. "I'm glad you called me, Bubbe. I love you."

"I love you, too. Give my regards to Luz. Tell her I love her because she took you out to supper."

"Okay, Bubbe, I will."

"All right, darling. Bye bye."

Shayna hung up the phone and tiptoed back to the bedroom, but Luz was wide awake. "She okay?" Luz held the blankets back so Shayna could crawl into them.

"Luz, have I died and gone to heaven?" Shayna shrugged off her robe and burrowed into Luz's warm, sleepy body. "First of all, look who I get to wake up with." She un-burrowed herself to give Luz a kiss. "And second of all, Bubbe approves."

"She likes me?"

"Of course she likes you. What's not to like? She called to apologize for hurting my feelings."

"You mean about what she said about you being a lesbian?" Luz had heard a teary recap of Shayna and Tzeydl's conversation in the car on the way home.

"Yep. She says she doesn't care. She said I could sleep with a dog and she'd still love me."

"Hey!"

Shayna laughed. "I'm sure it was nothing personal. Anyway, she sends her regards and says to tell you she loves you because you took me out to supper."

"You see that?" Luz cradled Shayna in her arms. "Your grandma is a wise woman."

"Why, because she loves you?"

"No, because she loves you." Luz tapped Shayna on the nose. "She loves you, no matter what."

"Yeah, she does." Shayna smiled. "I hope I'll be as wise as she is when I'm ninety-nine."

Luz chuckled. "Can't you just see us sitting on the porch of the old dyke nursing home rocking in our lavender rocking chairs..."

"With some cute baby butch feeding us mashed tofu and bananas because we don't have any teeth." Shayna sighed with contentment, now that her future was all mapped out. "Wait a minute," she said, sitting up. "I dreamed about rocking chairs last night." Shayna narrowed her eyes as if she could see her dream in the distance. "I dreamed Bubbe and your mother were sitting in rocking chairs, drinking a cup of tea together."

"You dreamed about my mother?" Luz sat up, too.

"Yeah, she looked just like the picture on your dresser. They had their heads together, like they were having this really private conversation, but I couldn't hear what they were saying." Shayna lay her head on Luz's shoulder. "What do you think it means, Luz? Do you think my bubbe will die soon?"

Luz wrapped her arms around Shayna. "I don't know, baby. But she is ninety-nine."

"Yeah," Shayna said softly, "but I don't want her to die."

"I know you don't." Luz kissed Shayna's forehead.

Shayna rolled onto her back and stared up at the ceiling. "I just wish I could do more for Bubbe."

"You're doing an awful lot."

"But it's not enough."

Luz put her head next to Shayna's on the pillow and looked up at the ceiling, too. "You talk to her every day. And we'll visit her as much as we can."

"But she's going to die anyway." A fat tear leaked out of Shayna's eye, rolled down the side of her face and dribbled into her ear. "Maybe she'll die sooner, now that she knows I'm getting married. She said that was what she was waiting for, to dance at my wedding. Now she doesn't have to worry about me being all alone."

Luz turned Shayna sideways so she could see her. "Your happiness isn't going to kill her, Shayna. When the time comes, she'll just go a little easier, that's all."

"You really think so?"

"Yes."

Shayna studied Luz through her tears. "How'd you get to be such a wise woman? You're only forty-one."

Luz shrugged. "Search me."

"Ooh, I'd love to." Shayna ran her hands along Luz's body searching for clues to her wisdom.

"Umm." Luz sighed with pleasure, and then stopped Shayna's hands. "Unfortunately, this wise woman wasn't wise enough to call someone to fill in for me this morning, honeycakes. I gotta go open the store. What time is it?"

Shayna rolled over to look at the clock, and then rolled back. "Eight-thirty-something."

"Too bad. We should have woken up earlier."

"If we'd woken up any earlier, we wouldn't have gotten any sleep at all."

"So? I wouldn't complain." Luz kissed Shayna's cheek and hit a tear track. "Umm, salt for breakfast."

"Is that a hint? I'll make you breakfast."

"You better. I told your grandma I never leave home on an empty stomach."

"Leaving so soon?" Shayna knew Luz had to go to work, but she couldn't help pouting. "I didn't think you were the love 'em and leave 'em type."

"You bet." Luz gave Shayna a deep kiss. "It's been swell, babe, but I gotta be moving on."

"Don't you mean moving in?" Shayna sat up and leaned over the edge of the bed to gather up Luz's clothes from the floor, where they had been so hurriedly dropped the night before. "Here's your shirt."

"Thanks." Luz put her arm through the sleeve. "Sure, I'll move in. How about next Thursday?"

"Isn't that rushing it a bit? Hey Tzimmy get off." Shayna shrugged Tzimmy off her robe and tossed it on the bed.

"You're right. How about next Friday?"

"Okay." Shayna watched Luz buckle her belt. "No, seriously Luz."

"Seriously," Luz sat down next to Shayna and bent over to put on her shoes. "We've got the rest of our lives ahead of us. A year of living apart won't be so bad."

"A year!" Shayna's voice came out in a squeak.

"Well, I just renewed my lease last month," Luz said, tying a double bow in her sneaker. "And we want to find a really nice place, don't we?"

"Yeah, I guess so," Shayna said with a pout.

"Hey, cheer up. It'll just prolong our honeymoon period and give us a chance to get to know each other better."

"You're so logical." Shayna sighed with both admiration and annoyance, for she had planned on giving her landlord notice that very afternoon, the hell with her security deposit.

Luz finished tying her other sneaker. "Tell you what. Tomorrow first thing, I'll move in…" She paused, "…a jar of instant coffee. How's that?"

Shayna considered Luz's offer. "Well, it's a start anyway."

"You think you could pick up some sugar next time you go shopping, sugar?"

"White sugar I gotta keep in the house? Oy vey iss mir, the things we do for love."

Luz straightened up. "Did you say love?"

"L-O-V-E, love? As a matter of fact, I did."

"I love you, Shayna." Luz stood and pulled Shayna to her feet.

"I love you, Luz."

They hugged for a minute and then Luz stepped back. "Here." Luz took Shayna's robe from the bed and held it out. "Madame."

Shayna put her arms through the sleeves and tied the belt around her waist. "So, what do you want for breakfast; scrambled tofu, a whole wheat bagel…"

"You." Luz took a nibble of Shayna's neck. "Never mind. I'll just get something on the way. I gotta stop home, anyway. You just rest."

"All right." Shayna walked Luz to the door. "Oh, look, it's raining. What a lousy day."

"No, it's a great day. We're in love." Luz bent down to kiss Shayna. "See you later, doll face."

"Bye." Shayna stood in the doorway watching Luz trot down the steps, fold herself into her car, wave and drive off. She went back into the house and looked around. Now what? I feel like my life is on fast forward, Shayna thought. Everything's happening so quick.

She opened a can of tuna fish and dumped it into Tzimmy's bowl as a peace offering. Tzimmy, being no fool ate the tuna, but then refused to jump into Shayna's lap and retired to the living room instead.

"Well, you better get used to it," Shayna called from the kitchen. "She's not going away."

There was a tapping at the screen door. "Who's not going away?"

Shayna started. "Oh, Mrs. Mamelinski. You scared me."

"You were expecting maybe Lucy Lawless?" Pearl came in and tossed Shayna's spare key on the kitchen table. "So, nu, Mrs. Bubbelinski, want to play with me today?" She unzipped her raincoat and hung it in the bathroom over the shower. "Pearl's Girls Construction Crew is once again a washout. Hi, Tzimmy." At the sound of Pearl's voice, Tzimmy had galloped into the kitchen right over to Pearl, like she was her long lost lover. "Hello, kitty. How's my old girl?" Pearl bent down to pet Tzimmy, who was weaving in and out of her ankles, purring louder than a chain saw.

"I get the point, Tzimmy." Shayna put the tea kettle on. "She's just mad at me because Luz slept over last night, and her royal highness had to sleep on the floor."

"Luz slept over?" Pearl got out two mugs and teabags.

"Not only that." Shayna turned from the stove. "Notice anything different about me?"

"Let's see." Pearl surveyed Shayna from head to toe. "Your hair's the same. I know, you're not wearing any earrings."

"That's because I just woke up. Guess again."

"Turn around." Shayna revolved slowly and then faced Pearl with her right hand splayed across her chest.

"So you did your nails. Big deal. I always knew you were a femme's femme through and through."

"You're getting warmer, Mrs. Mamelinski." Shayna wiggled her fourth finger.

"Oh, wow, Shayna, is it real?" Pearl stepped forward for a closer inspection. "It's gorgeous. Did your bubbe give it to you?"

"You better sit down, Pearl." Shayna eased Pearl into a kitchen chair, poured hot water into their cups and sat down at the table. "Luz gave it to me. After she proposed in the parking lot. We're engaged."

"Engaged? You mean you're getting married?"

"Isn't that what being engaged usually means?"

192

Pearl stood up, folded her arms and spoke loudly. "Shayna P. Steinblatt," she boomed. "The voice of reason has arrived."

"Yikes." Shayna put her hands over her face, pretending to cower.

"No, seriously, Shayna." Pearl sat back down. "You can't marry this woman. You've only known her a few weeks. You haven't even done it yet."

All of a sudden, Shayna got very preoccupied with spooning some honey into her tea.

"Shayna," Pearl put her finger under Shayna's chin and lifted her face. "Ah-ha," she said, pointing to the blush on Shayna's cheeks. "So you have done it. How could you not tell me? I've been sitting in this house for five minutes already. So nu," Pearl tilted her head to the side, "how was it?"

"Pe—arl!"

"What, you're shy all of a sudden?" Pearl fished her teabag out of her cup, wrung it out and placed it on the table.

"No, I'm not shy. This is different, that's all."

"How different can it be? Now everything's gonna change because you're getting married."

"No it won't."

"Yes it will."

"You're still my best-est friend." Shayna put her feet up on Pearl's chair and snuggled her toes under Pearl's thigh. "I never told you all the gory details of my sex life before."

"Oh yeah? How else would I know about the whipped cream caper with what's-her-name from Arizona?"

Shayna waved her hand. "Oh, you must have read about it in the paper."

"Fat chance."

"Hey, did you know a fat chance and a slim chance are the same thing?" Shayna looked at Pearl. "Personally, I find that fascinating."

"No changing the subject, Ms." Pearl tweaked one of Shayna's toes. "Did you do everything?"

"Sixty-nine times. Each."

"Really? Who went first?"

"Pearl." Shayna slapped Pearl's leg lightly with her foot. "No details. You'll have to use your incredibly vivid imagination. Luz is a very private person."

"She's more important to you than I am." Pearl punctuated her sentence with a pout. "We used to tell each other everything."

"She is not. It's just different."

"Well, it shouldn't be."

"Well, it is." Shayna looked out the window. "I bet you'd still be in bed with Deb instead of over here if she didn't have to go to work."

"I would not."

"Bullshit."

"Well, all right, maybe I would, but I still would have come over later to check on you."

"We're still best friends, Pearl, don't worry." Shayna turned from the window. "We'll still spend lots of time together."

"Maybe I'm jealous," Pearl mumbled.

"Why, Pearl darling," Shayna batted her eyelashes. "I never knew you felt that way."

"Oh Shayna, Shayna, Shayna." Pearl threw herself at Shayna's feet and pretended to sob uncontrollably. Then she got up, dusted herself off and sat back in her chair. "I'm just maybe a teeny weeny bit jealous that you found someone to settle down with, that's all."

Shayna was surprised. "But Pearl, I thought you said you weren't the marrying kind."

"Well, yeah." Pearl studied her teacup. "But you know everyone dreams of finding her Princess Charming and living happily ever after. Some of us would just live happily non-monogamously ever after."

"Well, not us, thank the Goddess." Shayna took a sip of her tea. "That's one of the first things we talked about."

"But how do you know she's the right girl?"

"I don't know, I just feel it." Shayna watched Tzimmy jump up onto Pearl's lap, turn around three times and then lie down and immediately fall asleep. "It's just like that," she said, pointing to the cat. "As soon as I said yes, I felt all peaceful inside, like I could finally stop running around in circles. You know, I was pretty happy the last nine months by myself. Well, up to the last few weeks anyway, but then it wasn't like I needed to be in a relationship, I wanted to be in one. You know, Pearl, as Bubbe so kindly pointed out to me, eppes, I ain't getting any younger. Maybe there's someone else out there for me, but Luz is here now, and that's what matters. From the first minute she wasn't afraid to show me how she felt about me."

Pearl shook her head. "The way to a femme's heart is always flowers. Gets 'em every time."

"No, it's not just the flowers, Pearl." Shayna looked into her friend's eyes. "She was just so open and vulnerable with me. I just feel like I've known her forever. It feels right and I'm ready to make the commitment. It doesn't feel binding at all. Actually I feel really free." Pearl still didn't look convinced. "Listen, don't worry. We're not moving in together for a year, or until we've had four fights, whichever comes first. See, we're not rushing into anything."

"Well, that's a big relief," Pearl said, rolling her eyes. "I feel so much better now."

"No, really Pearl." Shayna grasped Pearl's arm. "Listen, I know it sounds weird and believe me if one day out of the blue you told me you were getting married, I'd probably rush you to the emergency room for a CAT scan."

Pearl smiled. "Thanks. It's good to know I can count on you."

"I mean, I know this doesn't make sense logically," Shayna went on, "but both of us feel ready to settle down and that we won't find anyone better than each other."

"Oy, Shaynala, already you're talking in 'we'?" Pearl shook her head. "You are gone."

"Pearlie, here," Shayna pointed to her heart, "is more important than here."
She pointed to her head. "Bubbe taught me that. When I told Bubbe about it, she
ranted and raved for a while, but she came around."

Pearl shook her head. "You told your bubbe you were getting married?"
Pearl's eyes widened. "To a woman?"

Shayna filled her in on all the details. "And now I feel whole. I can be my lovable dyke self and still have my family. Well, my bubbe at least. I'm even kind of
getting used to being called Linda."

"So your bubbe approves, even though Luz isn't Jewish?"

"Yeah, it doesn't seem to matter to her."

Pearl sat forward. "And to you?"

"Well, I hate to admit you were right, Mrs. Mamelinski," Shayna wagged her
finger at Pearl, "but remember what you said about sharing our cultures?"

"Yeah."

"Well, we're going to have a Jewish wedding and a Puerto Rican honeymoon."

"Wow." Pearl leaned back in her chair. "Maybe I'll sew your huppa. Or at
least make the poles."

"That would be great."

"Lucky you, going to Puerto Rico," Pearl said. "Can I come?"

Shayna frowned at Pearl. "No way. This is our honeymoon."

"But you need a chaperone; oh never mind, you've done it already. Hey, I
thought this wasn't about S-E-X."

"Ah, S-E-X." Shayna's eyes glazed over with fond memories of a few hours
ago. "Well, we didn't mean to do it. I mean, we got back here and I didn't want
her to go home, so we got into bed with our pajamas on…"

"And the next thing you knew, your tit was in her mouth."

"Exactly."

"Death is a very sexy thing," Pearl said. "I mean your bubbe's not dead, but
she's starting her process about it."

Shayna sipped her tea. "Yeah, she talks about not having much time left."

"When Bobbi's sister was dying of cancer, she was jumping me every night."

"Pearl Gold, don't be so crass."

"Well, it's true."

Shayna picked up her spoon and started playing with it. "I wonder why."

"Well, pardon me for being so philosophical," Pearl stared at Shayna's spoon
which was balanced up on its edge, "but sex reaffirms life, which is what you want
when someone's dying." Pearl paused, looking at Shayna. "Hey, you're not marrying Luz to replace your bubbe, are you?"

"Pearl." Shayna shook her head. "They're hardly interchangeable."

"I know. But I mean so you'll still have family."

"Listen, I know this is hard for you to believe, because it's even a bissl hard for
me to believe, but this is what I've always wanted. We really fell in love at first sight,
and we're really getting married, and it's really going to be just fine. I know it."

Pearl put her hand on Shayna's arm. "I just don't want you to get hurt,

Shayna. That's all"

"Thanks Pearl." Shayna covered Pearl's hand with her own. "I won't. Really."

"Well, if you do, I'll be here to pick up the pieces." Pearl looked out the window at the rain, which was still falling steadily. "Hey, how about a little mall adventure?"

"On a Monday? I was going to look over my lesson plans." Shayna looked out the window, too. It was a perfect day for malling, but shopping on a Monday seemed so decadent.

"Don't try to fool me, Mrs. Bubbelinski. You could teach those classes with your eyes closed and one hand tied behind your back. What is this, your sixth year teaching summer school?" Pearl stood up. "C'mon. We gotta start working on your trousseau."

"Well, when you put it that way." Shayna got up, too and put their cups in the sink. "Pearl, will you be my dyke of honor?"

"I thought you'd never ask." Pearl followed Shayna into the bedroom. "Are you gonna invite your bubbe?"

"I don't think so. She's too old to travel this far."

"What about your parents?"

"Hell, no." Shayna opened her top drawer and pulled out a pair of purple silk bikini underpants. "You know how impossible my mother is. I told her I was dating someone and she got mad for even mentioning it since she has so much else to worry about."

Pearl pulled the blankets up on Shayna's bed with exaggerated modesty and delicately placed her tuchus on top of them. "So things haven't improved much on the Sylvia front?"

Shayna shook her head and slipped her arms through the straps of a black lace bra. "You know, Bubbe really is getting old. I can almost understand my mother putting her in a nursing home, but I'll never forgive her for the way she did it."

"Do you think if she'd given her the choice, your bubbe would have gone?"

"No. I don't know." Shayna fished a lavender cotton sweater out of her drawer and pulled it over her head.

"No good," Pearl said. "Your bra shows through."

"It's so much work being a girl." Shayna took off her sweater and replaced her black brassiere with a beige bra. "Sylvia could have gotten her a live-in nurse. Or moved her to some kind of senior housing complex. Or had her move in with them. They've got plenty of room. My bedroom's been empty for twelve years."

"Tzimmy, c'mon." Pearl patted the bed and Tzimmy jumped up and snuggled beside her. "Shayna, if something happened to your mother and she couldn't take care of herself, would you have her move in with you?"

"Goddess forbid." Shayna disappeared into her closet and came out with a pair of dark purple pants. "Does this clash?"

"We're only going to the mall."

"Yeah, but a girl's gotta keep up appearances. Maybe black pants would be better."

"Shayna." Pearl tapped her foot. "You're changing the subject."

"I am?" Shayna asked, all innocence. "Gee, I wonder where I learned to do that." Shayna sat down on the bed and stuck her feet through her pants legs. "I'd just like my mother to see what it's like to live in a tiny room and eat overcooked food with a plastic fork and not be able to go anywhere." Shayna stood up and zipped her pants. "You think she wouldn't carry on? Believe me, Sylvia Steinblatt would scream and holler plenty, and it would serve her right."

"Ooh, vicious." Pearl thought for a minute. "I think I know what the real problem is, Shayna."

"What?" Shayna was busy rummaging around in her jewelry for the perfect pair of earrings.

"I think you're mad at your mother because your bubbe is getting ready to die."

Shayna continued her search. "What are you talking about, Pearl?"

"I know you're mad at your mother for how she handled things, and don't get me wrong, you have every right to be." Pearl spoke to Shayna's back. "But beyond that, I think you're really pissed that your bubbe is getting to the end of her life and there's nothing you can do about it. So who do you blame? Your mother. I mean, besides the fact that she's your mother and she's to blame for everything." Pearl folded her arms. "She was the first one to do something tangible that acknowledged the fact that your bubbe's getting old. She put her in a nursing home, and you hate that."

"Oh Goddess." Shayna had stopped sorting through her earring collection as Pearl spoke, listening to what she hated to admit had more than a grain of truth to it. Now she came to sit on the bed next to Pearl with a pair of purple sea shell earrings in her hand. "I hate to say this, Pearl, but you're on to something. Maybe you should give up construction and go into therapy." She stuck an earring into her ear. "And you know, I think Bubbe's mad for the same reason. She can't do anything about getting old, and my mother putting her in the nursing home is just a reminder of that." She stuck her other earring in. "You know, Bubbe could go home if she really wanted to. She knows the bus routes in Brooklyn, or she could sneak out of there and call a cab. The super would let her in, her name's still on the lease." Shayna shook her head. "I think, deep down, she knows she has to be there, and she hates that, so she blames my mother."

"Mothers always get the shit end of the stick," Pearl said.

"Mothers and daughters." Shayna pulled on a pair of lavender socks and sat on the bed to put on her shoes. "Maybe I have been too rough on Sylvia. Nah," she said, tying her shoelaces. "I still say she could have done it differently. She could have brought Bubbe to Vey Iss Mir to live with them." She reached over Pearl to get her hairbrush from the night table.

"Would you live with your mother?" Pearl asked again. "Here, let me do it. Turn around." She took the hairbrush from Shayna and started brushing.

"My mother would drive me nuts, are you kidding? And anyway, I'm a dyke."

"So? Maybe your bubbe would drive your mother nuts, too. And," Pearl lifted Shayna's hair to brush the tangled underneath part, "since when have lesbians cornered the market on mother/daughter conflict?"

"I don't know, Pearl." Shayna leaned forward so her hair fanned out flat against her back. "But Sylvia really could have taken her in. She's got nothing better to do. She just sits around all day."

"How do you know?" Pearl stopped mid-stroke. "Maybe she's got a secret life you don't even know about."

"The secret life of Sylvia Steinblatt." Now Shayna was intrigued. "Maybe she's a numbers runner. Maybe she's an F.B.I. agent. Maybe she's an international spy." Shayna picked up Tzimmy, who had finally forgiven her, and petted the cat's back in time with the strokes of the hairbrush. "All right, maybe she does have a life. But I'm still mad at her. I don't know if she did the right thing or not. Did I tell you Bubbe's neighbor Tillie got mugged?"

"The one that made you breakfast and sent you home with that delicious mandelbrot? That's awful."

Shayna told Pearl the whole story. "So I can see why Sylvia got her out of that neighborhood, it really isn't the safest place in the world. But I hate how she's always saying that Bubbe is crazy. I guess she had to convince herself that Bubbe's lost it, to ease her guilt. And then Bubbe has to convince herself that Sylvia's crazy, or else she can't understand how her daughter could dump her into a nursing home full of strangers. And I'm in the middle of it. The two of them won't even talk to each other."

"That's sad." Pearl put the hairbrush down. "Want a french braid?"

"Sure."

Pearl ran her fingers through Shayna's hair, dividing it into sections. "So, you think you can forgive your mother?"

"I don't know. I can't imagine saying I'm so-so-sorry to her." Shayna practiced trying to get the word out. "But maybe I'll try to be a little nicer to her."

"Turn your head a little."

"Oh, but it's so complicated," Shayna said, as if turning her head made her see the other side of the story. "Then the whole lesbian issue comes up and she's just impossible. How can I be nice to her if she hates who I am?"

"Well, that certainly is a challenge," Pearl said, weaving Shayna's hair. "But someone's gotta make a friendly move here, and it sure ain't gonna be your mother. How old is she?"

"Sixty-one."

"So, she's a sixty-one year old little girl losing her mommy."

"Wow, what a concept." Shayna tried to visualize her mother as a little girl, but even though she had seen pictures, it was impossible. "Well, she could try a little harder to accept me. She's known about me being a lesbian for eight years already. I told Bubbe and she came around in less than twenty-four hours."

"Your bubbe must have had your mother late in life," Pearl said, obviously doing some quick arithmetic in her head.

Shayna saved her the trouble. "She was thirty-eight. She calls Sylvia her change of life baby."

"Did they always fight like this?"

"Oh, no." Shayna shook her head and Pearl tightened her grip on Shayna's hair. "Woah, Nellie."

"Sorry." Shayna held her head still. "Bubbe and Sylvia always got along okay, I guess. Bubbe's so emotional, though. Maybe Sylvia keeps everything on the surface as her way of rebelling. And then, I'm just like Bubbe, letting it all hang out."

"The old skipping a generation theory." Pearl patted Shayna on the keppie. "Go look at your hair."

"Nice." Shayna turned this way and that in front of her bedroom mirror, admiring herself. "Forget construction and therapy. Maybe you should be a hairdresser."

"Arf, arf."

"What's that?" Pearl and Shayna looked at each other and Tzimmy's ears swiveled back and flattened out against her head.

"Arf, arf."

"Is there a dog in here?" Shayna walked swiftly through the apartment into the kitchen where Luz stood, holding a bouquet of flowers. "Arf, arf," Luz barked again. "It's the dog your grandma doesn't mind you sleeping with." Luz handed Shayna three red roses and a sprig of baby's breath.

"Hey, don't you call my fiancé a dog." Shayna took the roses and gave Luz a kiss. "Umm. Smell." She extended the flowers to Pearl, who had followed her, and then turned back to Luz. "Just in time. The roses you brought me last week are all droopy."

"Let me see them."

"I hear congratulations are in order," Pearl said. "Mazel tov."

"Yep." Shayna came out of the living room with a carafe of sad looking white roses. "She snatched me up when I wasn't even looking."

"Women like you don't have to look." Luz took the flowers while Shayna beamed. "You got something flat I can lie these in?"

"Let me see." Shayna disappeared into the pantry. "How about a shoebox?"

"No, I have to fill it with water."

"Wait a minute." Shayna emerged holding a rusty bread pan. "How's this?"

"Pathetic."

"Okay, hang on." Shayna rummaged some more until she found a square casserole dish she'd never used. "How's this?"

"Perfect." Luz ran the water and trimmed the stems of the white roses. She filled the casserole dish and floated the flowers gently in it. "Leave 'em there for three hours and they'll be as good as new. In the meantime," she cut the new roses to size and arranged them in the carafe, "you'll have these."

"Thanks." Shayna looked from the roses to Luz. "You on your lunch break?"

"Yeah. I was on my way to get a bite, but first I had to see my girl."

"I can't believe it's lunch time already." Shayna looked at the clock. "Time went so fast this morning. When we were with Bubbe," Shayna said to Pearl, "it was like everything moved in slow motion."

"You still sad?" Luz put her arm around Shayna.

"A little. But Pearl's taking me to the mall, so that should do the trick. Need anything?"

"Nope." Luz looked at her watch. "I gotta run. Call me at the store later and I'll pick something up for supper."

"Okay." Shayna lifted her face for Luz's kiss.

"Bye. Bye, Pearl. Make sure she eats something." Another quick kiss and Luz was gone.

"Think we can clone her?" Pearl asked, leaning over to smell the flowers. "You've gotten more roses in the past few weeks than I have in my entire adult life."

"Pearl, I've told you a hundred million billion times not to exaggerate."

"'I'll pick up something for supper.' You two sound like you're married already. I have to admit, though, it does look good on you."

Shayna was still standing where Luz had left her, a dorky smile plastered across her face. "Yeah, this feels like IT all right." Shayna went into the pantry to look for an umbrella while Pearl put on her raincoat. "I think this one works." She came out with an umbrella covered in a newspaper motif.

"Don't open it in the house, it's bad luck."

"Okay. Let's go."

"Should we go to a bridal shop?"

"Pearl, are you kidding?" Shayna got her shoulder bag from the pile of stuff she and Luz had shlepped up from the car last night. "I'm not going to wear a long white dress."

"Well, what then?"

"I don't know yet. Let's see what's around."

"Well, remember the bride is the picture and the butch is the frame." Pearl held the door open for Shayna.

"Ooh, I like that." Shayna checked the door to make sure it was locked behind them.

"I think I read it in Vogue," Pearl said.

"Did it really say the butch?" Shayna opened her umbrella, which promptly turned itself inside out. "Oh, bother."

"C'mon, I'm getting soaked." Pearl grabbed Shayna's hand and hooked it through her arm. "Here comes the bride, here comes the bride," she sang as she escorted the lovely bride-to-be down the steps, into her waiting car.

Chapter Seventeen

The summer passed quickly with Shayna grading papers, writing a few articles, keeping her apartment fairly clean, and spending most of her waking hours (not to mention her sleeping ones) with Luz. They spent lots of time tending Luz's flower garden, going for long walks in the moonlight and cheering on Pearl's softball team. Shayna became quite fascinated with the art of photography, especially since Luz's favorite new subject to click pix of was none other than our ace reporter herself. Shayna could now pour over pictures of herself sitting at her desk writing, standing at the stove in one of Luz's T-shirts making coffee, and even lying in bed in an x-rated pose. They spent hours hanging out at each other's apartments, talking, talking, talking. And smooching of course. They talked about the wedding, which they decided would happen a year from that fall, and they talked about living together and decided to look for a place in the spring. They'd even had their first fight, which wasn't a heavy duty processing marathon about their cultural differences, as Shayna was afraid it would be. No, rather as Luz predicted, their fight was about something incredibly stupid: which way the toilet paper should go in the holder. Shayna liked to pull the paper from over the top, and Luz preferred it to come from underneath. Of course, being the good dykes they were, they decided, after an hour of discussing the pros and cons of both options, to alternate with each TP refill, and Shayna graciously volunteered to keep track. Shayna, who had started the argument, and who had come up with such classic lines as "It's my house, I get to have the toilet paper go the way I want," was somewhat embarrassed by the whole thing. "You won't hold it against me?" she asked Luz when the fight was over. "No, I'll hold you against me," Luz replied, and then they proceeded to make up for about four hours. Afterwards they'd gone out to celebrate their first fight ("One down and three to go," Shayna said, a note of triumph in her voice, which made Luz wonder if she'd staged the whole thing on purpose) with a romantic dinner, complete with a bottle of pink champagne.

The summer days flew by (Shayna never could understand how June, July, and August could disappear in the wink of an eye, while January, February and March dragged on for a century) and then before she could turn around and say, "Happy Year, Nu?" fall was in the air and Rosh Hashannah had arrived.

Of course Shayna was going to ring in the new year with her bubbe. She felt a little guilty that she hadn't seen Tzeydl as much as she'd wanted to that summer, but somehow the time had gotten away from her. They'd talked on the phone everyday and Shayna had managed to get down to Brooklyn four times, twice with Luz and twice by herself. Luz had brought her camera and taken some great shots of Shayna and Tzeydl: standing together outside the nursing home, taking a walk, and sitting on a wooden bench on the pier. Luz had taken a few shots of Tzeydl by her lonesome, and had even shown Tzeydl how to use the camera, though, of course, it had taken some effort to convince her to try it.

"Just look through here…" Luz held the camera in front of her pointing the lens at Shayna who smiled and waved, "…and press this button."

Tzeydl took one picture and then waved the camera away. "I don't want I should break it," she said. "One is plenty." And in this case she was absolutely right, for that picture was Shayna's all-time favorite photo of herself.

"She really captured me," Shayna said, studying the print with Luz.

"That's because when she looks at you, her eyes are full of love." Luz looked from the picture of Shayna to the real thing. "And your eyes are full of love for her. It's like she was looking in the mirror."

Luz helped Shayna frame the picture and wrap it up to send to Tzeydl. "Let's send one to your mother, too," Luz suggested, and Shayna reluctantly consented even though she suspected Sylvia would either hide it in the attic, or set it up in the basement to use as a dart board for target practice.

Shayna packed up other presents to send to Tzeydl too: a necklace made of seashells from Cape Cod; a pair of terry cloth slippers and a new bathrobe; a silk scarf to wear around her neck. But no matter how much she did, it still didn't seem like enough (though, as Luz pointed out, nothing short of moving into Rosenbaum Estate would seem like enough). Shayna wanted to give Tzeydl the world, including the moon, the stars, the sun and her youth, but clothing and a few choice tchotchkes would have to do.

Shayna threw her bags into the back of her car and carefully placed an autumn bouquet of mums and golden asters in the front. The flowers were Luz's new year's present to Tzeydl. She had brought them over last night, each stem encased in its own tiny tube of water.

Tzeydl had grown very fond of Luz during the summer. A few times when Tzeydl called Shayna and she was busy with something, Luz had answered the phone and talked to Tzeydl for a good twenty minutes before putting down the receiver and telling Shayna that her grandma was on the line. Tzeydl ended each and every conversation with Shayna in the same way: "I love you, Linda. Give my regards to Luz. Tell her I love her, too." Unlike Sylvia, who still couldn't bear to even say the woman's name.

Shayna pulled out of the driveway and headed for the highway. She had tried being nicer to her mother over the summer by sending her presents as well: a whale magnet from Cape Cod to add to her refrigerator magnet collection, and a mug that said EVERY MOTHER IS A WORKING MOTHER. Shayna had called once or twice, and they got along just fine, as long as she didn't mention the B word (Bubbe) or the L word (Luz). Which didn't leave them all that much to talk about.

Mrs. Steinblatt had been to Rosenbaum Estate twice that summer. She'd had a private telephone installed in Tzeydl's room and brought her a new color TV ("Such a fancy-shmancy television your parents bought for me," Tzeydl told Shayna. "All right, your father's a rich man, he ain't gonna mortgage his teeth.")

Mrs. Steinblatt had put venetian blinds in the window at Tzeydl's request, as well as a new bureau and a comfortable chair. But for all her interior decorating, Mrs. Steinblatt was far from earning her mother's (and therefore her daughter's) forgiveness.

Shayna could still hear the conversation she'd had with Sylvia on the phone earlier that week, after her second summer visit to the nursing home. "Your grandmother yells at me so," Mrs. Steinblatt said, "I get a headache the minute we walk in there. I bring her a present; a skirt, a blouse, a sweater, but does she appreciate it? No. She barely looks at it. I try to stay calm, to talk about the family, the people in the neighborhood, the weather, anything to take her mind off it. But once she starts in on me, she's like a broken record: 'Why am I in here? What did I do? Why can't I go home?' And what am I supposed to tell her, Linda? If only she would accept it, she's so stubborn, your grandmother, it's been five months already, then we could go out to lunch, for a ride, you know, have a nice time. But no, she just spoils it for herself. I can't sit in traffic for over an hour just to get there and be yelled at. And it's no good for her either, she only aggravates herself, and I'm afraid something shouldn't happen, especially since she's too stubborn to take her pills. And your father, he can't take it; this is not for his nerves, believe me. So what can we do, except turn around and go home?"

And a few minutes later, Tzeydl had called with her side of the story: "Your mother comes to see me and she stays maybe five minutes, such a hurry she's always in, eppes. And as soon as I open my mouth, she says it's enough already, we'll talk about it later. Linda, tell me, how much later have I got? Presents she brings me, a new shmate I need like a loch in kop, so many beautiful clothes I got at home. If only she'd say she was sorry, I'd forgive her already, but no, so stubborn she is, your mother, she won't even talk about it. So what should I do, sit there and talk about this one's children and that one's grandchildren, when all the while my heart is hurting me so..."

Shayna had called her mother back begging her to apologize to Tzeydl. "Please, Sylvia, it would mean so much to her, and it would make things so much easier. Just say you're sorry, even if you don't mean it."

But Mrs. Steinblatt wouldn't budge. "Say I'm sorry? Sorry for what? For taking such good care of my mother in her old age, a private room she's got with three meals a day and an army of doctors and nurses to wait on her hand and foot? I'm not sorry. I have nothing to be sorry for." It had been an exhausting morning, but luckily Luz was there to kiss away Shayna's tears, coax a smile out of her, and make sure she ate a little breakfast.

Luz. Shayna took her eyes off the road for a minute, to glance at the picture of her beloved, which she had put in a magnetized frame and stuck to the dashboard. They had had apples and honey for breakfast that morning so they'd have a sweet new year together. Luz had offered to come with Shayna, but the holiday was during the week and Shayna didn't want Luz to close the store on her account. And besides, Sylvia and Sol would surely visit Tzeydl for Rosh Hashannah and Shayna didn't think she was quite ready to have Luz meet the family yet. Shayna had been sure Sylvia wasn't looking forward to that fateful day either, because she had managed to avoid running into her daughter each time she had ventured down to Rosenbaum Estate. Not that Shayna had extended a golden invitation to her mother, mind you, but Tzeydl had.

"I just got off the phone with your mother," Tzeydl had said, on Shayna's last visit, after kissing her hello. "I told her she should come over; she's all alone in the house; your father works a whole day Saturday; she could be with her mother and her daughter and her daughter's friend. What could be better? But she got things to do, she says. What things? What could be more important than the family?"

Shayna turned on the car radio to drown out all these instant replay conversations going on inside her head. She found a good oldies station, and sang along with the Supremes, Aretha Franklin, and Patti La Belle at the top of her lungs until she got to the nursing home.

Tzeydl was in her room, waiting, her pocketbook on her lap. "Hello darling. How was your trip? What have you got there?"

"Hi, Bubbe." Shayna kissed Tzeydl's cheek. "There was hardly any traffic. Look, these are from Luz, from her store."

"Oh ain't they gorgeous, so many flowers." Tzeydl took the bouquet and looked around. "Where will I put them?"

"You don't have a vase?"

"A vase, where would I get a vase? At home I got so many vases, a green one, a white one... All right, maybe from the nurse I can get something."

"I'll go ask her."

"You sit. You're tired from your trip." Tzeydl pointed to the bed.

"I'm not tired, Bubbe."

"You wanna call your girlfriend?"

"Can I?"

"Sure, go on. Tell her you got here safe, she shouldn't worry. And thank her for the flowers. I'll go ask the nurse."

Shayna sat down and dialed the number to Petal Pushers. Luz was out on a delivery, so Shayna left a message.

As she hung up, Tzeydl came back into the room, carrying a styrofoam pitcher. "That's the best she could do," Tzeydl said, bringing the pitcher over to the sink.

"I'll take you shopping, I'll buy you a vase. Here, let me do that."

Tzeydl was futzing with the small tubes stuck on the flower stems, emptying them into the sink and saving them in a pile on top of her dresser, for Goddess only knew what purpose. "You rest, you're tired. We'll eat lunch and then you can take me shopping. I wanna get something for the nurses; I try to tip them a dollar for giving me a bath, for doing my nails, but they won't take it. They say they ain't allowed. And for the rabbi I want to get something too, for the holiday. Look what he did for me." She pointed to the door.

"What?" Shayna got up and looked at the door. "Oh, he put up a mezzuzah for you. That's nice." She touched the shiny brass mezzuzah decorated with Hebrew letters hanging on a slant in the doorway.

"He blessed the room and everything. Last week he came, he said I should have a happy new year and a healthy new year and many, many more. More years I need? I ain't lived long enough already?" Tzeydl sighed and turned from the sink with the pitcher of flowers in her hands. "All right, how long I live ain't for me to decide. Where should I put these?"

Shayna looked around. "How about on your dresser?"

"All right." Tzeydl moved aside some cards and some pictures. "This is from your mother and father," she said, holding up a card. "This is from your Uncle Ira. And this is from your cousin Abbie, she sent a card, too."

"So, what do you want to buy for the nurses and the rabbi?" Shayna asked, after dutifully reading the cards.

"The nurses I'll get a bag of candy. They gotta take that, for their children it is, I'll tell them. And the rabbi…" Tzeydl sat down on the bed across the room from Shayna, "…him, I don't know. Some handkerchiefs, maybe? A tie? What do you think, Linda, you know better than me."

"I know better? Bubbe, I never bought a rabbi a present in my life."

"Maybe clothes is too personal, he shouldn't get the wrong idea." Tzeydl thought a minute. "Maybe a bottle of wine for the holiday?"

Shayna turned from the picture of herself and Luz she was admiring on Tzeydl's dresser. "That sounds good."

Tzeydl wasn't sure. "He won't think I'm a shikker?"

Shayna laughed. "I don't know, Bubbe, how's your reputation?"

"My reputation?" Tzeydl laughed, too. "Well, you know me, such a big drinker I am, hoo-hah. Here they don't give you no wine, even if you ask for it. Grape juice they give you in the dining room. Come," Tzeydl got up, "let's go down for lunch."

"Okay." Shayna got her bag from the back of Tzeydl's chair.

"No, wait a minute, your mother wants we should call her."

"Did you talk to her?"

"No, she called when I was at breakfast, and a nurse took the message. She probably wants to tell us what time she's coming tomorrow." Tzeydl sat down on the bed. "Give your mother a call, Linda."

"Okay." Shayna picked up the receiver with a sigh. Sometimes, especially recently, she found herself wishing that Alexander Graham Bell had never invented the telephone. Nevertheless, she dialed and waited for her mother to pick up the phone.

"Hello?"

"Hi, Sylvia, it's your daughter."

"Linda, where are you?"

"I'm at Bubbe's. What time are you coming tomorrow?"

"Coming? We can't come, Linda, you know that. We can't ride in the car on Rosh Hashannah."

She had to be kidding. Since when had they gotten so religious? "Sylvia," Shayna said, making a gallant effort at keeping her voice steady. "I don't think God would judge you for riding in the car so you could be with Bubbe on Rosh Hashannah."

"My daughter, the religious expert. Since when are you an authority on the judgment of God?"

"Sylvia." Shayna shook her head. Obviously this wasn't going to be one of their better conversations. "Bubbe shouldn't be alone on the holiday."

"She isn't alone. She's with her favorite granddaughter. With me, she'll only get aggravated; with you at least she'll enjoy the holiday." Was that a note of bitterness in Sylvia's voice, a note of jealousy perhaps? Whatever it was, it disappeared as fast as it had come. "Linda," Mrs. Steinblatt said in a friendlier voice, "let's not start, all right? I want you to do me a favor."

"What?" Shayna asked, a little warily. She couldn't remember her mother ever asking her to do her a favor before.

"Listen, I talked to the social worker the other day, and he's not pleased with your grandmother's progress. He says by this time she should be doing more activities, socializing more. Once in a while if a volunteer brings her down, she'll participate, he says, but she's still very depressed. She isn't making the adjustment."

This was news? "So?"

"So I want you to tell her we're giving up the apartment."

"You're giving up the apartment?" Shayna's voice rose to a shrill pitch and dropped to a soft whisper at the same time.

"Now don't get excited, Linda. I didn't say we gave up the apartment, I'm just asking you to tell her that we did."

"Why?" Shayna glanced at Tzeydl, who was staring at her intently, and then looked away.

"Because maybe that way she'll get it into her head that she lives at Rosenbaum Estate. That's it, it's done, finished, period. Then maybe she'll stop hocking me to take her home, since there'll be no home to go to, and I can have a little peace."

"Oy, Sylvia." Shayna let out a deep breath, "Do me a favor."

"What?"

"Don't ask me to do you any favors."

"Linda."

"Sylvia, I can't lie to Bubbe. You know that." Shayna spoke in a frantic whisper. "Where would I tell her I sleep?"

"Tell her you sleep by me."

Yeah, and if she believes that one, I'll sell her the Brooklyn Bridge. "Sorry, Sylvia, I can't do it."

"Linda, it would be for her own good."

That's what you think, Shayna thought, but she knew better than to say it. "Is that what the social worker said?" Not that it mattered, really, but Shayna was curious.

"He said we should try to talk to her about it, and get her to give us permis-

206

sion to let it go, but what does he know? Your grandmother would never agree to it, and it would only upset her."

"She's upset anyway, Sylvia, maybe you should talk to her about it. She doesn't understand why you keep it anyway."

"I keep it because I can only cope with one thing at a time. Your grandmother never throws anything away, there's a lifetime of chazzeri up there, who's gonna go through all that junk?"

I'll give you three guesses, Shayna thought, and the first two don't count.

There was a pause, and then Mrs. Steinblatt added, "And I keep it for you, you should have a place to sleep when you come."

"You do?" Shayna was stunned, and her voice evidently gave her away, for her mother said softly, "Don't be so surprised. I ain't a hundred percent rotten, you know."

"I never said you were." Thought so maybe, but never said so. "Thanks, Sylvia."

"You're welcome. Now think about what I said, Linda, she would take it better if she heard it from you. Did she get our card?"

Shayna looked toward the bureau. "Yeah, she put it on her dresser, next to the picture of me and Luz I sent her. Did she show it to you?"

"The picture in the round frame?"

"Yeah."

"The one she keeps on the dresser next to her sewing box?"

"Yeah, that one."

"No, that picture I didn't see. Listen, Linda," Mrs. Steinblatt didn't pause for air. "Think about what I said, and put your grandmother on the phone for a minute. I want to wish her a happy new year."

"Okay, hang on." Shayna put down the phone and gestured to Tzeydl. "She wants to talk to you."

"Me she wants to talk to?" Tzeydl got up from the bed and picked up the receiver. "Hello?"

Shayna crossed the room to smell the bouquet she had brought from home, but her nose barely had a chance to graze the petals before Tzeydl started screaming into the phone, her voice pitched higher than Shayna had ever heard it.

"Happy New Year? You want I should be happy? How can I be happy in a home with all crazy people? Why did you bring me here, Sylvia? How could a daughter do such a thing to her own mother? Was I a bother to you? So much trouble I was, you had to get rid of me so fast? I was in your way, takeh, I was such a bother?" She paused for a split second, just long enough for Sylvia to get in one sentence no doubt, before she was off again, her voice even shriller. "Better for me? Since when does a daughter know what's better for a mother? What would be better would be if I was in my own house with my own things. Why can't I go home, Sylvia, I committed some kind of crime?"

Sylvia's answer was cut short with the the continuation of Tzeydl's tirade. "So, if I didn't commit no crime, why can't I go back to the apartment? What are you up to with the super there, with the wires on the fire escape? That super is no good, Sylvia, you should never have gotten mixed up with him, he made you crazy, eppes, you don't even know to listen to your own mother anymore, what's the matter with you?" She paused again and then all the life went out of her voice. "All right. Go."

"What happened?" Shayna came up behind Tzeydl, took the receiver she was still holding in her hand, and returned it to its cradle.

"Someone was ringing the bell, she said, she had to go answer it. Did she tell you what time she was coming?"

Shayna shook her head. "She isn't coming, Bubbe. She says they can't travel on the holiday."

"No?" Tzeydl didn't seem surprised. "Well then, that's the end of it. You see, you're the only one that still cares about her old bubbe. Come, let's go eat." Tzeydl picked up her pocketbook. "I need a sweater?"

"No, Bubbe, it's gorgeous out. It feels more like July than September. You want to go out for lunch? Come, we'll take a little walk."

"Walk? Sure, if I still remember how, we'll take a walk. At home I'd take a walk on the avenue everyday, you remember, but since I been in here..." She paused to look at herself in the mirror over the sink. "I look all right?"

"Yeah, you look great. When did you get your hair done?"

"Yesterday, for the holiday, you should have seen how busy it was down there, I'm telling you, everybody and her mother only wanted to get their hair done and a manicure. All right, come." Tzeydl turned from the mirror and took Shayna's arm. They took the elevator down and went out the front door.

"Let's go this way." Shayna steered Tzeydl to the left. "I'm pretty sure there's a diner on the next block." They made their way slowly up the street. When they got to the curb, Tzeydl stopped.

"You okay?" Shayna asked.

"It's nothing. I'm a little dizzy, eppes, that's all."

Dizzy? They hadn't even walked half a block. "Are you sure you're okay, Bubbe? Maybe we should go back."

Tzeydl waved her hand. "I'm all right, come. I'm not used to such a big walk, that's all."

They made their way up one more block and into the diner where they sat at a little table near the window.

"What do you want to eat, Bubbe?" Shayna asked.

Tzeydl shrugged. "Today I ain't so hungry, Linda. Take whatever you want."

The waitress brought their menus and Shayna tried to coax Tzeydl to eat something, as Tzeydl had coaxed Shayna so many times before. "Bubbe, want to split a sandwich with me? Or how about a bowl of soup? You want a hot dog maybe?"

"I don't want nothing, Linda."

"What about a knish?"

"Today I ain't got no appetite, eppes, but you take something."

"How about a cup of coffee at least?"

"No, I don't want no coffee."

No coffee? This was serious. Shayna studied the menu, taking periodic peeks at Tzeydl. She looked okay. Maybe she was just tired, but still she should eat something. Shayna read the list of appetizers, but the words blurred on the page, as an old Jewish saying she had read somewhere leapt to her mind: *when a father helps a son, both smile; when a son must help a father, both weep.* It must be true for grandmothers and granddaughters too, Shayna thought, or at least half true, for she couldn't tell if Tzeydl was crying, but she sure was. She closed her menu, wiped her eyes and pulled herself together, ordering and forcing herself to eat three blintzes, which she assured Tzeydl were nowhere near as good as hers.

The waitress came to clear her plate. "Anything else?"

"You want some dessert, Linda?" Tzeydl asked.

"No thanks, Bubbe."

"Take something, darling. Three blintzes ain't enough lunch for you."

"We got very good diet cheesecake today," the waitress said, turning toward the revolving glass dessert case up near the cash register. "With low calorie strawberry topping."

Diet cheesecake? Why bother? That sounded even worse than the tofu cheesecake Shayna pretended to enjoy. "I'll just have some decaf."

"With milk or cream?"

"Milk."

"Regular, low fat, or no fat?"

Was she kidding? "Never mind, just bring me some half and half."

The waitress left and Tzeydl unzipped her bag and handed Shayna a pastry wrapped in a napkin. "Go on, Linda. I saved it for you from this morning. Eat up."

"Bubbe."

"Linda, let me see you eat a little dessert, give me a bissl pleasure."

Well, when she put it that way… "All right." Shayna gave in and took a bite, just as the waitress came back with her decaf.

"What's that, a danish? That's a dollar fifty." She whipped her order pad out of her apron pocket and started flipping through it.

"No, no." Shayna swallowed. "We brought this in ourselves."

"What am I running here, an automat?" The waitress slapped their check on the table and left in a huff.

"Never mind, Linda. You just enjoy, that's the main thing." Tzeydl reached for the bill. "What's that say, seven dollars? I can't see nothing no more. Since I went in there, the eyes are no good, the ears are no good…"

"I'll take care of it, Bubbe."

They left the diner in search of candy for the nurses and the rabbi's bottle of wine. Again Tzeydl stopped after they had walked half a block. "You go, Linda. I can't walk no more."

"But Bubbe, look. There's a liquor store right across the street."

"I'll wait here, Linda. You go."

Shayna looked around helplessly. She couldn't just leave Tzeydl standing there in the middle of the street. I was stupid to suggest a walk, Shayna thought.

I forgot how old she is. Her eyes scanned the neighborhood searching for…for what? A taxi cab? A magic carpet? Something. She turned around and was relieved to see what she never in her life thought would fill her soul with gladness: a pair of golden arches. "Look, Bubbe, here's a McDonalds. Let's go in and sit down a minute."

Shayna led Tzeydl inside and sat her down in the nearest empty booth. "You want a drink?"

"You see, five months in that…that estate there, and I forgot how to walk already. Ach." Tzeydl shook her head in disgust. "Yeah, get me a soda or something, I'm thirsty, takeh. Here, take the money from me."

"You can owe it to me. I'll be right back." Shayna went up to the counter and got two containers of orange juice, knowing if she just got one, Tzeydl would make her drink it.

"You want to just go back, Bubbe?"

"No, I'll wait here a minute and you go." Tzeydl had opened her pocketbook to get her change purse out for Shayna. "Here, get for the nurses and for the rabbi. It ain't right to always take, take, take, everybody doing for me. I gotta give something, too." Shayna sat down, trying to figure out what to do. She wished she could carry Tzeydl on her back, and she practically could, her bubbe was so tiny. She's aged so much over the summer, Shayna thought, watching Tzeydl open a container of orange juice and unwrap a straw. I guess she seems okay now. I suppose I can leave her here for five minutes. But what if she gets mugged, like Tillie? Shayna looked around, checking out the situation. The place looked harmless enough; a few teenagers were eating french fries in the corner and a bored mother was watching her two kids romp around Ronald McDonald Land. But this was New York; you never could be too careful. And Shayna had to admit, tearfully, her bubbe looked awfully frail.

Tzeydl pushed a container of orange juice toward Shayna. "Here, darling, take a drink."

"Bubbe, how about if you wait here, and I'll go get the car and we'll just go back?"

"Linda, what are you talking about? I'll be fine. I want to get something for the rabbi, plenty hard he works, I wanna thank him. And the nurses, too."

"Okay. Wait right here." Shayna practically flew across the street into a liquor store, and next door to a pharmacy, where thank the Goddess, they had an early display of Halloween candy.

She was back in six minutes flat. Tzeydl hadn't moved. "Look, Bubbe, I got bags of little chocolates for the nurses, okay? And Manischevitz for the rabbi."

"Let me see." Tzeydl took the wine out of the bag. "Such a big bottle you got? All right, that's good, he shouldn't think I'm such a shnorrer."

"Are you ready to go?" Shayna put the wine and candy in one paper bag and left the other on the table. "Here, put your change purse back in your pocketbook."

Tzeydl put her purse in the appropriate compartment. "Sure, I'm all right now. I had myself a little rest. I was getting such pains here…" She pointed to her chest.

"Bubbe, maybe you should wait here while I go get the car."

"Don't be silly, Linda, I ain't having a heart attack." Tzeydl had read Shayna's mind. "Come, I'll take that." She reached for the bag.

"I'll carry it." Shayna helped Tzeydl from the booth and out onto the street.

"That's too heavy for you, Linda. Give it to me, it's a big bottle." Tzeydl grabbed the neck of the bottle through the paper bag and tried to wrestle it away from Shayna.

"Bubbe, stop. I'm a strong woman. I can carry it."

"Linda, give it to me. You're a young girl, it ain't right you should always be shlepping for me and doing for me, like I'm a baby."

Shayna stopped struggling. "Bubbe, you can't carry it, I'm sorry," she said firmly. "You're having chest pains. I shouldn't even let you carry your pocketbook."

"My pocketbook you want now too? Here, take it. Give it to your mother." Tzeydl threw her bag down in the street and continued yelling. "Everything else of mine she's got, she should have that, too. And the hair off my head take, already." Tzeydl pulled at her hair, which thank the Goddess didn't come off, as it was still her own.

"What's the matter with you today?" Shayna was mildly aware of people staring at her as she bent down to retrieve Tzeydl's pocketbook, which luckily had been zipped up tight. "Here, take your bag." She held it out and Tzeydl took it.

"C'mon, let's go." Shayna took Tzeydl's arm and led her slowly back to the nursing home. "I'm gonna have a nurse look at you when we get back."

"I don't need no nurse. You think I don't know why my heart hurts me? It hurts me because my daughter and my son don't care if I drop dead in the street, as long as I ain't a bother to them."

"I love you, Bubbe." Shayna didn't know what else to say, and she knew it was no use to defend her mother, even if she'd wanted to.

"You, you're my lucky charm. What would I do without you?" They got back to Rosenbaum Estate and Shayna made Tzeydl sit down on a bench outside because there was a commotion going on blocking the entry. Two men in blue uniforms were wheeling an old woman out of the nursing home and into the ambulance parked right outside the front door. Several people from the nursing home were sitting outside on benches, enjoying the warm weather, and watching.

"Did you ever see anything like it?" Shayna turned to see Minnie, who always seemed to be where the action was. "Someone's always coming or going around here."

"Nu, welcome to God's waiting room," Tzeydl said, turning away in disgust.

Minnie pondered Tzeydl's comment for a minute. "She's right," she said, nodding her head. "The bubbe's right. In here, out there," she pointed to the street where a flock of kids were pouring out of a yellow school bus, their books and lunch boxes flying. "God's waiting room," she repeated with another nod. "In here there's people, out there there's people, wherever there's people there's life. And wherever there's life…" She shrugged and pointed to the ambulance. "We're all waiting, takeh, and that's how it is." They watched the ambulance drive away. "I was in the hospital, too, since last time you was here, did the bubbe tell you?" Shayna shook her head. "You see how skinny I got?" She patted her stomach, which Shayna noticed did indeed look flat.

"What happened, Minnie?"

"Twins I had. Shmendrick and Shmendrick." She laughed and patted her stomach again. "They took my kishkes out. Gall bladder. A whole week I was there, but now, thank God, I'm all right."

"That's good. Minnie, will you watch my bubbe for a minute? Bubbe," Shayna tapped Tzeydl on the shoulder, "I'll be right back." Shayna disappeared into the nursing home and came out a minute later with a nurse who checked Tzeydl's pulse and listened to her heart.

"I'm fine," Tzeydl said, trying to shoo her away.

"Just a minute, Tzeydl, let me undo your collar." The nurse turned to Shayna. "See, she's sweating, it's too hot for this blouse today." Tzeydl, as usual was buttoned up to her neck in polyester. "Take her upstairs to rest. See if she'll lie down."

"Will she be all right?" Shayna asked the nurse. "She seemed kind of upset before."

"The walk was probably a little too far for her. Sometimes when something hurts them they get cranky, that's all. She'll be fine."

"Okay. Let's go upstairs, Bubbe. See you later, Minnie."

"A happy and a healthy New Year," Minnie called after them. "A gezunteh yontiff."

Shayna took Tzeydl upstairs and tried to get her to lie down, but Tzeydl wouldn't hear of it. "Rest, I don't need no rest." She sat down on the edge of the bed and looked at it. "Soon, takeh, I'll have plenty of time to rest, believe me. What'd you do with the wine and the candy?"

"It's right here." Shayna held up the bag.

"The nurses I'll give tonight, but maybe we should find the rabbi now and give it to him?"

"You sit. I'll go."

Shayna turned but was stopped by Tzeydl's voice. "No, wait. We can't give him in front of everybody, they'll get the wrong idea, they'll think I want from him a special favor."

"No they won't, Bubbe. Why would they think that?"

Tzeydl shook her head. "Linda, believe me, I know these people, I gotta live with them everyday. This one talks about that one, that one talks about this one… I don't want nobody should have what to say behind my back."

Shayna came over to the bed. "So what should I do with it?"

"You better lock it in the closet, they shouldn't steal it. I'll wait for the rabbi to come upstairs, then I'll give it to him." Tzeydl unzipped her bag to look for the key to the closet. Shayna noticed that the sleeve on her blouse looked funny. It was sewn closed with very uneven stitches, and a long thread was hanging off the end. Shayna bent down to inspect it. "Did your button fall off, Bubbe?"

Tzeydl took her hand out of her pocketbook and turned her sleeve around.

"Yeah, I must have lost that button somewhere, but never mind, my arm got so skinny, eppes, I sewed it closed and I can just push my hand through. I didn't have no yellow thread, so I used the white. It looks all right, don't it?" Tzeydl held her sleeve out for Shayna to see, and then went back to digging in her bag. "I should care what I look like in here," she mumbled.

Shayna stared out the window, letting her tears silently fall. The end of Tzeydl's sleeve looked like those cards children use when they're first learning how to sew; the ones with the big holes that a child would push a shoelace through and follow a pattern of a ship or a bunny. Well, maybe that's an exaggeration, Shayna thought, but not really, compared to what Bubbe's sewing used to look like. Stitches so fine and even, you would swear they were from a machine.

"Here." Tzeydl handed Shayna the key and studied the sleeve of her blouse again. "An hour it took me to thread the needle, Linda, would you believe that?"

Shayna opened the closet, not bothering to ask Tzeydl why she hadn't gotten the nurse to thread the needle for her, or better yet, find a button and sew it on. She knew the answer. "I'm putting the wine right here, Bubbe. Right next to your shoes."

"I hope I shouldn't forget about it, it shouldn't turn into borsht by the time I give it to him." Tzeydl laughed. "The candy leave out, I'll give them tonight. Oy, Linda," Tzeydl sighed. "I wish you lived a little closer to me, darling, we could help each other out."

"I do, too, Bubbe." Shayna locked up the closet and sat down next to Tzeydl on the bed. "Here's your key. Listen, I brought some New Year's cards in case you wanted to send any." Shayna got a package of cards out of her shoulder bag. "Look."

Tzeydl held the cards up to the light. "What's that, an epl?"

"Yeah, see, it's an apple and a piece of challah dipped in honey. On the inside it says, 'Wishing you a Sweet New Year.' You like them?"

"Sure I like them. Very nice." Tzeydl handed the cards back.

"You want to send them?" Shayna tore the plastic off the package.

"All right, we'll send them from me and you. Who should we send to?"

Well, there was always the obvious. "How about one to Sylvia and one to Uncle Ira?"

"Yeah, that's right."

Shayna started addressing the envelopes. "What should I tell them?"

"Wish them a happy and a healthy new year." Tzeydl watched as Shayna wrote. "And tell Ira he should send my regards to Sam, he shouldn't get himself killed over there, and he should kiss Abbie and the baby for me, and they should come and see me soon, I'm an old lady, eppes, I ain't getting any younger."

"Okay." Shayna sealed up the envelopes. "Anyone else?"

"Send one to Tillie. She must be by her son in Jersey, but all right, a card keeps, it ain't gonna go bad like a banana."

"What should I say to her?"

Tzeydl thought for a minute. "Wish her a happy and a healthy new year, too, and tell her I don't call because I can't hear over the phone no more. Tell her maybe her son could bring her to see me."

"Okay." Shayna added a P.S. from herself, telling Tillie she had heard what happened on the avenue from a neighbor and that she hoped Tillie's arm was getting better.

"You got stamps and everything?" Tzeydl watched Shayna lick the envelopes and put on the stamps. "Boy, what you don't think of, I'm telling you."

"Anyone else, Bubbe? You got two cards left."

"Can we send one to your girlfriend there?"

"To Luz?" Shayna was thrilled. "Sure, she'd like that."

"She ain't Jewish," Tzeydl said, in case Shayna didn't know, "but all right, she deserves a happy new year, too."

"What do you want to tell her?" Shayna asked, pen posed.

Tzeydl thought for a minute. "Tell her thank you for the flowers, so beautiful they are. And thank you for letting me borrow Linda for a few days, I enjoyed having her." Shayna smiled as she wrote. "And tell her all right, we'll make believe she's Jewish too, she should have a happy and a healthy new year."

Shayna finished writing. "How should I sign it, Bubbe? Mrs. Zimmerman?"

"Mrs. Zimmerman? No, that's too formal."

"What then, Tzeydl?"

"No, that ain't right, either." Tzeydl searched Shayna's face for the answer. "Sign it Bubbe, she can call me Bubbe, too, no?"

"Sure, if you want her to."

"Linda," Tzeydl put her hand on Shayna's arm, "she won't be insulted?"

"No, Bubbe, why would she be insulted?"

"She'll know who it's from?"

"Yeah, I think so. She doesn't know any other bubbes."

"You better put Bubbe Tzeydl, just in case."

"Okay." Shayna wrote it down. "I'll mail these on my way out."

"Listen, Linda, take some money for the stamps, and for your time. I gotta pay you, nobody works for nothing." Tzeydl unzipped her bag again. "What's this, Linda?" She handed Shayna a typed form. "This they gave out at breakfast."

Shayna looked it over and explained, "This is for the yarzheit, for Yom Kippur. You fill in everyone you want to remember, see there's a space for husband, wife, father, mother... you want me to fill it out?"

"I don't know." Tzeydl looked at the form in Shayna's hand. "You think I should?"

"Sure, Bubbe. The rabbi will probably say a blessing for them. What was your father's name?" Shayna asked, even though she knew.

"My father? Chiam Shiplitsky. And my mother was Leah Shiplitsky, you was named for her, darling. And put down grandpa, too. Benny Zimmerman."

Shayna wrote down the names. "You want to put in your brothers and sisters, too?"

"That's enough. Oy, so many people." She closed her eyes. "Wait, put down my sister Tzivia," she mumbled, "and my sister Rukhl and my sister Libye. And put my brother Moishe and my brother Ya'acov. Oy, I'd give the whole world to see them again. And my mother." Tzeydl opened her eyes and looked in her bag for a tissue. "What I wouldn't give to see her again. My own hand I would cut from my arm." She made a chopping motion with her right hand against her left wrist. "Just once more to talk to my mother." She found a tissue and wiped her eyes with it. "Linda, maybe you should go by your mother to sleep; why should you be all alone in the apartment by yourself? Tomorrow you'll get up with the family, you'll go with them to shul. On a holiday the family should all be together."

"But Bubbe, I'm here with you."

"With me? Me, I'm an old lady. What good am I? You should be with your mother and father; what's gonna be when I'm gone? You won't have no family."

"I'll have Luz."

"Sure, your girlfriend is very nice, but family is family." Tzeydl tucked her tissue up into her sleeve and Shayna winced at the sight of the crooked stitches, as though they were a wound. "Listen, Linda. Whatever it is between you and your mother, you should forgive her already. You know me, I don't stand on ceremony, and you shouldn't either." Tzeydl patted Shayna's arm. "Very special days are coming now, the days between Rosh Hashannah and Yom Kippur, the Days of Awe, they call them, like magic they are, wonderful things can happen. All the Jews all over the world try to make peace in those days. So make me happy, and make your mother happy and go sit by her in the shul. It's a brand new year, you should start it off on the right foot."

"But Bubbe, I want to go to shul with you. They're having services at ten o'clock, it's posted by the elevator. And besides," Shayna knew what would save her, "I don't have a ticket. You know at Sylvia's shul you need a ticket."

"Oh yeah, the tickets I forgot about already. See, what can I tell you, Linda, it's no good no more. I'm like a book that can't spell. Nu," Tzeydl sighed and looked into Shayna's eyes. "When I was young, so active I was, just like you, coming and going with this one, with that one. Now it's no good. Now all day I sit with nothing. You know, my mother used to look at me and say life is like a dream." She took Shayna's hand. "She used to say to me, 'I look at you and I see myself.' That's how it is, Linda, I look at your mother, I look at you, takeh, and I see myself. I look in the mirror and a stranger looks back at me. Where did all the time go?" She patted Shayna's hand. "Years ago, there was no time for nothing, what with the cooking, the shopping, the cleaning, the washing. Every time I turned around, this one was getting Bar Mitzvahed, that one was getting married; it was time to fast for Yom Kippur, time to light the Chanukah candles; time to change the dishes for Pesach; time to bake hammentaschen for Purim...," her voice trailed off. "Then the grandchildren was born and it was time to sit shiva for your grandpa, alav ha sholom; then more grandchildren was born, then great-grandchildren already...never a minute to myself and now I got all the time in the world and I ain't got no koach, no strength, takeh, so what good is it?"

Shayna had no answer for Tzeydl, but she didn't really need one. "Listen, darling, I want you should have my dishes, a whole set I got, you should use them. You took the silverware I had for you, right?" Shayna nodded, numb.

215

"Take my jewelry, what's in the top drawer, and send something to Abbie, and something for the baby, they should have what to remember their old bubbe. Sam, I don't know what to send him, you pick something, all right? My watch and my medal your mother has, I'm sure. Ask her for it, and my crystal bowl, too. Linda, you're listening?" Shayna nodded.

"Take my pocketbooks, so many beautiful bags I got. Shoes to match, take them, Linda, your feet are the same as mine. In the closet they are. And my winter coat, take; your grandpa had that made for me special, such a warm coat that is, take that, too."

"Bubbe, you'll need your coat this winter. I'll bring it to you."

"Where am I gonna go, I need such a heavy coat? Almost thirty-five years I spent the winter in Florida, you think I can go out now in the snow?"

"I'll take you out when I come."

"Linda," Tzeydl patted her hand. "Take the coat, take the shoes, take whatever you want. Take the pots and pans, I ain't gonna cook no more. Your mother's gonna give up the apartment soon, then you'll have nothing. So take what you want."

I want you, Shayna thought, squeezing Tzeydl's hand. "She's not going to give up the apartment."

"You think she's gonna pay to have empty rooms standing forever? Take my things, Linda, I want you should remember your bubbe."

Did she hear what Sylvia and I were talking about, Shayna wondered. "They're not giving up the apartment," Shayna said, despite what her mother had asked her to do.

"To tell you the truth, I don't care. They ain't gonna let me go home no more." Tzeydl's voice was weary. "I'm tired, Linda."

Shayna felt her stomach curl. She had never heard Tzeydl say those words before. "You want to take a rest, Bubbe? Here, lie down." She got off the bed. "Put your feet up." Shayna took off Tzeydl's shoes. "You want me to tell the nurse to bring up your supper?"

"The supper I don't care about. You go down and eat it."

"I'm going to talk to the nurse, Bubbe. I'll be right back." Shayna left the room, closing the door behind her. She spoke to the third floor nurse, who assured her she would keep an eye on Tzeydl, but refused to allow Shayna to sleep on a cot in her room. "It's against regulations," she explained. Shayna went back to Tzeydl's room and sat down in the chair by the telephone, watching her sleep. She looked so delicate there, so tiny. When Shayna was a little girl, her bubbe had seemed so big; big, round and soft just like the earth. And now she seemed fragile as a china doll.

After a little while Tzeydl opened her eyes. "Go Linda. I don't want you should travel in the dark by yourself."

"Are you sure you'll be okay?" She knelt down beside the bed. "The nurse said she'll tell them to bring up your supper."

"You eat something, Linda. Get something on the avenue. What time are you coming tomorrow?"

"Ten o'clock."

"Come a little before. And bring me my skirt, the black one, it's hanging there in the closet."

"Okay, Bubbe." Shayna leaned forward and kissed her cheek. It was soft as baby skin. "I love you, Bubbe."

"I love you, too, darling." Tzeydl didn't offer to walk Shayna to the lobby, so she took her aching heart out to the elevator alone.

Chapter Eighteen

When Shayna got to the nursing home the next morning at nine-thirty, she was relieved to see Tzeydl sitting in her chair waiting, her pocketbook on her lap, just as she had been the day before. "Hi, Bubbe. How do you feel?"

"Me? I'm all right. Sit down, I saved some breakfast for you."

"Here's your skirt." Shayna put Tzeydl's black skirt on the bed.

"Sit down, Linda. I got milk and cereal. Here's a shissl and a spoon." As Tzeydl spoke, she moved aside her telephone and set a place for Shayna, as though she was back in her apartment. "Eat something, mamela, I know you didn't have no breakfast. In the meantime, I'll get dressed."

"Did you sleep okay? I was worried about you." When she got to the apartment, Shayna had discovered that her mother had already disconnected Tzeydl's telephone, so not only had she no way of reaching Luz and Pearl, but worse yet, if something happened to Tzeydl during the night, the nursing home would have no way of reaching her.

"I slept all right, Linda. You don't gotta worry about me; you're young yet; you shouldn't have what to worry."

"But you didn't feel good yesterday."

"Listen, when you're old like me, some days are good days and some days are not so good days." Tzeydl got her key from her pocketbook, unlocked her closet and started looking through her blouses. "Would this look all right with that skirt?" She held up a black velour top with turquoise and cranberry diamonds splashed all over it.

"Sure, that's nice." Shayna sat down at the table, opened her Special K along the dotted lines, and poured some milk right into the single serving box, just like when she was a little girl.

"Maybe it's too loud, you know, for shul." Tzeydl hung the pullover back in the closet and took out a white cotton sweater. "This is better, no?"

Shayna considered it. "Yeah, I think that would be good."

"All right, what do I care what I look like, it ain't a real shul anyway." She took the blouse off the hanger and laid it on the bed. "I gave all the nurses the candy, some last night and some this morning, you know, different ones work in the night and the day. The rabbi came upstairs this morning too, but the wine he didn't take. He says he can't carry nothing on the holiday."

"You'll have to give it to him next week, I guess." Shayna finished her cereal

218

and watched Tzeydl get changed, literally sitting on her hands so she wouldn't offer to help. Tzeydl slowly unbuttoned each button of the blouse she had on, took it off, folded it neatly and laid it on the bed. Then she held onto the edge of her bureau with one hand to slowly step out of her pants. Shayna almost told her to sit down and do that, she shouldn't fall, Goddess forbid and break her hip. But she stopped herself, for, after all, Tzeydl had been getting dressed and undressed for ninety-nine years without her granddaughter's help, and so far she'd done just fine. Tzeydl caught Shayna looking at her body, and looked down at herself as well. "Look how skinny I got," she said, holding both arms straight out from her sides. She wasn't shy, that's for sure, standing there in just her brassiere and panties. "So skinny like this is no good. Like half a person I am." She did look small to Shayna's eyes, which were used to seeing a much bigger bubbe. Tzeydl still had a round, soft belly and sturdy legs, but her arms were thin and her chest was caved in and frail looking. Still, to Shayna, her body was a beautiful collage of wrinkles and age spots. Shayna watched Tzeydl pull her skirt over her head, adjust the elastic waist band around her middle, and pull on the white sweater, blousing it out over the skirt. "There," she said, turning for Shayna's inspection. "How's that?"

"Very nice, Bubbe. You got stockings?"

"Stockings I got, you know the ones that go up to the knee." She opened her top drawer and sorted through her nylons. "Black ones is good, no? You think up to the knee is all right? I ain't got no pantihose."

"Bubbe, look." Shayna lifted her skirt, which she'd worn to please Tzeydl, and revealed a shapely leg covered with knee-highs as well. "See, I got the same kind."

"Yeah? If you got them, Linda, then they must be all right." Tzeydl sat down on the edge of the bed to put her stockings on. "Oy, do my feet hurt me, eppes, that foot doctor they got down there is no good. He cut my toenails and he cut off my corn, see, but he only made it worse. Oy, this is a life, I'm telling you." She put on her shoes, and Shayna wondered for the millionth time how Tzeydl could walk at her age in patent leather toeless slingbacks with two inch heels. Shayna had tried to get Tzeydl to wear shoes that were better for her feet a hundred times: moccasins, sneakers, flat lace-ups, even a pair of Birkenstock sandals. But every time she brought shoes for Tzeydl, Shayna wound up taking them home for herself. "I ain't used to such a flat heel," Tzeydl would say. "I'm afraid I shouldn't fall and break my neck in those shoes." And Shayna was afraid, after so many years, that she was probably right. Tzeydl stood up and walked over to the mirror above the sink to inspect herself. "Linda, put on a little lipstick, here, I got some for you." She took a white plastic tube out of a paper cup standing on the edge of the sink.

"Where'd you get that, Bubbe?"

"Downstairs I got it, from playing Bingo. I won it."

"You played Bingo?" Shayna was surprised. "Did you like it?"

"Did I like it? It was something to do, that's all." Tzeydl turned from the mirror to address Shayna. "One day I decided to try it. I'm sitting up here all by myself, a person could go off their mind, all day long sitting, sitting, sitting, and it's spinning in my head like a wheel, what they did to me, how they threw me in here with nothing, how they never took me back to the apartment. So I went down." Tzeydl turned back to the mirror, took the top off the lipstick and applied it to her mouth. "I couldn't see the numbers on the card and I couldn't hear what they were calling out, but all right, I won anyway. They don't give you real money, they give you tickets like, and then the tickets you trade for prizes they got there. So I traded my tickets for a lipstick and then I asked them to give me an extra one for you."

"You didn't have to get me one." Shayna came over and took the lipstick from Tzeydl.

"Wait, I have another one here." She reached into the paper cup. "Here, this one's lighter, that's better for a young girl."

"All right, I'll trade ya." Shayna exchanged the Ruby Dooby Red in her hand for Pearly Pink Pizzazz.

"First they said no, I only got enough tickets for the one lipstick," Tzeydl said, blotting her lips with a tissue. "But you think I'm gonna be finished with them, just because they said no? I says I need a lipstick for my granddaughter, I ain't got no more tickets so I'll pay with money, how much could one lipstick be?" Tzeydl, having wiped off most of her lipstick, now touched up her mouth again. "They said no; I says yes, and finally they gave it to me, I should only stop hollering. They know I can't go out shopping, so they got the lipstick, I got the money; we made a deal and everybody was satisfied." Tzeydl turned once more to the mirror. "I look all right?"

"You look great. C'mon, let's go down. They're probably starting."

"All right, you got your bag? We ain't like the rabbi, we gotta carry our things, even on Rosh Hashannah they shouldn't steal them." Tzeydl took her pocketbook and they rode down the elevator to the second floor, where some of the offices and activity rooms were. Shayna noticed the nursing home was fairly empty.

"Did a lot of people go home for Rosh Hashannah?" she asked Tzeydl.

"What do I know where they went?" she said, peering down the hallway. "Which way do we go?"

"I think it's over there." Shayna led Tzeydl in the direction of the low chanting voices she heard coming from behind a closed door. They opened the door and saw the rabbi standing in front of the 'Nature Room' as a hand-painted sign announced in big letters over his head. A group of men sat at a round table in front of the rabbi, two of them in wheelchairs. Several other men sat behind them, and to the left of those men were a group of women, sitting on folding chairs. Everyone was in their yontiff best: the men in ties and jackets, the women in skirts and blouses, with bits of lace bobby-pinned to their freshly washed and set hair. Along the wall were shelves lined with "nature" items: pine cones, rocks, dried flowers and sea shells. And various posters hung here and there: an owl, a polar bear, a humpbacked whale. Not your typical shul.

"Over there," Shayna whispered, steering Tzeydl to the women's section. She picked up two prayer books on the way and handed one to Tzeydl.

"What page are we on?" Shayna asked, sitting down next to a woman in an orange flowered dress. The woman pointed with a matching orange fingernail to the number at the bottom of the page of her open prayer book. "Page one-seventy-one," Shayna whispered loudly to Tzeydl.

"I can't see no more, I can't read it." Tzeydl put the closed book down on her lap on top of her pocketbook. Shayna opened her book and followed along from right to left as best as she could. A few years ago she had asked a friend to teach her the Hebrew aleph-bez so she wouldn't feel like a complete imbecile when she went to shul. She still couldn't understand what the rabbi was saying, which was probably just as well, since Shayna didn't go in for all that God the Great White Father stuff, but at least now she could pronounce the words and sing the old, familiar melodies. There was something about hearing the prayers she'd heard every year since she was a baby, and knowing that Jews all over the world at this very moment were reciting them too, that filled Shayna's soul with a peaceful feeling, even if the meaning didn't quite jive with her politics.

The prayer ended and Shayna looked up at the rabbi, who was stepping aside to let an old man take his place at the makeshift bima, which appeared to be a milk crate covered with a folded blue paper tablecloth. Shayna almost gasped out loud, for the man taking the rabbi's place was none other than Murray Perlman. Shayna was stunned, for even though Murray was never able to remember what room he was in, or how to look on his hospital bracelet to find out, there he was, standing at the bima with a yarmalke on his head and a tallis draped over the sweater his wife had made with her goldeneh hands, reciting the Hebrew blessings in a loud, clear, confident voice.

"Bubbe, look," Shayna whispered, eager to inform Tzeydl of this amazing fact, but she stopped at the sight of tears streaming from Tzeydl's eyes. "Are you okay?" she whispered a little louder. Tzeydl replied by unzipping her pocketbook, handing a crumpled tissue to Shayna and keeping one for herself. I wonder what's making her cry, Shayna thought, wiping her own eyes. She knew she was crying because her bubbe was crying, but why was Tzeydl upset? Because she missed her mother and father? Because she missed all her sisters and brothers? Because she missed her husband? Because she missed her daughter and her son who never came to visit? Because she hated living in a nursing home? Because this very well might be her last Rosh Hashannah on earth? When you think about all the things she does have to cry about, Shayna realized, it was a wonder that there was any time she spent dry-eyed at all.

"Listen, Tzeydl." A woman behind them tapped Tzeydl on the shoulder and spoke in a loud whisper. "What's with all the tissues, what are you crying for? On Yom Kippur we'll cry plenty, believe me. On Rosh Hashannah we should be happy."

Tzeydl smiled. "She's right," she said to Shayna, who had also turned around and was now staring at two women at the back of the room who were watching a hamster in a fish tank running on an exercise wheel. "Enough with the crying," Tzeydl said. She blew her nose and tucked the tissue into the sleeve of her sweater with a sigh.

"Look, he's going to blow the shofar," Shayna said, pointing to the rabbi who stood in front of the bima again, holding a curved ram's horn up to his lips. This was Shayna's favorite part of the service; she loved hearing the ancient sound. The rabbi blew a series of long and short high-pitched notes, turning all red and working up quite a sweat in the process. When he was finished, Shayna turned to Tzeydl. "What'd you think?"

"Very good. He blew it very good. Come, we'll go down." Tzeydl stood up and Shayna followed her out to the hall where a group of people were waiting for the elevator.

"Watch it, watch it," someone called as the door opened and there was a rush to get on.

"Did you ever see anything like it? Worse than the subway this is." Tzeydl held Shayna back by the arm. "We'll wait for the next one."

"Take your time," a man in the elevator called to a woman who was slowly inching her way forward with a walker. The elevator door started to close, so Shayna stepped up to press the down button to hold it. "Take your time and hurry up," the man called again. Finally the woman got in, the door closed and Tzeydl and Shayna were alone in the hall.

"You wanna take the stairs, Linda? Look they're over there." Tzeydl pointed to a red exit sign.

"No, let's wait, Bubbe."

"Wait? Till they send the elevator back up, it'll be Yom Kippur already." Tzeydl started down the hall. "Come." She motioned for Shayna, holding open the door, then slowly made her way down the steps, holding onto the banister, her pocketbook dangling from her elbow, her heels echoing loudly in the empty stairwell. They got to the bottom and walked through the lobby into the dining room.

"Sit, sit." Minnie, seeing Tzeydl and Shayna approaching, waved them over. "The granddaughter can sit in Mrs. Chocolata's place. She ain't here today."

They sat at the table which had been decorated with blue and white placemats and plastic flowers for the holiday. At each setting was a piece of challah, a salad, and a piece of honeycake.

"Gut yontiff." The man sitting next to Minnie, who even today wore his baseball cap, smiled.

"Shana tova," Shayna answered. "You didn't go to shul?"

"Shul? No, that ain't for me." The man pushed up the left sleeve of his sweater and extended his forearm, which had a row of blue numbers tattooed on it. "I don't believe in that no more."

"Oh, I'm sorry." Shayna stared at the numbers and then looked away.

The man smiled again as he pulled down his sleeve and it was absolutely the saddest smile Shayna had ever seen. "All right, that was a long time ago, you don't have to be sorry. You wasn't even born yet."

"She was a twinkle in the bubbe's eye, right, Bubbe?" Minnie asked loudly, taking a bite of honeycake. "Oy, is that good, granddaughter. Take a piece."

222

"I don't know, I ain't got no appetite." Tzyedl mumbled to no one in particular, staring at the plate of food that had just been placed in front of her.

"Eat a piece of challah at least," Shayna said, handing her a piece she had just shmeered with butter.

"Eat the honeycake," Minnie said with her mouth full. "For a sweet new year they gave us, we gotta eat it."

Shayna dug into her food with zest, hoping Tzeydl would follow her shining example, but she didn't.

"All right." Minnie stood up and put a piece of challah and a slice of honeycake into her bag. "I'm going up."

"Wait, I'm coming, too." The man in the baseball cap stood up. "Nice to see you again."

"Bubbe, eat a little cake with me for the new year at least." Shayna broke off a piece and gave it to Tzeydl.

"All right." Tzeydl took what was offered. "Listen," she said, mid-chew. "The holiday is two days, maybe you could spend one with me and one with your mother?"

"Bubbe, I want to spend the holiday with you."

"Linda, I ain't gonna go up again. That ain't even a real shul." Tzeydl sighed and stared at a woman in a wheelchair maneuvering herself out of the dining room. "You shouldn't be with all old people so much. It ain't good for you."

"It's good for me to be with you."

"Me, never mind me. On a holiday a girl should be with her mother."

"I know," Shayna said, suddenly inspired. "I'll go if you come with me."

"What are you crazy, Linda? I'm too old for such a long trip."

"No you're not. It's only an hour."

"Linda, just do me a favor and go."

Oy, again with the favors? "Bubbe," Shayna looked up from the table. "Are you trying to get rid of me?"

Tzeydl laughed. "I should cut off my own head first before I would get rid of you." She patted Shayna's knee. "Listen, darling, your mother's not feeling too good. It's hard to lose a mother, mamela, believe me, I know, but it's harder yet to lose a daughter. Go sit with her in shul and make her happy."

"What do you mean, lose a mother?" Shayna looked at Tzeydl with anxious eyes.

"I ain't gonna live forever, Linda. I'm an old lady, I'm tired."

"Come, I'll take you to your room. C'mon, I want you to lie down." Shayna led Tzeydl through the empty lobby and pressed the elevator button. When it arrived, she took Tzeydl's arm and helped her to her room. Shayna sat down on the easy chair and Tzeydl perched on the edge of the bed.

"You wanna go down to the services, Linda? They're probably starting them again."

"No, Bubbe, I'll stay here and take a rest, too." Shayna kicked off her shoes and curled into the chair, hoping Tzeydl would follow suit.

"You wanna rest? Sure, you're tired. Here, lie down." Tzeydl got off the bed.

"I knew you was tired."

Well, so much for that strategy. "Bubbe, you lie down."

"Linda, I ain't gonna rest with you sitting there with nothing to do. What kind of holiday is that for you?"

This was getting ridiculous. Shayna sighed. "All right then, what should we do?"

Tzeydl sat back on her bed. "You should go be with your mother."

"Bubbe."

"Don't 'bubbe' me. Didn't I do something for you, you should feel good, I took your girlfriend right into my heart like she was my own granddaughter?" She pointed to the framed picture of Shayna and Luz on her bureau. "Now I want you should do something for me. Go visit your mother and father and make them happy on the holiday. Don't sleep in the apartment all by yourself, I should worry about you a whole night long. Go be with the family."

Shayna sighed again. She could see Tzeydl was never going to get any rest with her sitting there. And even though she looked better than she had yesterday, she did look tired. And yesterday had been more than a little scary. Maybe she just wore out in the afternoon. Morning always was her best time. Shayna remembered when she was in junior high and Tzeydl would come visit, she was always up at six, washing the dishes and scrubbing the floors. By the time Shayna stumbled downstairs at eight-fifteen, she'd have a complete pancake breakfast waiting for her, she shouldn't go off to school on an empty stomach. Come to think of it, Tzeydl often did take a nap in the afternoon; frequently Shayna would come home from school at three-thirty and find Tzeydl snoring on the couch, lulled into sleep by the tunes of Lawrence Welk.

"All right, Bubbe, I'll leave," Shayna said, "but I want you to rest." Shayna would leave all right, for the sake of Tzeydl's health, but she wouldn't go so far as to spring a surprise visit on Sylvia and Sol. No, if she wasn't going to spend Rosh Hashannah with Tzeydl, she'd spend it with Luz and Tzimmy, and maybe Pearl if she was back from visiting her family in Boston. "But I'll be back for Yom Kippur, Bubbe, okay?"

"All right, so I'll see you in a week." Tzeydl patted the bed beside her. "You're a good girl, Linda, I appreciate it and your mother will appreciate it, believe me. Sit down a minute, I want to tell you something." Shayna sat down and Tzeydl took her hand. "Remember, if you make a dollar put fifty cents in the bank and keep the rest, except for a nickel. The nickel you give to charity. Even if you only make a dime, a nickel you put in the bank just in case, four pennies take out for yourself, and one penny give away. Even if you got next to nothing, you can always find someone who got less than you. And your health is the most important thing. As long as you got your health, you got everything." Tzeydl stared at Shayna's face for a long moment, as though she were memorizing it. "And enjoy yourself, that's the main thing. Life is very short, mamela, too short to worry. Don't worry about nothing. Just enjoy. And eat a good supper." She squeezed Shayna's hand. "Ooh, such a soft little hand you got. I don't wanna let go of that hand." She looked at Shayna for another long moment and then stood up.

"Goodbye, darling," she said, bending down to kiss Shayna's cheek three times.

Shayna looked up at her grandmother and felt like a little girl again. "I love you, Bubbe," she said, throwing her arms around Tzeydl's shrunken middle, and hugging her tightly, and then not so tightly, for she felt so frail. Shayna could feel Tzeydl's body shaking and hear her voice crack with tears. "Oy, I love you, too, shayneh maideleh. I'll always love you. Never forget that. And your girlfriend, too." Shayna's tears soaked into Tzeydl's sweater, and Tzeydl's tears slid down her cheeks and dripped from her chin into Shayna's hair. "A laybn on dine kop," she said, stepping back. "Come, it's time."

Shayna stood up. "Bye, Bubbe," she said, her voice a whisper.

"Goodbye, darling. Thank you for doing this and thank you for everything else you done for me. Now your bubbe will get a nice long rest."

"I love you, bubbe," Shayna said again turning to Tzeydl for one last hug.

"I love you, too. Tell your mother a happy and a healthy new year for me."

"I will, Bubbe," Shayna said. It was the first and last time she ever lied to her.

Chapter Nineteen

The call came at ten after twelve, just as Shayna was setting the table for lunch. She was having hummus and whole wheat bagel chips and Luz was having whatever drek she was picking up at McDonalds on the way over from the store. Shayna's stomach clenched into a fist at the sound of the telephone. She'd had a bellyache all morning, which she knew had to do with the fact that Tzeydl thought she was sitting in shul with her mother like a good Jewish girl, and instead, here she was about to have lunch with her goyishe lover, who would probably bring over, of all things, a cheeseburger. Shayna hadn't called Tzeydl last night to assure her she'd arrived safely, for she'd arrived home, not in Vey Iss Mir, as she'd led Tzeydl to believe. And if she had called, Tzeydl surely would have asked to speak to Shayna's mother, and what was she supposed to do then, have Luz do a Sylvia Steinblatt imitation? Shayna put down the napkin she was folding, went into the living room and picked up the phone.

"Hello, is this Linda Steinblatt?"

"Yes." Shayna sat down, for whenever anyone except her bubbe called her Linda, it always meant trouble.

"This is the third floor nurse from Rosenbaum Estate." She paused and Shayna stopped breathing. "Your grandmother was taken to the hospital a little while ago."

Shayna clutched the phone. "What happened?"

"We're not really sure. She collapsed, but she did start to respond when they put her in the ambulance."

I'll bet she started to respond, Shayna thought. "Should I come?"

"Not yet. There's nothing you can do at the moment," the nurse said.

"Well, is Alan Meyerhoff there?" Shayna wanted a second opinion.

"No, he's not working today because of the holiday."

"All right. Well, call me as soon as you know anything. I'll be home all day."

"We really should be in contact with your mother. She's her next of kin. But we can't seem to reach her. Do you know where she is?"

Shayna glanced at the clock. Twelve-fifteen. "They're probably still in shul."

"All right. I'll be in touch with you then."

"Okay. Thank you." Shayna hung up the phone and sat there shaking. She stared across the room and her eyes fell on her cat. "I need you," she called to Tzimmy, who was not pleased at being woken up from her tenth nap of the day by the ringing of the phone. Shayna crossed the room on wobbly legs, picked up Tzimmy and lay back on the couch with the cat purring on her belly like a live heating pad. No wonder my belly's been upset all morning, Shayna thought, for in her gut, she knew.

"What should I do?" Shayna asked Tzimmy. "I could drive down there, it's not like I have any wild plans for the day or anything. I could make it in three hours if I don't get caught in traffic or stopped for speeding. At least I'd be doing something, instead of just sitting here waiting by the phone. I wish I had a carphone." She scratched Tzimmy between the ears. "What do you think?" Shayna stared into Tzimmy's green eyes which blinked once slowly in a mute reply. She flung her arms over her head and ran her fingers through her hair. "Okay, world, let me know what to do." She closed her eyes.

They flew open instantly, however, for Shayna was suddenly hit with a wave of deja vu. Something felt very familiar. What was it? "I know, Tzimmy. Remember when the guy from the phone company called? I couldn't reach Sylvia and Sol then either." Shayna sat up. Was that only five months ago? Goddess, it seemed like five years.

Shayna went into the kitchen and took two smooth white Shabbas candles out of the last cabinet on the left. She pushed aside the place settings, placed the candles in Tzeydl's candlesticks and put them on the table. Then she went into her study and got the picture of her and Tzeydl laughing together on the board-walk and put that on the table, too. She lit the candles and stared at the picture, which blurred and cleared as tears rose and fell from her eyes. "Brucha Aht Shekhina, Elohanu, Malka Ha Olam. Blessed Art Thou, oh Lordess, Our Goddess, Queen of the Universe, Whoever You Are. Please take care of Tzeydl Zimmerman, also known as Sally Shiplitsky, also known as my bubbe. Bubbe," Shayna whispered softly, tracing the shape of her grandmother's cheek with her index finger. "Don't worry about me, Bubbe. I'm all right, I'm not alone. If you need to go, you should go. It's enough already. It's enough." Shayna's voice cracked with tears and she could barely get the words out, but she knew she had to say them, and that somehow Tzeydl would hear them.

"Go, Bubbe. You don't have to fight anymore. Go rest. Your mother's wait-ing for you, and your father's waiting for you, and your sisters Tzivia, Rukhl and Libye are waiting for you, and your brothers Moishe and Ya'acov. And grandpa's waiting, too. I'll be all right. I'll miss you, but I'll be all right. Go rest now. You've earned it. You deserve it." Shayna wiped her soggy face with the back of her hand. "I love you, Bubbe. I'll always love you, you know that. And Luz, too. We'll always remember you. But it's enough already. You can stop now. You can rest now. Enough is enough. You can go." Shayna put her head down on the table, letting herself wail into her arms, and that's exactly how Luz found her when she walked in the door at twelve-thirty on the dot.

"Honey, what's the matter?" Luz knelt down, dropping her McDonalds bag on the floor.

"It's Bubbe. They took her to the hospital. She…she—" Shayna's words were cut off by a sob. "She collapsed. They said they'd call when they knew anything."

"Well, at least she's still alive then." Luz fished a handkerchief out of her back pocket and wiped Shayna's face with it. "She's a fighter. Maybe she'll pull through."

"No." Shayna took the hankie and blew her nose. "No, I told her to go if she wanted to." Shayna looked at the photo on the table. "See, I lit her candles and I told her she didn't have to worry about me; I'd be all right and it was enough already."

"That was brave of you."

"I don't feel brave. I just don't want her to suffer anymore."

As if on cue, the phone rang, sending a chill up Shayna's spine. She froze, staring at Luz.

"Want me to get it?" Luz asked softly.

"No, I better." She got up and Luz followed her into the living room. "Hello?"

"Hello, is this Linda?"

"Yes."

"This is the third floor nurse from Rosenbaum Estate again. I'm very sorry to tell you that your grandmother passed away this afternoon at twelve-twenty-five."

"All right," Shayna said, even though it wasn't.

"We still haven't been able to reach your parents."

"I'll take care of it. Thank you."

"Wait a minute. There's someone here who wants to talk to you."

Shayna waited until a shaky voice came onto the phone.

"Hello?"

"Yes?"

"Hello, granddaughter? It's Minnie. I'm so sorry about your bubbe, grand-daughter, oy am I sorry."

Shayna could hear that she'd been crying. "Do you know what happened, Minnie?"

"We was sitting down in the shul, you know, she didn't wanna go with me, but I says to her, 'Tzeydl, you got something better to do?' So we go down and we're sitting, and the rabbi is davening there, and then he picks up the shofar and he blows in it, one note he makes, and your bubbe falls over, I'm telling you, like God himself is calling her."

"Was she in any pain, do you think?"

"I'm telling you, bubbeleh, she got dressed, she came down for breakfast, she ate something, she went back upstairs, she walked with me down the steps to the shul, nothing. And then all of a sudden, just like that." Minnie heaved a big sigh. "Oy, we're all gonna miss her, that's for sure. So full of the devil she was. Full of the devil, and she died like an angel."

Shayna smiled through her tears. "It was a pleasure to know you, Minnie. Take good care of yourself."

"Listen, you can always come visit Minnie. I'll be here, you can always come."

"Thanks."

"Listen, granddaughter, maybe you'll send me something for a remembrance like?"

Shayna was touched. "Sure, Minnie, I'll look through her things and pick out something."

"I got pierced ears, remember. And silver I like, not gold, it goes better with my skin."

"Okay, Minnie. I'll send you something."

"Wait, wait a minute. Jack wants to say a word."

"Okay." Shayna sat down on the couch and Luz settled beside her with an arm around her shoulder.

"Hello, this is Jack from your grandma's table. You remember?"

"You always wear the baseball cap, right?"

"My cap? Yeah, that's right, that's me. Listen, I'm so sorry about your grandmother. Such a nice lady she was, such a smart lady. She loved you so much, she was always talking about you. We always knew when you was coming, her face lit up like the sun."

"Thank you."

"Look, at least she didn't suffer. That was the best way she picked to go: one-two-three."

"I guess so."

"It was always a pleasure when you ate by the table. Come anytime, there'll always be a place for you."

"Thanks."

"Wait, wait, here's Manny." Manny gave his condolences, as did a few more people from Tzeydl's floor. Finally the nurse got back on and Shayna assured her she'd get in touch with her parents as soon as possible.

Shayna hung up the phone and melted into Luz's arms. "My bubbe's gone."

"She's not all gone. She's still in here." Luz rubbed Shayna's heart.

"But she's dead." Shayna cried and cried, rocking back and forth, letting out deep moans.

"That's it, Shayna. Let it out. Let it all out." Luz held her tightly, stroking her back round and round.

"That's why she wanted me to leave yesterday," Shayna said when she could talk again. "I knew I should have stayed with her and had the nurse look at her. Why didn't I?"

"My poor Shayna." Luz smoothed back Shayna's hair. "You did the right thing, honey. She was ready to go and if you were there it probably would have been too hard for her."

"She would have been too worried about me," Shayna said, searching for a dry spot on Luz's hankie. "She died thinking the family was all together and we weren't. Do you think that's okay?"

"Yeah, it made her happy." Luz stroked Shayna's cheek. "I'm glad you were here with me, though."

Shayna let out a deep breath. "Me too. After the nurse called, I looked at her picture and told her to go. Do you think she heard me?"

"I'm sure he did."

"Do you think she knew yesterday, and that's why she wanted me to leave?" Shayna gave up on the hankie and wiped her nose on her sleeve.

"Probably. She was a very wise woman."

"She still is. Not was." Hearing Luz use the past tense to refer to Tzeydl brought a fresh batch of tears to Shayna's eyes. She wiped them away and sighed. "I guess she didn't suffer, anyway. She just keeled over in services when she heard the shofar. Talk about the Days of Awe." She shook her head and looked at Luz. "What do we do now?"

"Well, the first thing we do is call my employees and tell them I need a few days off." Luz reached for the phone.

"What are you going to tell them?"

"The truth."

"That your girlfriend's bubbe died?"

"That there's been a death in my family." Luz made a few phone calls. "I got things covered till Monday." She pushed the phone toward Shayna. "Ready to call your mother?"

"Not yet."

"Baby, you have to."

"I know." She stared down at her hands. "They'll just turn it into a three ring circus with their fancy funeral arrangements, and all their friends who never came to see Bubbe in the nursing home when she was alive." Shayna's voice was bitter. "They'll probably all show up at the funeral though. And Sylvia will be hysterical." Shayna shook her head. "Bubbe was smart to pick Rosh Hashannah. If the nurse had reached my parents, they'd probably have gotten killed themselves, rushing into Brooklyn to get to the hospital in time. At least she didn't have to worry about that."

"I'm sure she would have wanted you to know first," Luz said, taking Shayna's hand.

"Yeah, I'm glad I didn't hear it from them. They should hear it from me."

"Well, you're the one who really took care of her. She really loved you."

"She loved you, too." Shayna stared at Luz's hand, clasped in her own. "She sent you a card for Rosh Hashannah. She had me write it out yesterday. You'll probably get it tomorrow. And," Shayna squeezed Luz's fingers, "she told me to sign it, 'Bubbe Tzeydl.'"

"She did?"

"Yeah." Shayna looked up to see two fat tears spill out of Luz's eyes. "Oh, Luz, don't cry."

"I'll miss her, too. She was really nice to me. You know, I never had a grandma before."

Shayna kissed Luz's cheeks. "Well, you got one now. The world's greatest bubbe. She even had a cup that said so on it. I gave it to her last Chanukah."

"I should get you a cup that says 'world's greatest granddaughter on it,' Luz said. "You really did a lot for her."

"Well, she meant a lot to me," Shayna wiped her eyes with the back of Luz's hand and then kissed it. "Want your lunch?"

"Only if you'll eat yours."

"I'm not hungry."

"Wouldn't your grandma want you to eat something?"

"I guess so. Come." Shayna got up and took Luz by the hand into the kitchen, only to find Tzimmy, up to her elbows in a box of chicken McNuggets. "Oh, no. Tzimmy Steinblatt, you little goniff, get out of there." Shayna shooed Tzimmy away. "I'm sorry, Luz. You want some bagel chips and hummus?"

"Not really." Luz opened the refrigerator and stared into it. Except for the bottle of orange soda and the box of Sara Lee chocolate brownies she had brought over recently, she didn't recognize a thing.

"I got some eggs you could fry up," Shayna said, opening the dairy compartment on the door.

"Okay." While Luz cooked, Shayna sat at the kitchen table and stared out the window. She watched some birds flitting across the lawn and two squirrels chase each other around the trunk of a tree. Didn't they know her bubbe was gone? How could the world just continue on, business as usual, as if everything was the same? It wasn't the same at all. Tzeydl Zimmerman was gone. Not only gone, but dead. Dead meant forever. Forever meant never. Shayna would never see Tzeydl's face again, or hold her hand or kiss her cheek or laugh with her, or fight with her, or cry with her. Never. How could it be?

"You should eat something." Luz moved aside Tzeydl's picture and candlesticks, and set her plate down. She spooned some hummus onto Shayna's plate and shook some bagel chips out of the bag. "C'mon. Try." Luz sat down and dug into her eggs. Shayna took a small bite but her throat closed up with grief. "I can't. It hurts."

"Okay. You don't have to. Want some tea?"

"No thanks."

Luz finished eating and did the dishes. "You wanna call your mother now?" she asked Shayna.

"No, but I guess I have to. If I wait too long, she'll get mad at me."

They went back into the living room and Shayna dialed. There was no answer. Shayna hung up and looked at Luz. "They're not there. What time is it?"

Luz looked at her watch. "One-thirty."

"They should be home from shul by now. Maybe I dialed wrong." Shayna tried again but there was still no answer. "Oh, no."

"What?"

"I know what it is. Mr. and Mrs. Observant don't answer the phone on the High Holy Days."

"Would they answer the door?" Luz asked. "Maybe you should call a neighbor to go over."

"Maybe." Shayna dialed her parents' house again, letting the phone ring and ring. After fifty-seven times (she counted) her parents' annoyance level won out over their religious beliefs, as Shayna suspected might happen, and her mother picked up the phone.

"Hello?"

"Hi, Sylvia, it's your daughter."

"What's the matter?"

Shayna tried to keep her voice from quivering. "Sylvia, they took Bubbe to the hospital. She died about an hour ago."

"Oy, Gottinyu." Mrs. Steinblatt was stunned for a moment, and then regained her composure. "Well, thank God she wasn't by herself in the apartment, she could have laid there rotting for days, God forbid, before anyone would find her. You see, Linda, didn't we do the right thing?"

"Yeah, Sylvia." Shayna was too sad to fight, and besides, what did it matter anymore?

"Are you all right Linda?"

Just jim dandy, Shayna thought. "Yeah, I'll survive."

"What happened?"

"They're not sure. She collapsed at services and she died right after that."

Mrs. Steinblatt gave her official diagnosis. "Sounds like a heart attack. You were with her?"

"No."

"What happened? I thought you were spending Rosh Hashannah with her."

"I was there all day yesterday. I came home a day early." Shayna didn't feel like explaining, and luckily her mother didn't press her.

"She should have waited a few days, we were gonna go see her before Yom Kippur. Your father will have to make all the arrangements, we can't do anything today on account of the holiday." Mrs. Steinblatt was thinking out loud. "Ira will have to fly in. Are you coming tonight, Linda?"

"I don't think so, Sylvia. Call me when you know about the funeral."

"What's today, Wednesday? It'll probably be Friday, but I'll let you know. You'll stay here?"

Shayna glanced at Luz. "We'll probably just drive down for the day," she said, emphasizing the *we*.

"All right. I'll call you later."

Shayna hung up and lay back on the couch. The rest of the day passed in a blur of tears. Luz stayed close by, fielding phone calls and administering lots of TLC and Pearl came over with a tall white yarzheit candle, an Entemann's sponge cake and a jar of gefilte fish. She covered all the mirrors in the apartment, which was no small feat, while Shayna explained the ancient Jewish tradition to Luz.

"We're supposed to feel free to grieve without worrying about how awful we look," she said as Pearl threw a bath towel over the mirror in Shayna's bedroom. "Some people don't even bathe or change their clothes for a whole week. All they do is grieve."

Pearl came back into the living room. "Look what else I brought, Shayna."

"What?" Shayna barely lifted her head from the couch she was lying on.

"Well, you might think it was a pocketbook," Pearl held up what indeed looked like a pocketbook: a black patent leather box-shaped container with a mother-of-pearl handle. "But, as we all know, things are not always what they seem." She unsnapped it. "Look, Oma's prayerbook. Want to say kaddish for your bubbe?"

"Yes." Shayna got up and she and Pearl recited the ancient words: "Yit-ga-dol ve-yit-ka-dash, she-mei raba..." When they finished, Shayna hugged Pearl tightly. "Thanks, Mrs. Mamelinski."

"You're welcome, Mrs. Bubbelinski." Pearl turned to Luz. "Take good care of her in New York," she said.

"I will." Luz put her arm around Shayna.

"I'll be all right," Shayna said.

"Well, be careful. Grief does strange things to people; anything can happen."

"What do you mean, Pearl? You don't think I'll be all right?"

"It's not you I'm worried about, it's your family. You know, a crisis either opens people's hearts or closes them." She snapped her grandmother's prayerbook shut. "When Oma died, my mother let me and Bobbi sleep in the same bed under her roof. I think she was just in shock. On the other hand, all these relatives I had never even heard of came crawling out of the woodwork and descended like vultures: this one wanted her wedding ring, that one wanted the diamonds she had sewn into her quilt and smuggled over..."

Shayna walked Pearl to the door. "Well, Luz and I aren't sleeping there. And I can't imagine my mother or my Uncle Ira want anything. There really isn't much that they would find valuable."

"Well, just take care of yourself. And don't worry, I'll do Tzimmy patrol." Pearl kissed Shayna's cheek. "Call me when you know when you're going down."

"Okay, I will. It'll probably be Friday."

"You want to hold onto this for a while?" Pearl held out the prayerbook.

"That would be great. Are you sure?"

"Sure I'm sure. Here."

"I'll take good care of it. Thanks." Shayna hugged the small book to her chest.

"See you later. Bye, Luz," Pearl called and Shayna shut the door behind her.

The funeral was set for Friday at two o'clock. Shayna put on a black dress Friday morning and pinned a piece of black ribbon onto it, which she cut, explaining to Luz the tradition of rending one's garment as a sign of mourning. "Bubbe wouldn't want me to ruin my dress on her account," she said, pulling down her slip and making sure it didn't show. "The rabbi will give my mother and my uncle a black ribbon to tear at the funeral, but he probably won't give me one. I'm just a granddaughter, not a daughter. I'm not immediate family."

"Seems to me you're about as immediate as you can get." Luz said. "Will any of your cousins be there?"

"I doubt it. My cousin Sam's still in Israel and Abbie's kid is kind of young to take on a plane. Probably just my Uncle Ira will come."

Shayna picked up her shoulder bag which had Pearl's grandmother's prayerbook in it. "I'm ready."

"Okay." Luz took Shayna in her arms and kissed her gently. "I'm with you all the way, you know."

"I know. You've been great, Luz."

"Hey, what are wives for?" She smiled at Shayna. "I love you, Shayna."

"I love you, too." They kissed again and then Shayna pulled away. "We better go." They ran to the car because it was raining out, a heavy, steady rain with thunder and lightning, too.

"This is incredible," Luz said, turning on the windshield wipers, headlights and defroster. "This isn't September weather."

"Bubbe's still mad," Shayna said, buckling her seatbelt. "She's getting her last licks in."

They drove slowly to the Horowitz Funeral Home in Brooklyn. Luz had to pull over twice because the rain was coming down in absolute sheets. They got there at one-forty-five and pulled into a parking space in the huge lot. "Ready to meet the family?" Shayna asked, as Luz cut the motor.

"I guess." Luz checked her hair in the rearview mirror and ran a comb through it.

"Don't worry. They can't cause a scene at Bubbe's funeral. And she would want you to be here, I know that for sure." They ran through the rain into the funeral parlor, and entered a somber looking mahogany paneled hallway. A door to the left was open and Shayna and Luz walked toward it cautiously. Shayna peered in to see a few people sitting stiffly on chairs and a polished coffin in front of the room. She felt like she had stumbled onto a movie set, until she realized that one of the chief players sitting there was none other than Sylvia Steinblatt herself

"This is it. C'mon." Shayna walked in quietly with Luz right behind her. "That's Sylvia," Shayna whispered, indicating a thin woman in a maroon dress with a bit of black lace pinned to her hair, talking to a man Shayna didn't recognize. Shayna's hand flew up to her head. "Oh, I should have brought a shmate or something," she whispered.

"I saw a box of black caps when we came in," Luz said. "Can you wear one of those?"

"Not in this crowd." Shayna was still whispering. "Those are yarmalkes. For the men."

Sylvia Steinblatt looked up just then and caught her daughter's eye. "Hello, Linda."

"Hi, Sylvia." Shayna walked over and Luz followed.

"How was the driving?" Mrs. Steinblatt asked. "Isn't this rain terrible? I've never seen anything like it. Yesterday was nice, a little cold maybe, but not like this."

I can't believe she's still talking about the weather, Shayna thought. Will she ever stop? She dutifully kissed the cheek that her mother extended to her and then stepped back. "Sylvia, this is Luz."

"Hello," Luz said.

"Hello." To her complete and utter amazement, Shayna watched her mother offer her hand to Luz. "Thank you for coming. I know my mother was very fond of you," she said, as Shayna's jaw dropped. Pearl had said to be ready for

234

anything, but this was above and beyond Shayna's wildest dreams.

"Hello, Linda, remember me?" The man who had been talking to Shayna's mother stood up. "I'm your Uncle Ira, remember, Sam and Abbie's father,?"

"Hi."

"Thank you for taking such good care of my mother," he said, pressing Shayna's hand and giving her her second shock of the day. "You did a lot for her and we all appreciate it."

"Hello, Linda." Mr. Steinblatt came up to Shayna with a couple in tow. "You remember the Jacobsons, don't you?"

Not really, but Shayna smiled at them anyway. "Hello."

"I haven't seen you since you were this high." Mrs. Jacobson bent over a little so that the palm of her hand lined up with her knee. I can't believe she really said that, Shayna thought, a pseudo-smile frozen on her face. "You look so gorgeous, Linda," Mrs. Jacobson went on. "So tell me, what have you been doing with yourself lately?"

"Look, the Brombergs just walked in. Hello Irving." Shayna's father led the Jacobsons away before Shayna could answer their question. She and Luz stood off to the side a little, watching as more and more people came into the room. Shayna hardly recognized anyone. Everyone was hugging and kissing and chattering away, and if it wasn't for the coffin in front of the room which not a soul was anywhere near, and the fact that she'd never been to one, Shayna would swear that she and Luz were at a cocktail party instead of a funeral. Finally the rabbi came in and asked everyone except for members of the family to leave.

"What should I do?" Luz whispered.

"Stay with me," Shayna whispered back.

They watched the rabbi pin a black ribbon on Shayna's mother and Uncle Ira. The rabbi said a prayer and then asked if they would like the coffin opened. Everyone turned to Shayna, as if they had rehearsed it and she shook her head no. "Would you like to say a few words about your grandmother before we go into the chapel?" the rabbi asked Shayna, who everyone was still looking at. "I understand you knew her best."

Shayna looked at her mother, who nodded, and with that nod, Shayna realized it was she who had told the rabbi to give Shayna the chance to speak. "My bubbe was the most important person in my life," Shayna said, her voice clear and strong. "She taught me many things: to be patient and generous and forgiving and strong. She taught me life is short and sweet and precious, so I should always enjoy myself and take care of myself. And," Shayna looked at the circle of faces staring at her, "she taught me the true meaning of love. She taught me that it doesn't matter if you disagree with someone, or don't understand them, or come from two different places, or even if what they're doing goes totally against what you believe. If you love them, you love them and nothing else matters." She looked around at her mother, her father, her Uncle Ira, the rabbi and Luz once more. "That's all."

"Thank you," the rabbi said. "This way."

"I'm proud of you," Luz whispered as they filed into the chapel and filled the front row. Shayna only heard bits and pieces of the rabbi's eulogy: "devoted wife and mother...loving grandmother...proud great-grandmother..." She just listened to the rain and someone two rows behind her who kept sniffing and blowing their nose. Soon it was over and they were in the car again, heading for the cemetery.

"You okay?" Luz asked, turning on the headlights.

"I don't know. I'm pretty numb." Shayna watched the rain splatter on the windshield, seeing Tzeydl's face in every drop. They pulled onto the highway, Luz's little red car surrounded by big Oldsmobiles and Cadillacs.

When they got to the graveyard, Shayna watched her parents get out of the hearse, her father holding an umbrella over her mother. Several people were already standing at the open grave.

"You ready, honey? I think I have an umbrella." Luz reached into the back seat, but she needn't have, for as soon as Shayna opened her car door, the rain came to a screeching halt.

"How about that?" Shayna asked, taking her pocketbook off the front seat.

"She's a pretty powerful woman," Luz said looking up at the sky.

"My bubbe would never let her favorite granddaughter catch a cold at her own funeral." Shayna took Luz's hand and they walked to Tzeydl's grave. It was wedged between that of Leah Shiplitsky and Benny Zimmerman. "See, that's her mother, my great-grandmother, and that's my grandpa, her husband." Shayna pointed as Tzeydl's casket was lowered into the earth. "She's going right between them."

"Where's her father?" Luz asked.

"He died in Europe. Goddess only knows where he's buried." Shayna lifted both palms to the blue sky. The rabbi came over and gave all the men little cards with the mourner's kaddish printed on it. That Pearl, she's always one step ahead of me, Shayna thought, as she got the small prayerbook out of her shoulder bag. She turned to the earmarked page and recited the words along with the men: "Yit-ga-dal ve-yit-ka-dash she-mei ra-ba..."

When they finished the prayer, Shayna's parents turned to go back to the car. "You'll come to the house for a little nosh?" Mrs. Steinblatt asked.

"Sylvia, wait. Aren't we supposed to throw the first shovelful of dirt on her coffin?"

Mrs. Steinblatt looked over her shoulder. "It's so muddy."

"Well, I'm going to." Shayna handed her shoulder bag to Luz and took a shovel that was propped up in the dirt over to Tzeydl's grave, ignoring the mud that was oozing around her shoes. She looked at Tzeydl's casket, plunged the shovel into the dirt, and threw some clumps of soil onto the coffin, listening to the thud of earth against wood. "I love you, Bubbe," Shayna whispered. She turned and walked away, joined by Luz, who put her arm around her, and led her back to the car and onto the highway again. Shayna watched the world speed by: cars, trucks, streetlights, trees. Would everything just go on like this after she was gone, too? "I wonder where Bubbe is," Shayna said, resting her head against the cool window.

"I think it takes a little while to get to heaven," Luz said, keeping an eye on the Steinblatt sedan in front of them.

"Yeah, she probably had to stop and get her hair done first," Shayna said to the window. Then she turned to Luz. "I don't even know if Jews believe in heaven."

"Well, you believe in God, right?"

"God or the Goddess, as the case may be. And the Kingdom of Heaven, or the Queendom, I suppose." Shayna thought it over."I know we don't believe in hell. I should have asked the rabbi."

"Don't worry," Luz said. "Your grandma will let you know where she is."

Shayna smiled. "What do you think, she'll send me a postcard?"

"No, you'll see. Like the rain ending when you got out of the car. She's still keeping an eye on you." Luz pulled off the highway and chased Shayna's parents down the exit ramp.

There was already a small crowd of people gathered at chez Steinblatt. The men were in the living room drinking soda water out of plastic cups, and the women were in the kitchen pulling cakes out of boxes and taking Saran Wrap off serving platters. Soon everyone was rotating around the kitchen table, holding a paper plate and piling it high with hard-boiled eggs, gefilte fish, chopped liver, creamed herring, bagels and cottage cheese.

"Bubbe would want us to eat a good lunch," Shayna said, handing Luz a plate.

"Don't talk about her, Linda, we'll only cry," Mrs. Steinblatt said, spearing a piece of lox.

Shayna and Luz sat on the couch in the living room and ate, or rather Luz ate and Shayna pretended to. She listened to her father and her Uncle Ira have a long less-than-fascinating conversation about computers and then football. After a while she wandered into the kitchen where her mother was putting out yet another sour cream chocolate chip coffee cake.

"Try some of this, Linda," Sylvia said, breaking off a piece with her fingers. "It's very good, very moist, and it has no cholesterol."

"Entemann's is coming out with a new low-cholesterol line," said Mrs. Weiss, one of the few Steinblatt neighbors that Shayna did remember.

"No, I think that's Freihoffers," Mrs. Steinblatt said over her shoulder. "I read about it in the paper."

Shayna sighed. Clearly it was time to go. "Sylvia, we're going to take off."

"Already? All right." Shayna had expected her mother at least to pretend to put up a little fuss, for Mrs. Weiss's sake if nothing else, and was slightly disappointed that she didn't.

"Come upstairs a minute, Linda. I have something for you."

"One second." Shayna ducked into the living room to check in with Luz and then followed her mother upstairs. Mrs. Steinblatt led Shayna into her old bedroom, which had a few cardboard boxes strewn about the floor.

"Your father went and got her things yesterday," Mrs. Steinblatt said. "The clothes I told him he should just donate to the nursing home, they got people there that can use them, I'm sure, but everything else is here. You want to go through it?"

Shayna knelt down and opened a carton. "Her pocketbook I want, and her sewing kit." She laid them aside.

"Here, I saved an empty box for you." Shayna's mother brought over a carton.

"This wine we bought for the rabbi, for the new year," Shayna said, lifting the bottle. "Bubbe really wanted him to have it."

"Your father can bring it back, he has to go next week for the television. There wasn't room in the car for everything."

"What's this?" Shayna unwrapped something in tissue paper. "Oh, her mezzuzah. The rabbi put that up for her. I'll hang it in my new apartment."

"You're moving?"

"In the spring." Shayna carefully re-wrapped the mezzuzah. "Luz and I are moving in together." Her mother was silent, which Shayna supposed was better than a nasty comment, or yet another weather report. "What's this?" She opened a small box to find some jewelry. "Her pearls I'll keep. These earrings I'll send to Minnie, she asked me for a remembrance. And I'll have to call Tillie from her building." Shayna put the box down and looked up. "What about her apartment, Sylvia?"

"The rent is paid until the end of the month. You think that'll give you enough time to go through it and take what you want?"

Shayna nodded. "Don't you want anything?"

"No, I got a whole house full of junk, what do I need more for?" Mrs. Steinblatt spread her arms. "Take her dishes, Linda, she's got a full set, you'll make good use of them. And we just bought her an electric frying pan last year, take that, too. And a new toaster. You'll see when you go, it's all there." She's giving me a dowry, Shayna thought, standing up . If only I could tell her. Well, maybe someday. She bent down to lift the box she'd just packed.

"Don't pick that up, Linda, you'll hurt your back. I'll get your father to do it."

"I can do it, Sylvia."

"Come into my bedroom a minute, I have something for you." She led Shayna across the hall. "Here's her crystal bowl, I packed it up good and tight for you, it shouldn't break." She pointed to a box on the bed covered with silver tape.

Shayna sat down and rested her arm on it. "Thanks."

"Wait a minute. Here." Mrs. Steinblatt took a red velvet box out of her top drawer and handed it to Shayna.

"What's this?"

"Open it." Shayna opened the box. "Bubbe's watch," she gasped, staring at the small gold face of numbers. "And her medal." She lifted them out of the box and felt the cold gold against her skin. "She's gone. She's really gone." Shayna began to cry, unable to hold back the tears any longer, though she'd sworn to herself she wouldn't break down in front of Sylvia. "I don't want these," Shayna said, flinging them back into the box. "I want Bubbe. Bubbe," Shayna shrieked, her whole body shaking. "I miss Bubbe. I want her."

"I know you do, sweetheart." Mrs. Steinblatt put her arms around Shayna. "We're all going to miss her. She loved you very much." She paused and then added softly, "I know it's no great consolation, but I'm still alive, you know."

"Mameh." Shayna buried her face into her mother's rayon covered breast and sobbed for a long time. When she could finally catch her breath, she sighed deeply and sat up. "You take her medal," Shayna said, getting it from the box. "You should have something."

"But she wanted you to have it, Linda."

"But I want you to have it. I have her watch, I don't need both." Shayna extended the pendant as a peace offering which her mother accepted.

"All right, someday you'll have it back anyway," Mrs. Steinblatt said. "And her wedding band, she wanted me to take it apart and give each grandchild a diamond." She looked at the gold charm in her hand. "You remember what the letters stand for?"

"The Ethel Rothman Aid Society."

"When I was a little girl, my mother used to let me play with it." Mrs. Steinblatt stared at the necklace. "I used to sit on her lap and read the letters. I pretended the S was for Sylvia." She put it back in the box and sighed. "She had this medallion since before I was born and she was so proud of it, it killed me to take it away from her. But the director of the nursing home himself told me not to leave any valuables with her, just in case something would happen." A tear trickled out of her eye. "Oy, it hasn't been easy these past few months, that's for sure."

"I love you, Sylvia," Shayna said, following Tzeydl's advice to not stand on ceremony.

"I love you, too." Mrs. Steinblatt hugged her daughter. "Call me when you get home so I shouldn't worry."

Shayna looked up, surprised. "Since when do you worry?"

Mrs. Steinblatt shrugged. "Can't a mother worry about her own daughter?"

That's Bubbe's job, Shayna wanted to say, but Bubbe wasn't around anymore and Shayna supposed somebody had to fill the vacant position. "I guess so."

"Listen, Linda, I know I'm not your grandmother, but maybe we can try to be friends. She would want that, don't you think?" Mrs. Steinblatt took Shayna's hand, but Shayna wasn't won over so easily.

"What about Luz?"

Shayna saw her mother's jaw tighten. "I can try, Linda, that's all I can tell you."

Close, Shayna thought, but no cigar. "We're a package deal."

"Linda, I'll do the best I can, all right? Give me a little time."

"Okay. What time is it anyway?"

"Look on your new watch."

"It's running?"

"Of course. I had it cleaned for you."

Shayna took her bubbe's watch out of the box and slipped it on her wrist.

"Four-thirty," she read. "I'll give you about an hour."

"Gee, can you spare it?"

"Barely. Life is short, Sylvia."

"You said it." Mrs. Steinblatt took Shayna's hand again and looked into her eyes. "I don't know where the time goes, Linda, it's like a dream, I'm telling you. I look in the mirror, eppes, and I see a stranger. I look at you," she patted Shayna's hand, "and I see myself."

Shayna stared at her mother. "That's just what Bubbe used to say."

"You see that? My mother's barely cold in her grave and already I'm turning into her, takeh." She squeezed Shayna's hand and let go of it. "Fix your face and let's go down." Shayna stood up to look at herself in the mirror hanging over her mother's dresser, but it was covered with a tablecloth. To the right of it hung the picture Tzeydl had taken of Shayna during the summer.

"My picture," Shayna said, astonished. "You hung it in your bedroom?"

"Why not?" Mrs. Steinblatt got up and came over to her daughter. "After your father, you're the first thing I see every morning and the last thing I see every night. It's a beautiful picture and you're my beautiful daughter."

"Oh, Sylvia." Shayna's eyes filled with tears again, for she'd been waiting thirty years to hear those words. Then she recovered quickly. "Bubbe took that picture, you know. With Luz's camera; Luz showed her how." Using the L word twice in one sentence was maybe pushing it a little, but Shayna was certainly not going to miss this golden opportunity to get her girlfriend a few brownie points.

"I'll try, Linda, I'll really try, okay?" Mrs. Steinblatt said softly. "Come, let's go down, they'll wonder what happened to us already. You'll call?"

"I'll call."

"Come then." And together, mother and daughter descended the stairs.

Chapter Twenty

"Luz, wake up," Shayna whispered to the sleeping beauty in bed beside her. "I just had the most amazing dream." Luz didn't respond, so Shayna sat up and rubbed her eyes, disturbing Tzimmy, who had somehow managed to crawl between the sheets. For a minute Shayna thought she was still dreaming, because her bedroom, and what she could see of the living room was cluttered with large, unfamiliar objects. As Shayna's brain came into focus, she began to recognize shapes in the early Monday morning light: Tzeydl's bureau pushed against her own; Tzeydl's plant sunning itself on her windowsill; Tzeydl's end tables balanced precariously one on top of the other in a tall, lopsided stack. Shayna and Luz had borrowed a truck from one of Pearl's construction cronies and gone down to Brooklyn over the weekend, right after Yom Kippur, to clear out Tzeydl's apartment. It had taken them most of the two days to sort through her bedroom, her kitchen, her living room, her closets, her books, her papers and her clothes. Shayna couldn't get over it: a whole lifetime of ninety-nine-and-a-half years, gone in only two days. What she didn't want, she packed up carefully for Goodwill, except for Tzeydl's kitchen table and chairs which she and Luz shlepped down the hall for Tillie, who had returned to her apartment and was now living with a full-time, hired companion.

When they were finished, they took a walk on the beach, and cast the keys to Tzeydl's apartment into the sea. The three keys flashed on the surface of the water for an instant like precious jewels before sinking out of sight forever. Shayna held Luz's hand and looked out over the water, seeing nothing but sand, sea, sky and a circle of seagulls overhead.

Birds, Shayna thought, remembering. I dreamed about birds. "Luz wake up," Shayna said again, a little louder this time. "I had a dream."

"A bad dream?" Luz instantly sat up and encircled Shayna in her arms.

"No, a wonderful dream. I don't know why, but I feel so happy all of a sudden."

"Tell me." Luz sat back against a pillow.

"Well, I was back in Brooklyn, in Bubbe's neighborhood and I was driving around in circles because I couldn't find a place to park."

Luz laughed. "That wasn't a dream, honey. That was yesterday."

"No, listen." Shayna lay down on her back and looked up at the ceiling as if it were a screen that was showing the movie in her mind. "I parked the car, finally, and then I got out but I didn't know which way to go. I looked up the block one way and I saw all these stores and a deli and lots of apartment buildings, so I knew that wasn't right. Then I looked down the block the other way, and I could see the beach. I saw the ocean and the sand and there were these two white cranes, a big one and a little one, standing right by the water. They were so beautiful, so majestic looking..." Shayna turned her head on the pillow and looked at Luz. "That's it. I don't know, I just have such a happy feeling inside. Right here." She put her hand over her heart. "I know it was Bubbe."

"It's your sign," Luz said, tucking a strand of Shayna's hair behind her ear. "What do you think she was trying to tell you?"

"That she got there. Wherever there is. And she's happy. She's safe. She's at peace." Shayna smiled into Luz's eyes. "The big crane was Bubbe and the little crane was me. See, I'm still with her. Oh, I'm so happy." Shayna hugged her knees.

"That's because she's still with you, too." Luz gathered Shayna up in her arms. "She's just gonna talk to you in different ways now. Like in your dreams."

"Yeah." Shayna nuzzled into Luz's warm sleepy neck and Luz kissed the top of Shayna's head.

"Listen, honeycakes, I had a dream, too."

Shayna backed up a little so she could see Luz's face. "Tell me."

Luz stroked Shayna's hair, smoothing it down her back. "I dreamed I woke up next to the most wonderful woman in the whole wide world and she said she'd spend the rest of her life with me."

Shayna smiled. "That's not a dream, Luz. Be serious."

"I am serious. She had curly brown hair, almost down to her tuchus, and big green eyes and beautiful lips, and a nice...um, don't tell me...a nice, zaftig body."

"Very good," Shayna the Yiddish teacher said.

"And," Luz continued, "she was a little sad because her grandma had just died, and she loved her grandma more than anybody in the whole wide world. But then she had a dream about her, so she knew she was okay. And then in my dream, she woke up and told me her dream, and then I took her in my arms and she gave me a great big kiss, and then..."

But Shayna never heard the end of Luz's dream, because she was too busy making it come true.

a laybn on dine kop: a blessing on your head
ainekal: grandchild
alav ha-sholom: may he rest in peace
aleha ha-sholom: may she rest in peace
aleph-bez (H): alphabet
alevei: I hope; it should only be so
aveck: away

babka: a special kind of cake that's very light, often made with sugar and cinnamon
babushka: a scarf worn around the head
balaboosteh: an excellent cook and homemaker
Bar Mitzvah (H): ceremony commemorating a boy reaching adulthood at the age
        of thirteen
Bat Mitzvah (H): ceremony commemorating a girl reaching adulthood at the age
        of thirteen
bima (H): platform in front of the synagogue from which the Torah is read
bissl: a little
blintzes: crepes wrapped around a filling such as farmer's cheese or fruit and then
        fried, served with applesauce and sour cream
borsht: beet soup
Brucha Aht Shekhina Elohanu Malka Ha-Olam: Blessed Art Thou Oh Lordess
        Our Goddess, Queen of the Universe
bubbe: grandmother
bubbeleh: endearment (literally "little grandmother")

challah: the beautiful braided bread eaten on Shabbas and holidays
Chanukah (H): Festival of Lights which lasts eight days, commemorating the
        Maccabees' victory over the Syrians and the rededication of the temple
        at Jerusalem
chaynik: teapot (to hock someone's chaynik is to bother them)
chazzan: cantor
chazzeri: filth, mess (slang: junk food or just plain junk)
chup: snatch
chutzpah: nerve
cockamammy: mixed up; ridiculous

---

*Hebrew words are denoted with (H). Yiddish spellings are not "official" as the only correct way of spelling a Yiddish word is with Hebrew letters; instead the words are transliterated according to the author's ear. Likewise, the usage of Yiddish words may vary according to where one is from. Lastly, many Yiddish words have adopted English suffixes (shlepping, plotzed) as Jews who came to America learned to speak English and sprinkled this new foreign language with words from the mameh-loshen (mother tongue) which really do lose something in the translation.

daven: to pray

derma: intestines (stuffed derma is a delicacy)

draydl: a spinning top played with on Chanukah, inscribed with four Hebrew
   letters that stand for "A great miracle happened there."

drek: garbage

du: you

du hearst: you hear

epl: apple

eppes: for some inexplicable reason

ess a bissl: eat a little

essen tummult: eating commotion

fahshnotzed: stuffed up

fancy-shmancy: not so fancy (In Yiddish it is common to dismiss a word by
   repeating it starting with an SH sound)

farpotshket: messed up

farshimmeled: confused

faygeleh: little bird

feh: ugh

fenster: window

fleishig: meat

futz: fuss

gantzeh: whole

gantzeh megillah: the whole story (see megillah)

gatkes: underwear

gefilte fish: ground fish cakes

gelt: money

gershray: scream

gevalt: an expression of fear, sorrow, surprise, etc.

gey: go

gey aveck: go away

gey shlufen: go to sleep

gezunt: health, healthy

gezunteh yontiff: a healthy holiday

goldeneh: gold

goniff: thief

Gottinyu: oh my God

Gottsedanken: thank God

goy: a non-Jewish person (plural: goyim)

goyishe: non-Jewish

groyseh: big

gut: good

gut yontiff: good holiday

Hadasshah (H): a Jewish woman's organization (literally "Esther")
hag samayach (H): happy holiday
hammentaschen: a three sided pastry eaten on Purim
hock: bother
hoo-hah: an expression of scorn
hora: a circle dance
huppa: marriage canopy

in dem bays ha mik-dosh: in the Holy Temple (opening words to the song
      "Rozhinkes mit Mandlen")

Kaddish: the mourner's prayer
kasha: buckwheat groats
kasha varnishkes: a dish of buckwheat groats and noodles
keppeleh: head (affectionate)
ketuba (H): Jewish marriage contract
kibbutz (H): farming collective in Israel
kichel: a small plain cookie
kinehora: a phrase used to ward off the Evil Eye
kishkes: intestines
knaydl: matzo ball (plural: knaydlech)
knishes: a pastry filled with potato, kasha, spinach, etc.
koach: strength
kop: head
kosher: Jewish dietary law (slang: all right)
kvell: take pleasure in
kvetch: complain

l'chiam (H): to life (a toast)
latkes: potato pancakes
loch in kop: a hole in the head
lokshen: noodles
lox: smoked salmon

machatunim: related by marriage
macher: a big wheeler dealer; a show off
maidl, maideleh: young girl
mameh: mama
mamela: endearment (literally, "little mother")
mandelbrot: almond cake
mandlen: almonds
matzo: unleavened bread
matzo brei: fried matzo
mazel tov (H): congratulations; good luck
megillah (H): the Book of Esther (slang: a long drawn-out story)

menorah (H): eight-branched candle holder used on Chanukah
mensch: a human being
meshugas: craziness
meshugeh, meshugeneh: crazy, a crazy person
mezzuzah (H): small oblong container affixed to the door post of a Jewish home, holding parchment with Biblical passages
milkhig: dairy
mit: with
mitzvah (H): blessing
momser: bastard

naches: pleasure
nogoodnik: someone who is no good
nosh: snack, nibble
nosh a bissl: eat a little something
nu: so, well
nudnik: a pest

Oma (German): grandmother; used by some German Jews
oy: an expression of surprise, sorrow, pain, fear, excitement, etc.
oy vey: oy and then some

partniker: partner
Pesach (H): Passover; the eight day holiday commemorating the Exodus of the Jews from Egypt
pesadikha: fit to eat on Pesach according to Jewish dietary law
pish: urinate
plotz: to collapse or explode
potch: a slap
punim: face
pupik: belly button
Purim (H): holiday commemorating the rescue of the Jews of Persia from Haman's plan to exterminate them
putz: a jerk

rebbe: rabbi
Rosh Hashannah (H): Jewish New Year
rozhinkes: raisins
"Rozhinkes mit Mandlen": "Raisins and Almonds," the title of a popular Yiddish lullaby
ruggelech: small pastries usually filled with sugar and cinnamon

seder (H): the Passover meal (literally "order")
Shabbas: the Jewish Sabbath
shah: shhh

shah shtill: keep quiet
shalom (H): peace
shana tova (H): a good new year
shayneh: beautiful
shayneh maideleh: beautiful girl
shep naches: reap joy
sheytl: wig worn by married women
shiddach: marriage match
shikker: a drunk
shiksa: a girl or women who isn't Jewish (not complimentary)
shissl: bowl
shiva: seven day mourning period for the dead
shlemiel: a fool
shlep: to drag or carry
shlock: junk; something that is cheaply made
shluf, shlufen: sleep
shluf-zhe yideleh shluf: sleep now, little boy, sleep (refrain from the song
          "Rozhinkes mit Mandlen")
shmaltz: excessive sentimentality (literally "rendered chicken fat")
shmate: rag
shmechle: smile
shmeer: to smear
shmegeggie: a jerk
shmendrick: a loser
shmutz: dirt
shnapps: any alcoholic beverage
shnorrer: a cheapskate
shnozzola: nose
shofar (H): a curved ram's horn blown during the High Holy Days
shpeel: speech
shpilkes in tuchus: ants in one's pants
shtup: to fill or stuff
shvitz: to sweat
shul: synagogue
sukka (H): a hut in which meals are enjoyed during the festival of Sukkot
Sukkot (H): Festival of Tabernacles

takeh: really
tallis (H): prayer shawl
tateleh: endearment (literally "little father")
tchotchkes: knicknacks
tochter: daughter
tsouris: troubles
tuchus: buttocks
"Tumbalalaika": the title of a popular Yiddish folk song

tummult: commotion
tzimmes: a stew of sweet potatoes, carrots and prunes

unkosher: unfit to eat according to Jewish dietary law (slang: not all right)
utz: to nag; to move along

vey iss mir: woe is me
vildeh chaya: wild beast
Vilstu a knish?: Do you want a knish?

yarmulke: skull cap
yarzheit: anniversary of someone's death
yiddishe kop: a Jewish head
yideleh: a little boy
Yit-ga-dal ve-yit-ka-dash she-mei ra-ba (H): opening words of the mourner's
        Kaddish
Yom Kippur: Day of Atonement
yontiff: holiday

zaftig: plump, juicy
zei gezunt: be well
zetz: a strong blow